FREE TO JUDGE

AN ENEMIES-TO-FRIENDS-TO-LOVERS, SECRET
IDENTITY, FAMILY SAGA

AMARYLLIS HERITAGE
BOOK 2

TRACEY JERALD

FREE TO JUDGE

ISBN: 978-1959299769 (E-book)
ISBN: 978-1-959299-43-1 (Paperback)
ISBN: 978-1-959299-44-8 (Discreet Cover)

Tracey Jerald
101 Marketside Avenue, Suite 404-205
Ponte Vedra, FL, 3208
https://www.traceyjerald.com

Editors: Melissa Borucki , A. Rhodes, K. Lira
Proof Edits: Holly Malgieri, Comma Sutra Editorial
Cover Design by Tugboat Design
Photo Credit: Wander Aguiar
PR & Marketing: Foreword PR

DEDICATION

To Amy and Kristin.
Comma.
Enough said.
I love you both.

PERSONAL CONTENT WARNING

As you progress through this story, please note the possible items which may be a source of discomfort to you as a reader. As always, to enhance your experience, please check the author's website for any personal comfort triggers for the entire series.

PLAYLIST

Phil Collins: "In the Air Tonight"
Nathaniel Rateliff & The Night Sweats: "Get Used to the Night"
Post Malone, Morgan Wallen: "I Had Some Help"
Sarah McLachlan: "Forgiveness"
John Mayer: "Say"
Enya: "Book of Days"
Dua Lipa: "IDGAF"
AWOLNATION: "Sail"
Rihanna: "S&M"
Edwin McCain: "Solitude"
X Ambassadors: "Renegades"
Taylor Swift, Post Malone: "Fortnight"
Sarah McLachlan: "Hold On"

ALSO BY TRACEY JERALD

AMARYLLIS HERITAGE SERIES

Free to Fall

Free to Judge

Free to Taste (Coming in 2026)

AMARYLLIS SERIES

Free to Dream

Free to Run

Free to Rejoice

Free to Breathe

Free to Believe

Free to Live

Free to Dance

Free to Wish

Free to Protect

Free to Reunite

SEVEN VIRTUES SERIES

Coming Soon!

MIDAS SERIES

Perfect Proposal

Perfect Assumption

Perfect Composition

Perfect Order

Perfect Satisfaction

Perfectly Free

Perfect Pitch

Perfect Pursuit

Perfect Secret (Coming in 2026)

GLACIER ADVENTURE SERIES

Return by Fire—Available in audio!

Return by Air—Available in audio!

Return by Land

Return by Sea

DEVOTION SERIES

Ripple Effect

Flood Tide

Troubled Water (Coming in 2026)

NEW YORK MINUTE (INDEPENDENT STANDALONES)

Close Match

The Ultimate Challenge

Go to https://www.traceyjerald.com/ for all buy links!

EPIGRAPH

Love is the absence of judgement.

DALAI LAMA

PROLOGUE
SEVEN YEARS AGO

I should focus on the pomp and circumstance occurring in Holmes Field and the Tercentenary Theatre at Harvard University, but instead, I'm captivated by the chocolate brown eyes that bore into mine when I allow my gaze to sweep past his every few minutes. The face they're attached to is distracting—chiseled jaw, light beard, dark, thick hair that begs a woman to run her hands through it. He screams "heartbreaker" and "take me home tonight" without saying a single word.

If today wasn't my last day in Cambridge...

If today wasn't the start of a future I'd been born into...

Hell, if my life wasn't perfectly planned down to the minute after I cross the stage, I might take him up on the invitation he's openly throwing in my direction.

It's too bad, really. He checks off all the boxes that make my insides quiver—tall, dark, with an air of danger. After all, who could blame me? I grew up around men who embodied those attributes like a second skin. With a mental shrug of my shoulders, I bid *adieu* to a man who I'll tuck away in the recesses of my memory. Someone who'll have a starring role in my fantasies later. *It's too bad you weren't around in the last six months. I could have used a distraction as I waited for this day to arrive.*

After all, despite the hard work and long hours, it felt like the beginning of the rest of my life would never get here. And now? I'm so eager for it I can barely remain seated as I wait for my name to be called.

Allowing myself a moment of weakness, I sneak a glance to my left. Yep, he's still checking me out. Well, to be fair, so is everyone else who is sitting, standing, or remote viewing the temporary stage set up near Widener Library.

Slowly, my heartbeat increases as time inches closer to my moment in the spotlight—a moment delayed because I was running after a different dream.

During our commencement, we are honored when the current Director of the National Counterterrorism Center—a Harvard Law graduate herself—urges us to use our power and influence to make a difference in the world. I feel drawn in by her background—a military father and a mother who suffered great abuse at a young age.

Much like my own.

Still, when the director returns to her seat to resounding applause, her closing comments of, "No matter what you face in the future, utilize the wisdom you learned within these hallowed halls. Judge carefully. Rule righteously. Ensure your heart, your mind, your expertise, and above all, the law you've studied to uphold will ensure future generations can live the life they deserve," ring on repeat in my mind.

Judge carefully.

My eyes stray to the dark-haired man again. I'm an exceptional judge of character. Between that and the arc of electricity racing along my skin every time our eyes meet, I don't need something notarized to tell me we'd burn up the sheets if there was time to make a move.

Too bad my schedule won't allow for it.

My lips twist in a smirk my mother swears I was born with—a fraction of my Marshall heritage. A legacy that's had me judged since the moment I arrived on campus, if for nothing more than my last name and the extended family I was born into.

Marshall. Freeman. The blood of both runs through my veins. To the outside world, our family is the epitome of the American dream— wealth, privilege, influence. To those who are let in, they understand we're about pride and determination. Family first.

Family always.

The love of all our extended family names is imprinted onto the core of who I am—much like the Amaryllis legend tattoo I sport on the arch of one foot. A tattoo inspired by a different legend resides on the other.

A legacy I alone am a part of, even among the elite.

Early on, it was impressed upon me that not everyone has had the comfort and security I've been blessed with every day. As the first-born daughter of Keene Marshall and Alison Freeman-Marshall, I understand their overprotective natures. They suffered through individual traumas before being able to set them aside long enough to fall in love.

Almost a quarter century later, my father can still barely tolerate letting my mother out of his sight. Twisting away from the eye candy that's captured my attention, a quick glance into the audience shows Daddy has Mama wrapped protectively in his arms, even with the agents from the investigation agency he co-owns with my Uncle Caleb hiding in plain sight around the perimeter of my graduation ceremony.

Let's face it, nothing my dad does shocks me anymore. Our eyes meet and hold. I catch the sheen in his, even as his lips curve. His free fist presses against his heart.

I lift mine in a similar salute before rising along with my classmates, readying to cross the stage. My attention is once again grabbed by the face in the crowd. His lips curve upward as I approach the stairs. My heart thunders in my chest, and I'm not certain if that's due to excitement over getting my degree—finally—or because of the sexual charge between me and Mr. Unknown.

Two more people, then it's my turn.

I inch closer and catch a high-powered external flash unit illuminate— preparing to add brightness to what the news media must feel is an insufficient light source. Internally, I let out a sigh despite the smile plastered on my face.

The paparazzi. There isn't one single moment of my life where they're not invading my space. Not anymore.

To the vast number of people who read about me in the tabloids, I'm glorified as a product of privilege—an heiress to a legacy I hadn't truly earned. But they don't have a right to cast aspersions on me—on any of us.

People don't appreciate how my family got where we are today. Me and my cousins? We're a legacy of love more valuable than the billions we stand to inherit. But, much like the scales of justice I am prepared to uphold, there's an equal amount of tragedy that shaped who we are.

A past we hope few have to endure.

Our family's lives were a trial by fire. For some, they were sentences of agony. But since our lives play out in the court of public opinion, we know one thing for certain. Love, the kind that truly matters, is worth sacrificing anything for.

I'm next.

Pressing a hand to my stomach, a familiar churning sensation rolls through my gut. A reminder I'm ready for the next step in the marathon called life I'm about to endure.

I recognize the feeling because I conquered it time and time again as I waited for a gun to signal the start of some of the most important races of my life. Each race in high school. At the University of Connecticut, when I raced for my mother's alma mater. Later, during my first year of law school, when I won the Boston Marathon, which qualified me to be a part of the US Women's Olympic Team.

Just before I went on to medal at the Games.

Like that moment when they slid the ribbon with those famous rings embossed on it over my head, tears prick my eyes as my legal name rings through the air. Thunderous applause bounces off towering marble columns as I step to the edge of the stage. The weight of the moment presses against my chest—not from nerves, but from the sheer gravity of what I am about to finish.

"Katherine Laura Marshall. Juris Doctorate, Master of Business Administration. Summa cum laude."

Even as I saunter forward, eyes on the dean, I hear my mother, father, and sisters shriek my name, "Kalie!" with pride. Above all, with love.

My head is held high, my hood flops behind me—designating me as one of the elite. Not just because I am graduating from one of the most prestigious institutions in the world, but because I did so with a dual degree and with one of the highest grade point averages.

I earned this.

Suddenly, the nights I spent in the Harvard Law Library with my head buried in corporate case law are worth it. The relentless drive that pushed me past exhaustion, past my own limits, is now worth it.

I did it.

Quickly shaking the dean's hand, I pose for a picture and beam at my family, knowing this is just the start of the rest of my future. As I cross the stage, I catch the handsome stranger's eye. His smile is broad, his head nodding in slow motion. It doesn't occur to me until now, I have to pass him in order to return to my chair. When I do, his husky, "Congratulations," sends chills down my spine.

I twist my head around and beam in his direction. "Thank you."

His cocky expression falters for a moment, and it makes me wish I had more time here in this world before real life kicks in. All too soon, the ceremony ends, and my family scrambles forward to bombard me with hugs.

Their pride is practically tangible, and it means more to me than anything. Certainly more than any medal packed away. Those were moments of temporary glory. This is proving I belong where I always knew I was meant to be.

By my mother's side, as associate counsel at Amaryllis Events.

I set the dark haired stranger to the back of my mind and welcome the weight of my family's legacy as it settles over my shoulders, not as a burden but as a privilege.

Now, I'm ready to carry it.

CHAPTER ONE

FOUR YEARS LATER

I STAND BEFORE THE WINDOW IN DIRECTOR HOLDER'S OFFICE, fists shoved deep into my pockets, my jaw clenching tight enough to snap any second. The room assaults my senses with a twisted scent of burned coffee and raw desperation—a scent that, perversely, offers a grim comfort. The director wisely avoided the harsh glare of the fluorescent light, opting instead for a dim lamp, shrouding our forms behind drawn blinds. No one must see me.

Pivoting sharply to face him, I brace for his judgment.

Director Holder lets out a weary sigh as he rubs his battle-worn face—one that's witnessed too many brutal choices, including the one he's about to sanction. "You certain you know what you're doing, Dec?" he rasps, every word strained with fatigue, yet his black eyes cut through my armor with fierce precision.

I recall when he used to do that when I was a little boy. Growing up next door to an FBI agent, it was Holder who would chide me when I got too unruly for my mother—my father being long gone from our lives. When she died, he stood by my side at her small service. He stepped in to become my mentor, my boss, and my father figure, all rolled into one.

Thus why he's the one I'm turning to before I take on my biggest challenge to date. Nodding slowly, I answer, "I do."

Sitting forward in his chair and resting his elbows on his desk, he continues, "Let's lay all the cards on the table."

"Fine."

"If you do this, they'll think they own you."

A wry smile twists my lips. "They think that already. They've planted enough evidence to play a game of cat and mouse with me. I have a choice—capitulate to their demands and release information about our agents in the field, or they'll release the information that I did it anyway."

He considers my words. "But by leaving—"

I pick up where he left off. "I'll be a part of something."

He looks at the card I laid beside the open folder on his desk. "There are good men and women who work there. Fortunately for you, they'll give you a lifeline."

I nod in agreement. I might be going so deep undercover that I won't recognize myself, but I can still get out. That is, if I'm alive to make the call.

Holder goes on, "If this spirals out of your—their—control, there won't be a team ready to storm in and rescue you."

Ice chills the fire of revenge fueling the blood in my veins. "I accepted that before I chose this."

A grim silence hangs between us until he lands the final blow. "You'll cease to exist in the department."

I scoff. "I cease to exist now."

"Fair point. The rumors have spread like wildfire."

"You've got a mole, Ace."

Leaning back heavily in his chair. "Tell me something I don't already know."

"You need to flush him out."

"Which is what I'll be doing while you"—he lifts the folder—"go to work on this."

The breath leaves my body. Some part of me thought he'd force me to wait for acknowledgement from the bureau of my innocence. But the evidence is too damning. The Irish Mafia is too damn good once they have you in their sights.

And they planted just enough evidence about me to make doing my job impossible.

"There's one thing."

"What?"

He points back and forth between us. "To every man and woman here at the agency, in uniform, you'll have become one of them—the enemy."

"I know." That burns. These are people I've gone into hot spots and cold missions with. I've never made them doubt me.

But the mob has.

"Dec, I can't publicly acknowledge what you're doing until it's all over. Do you understand what I'm saying?" His eyes meet mine. "Even if I consider you to be the son I never had."

His declaration hits me like a vicious blow to the gut—confirming everything I already feared. "Ace, do you think I'm doing the right thing?" I anxiously await his verdict. Every movement I've made since graduating from Harvard Law all those years ago, including being assigned to the FBI's Organized Crime and Racketeering Section, he's been by my side.

But this? I stare as he flips through the file again.

What will I do if he disagrees? Give up on my vow? I think bitterly. Yet here I am, forced to accept that I might just do that. The vow I made in the vestige of an agent's blood and the danger lurking in the shadows waiting to strike at any moment propel me to move forward even if it's not quite within the lines of justice.

For now.

A few weeks ago, I was at home when my doorbell rang. *Ding, dong.* It wasn't UPS leaving a package. No, instead of something I ordered from Amazon, I had a visit from the Byrnes family—founding members of the largest Irish Mafia operation on the Eastern Seaboard.

The enforcers weren't there to deliver a message. They were there to recruit me. They need help, and apparently, I'm the one they've chosen for the position. I tried to decline their "interview," but all I received for my efforts were three cracked ribs and bruised kidneys that caused me to piss blood for days.

After they left, I made a call to someone I knew would be *very* interested in who stood back and watched while I had my ass handed to me by not one but four of the Byrnes best. He agreed with their unanimous vote—I should fill that position, but for an entirely different reason.

The company I recently started working for planted the necessary seeds. They did this carefully. Meticulously. We, the few in the know, understand the security around the Byrnes inside, but still, someone managed to get that man in. Worse, someone's keeping him from being found out.

The only way to discover the truth is to get past their stronghold undetected.

Still, it means there's information about me in federal databases that's about to disappear. My new boss assured me the hacker he has on staff is wiping away the electronic evidence even as we speak. In a matter of hours, I'll be able to operate from inside the Byrnes' operation in a do or die attempt to bring the entire empire down, desperately hunting for a redemption that may be forever out of reach.

"Burning their organization down from the inside out is the only option," I growl. "The Byrnes will believe I've truly flipped sides when they see I abandoned my post at a moment when it suited them."

A cold, grim silence hangs between us until he lands the final blow. "Dec, you can lose everything representing them. Hell, you could be arrested yourself."

"If they commit a crime against the legal advice I provide, essentially ignoring my counsel, then I can be excused under the crime-fraud exemption," I remind him.

"True. But by then, they'll have you so ensnared in their business dealings you'll have to go down with them first. You could end up disbarred. Worse yet, the testimony could be thrown out."

I jerk my chin. "That's why you're going to call that number."

Ace picks up the card again. Turning it over and over in his fingers, he flicks it back on his desk. "I don't have to. They reached out earlier, and their lawyer sent over the paperwork."

A shiver of cold travels up my spine. "Are you going to sign it?"

He closes the file. "I already did."

My breath releases in a rush. Just as I'm about to express my gratitude, he reminds me of what to expect. "Once you leave my office, you'll become one of them—a traitor. You know defense attorneys for criminal groups of this ilk are often as guilty as their clients."

His declaration hits me like the vicious blows I took to the gut when I first turned down the Byrnes enforcers—pain so sharp, I'd never felt anything like it before. Only this time, the pain isn't a physical ache making me want to vomit all over myself, it's a realization of loss.

"Burning every bridge is the only option," I growl.

Ace drums his fingers on the desk, absorbing every biting word I've spat out over the last hour. Finally, he relents. "When I can, I'll keep an eye on you and pull a few strings."

"Don't get yourself entangled in this," I snap, warning him. The last thing I need is for him or anyone else I remotely care about to become collateral damage when one of the very reasons I'm plunging into the Byrnes' shadowy hierarchy is already gone.

He presses on, oblivious to my protest. "But if they ask you to do something too... messy. If you cross lines that aren't meant to be crossed, Dec? There's no way for me to protect you."

My lips curve, but my smile never reaches my hardened eyes. "I've never needed help in that department before."

"Bullshit. We've always had your back. You know that."

He's right, of course. My team, the department, even the man in front of me—they've covered my ass countless times. Still, I've felt the burning stares and heard the abrupt shifting of conversations as the lies deliberately planted began to spread.

If the suspicious glares during Office of Professional Responsibility meetings are any indication, the storm that will rage if all the fabricated evidence is revealed will be devastating. If I don't capitulate under my own terms, the "proof" the Byrnes have manufactured is tainted enough to set us back years and will have OPR scrambling for that long to uphold any arrests I've made as an agent.

Still, I have to prove myself. Right now, I'm being tested. Aside from their business holdings, the Byrnes' top priority for me will be to negotiate a marker with their compatriots, the Tiberis—a faction of the larger northeastern Italian mob located in Darien, Connecticut.

Most of the higher ranking officers are hanging on by a thread in the federal penitentiary because of charges ranging from B&E to stalking, kidnapping, assault with a deadly weapon, and attempted murder. One is charged with multiple counts of murder.

At first, I couldn't figure out why the Byrnes wanted me involved until I realized their interest is money driven. Money that has dried up with the key Tiberis in jail. They need me as a go-between. What they don't realize is by appointing me as their liaison, they're giving me unfettered access to the ins and outs of their operations under the guise of legal necessity.

I'll be a federal prosecutor's wet dream. Eventually.

"This case…," his deep voice rumbles. "The weight of media frenzy is practically tangible over anything having to do with Irish mob revelations."

"I know."

"No, you think you know. The people you work for now? They're hungry for retribution. In a dark alley, I'm not certain who I'd fear facing —them or the Byrnes. They're no one to fuck with."

"I understand." Do I ever. The moment I was approached with the offer, I knew what stakes were on the line. I was about to dive so deep into a pit of mud, I'm certain I'll never be clean again.

He leans in, voice lowering dangerously, "If you take this path, you're not just abandoning your badge—you're forsaking every ounce of protection it once provided."

Unable to contain my fury, I slam my fist onto his desk. "Unless I do, we don't gain anything! Have you considered that?"

Rubbing his temples in resignation, he challenges, "At what cost, Dec? What will it cost you personally?"

My head hangs low, the weight of his despair and desperation making it hard to hold up. "Maybe that's exactly what's needed. I failed to save her. I lost her. How many more lives won't be saved if I don't take this next step?"

"We all lost Tanya, Dec. Not just you."

I flinch and can't reply because while I know he's right, he's also wrong. She was *mine* to protect. Something in my face must reflect that because Holder swears under his breath. After a long moment, he reaches into his desk, pulling out a packet of matches. Without any further discussion, he lifts the file we've been discussing, drops it into the trash, strikes a match and drops it atop of it.

Together, we watch as a list of my accommodations and the crucial paperwork OPR has been cultivating about my life turns into ash. When the fire smolders out, he hands me the metal bucket.

I stomp down on the remaining embers, each movement obliterating my ties with the FBI more so than the simple resignation letter he received in his email earlier today. Then I head into his en suite, fill the bucket with water, and transform the blackened remnants into useless sludge before flushing the slime away.

> UNKNOWN
>
> The files are gone for good. No chance of recovery.

When I enter back into his office and hand over the bin, I meet his gaze. Regret is heavy in my voice when I show him the text, "There's nothing to stop it now."

He winces before ordering, "Get the hell out of my office before someone catches us."

I jerk up my chin. Just as my hand touches the knob, I hear him call out, "Dec?"

I don't turn around. "Yeah?"

"See you on the other side. We'll make this okay, yeah?"

Without another word, I open the door and vanish into the night, each silent step affirming that there's no turning back—a haunting promise that nothing will ever be the same again.

CHAPTER TWO

ONE YEAR LATER

DECLAN

BOSTON SMELLS LIKE FILTHY SNOW AND BACK-TO-BACK CARS IN the winter. It doesn't matter if it's morning, noon, or night—the white crap that falls from the sky absorbs the scent of exhaust from the vehicles that trudge their way into the city at all hours of the day.

I keep my head down, walking carefully over the salted and cracked sidewalk from my apartment toward the front office of Byrne Litigation —a clean front for the laundering operation buried underneath.

Technically, I work for them now. Or at least, they think I do.

The reality is that I'm here to help Hudson Investigations clean house, investigate a string of dirty contracts and politicians getting rich off their name.

Not blow my cover.

Not get noticed.

Unfortunately, I'm good at my job—too good. And I spent the night out on my freezing balcony trying to make certain the backstory about my case history would substantiate what I found in the files I've been reviewing—that one of their own had been systematically ripping them off for years.

While I'm not here to make friends, I'm definitely not trying to get killed. Coughing into my gloved hand, I'd also like to avoid too many conversations in below zero weather unless I want to pay for a trip to urgent care. As tough as I know I am, it's been years since I've gone through any kind of arctic training.

I stop to hack up a lung in front of an electronics store, causing the people in front of it to scurry by as if they're afraid they'll catch the plague. I want to reassure them what I have isn't contagious, but something catches my eye from the wall of television screens through the glass.

And it's not the StellaNova logo playing on each one.

It's her.

Over and over.

She's posing on the red carpet in an intricately pleated dress that shimmers navy and purple beneath the camera lights. Her black hair, piled high, gleams as brightly as the jewels wrapped around her neck. When she turns to give the paparazzi a better angle of the masterpiece she is, my tongue thickens in my mouth at the sight of all her creamy skin on display.

Someone says something to her off camera, and her eyes light up. Her smile broadens and her head falls back with genuine laughter.

I knew from the moment I saw her she was a force of nature. Seconds later, when her name flashes on the screen, I read aloud, "Kalie Marshall

—Heiress to Lockwood Industries Fortune. Sports icon, philanthropist, and renowned attorney."

I can't move. Can't breathe as I put the pieces together of who she is in my mind.

The household heiress mentioned in the news for her good deeds and charitable work, is Katherine Laura Marshall—the same womanI couldn't take my eyes off during that long-ago Harvard Law graduation.

Still, I didn't put it together until just now when I saw her name displayed on a wall of televisions. After all, Kalie Marshall isn't a name you forget. Not anywhere in the Northeast—hell, not anywhere in America. The Lockwoods and Marshalls are as intrinsic to the history of American wealth as the Waltons. The family's fortunes stem from their business empire built over generations and continues to grow year after year.

I force myself to back away from the televisions, muscles taut. I can't think about that day right now. There are too many balls to juggle. Balls that, if they splat on the ground, will have my head lying next to them bloody soon after. Today, I need to don the mask of skirting the law without actually breaking it.

Pushing forward, cold air scraping at my throat, I wonder how much my boss cringes every time his daughter is front and center of the world's attention. Though, knowing her family, the banner from StellaNova likely has subliminal messages screaming "Stay away!" built within them.

There's nothing they won't do to protect their family, including hiring someone to blow up the mob from the inside when one of their own is threatened.

I trudge a few feet down the street before something compels me to twist my head back. All the monitors have zoomed in. Amid too many people, I fight through the bobbing heads and see only her. For all intents and purposes, the only two people on the street are me and her gorgeous face.

Just like we were for those precious seconds that day at the Tercentenary Theatre.

I wasn't supposed to meet anyone like her. Hell, I technically don't exist in her family's world, even if I'm on their damn payroll.

If anyone knew, it could blow apart everything we're trying to do, and I could end up dead.

A bad combination for a man who relies upon working the shadows to stay alive.

For now.

CHAPTER THREE

PRESENT DAY

My sisters and cousins have all gathered around the flat screen. On the coffee table, I've strategically placed bowls of snacks to be munched on as we catch up on gossip for the first time in forever.

"All right, ladies! I've got wine. I've got booze. Let's get our StellaNova game faces on!" I proclaim as I pass a heavily laden tray full of cocktails around.

My cousin, roommate, and one of my best friends, Grace Bianco, announces to the room at large. "Growing up, did any of us ever imagine our cousin would turn to the dark side?"

I chuckle. "You mean Chuck going to work for the paparazzi that have stalked us our entire lives?"

Grace waves her glass in the air. "Exactly."

"Did you ever imagine we'd actually be excited to watch Chuck's first solo celebrity interview on StellaNova?" I muse. StellaNova, the most intuitive—and sometimes intrusive—of the media moguls, has somehow made its way into our lives, not just through my cousin.

"I can't believe it. He's all grown up." Grace swipes an imaginary tear from beneath her eye.

Our other cousin and former housemate, Laura Lockwood, sips her drink. "It's hard to imagine he's the same pain-in-the-ass little brother who used to crush on all our friends. Gracie, remember your and Kalie's senior prom when he was mouthing off about trying to get laid, and Mama lit into him?"

That sets the three of us whooping in hysterical laughter. Grace chortles, "Chuck was scolded by Aunt Cassidy so hard, we called you at college from my bedroom to tell you all about it."

Laura cackles, "Even before you left for prom!"

One of my twin sisters, Regina, who somehow turned doodling in the margins of her homework into a worldwide phenomenon of home tile designs used by high-end kitchens all over the world, snags the chilled bottle of Grey Goose off the table. "Let's not talk about getting laid. It's been a bitch of a week."

Reggie's twin—my other sister, Valerie—rolls her eyes at Reggie's flair for the dramatic. "Why? Did you not get your insides ground up by your favorite Coffee Shop boy toy?" Val names the small breakfast stop in Collyer near my office, which I swear fuels the blood in my veins and apparently is Reggie's spot to troll her latest conquest.

Reggie tosses back her shot of vodka before offering Val a killer glare. "Jealous much? Cobwebs not getting cleared out, so they're about to reaffirm you as a vestal virgin?"

Val reaches over and snatches up one of our cousin Nicole's infamous chocolate caramel brownie bites and cocks her arm back—her intent obvious. Before she can break a sacred family rule—waste no food baked by our Aunt Corinna or Nicole—I snatch it out of her hand and pop it into my mouth. Then I stare down my two sisters and nod in the direction of my front door. "If you two can't hold your liquor, call a cab, and don't let the door hit your ass on the way out."

Reggie pouts, and Val tries for an air of innocence.

Story of my life with these two.

Still, after I take them down a peg or two, we settle in to watch Chuck's debut on national television. I relax back into the cushion of the couch with a content sigh. It's been a long year and we're well overdue for a night like this, where we can just be us again. Casting a glance in Laura's direction, my heart trembles. I have to keep repeating to myself, you didn't lose her. You didn't lose her. None of us did.

Almost two years ago, Laura worked on saving the life of a man in the ER. When he didn't make it, his family took revenge by shooting up her ER, killing colleagues and friends. Not long after, she was stalked and almost died when they captured her and her soon-to-be stepdaughter. Both were held hostage for hours by the monster's family. She escaped relatively unscathed, but it forced us to accept the monsters our family had told us about, as their origins still lurk in the shadows, ready to strike at any moment without provocation.

Now, sitting here drinking wine and laughing, you'd never believe Laura's fine and planning her wedding to the man she worked for as a medical nanny for his daughter while she recovered. She's declared more than once she refuses to be coddled by what happened to her— much like the traumas that shaped the rest of our family.

No, none of us are defined by those; we're defined by something much more profound—love.

Gracie snickers as she tucks her feet beneath her. "Let's talk about something more important."

"Like what?" Reggie asks.

"Like how did Chuck get the scoop on how Snowy T thought this was a good idea? I mean, a grand gesture is one thing, but he proposed to his girlfriend in front of a thousand wedding guests using a skywriter where he was the best man. Isn't there some sort of unwritten rule that this kind of nonsense gets you sent to best friend jail?"

"Bitchy bride jail, if nothing else," Laura concurs. Then she drops some gossip of her own into the mix. "I heard a rumor he contacted Amaryllis Events to see if Mama and the rest of y'all are available to plan the wedding."

I somehow manage to suppress the smug grin that wants to spread across my face, not only because I know Chuck's about to announce that on his news show tonight, but because of the lightness in Laura's voice. I lift my drink to my lips to avoid giving the scoop away when I spy a banner running along the bottom of the television screen. My insides churn when I snap, "Gracie, rewind now!"

She fumbles for the remote. Silence descends on the room when the distinctive midnight blue and white banner StellaNova uses for up-to-the-minute celebrity news displays information I never expected. It rips through the lightheartedness of the room before reaching into my chest and squeezing my heart.

Attempted murder charges dropped against Sal Tiberi.

"Turn up the volume, Gracie," Laura orders softly.

My eyes cut over to her. "This can't be happening." My words are barely heard over the StellaNova celebrity gossip desk's somber proclamation.

"Earlier today, a controversial court ruling led to the release of an alleged mob consigliere in the Tiberi family. One of the men accused of the attempted murder of billionaire heiress Laura Lockwood had the charges dropped against him due to a chain of custody errors in handling key evidence. The judge ruled that..."

I stare at the television as video footage of the Tiberi defense attorney, Declan Conian, making his way down the Superior Court steps and through a madhouse of paparazzi, flashes across the screen. When the phone rings, pulling me out of my shock, a bitter laugh escapes me.

"Who wants to bet that's the courthouse calling to tell us about the release?"

Laura's glass trembles violently in her hand. Reggie leans over and hugs her from behind, carefully maneuvering the glass away before she can hurt herself any more than she already has been. Moments later, the entire front of our home is lit up like it's daylight as news crews do everything short of trespass to get a shot of the place where the events Declan Conian is working to erase occurred.

Her own home.

Gracie mutters, "Son of a bitch."

I couldn't agree with her more.

Laura's frozen in place. I practically levitate from my position on the couch and make my way over to her. "Look at me, Laura."

Her wide eyes, glassy with tears she refuses to let fall, meet mine. "He's free. He can try again."

"Liam won't let him," I remind her of her fiancé waiting at home. "Neither will your dad or my dad. Our family. Remember all the people who love you who have your back." My voice is fierce.

I reach for the remote to mute the sound, but Laura says, "Is there anything I can do, Kalie? I need to know."

I swallow down the bile even as I give her the truth. "Unless there's new evidence, they can't try him again for the same crime. It would be double jeopardy."

Laura wraps her arms around herself and rocks. "He gets to walk." She shoves to her feet and mumbles, "I...just need a second."

Helpless, we sit by as she hurries up the stairs to her old bedroom—now my home office. I hear the door click shut behind her before I say what I'm really thinking. "Fuck."

I know the law. I studied it. But tonight, I feel like justice failed. We were judged and found lacking, and I don't know how we're going to live with that.

But I need to try.

Hours after everyone left, I can't help but draw up the memory of Declan's flirtatious smile on the day of my law school graduation. Gorgeous and intense, instead of luring me in, his immediate interest in me—a complete stranger—should have been a clanging of warning bells. It's hard to reconcile the man—a man I've fantasized more than once about before I found out who he really was—could be so calculating, so ruthless.

I can still recall reading the news article where he'd been named as the counsel of record for the Tiberi family. The night before, I'd had a particularly lucid dream about running into him again—and what had happened with him when I had. He'd dragged me into an alley, fumbling with his belt, and my skirt rucked up around my waist. I flush at the memory as I stare down at my pillow.

A media circus ensued once his name was tied to the case. But my unease wasn't full blown until I saw news articles with photographs of him at hearings with Tiberi family members at his side, challenging evidentiary rules being violated.

Despite everything, justice continued to be upheld. It withstood scrutiny. Until today.

CHAPTER FOUR

Kalie

If I thought the events from the night before were a bad dream, then work the next morning proved me to be sleepwalking. I can't seem to awaken from this nightmare that's happening to my family.

"He did what?" My mother's shriek outside my office cuts through the static of my phone call with a recalcitrant client. Hunched over my cluttered desk, I'm trying to wrap up the conversation while my heart thuds against my ribs. Through the window, the gloomy Friday the Thirteenth sky looks as if it's holding its breath—a day we normally keep free at Amaryllis Events because even we're not immune to human nature and its superstitions.

When I joined the company fresh out of Harvard, my early days were less about practicing law and passing the bar exam and more of a crash course in the corporation's unspoken rules. First, I learned to keep Uncle Phil far from anything with a power cord—if he touched anything electronic, disaster was inevitable. Second lesson, never underestimate a bride on a budget who's determined to see her vision come true. And third, I realized my very existence depends on the meticulous drafting of a contract—a document only as strong as the words etched into it.

Still, that doesn't mean a contract is always honored—much like a guilty verdict, or so I've learned in the last twenty-four hours. While Amaryllis Events has always stuck to our contractual terms, we've experienced more weddings than most, facing couples attempting to circumvent our ironclad clauses.

Now, a throbbing headache builds behind my eyes while I try to pacify the father of a bride over the phone. His deep, grumbling voice buzzes with anger. "I don't care what the contract says. If the country club canceled, then find me another site. My daughter isn't getting married under some flimsy wood slats they happen to have cobbled together on their grounds."

I pinch the bridge of my nose, calculating in my head. If I were a billable attorney, this call alone would earn a thousand dollars. Mr. Jones, the bride's father, is a maelstrom of fury and obstinacy, refusing to listen to a single word I've said even though the changes are in his favor. "Mr. Jones, the contract you signed clearly states that in the event of unforeseen circumstances, the venue reserves the right to relocate the event to a comparable space."

He cuts me off, voice rising like steam from a locomotive. "You don't get it. My daughter's in hysterics, my wife's in tears, and you're just hiding behind fancy legal words. I'm going to own your ass."

My jaw tightens as I try to interject, "Mr. Jones—"

"Listen, sweetheart." His tone drips condescension and disdain. My teeth grind together at the derogatory term. "I get this might be the only job a paralegal like you ever landed, but can you get a real fucking attorney on the phone?"

It takes every ounce of self-control not to fire off a snide email that flaunts my law degree and bar association number to this raging tyrant. Through gritted teeth, I press on, "Would it help your wife and daughter if I let you know that the wait list for the rotunda and grotto is longer than that of the ballroom? It's considered more exclusive."

A heavy silence falls before his voice wavers with uncertainty. "It is?"

At last, a breakthrough! "Yes. Additionally, due to the inconvenience to your daughter's vision"—I add a mental note to thank Uncle Phil for pontificating about the bride's questionable taste and flower choices so I can speak to it with ease—"the venue has arranged for additional decor enhancements for the rotunda and will contact you later today to upgrade your catering package at no extra charge."

His anger deflates significantly, replaced by the pragmatic tone of vanity and fiscal logic of the man I initially dealt with. "Those are very reasonable terms. Why didn't you just say so?"

I fight the urge to burst into hysterical laughter. We finally wrap up the call as I promise to send him the amended contract by the end of the day. No sooner have I disconnected than my mother, dressed immaculately in a trim blue suit and towering heels, strides into my office. As General Counsel and Chief Financial Officer for Amaryllis Events, she carries an air of command and grace. "You deserve a medal for not verbally annihilating Mr. Jones."

I lean back in my chair, admiring the way her light hair spills perfectly around her face, her peaches-and-cream skin glows, and her athletic runner's build makes her look two decades younger than she actually is. "Barely earned it, but thanks," I reply.

She chuckles knowingly. "When I was your age dealing with such imbeciles, I'd just let them sue us."

"Did you win?" I ask, arching an eyebrow.

"Most of the time," she admits with a wry smile. "Even then, I was obsessive about covering our proverbial asses with meticulous paperwork." Her lips curl with amusement as she adds, "There was one bride who sued us because she'd forgotten she was actually getting married. It's Cass's favorite story to tell."

My jaw falls open. "We send out like a million reminders and…"

Mama shrugs, her tone shifting to a playful chastisement. "Yet, we still can't help people who don't know what day of the week it is." Her voice rises to taunt someone she knows is within hearing distance. "You know, like Phil."

A faint, indiscernible mutter from just beyond my door makes me smile, and my mother laughs softly. With a come-hither gesture, she beckons me. "Come on. Meeting time."

I rise from my chair and reach for my laptop. "What did Uncle Phil get into this time?" I ask, a note of apprehension creeping into my voice.

"You won't need that," she nods at my laptop.

"What's this about?"

Her face, so usually animated, suddenly hardens into a mask of solemnity. "It's better if we tell you all at once."

Leaving my office with a sense of dread, I trail behind her to the conference room. Normally, I love spending time in this room, which has borne witness to so many of our family's celebrations and milestones. From the deep, rich mahogany woodwork to the stained glass with its perfectly centered amaryllises, it embodies the vision my family had decades ago for the type of legacy they wanted to create—strong and enduring.

The moment I step inside, I realize this isn't another issue related to Uncle Phil's shenanigans with electronics, or even Amaryllis Events, for that matter. Instead, my cousins are huddled together—Laura, with her ER doctor's steady gaze, and Grace, an anaplastologist whose skilled hands speak of delicate precision—along with every member of our immediate family who calls this town and its surrounding areas home. Before I can muster a question, my mother strides purposefully toward Aunt Cassidy.

It's then I spot my father and Uncle Caleb standing at the head of the table, their presence as imposing as the reputation of their investigative agency. Flanking them is Laura's fiancé, his expression unreadable.

Suddenly, the explosive words I had heard while on the phone are far more ominous. Quietly, I murmur to myself, "This is going to be bad," and make my way toward my cousins, silently ready to offer my support.

An hour later, I find myself wishing I had been mistaken—wishing fervently that someone had pulled a Friday the Thirteenth prank.

But reality is far more grim.

My father and others, who are up to date on their Hudson bro code, have come into the office to explain the details regarding Declan Conian's demand for the recent release of the Tiberi consigliere based on the technicality we heard about on the news last night.

Like I thought, there's nothing we can do about it.

My nails bite into my palms as I make a fist, imagining what I would do if I had five uninterrupted minutes with Declan Conian.

Too bad they're different from what I imagined doing to him at my college graduation.

CHAPTER FIVE

Kalie

IF I HAD A DO-OVER AND PAUSED TO LOOK PAST THE SMUG GRIN ON his gorgeous face, would I have cursed first and hit second? I'm not sure. Either way, I'm confident the result would be the same. Struggling against the officer, I screech, "You're putting these on the wrong person! That bastard helped the son of a bitch who hit my niece get off scot-free!"

That gives the officer a moment's pause but doesn't deter him. Crap.

Then I spy a familiar face across the breezeway and shout, "Jon! Get this goon to take these cuffs off me!"

My cousin's eyes narrow before he leaves the group of people he was conversing with to bolt my way. Not even breaking a sweat in his bespoke suit, his "What the fuck, Kalie?" is heard by every person in the small circle around me, many of whom have cell phones up since the sinfully rich and equally gorgeous Jonathan Lockwood is in their presence. I roll my eyes. This ridiculously handsome playboy is the same child my cousin Laura and I would force to eat our mud pies. One would think they'd be more impressed that a dainty brunette in four-inch heels managed to knock out a man built like a linebacker with one solid punch.

Not.

I make a mental note to thank Mama and Daddy for my pugilist skills. They made certain all their "girls" could protect themselves in any situation. Whether it was running or self-defense, one of the Marshall clan's more annoying tendencies includes a never-ending competitiveness.

Those feelings festered and flourished in me—the first-born daughter to a man who openly admits he was born into a family that encouraged his being a sanctimonious prick. Not that I can blame my parents for my current predicament. I shake my wrists, feeling the cold steel against them—not a good look with the designer suit Aunt Em made me that I'm wearing for court.

A groan from the floor causes my insides to quiver. Glaring at me, Jon—the traitorous jerk—leans down and offers the prick a hand. I'm not sure my mouth can fall open any farther when the son of a bitch clasps my cousin's forearm and says, "Thanks for the assist."

"Excuse me? What the hell is happening right now?" I snarl at both men.

That's when furious chocolate brown eyes bore into mine before my victim snaps, "That's what I'd like to know."

Hearing his smooth voice sends bitter shards of fury to pump through my veins even as it makes my thighs clench together in sweet agony. Damn him. Damn, Declan Conian. I never imagined what it was like to curse in a violent rage until I read a news article about my cousin's trial one day and saw him with the people who harmed her.

Now, a face that used to cause tingles down my spine became a face I memorized in the hopes of achieving sweet, sweet vengeance if I ever happened upon the opportunity.

Yet, here he stands in a six-thousand-dollar suit, dabbing his split lip like he's the one who has been wronged. But I know better. Underneath the polished exterior made possible by blood money, by lying with the filth of the criminal underworld, is a man who deserves to face a judge for crimes against humanity.

Regretfully, I won't be able to file the paperwork to prevent Amaryllis Events from being sued, which was my intention before I entered the courthouse. No, instead, I let my temper get the best of me in front of two court officers. I have a one-way ticket to the pokey, and I somehow suspect this man isn't going to stop me from rotting in a cell. After all, he's intent on making my family relive our most recent nightmares.

And I, for one, haven't forgotten a single second of it, even if my cousin's appalled face indicates he might be wavering toward the enemy. I yell at Jon, "Since when did you start assisting the shyster who threatened our family?"

He tries to placate me, "Now, Kalie..."

My eyes narrow at him. "Don't, Jon. Don't you dare justify your actions right now."

"Declan wasn't directly involved with what happened," he tries to reason. Meanwhile, I'm debating never speaking to my own blood cousin ever again for treason against his own.

Laura was harmed by the clients this man represents and he wants to stand here splitting hairs about ethics? About a man who will defend their innocence, yet he claims Declan isn't playing a part in harming his sister? Like I care about the difference between whether someone physically or mentally injures one of our family?

In our family, we know better than most that pain causes scars. It lingers in the soul's crevices. It agitates the subconscious. And just because you can move past it doesn't mean it's never going to rise back up and demand retribution.

Recalling the memories of how it felt to return after our home was violated, my breath releases in short, choppy bursts. My muscles tighten with the force of my fury. I refuse to be victimized anymore. Still, this bastard's unreadable expression holds mine.

It's quite different from the look he gave me over and over on one of the most important days of my life, when he charmed me from half a tent away. Fury builds up inside me as I recall the way I wanted to stay behind for him, causing me to shout, "You asshole!"

"Jesus, Kalie!" Jon admonishes, but I'm so beyond caring what my traitorous cousin thinks. Knowing another member of my extended family will bail my ass out, I ignore my cousin. My heel slips slightly as I struggle against the officer's increasingly tightening grip as I let my venom spew. "You have a lot of nerve to show your face in this town, Conian."

He quirks his brow at my cousin and asks, "Who is this...individual, Lockwood?"

Jon growls, "My cousin."

"Ahh. That...explains so much." He dabs at his lip one final time before announcing, "You look good leashed up, sweetheart."

"Why you, son-of-a..."

"Mr. Conian, I suggest you walk away if you don't want a judge to believe Ms. Marshall had provocation to attack you," the officer suggests.

My head whips around. "Why am I not surprised he has a few of Darien's finest tucked in his pocket right next to the dick you're likely sucking?"

Jon scrubs his hand down his face. "Kalie, stop digging your hole any deeper."

"Jon, I hope when I tell the family, they'll be proud of you for turning to the dark side." I jiggle my hands at the officers, and in a saccharine sweet tone, I say, "If you're going to do more than tease me with these, do it already. I don't like to be held down for too long."

At that, Conian chuckles roughly. "I'd love to see who has the balls to do that to you."

My smile is diabolical. "Any man other than you."

"Kalie," Jon warns. "Let me just call your father."

"Aww, ain't that sweet—a daddy's girl. Explains so much," Conian mocks me.

"Why you..."

"Maybe I should meet your father to offer him some pointers about how to raise his little girl."

A hush envelops the crowd. My smile is lethal. "You really want to meet my father?"

"I don't think you want me to answer that."

Something in his tone sends a shiver down my spine. I refuse to admit it's fear. Before I can lash out again, the officers are dragging me away, beginning their recitation. "You have the right to remain silent. Anything you say can and will be used against you in a court of law. You have the right to an attorney..."

I snarl, "I am one."

Conian lets out a frustrated sigh, "Then you should have known better."

"Go to hell and take my traitorous cousin with you!" I spit back with venom.

He casts a withering glance over me one last time before turning his back, engaging in a cold, calculated discussion with my cousin—his face a mask of indifference. I snap my head toward the officers as they finish reading me my *Miranda* rights. "Yes, I understand my rights. But before I utter another word, I demand my right to a phone call."

The devil remains unfazed as I am dragged toward lockup. Not a single flicker of concern crosses his face. But he should be worried.

This battle is far from over. Not as long as I have a breath to fight with.

CHAPTER SIX

HER DAZZLING BLUE EYES BORE INTO MINE WITH A SEARING FURY, so incredibly different than the last time I looked into them seven years ago. Christ, has it been that long?

I was too stunned to fake my reaction when her fist collided with my face. I didn't resist, letting the motion carry me to the floor. I let her channel all her raw anger into me, knowing she needed to unburden herself to stay strong for those around her. Besides, enduring her dainty fist to the face was a lot easier than putting her in danger by explaining the truth—that I'm not the enemy she believes me to be. Still, I admire the fact Kalie has such a strong moral code she believes in.

I just hate I'm on the side of it she abhors to such a degree she lost sight of her own safety in the process.

"Mr. Conian."

I snap around. A court officer eyes me with thinly veiled disgust. "You pressing charges?"

I let the thought circle in my mind. Then, like a ruthless sovereign, decree Kalie Marshall's fate. "Take her to the station. I'll let you know."

The officer's sneer cuts through the tension. "I figured you'd say something like that."

I don't say anything. Choosing—as is the better choice in the world I presently inhabit—to let my silence speak for me.

He snickers. "Still, the lady's right hook is something else."

I glare as fiercely as I can, forcing him into a hasty retreat. Deep down, I admit he's right. I never would have imagined my attending a Harvard Law graduation just so I could hear a speaker would lead to my meeting a woman.

Nor did I predict the way our lives would diverge in the manner they have now.

I rub the unexpected ache in my jaw. The raven-haired dynamo packs a shockingly powerful punch. It wasn't as brutal as the beatings I endured while working for the bureau, nor the torturous trials I took back in the early days proving my "loyalty" to the Byrnes scion. Yet, I'm still caught off guard that Kalie managed to clip me, but good.

I was unaware of the vicious torment occurring to Kalie's cousin—an exceptional ER doctor. Instead, under my cover as the Byrnes' family's lawyer—silently passing along information to my actual boss—I began building up a reputation for being able to get their soldiers and enforcers off using my brains instead of threats.

It got me noticed, giving me more access and helping to facilitate my own agenda.

Still, I wasn't expecting what happened next. Since there was a business tie between the Byrnes and the Tiberis, they called in a marker. Suddenly, I was being ordered to represent the *pezzi di merda*. Since I wasn't in any way associated with the raid in Darien—something the Tiberi *famigilia* considered fortunate—it appeared to be a legitimate business transaction.

The only benefit is the extremely long leash the Byrnes gave me by sending me to Darien after they entrusted me with the defense. In fact, this case has taken so long that I've been asked to check up on their business interests "as a favor."

The Byrnes ordered me to do it.

Favor, my ass. With most of their crew either dead or behind bars, the entire outfit is in danger of crumbling. Which is just how my *real* bosses want it.

As much as their family may be in the dark, the late-night strategy sessions I've had with my true bosses led to the necessity of getting Sal Tiberi released to keep the least dangerous of the rackets functioning without getting my hands any dirtier than they are while we continue to funnel more critical information to the Feds.

While avoiding having my head chopped off in the process.

Now, the Byrnes assume I'm playing nice with the Tiberis. The Tiberis are overjoyed I managed an actual break in what was presumably an airtight case. Neither has the slightest idea that I'm secretly aligning with federal prosecutors to bury them so deep in the penal system that retribution becomes impossible.

Still, as Kalie is dragged away in handcuffs, bitter remorse tugs at me— hating how her unwavering loyalty to her family has snared her into this mess. The reality is, I do know members of her family far better than she would appreciate. I suspect by the time she's done being fingerprinted, her connections will bail her out—long before she ever sees a real holding cell.

Impassively, I continue dabbing at my lip as the crowd disperses, and only when they vanish entirely does the tension leach from my muscles. The last thing I need is further attention.

Not now, of all times.

"You okay?" my direct supervisor, Jonathan Lockwood, asks quietly. I've been on the Hudson Investigation payroll for years now, trading my badge for a broader, potentially lethal cover that let me weave through the murky depths of the Byrnes family's operations.

My thoughts flash back to the long-ago night at Director Holder's office when I received a text from a shadow account. Without the tech wizards at Hudson Investigations, it's a certainty my cover would have crumbled under the first computer upgrade.

But here I am, years later, still alive.

"I didn't expect to run into your family," I murmur.

Jon's heavy exhale bristles with frustration. His reason for being at court today to testify for another case gave us an opportunity to meet in person. While we try not to meet in public too often, it would seem odd if our paths *never* crossed. "Yeah. If I'd known Kalie was going to be here, I wouldn't have paraded you around."

I work my jaw from side to side slowly, barely concealing my dark amusement. "Who would've thought the biggest reaction to seeing me would come from your cousin?"

"You'd be surprised," he replies, his eyes deep with unspoken history I can't penetrate. "Sometimes you have to worry most about the smallest members of my family."

I maintain a blank face, but her word "traitor" echoes violently in my mind, repeating over and over.

That label has haunted me since the rumors began to swirl about me. It hardly mattered if they were whispered, shouted, or spat in a thousand tongues. It was the price I agreed to pay to find out what happened to Tanya. Worth every ounce of pain, in my opinion. Yet those in the know —those who'd have a target in between their eyes if the truth escapes before we're done—know I fought for something far larger than my own judgment.

"We've got your back," Jon murmurs.

"I know." And it's that knowledge why, when Hudson Investigations approached me, I leaped at the chance to not only utilize latitude to take these bastards down, but to join a team of men and women from varying backgrounds who all have the same mission.

Protect the innocent.

The company founded by Jon's father and uncle admittedly wants retribution for what happened in the recent past. But they're ravenous for an opening into the human trafficking ring there are whispers about the Byrnes being involved in.

For decades.

I not only supplied enough information for them to start their search, but I've become the weapon Hudson has selectively aimed to dismantle that sinister pipeline by writing contracts my "bosses" are signing in their arrogance without understanding. Teams of agents are now capable of rescuing children snatched from exclusive homes across the country because of the intelligence I'm able to provide.

It might not make up for receiving a cooler filled with the severed head of a woman I deeply cared about, but it's something.

Jon's firm hand on my shoulder shatters my introspection. "We've got bigger problems than Kalie."

"What now?"

He maneuvers me through the bustling crowd—a sea of people oblivious to the spectacle of a man sucker-punched by a woman half his size. His eyes dart wildly until he pulls me away, grumbling, "I told you not to get near my family, Conian!"

My lips harden into a sneer—a barely hidden threat beneath a veneer of controlled calm. "Then keep your rabid cousin away from me."

Jon growls but relents the moment we disappear from the view of the courthouse's chaotic hallway. He flips his phone around to reveal a text message:

UNCLE KEENE:

Office.

Now.

I let out a sharp exhale. Yes, I'd anticipated this reaction from the protective father—not my demanding boss. Keene Marshall is nothing if not predictable. The second he realized his perfect princess had endangered herself—whether on purpose or not—I suspected I was going to go a round or two with him. But I refuse to let her emotional outburst derail years of struggle slogging through filth for one resolute goal.

Retribution for Tanya.

With that purpose still burning in my veins, I follow Jon out after a brief meeting with the court officers who want to take my statement. They seemed terrified that I'd unleash holy hell, sending some of my "family" in their direction. What they don't realize is I have more respect for them than they could possibly imagine. After giving Jon a signal to meet me at Hudson, I step out of the courthouse before subduing my groan at the number of paparazzi on the steps.

"Mr. Conian!"

"Do you believe you'll be able to get all the Tiberis exonerated?"

"What happened in the rotunda?"

"Do you plan on pressing charges?"

Answering each query from the media with a curt, "No comment," I slip into the back of an armor-plated limousine waiting at the courthouse's base. In the vehicle's shadowed confines, I exhale sharply after giving the driver precise directions.

So far, everything is unfolding exactly as planned.

Except for a thorn on the perfect rose that is Kalie Marshall.

Groaning, I massage my jaw, already hearing the thunderous disapproval of her father. I hope the man is brief—I have work to do.

And it wasn't my fault the fight ignited.

With this thought, I slump back into the seat. Keene is a reasonable man. He'll understand.

I hope.

CHAPTER SEVEN

DECLAN

Striding into Hudson Investigations half an hour later, I'm immediately swept underground into a secure space that only individuals with the highest credentials can access. I'm temporarily transported back to the early days of working for the agency before I became entangled with the treacherous Byrnes family.

Every step I take electrifies my spirit as I absorb the pulsing chaotic energy. Whispers say Keene built this very office to be near his wife when her pregnancy with their eldest daughter was first discovered. A sly smirk curls my lips. After today, I can completely imagine a tiny Kalie in utero throwing punches even before birth.

"Why are you smiling?" Jon growls in a low, demanding tone after catching up to me.

I let him in on my inner thoughts. He bursts out laughing before warning, "I'd keep that story to yourself since we're about to chat with Uncle Keene."

We push through the open office space amid the rapid-fire greetings from colleagues—some rallying from our team. Our path takes us past a glass-walled conference room where Liam Payne, Jon's soon-to-be brother-in-law, is mercilessly tongue-lashing a few miscreants. After listening for a few minutes, Jon and I chortle when we realize it's over an un-expensed stop at a food truck for one of the company's higher profile clients.

He elbows me with a wicked glint. "Doesn't this make you wonder what's going to blaze across the front page of StellaNova in the morning?"

I scoff, my voice laced with biting sarcasm. "Not a damn thing if they value their jobs."

"What do you think's going on?"

I observe Liam more closely as he waves a stack of papers in his hand. "Twenty says it's because they didn't fill out their paperwork in triplicate. He was always a pain in the ass about that in the bureau too."

Jon bellows out a laugh. "Probably."

"Still, I imagine if your father gets wind of this, it will give him something to mock him over at your twisted spectacle of a family dinner." I haven't let myself experience real family in years—not since Tanya opened hers up to me.

And then they cut me off after her brutal murder.

"For all the theatrics you've dealt with today pertaining to my family, you'd have one hell of a story to sell to StellaNova. That, or you're getting used to us."

I stop dead in my tracks. "Take that back."

Jon's brow furrows. "You don't want to be like us?"

"Be like you? Hell, I figure by the time I'm done, you're just going to assimilate me or kill me."

He howls with laughter as I demand, "Tell me I'm wrong, and your family isn't like the Borg?"

"I can't. They're worse. They breed more chaos."

"Point made." We walk a few more feet when a clearly pregnant Rachel Aiken, daughter of one of Hudson's owners, sends us a brisk wave before diving into a corridor that's so secure that if your biometrics aren't stored, or if you're not invited in, you may not make it out alive.

Jon shudders. "She scares the crap out of me."

I nod. "Her husband has balls of steel."

"He needed them a few years ago."

I know there's a story there, but Jon goes on to tell me what to expect when we meet with Keene. I interrupt. "You know, I have dealt with the man."

"Yeah, but this is his daughter," he warns me.

"Then she should have better control over her emotions."

"That's not the defense I would go in with."

"I'm not that suicidal. Plus, you'd have a hard time hiding my body. Every move of mine is being tracked by some media hound with a Mafia fetish—particularly the romance readers on TikTok," I add, arching an eyebrow at him.

"Better you than me."

"That's right. Your pretty face was exposed, so no more gritty fieldwork for you."

Jon snarls a response. The truth stings him and I immediately feel bad for the dig. Jon was a true chameleon, ever shifting, until that notorious night when Tanya's life ended and the score Jon and I agreed to settle together began. Still, he's one of the few people I call a friend. I try to lighten the mood. "After today's display, I'm leaning toward believing the stories you've told me about them."

"I can't make this shit up. Ask Liam if you don't believe me."

"I know you have enough money, so give me the license to market this. I can't be the only one who should get a front row seat to the reality show you call your life."

He snickers, a grudging smirk playing on his lips. "You'd cash in big if you could convince my family to star in one."

"If even half your stories are true—especially the part about your relatives dancing on tables—the possibilities are endless. We'd wind up with a wild mashup of *Say Yes to the Dress* meets *Dancing with the Stars*," I retort.

"I tell no lies. Now, speaking of truth versus performance art, how's your cover holding up?" Jon challenges.

I extend my arms, showcasing every seam of my impeccably tailored three-piece Brioni suit—a suit that costs as much as a down payment on a luxury car. It's almost surreal to think that seven years ago I wouldn't have known a Brioni from Macy's nor would I have been close to a man of Jonathan Lockwood's caliber. Yet today, both are lifelines that keep me in this brutal game we've orchestrated.

At least until I uncover the full, vile truth of who ordered the takedown of a federal agent. Sure as hell, he's one of the few who know why I'm playing to begin with.

We reach my desk, and I collapse into the chair amid a chaotic mess of papers—a deliberate, explosive chaos that only I can decipher. Jon leans casually against the cubicle wall, his presence a welcome distraction from the looming tasks.

"You should see it firsthand," he murmurs, as if the words barely carry the weight of impending doom.

My stomach churns. Part of me yearns to detach from this underworld of raw filth and ruthless brutality, yet another part trembles at the thought of feeling vulnerable at that table—a tempting reason to shatter my hard-won resolve.

"One day," I reply diplomatically.

Jon arches an eyebrow, but before he can press further, a voice booms from down the hallway. "Look who finally decided to show up!"

I don't even need to stand to know who it is. The combined silence and the way everyone snaps their mouths shut tells me all I need to know: Keene Marshall—sanctimonious prick extraordinaire and everyone's despised boss—has descended into our war room.

I can almost hear the collective groans echo in my head as everyone within earshot wonders, *Who screwed up this time?* The answer, glaringly clear, is me.

Knowing I'm about to take the massive fallout for the team, I rise and extend my hand to the older man. "Miss me that much?"

He scoffs derisively. "Hardly. Just wondering if you're finally going to file any of your past due expense reports." He gestures at my chaotic desk. "Or if this is just another miserable social call."

Before I can retort, Jon cuts in, "It's not nearly as bad as it looked, Uncle Keene."

He arches a brow—then his tone shifts, slicing coldly, "What wasn't?"

At that instant, Keene's cell rings. He picks it up and for just a moment his countenance softens before muttering with exaggerated disgust, "It's Kalie. I wonder which of my relatives I need to post bail for this time."

Jon whispers, "Holy hell. He doesn't know."

"I don't know what?"

Damn it. A shitstorm is approaching fast—too quickly for us to avoid it. I snap at Jon, "You didn't tell him yet?"

Jon waves his phone, exasperated. "I thought he already knew! You saw the text. I thought we were being summoned because of it."

That's when Keene answers the call that might seal our impending doom. "Hey sweetheart."

At that moment, if I still clung to any hope of redeeming myself before destiny, I'd be praying hard. Keene's veneer of amicability shatters, his calm morphs into rage as he bellows, "What the fuck do you mean you were arrested, Katherine Laura?" His green eyes turn into shards of green glass, lethal and aimed directly at me. "I see."

The way Keene handles his oldest child being apprehended reveals I must have taken a far worse hit than I initially thought—unless I'm completely unhinged. Perhaps a brutal mix of both.

Before I can muster a defense, Keene clamps down on his temper long enough to order, "Don't say another fucking word, Kalie. I'm sending your godfather to bail you out." He pauses for a moment before continuing, "No, don't argue. And don't, under any circumstances, accept any favors the chief offers." Then his voice softens moderately. "Stick to the damn book, sweetheart."

Jon groans, pain and tension etched in every line of his face. He has every right to be terrified. I manage to gulp down what may be my final few breaths. Despite the fact I'm a lawyer for one of the largest crime families on the East Coast, they still don't make me want to shit in my pants the way Keene does when he's angry. Right now, angry was left down the road a ways back.

After he ends the call, he fixes his steely gaze on both me and Jon before coldly ordering, "My office. Now."

Without waiting for an answer—because neither of us dares defy him— Keene spins on his heel and storms toward the elevator, leaving behind an electric void of impending doom. On the way there, Keene unleashes a torrent of wrath upon his nephew, momentarily sparing me the lethal laser beams of his glare, leaving me to wonder what's going to be my fate when we're behind closed doors.

I don't have long to find out.

CHAPTER EIGHT

Kalie

My hands rest on the cold metal table in front of me. I can feel the chill seeping into my skin. The air is a strange blend of tattered paper, stale coffee, and the acrid sweat of exhaustion. I take a sharp inhale, clinging to a semblance of memory in that smell. Even as furious as I am—both with myself and with Declan for merely existing—a part of me yearns for the days when that smell lived in my brain.

It was a time when I dreamed of something more noble—like when I spent hours arguing about how the treaty written by Thomas Jefferson was a tangible piece of justice. I recall the hours I spent hashing out torts, and right now, a part of me longs for the ease of those days. I wouldn't be in this mess, but that wish drifts away as quickly as it came.

I'm a Marshall. We, more than most, know life happens.

Besides, my current accommodation isn't the Harvard Law Library, and I'm not cramming for a Constitutional Law final. I shift uneasily in my seat, crossing one leg over the other, trying in vain to find comfort in the unfamiliar surroundings. Despite coming from a family steeped in the intelligence and investigative fields, I've never been drawn to criminal law the way I was to contract law. Though I know every protocol by heart.

I admire the officer's efficiency. If I had a way to rate them on Yelp, I'd be dishing out five stars—but my perusal of the holding room reassures me their rating would drop on decor that might send Uncle Phil into apoplexy. An ancient fluorescent light hovers overhead, its eerie glow making the coolness of the room all the more palpable.

The worst part is how utterly dirty I feel. Not just because of where I am but because of how seeing him again made me feel. Declan Conian. For years after my graduation, he starred in any number of my fantasies —those hypnotizing eyes, his challenging smile.

Then there's his voice that raises the hair on my skin like he's physically touching me.

It was like that even the first moment we interacted.

I can't help but recall the way the air between us seemed to suck us into our own vortex. For just a moment, when his eyes met mine when he was prone on the floor, I'd swear there was a flicker of admiration in his dark eyes before he masked it.

But why?

Flexing my fingers still bound by cuffs, I give myself a single moment to wonder what would have happened if I had stayed that day in Cambridge. Would Declan have put his charm to good use? Plied me with sweet words and promises that meant nothing? Put his lips and hands on my body?

Would it have felt as good as I imagined? Or—I stretch my aching hand out to assess the damage—why did the way I touched him today make me feel so much more satisfaction?

Still, if I'd known I'd have only gotten in one punch, I'd have gone for the soft cartilage of his perfect nose.

Conflicted satisfaction bubbles up as I remember the flawless execution of my punch, my controlled fury that sent a clear message. There's a part of me that relives the fantasy of landing blow after blow on his perfect jawline—a twisted retribution, to be sure. Admittedly, he's just doing his job as a defense attorney, but because of him, my family can't move past what happened.

With the thought of my family, a chilling realization hits. I now have to call someone to bail me out of my present situation. There are dozens, if not hundreds, of numbers I can dial but there's really only one when it comes down to it. I dread placing the call, not because I fear him, but because I've always feared letting him down.

While Dad's the one who can orchestrate an escape from this mess with minimal fuss, I still hesitate. My mother will completely understand my impulsiveness, but something of this magnitude will inevitably lead her to contact him anyway. I cringe at his reaction, unable to fathom what he's going to say.

Before I spiral further into my thoughts, a uniformed officer—the baby-faced type who seems more suited to guarding our prom dress selection than delivering *Miranda* rights—enters the room and slides my cell phone across the table. "One call. Make it count."

"He hasn't dropped the charges?"

"He hasn't decided."

With a frustrated shake of my head, I pull up my father's number. As the phone rings, I recall the time I was home from college, when my parents sat me down and unraveled our family's true history. Despite the broken homes and past betrayals, Alison Freeman and Keene Marshall did everything they could to ensure me and my twin sisters never had the torment that touched their lives touch ours.

I'll never forget the pride that surged through me when I finally understood why every adult in our family still carries a fragment of the Amaryllis legend inked on their skin. It's not just about a flower or an arrow symbolizing resilience; it's about our history flourishing against treachery and pain. Family first, family always—that's our creed.

And exactly why Jon's betrayal ignites my inner turmoil.

Within seconds, his calm voice answers. "Hey sweetheart." There's something low and steady in his tone—a surprising calm that makes me question everything I feel. I don't hesitate. "Daddy, I was arrested."

Clearly, I decided to throw privacy to the wind with my bold opening statement. I wonder if that was the best course of action since his bellow might echo beyond the observation window. "What the fuck do you mean you were arrested, Katherine Laura?"

I wince, my pride stung. "They arrested me for assault." I almost stop there, but then I tack on, almost as a challenge, "For punching Declan Conian."

I brace myself for the explosion of disappointment in his response. I expect a storm of fury. Instead, he locks his temper down before replying, "I see."

Where's the surprise? The anger? I know my father too well. Something in his voice today is off—a mix of resignation and something I can't quite put my finger on. Unable to let it go, I press on, "I'm sorry." *Only about being caught,* I tack on in my head.

The officer in front of me stiffens, as if trying to determine whether my words can be used as a confession. My heart pounds fiercely, chastising myself. As a lawyer, I know better than to give even an inch of leverage when charges are still officially pending. "Dad—"

"Don't say another fucking word, Kalie. I'm sending your godfather to bail you out."

"But Dad, there's absolutely no reason I can't—"

He interrupts again, his tone steely. "No, don't argue. And don't, under any circumstances, accept any favors the chief offers. Stick to the damn book, sweetheart."

The call ends abruptly, leaving me alone with the receiver and a storm of conflicted emotions. My pulse thunders in my ears as I realize the full weight of what I've done. My father isn't just angry because I got arrested; he's furious about who I hit—and part of me isn't even sure why that matters so much to him.

I'm left questioning everything. What exactly have I done?

Deep down, I know my father understands all too well who Declan Conian is. I feel the full burden of the trouble I've stirred up—a burning conflict between what I thought was justice and what might actually be my downfall.

Pushing my phone back, I inform the officer of what will be occurring.

Then, I just wait.

Knowing my godfather, the fun's really going to begin when he arrives.

CHAPTER NINE

DECLAN

"I CAN'T BELIEVE YOU FUCKING JACKASSES COULDN'T AVOID dragging my daughter into your op!" Keene roars, his voice slamming into the room like a sledgehammer. Jon and I aren't simply being harangued by every member of Hudson Investigations' executive team; we're being ground into the carpet like worthless insects instead of the elite agents we are.

In the room with us are Caleb—Jon's father—and Liam. Via teleconference, Keene brought in Calhoun Sullivan.

Cal is one of the five owners of Hudson and oversees the command of the Missing Persons division personally. He outranks Jon and gives two fucks for the fact he deals with the heir apparent. From the moment we met, I've had mad respect for him. Now, his seething anger and crushing disappointment weigh on me like an unyielding anchor dragging me to a suffocating depth.

Jon, as if his Ivy League education never covered the nuances of diplomacy, explodes, "I thought someone would've handled it before it got so far!" His voice cuts through the tension.

Caleb fixes a venomous glare on his son. "How? Kalie went off assaulting a 'private' citizen for no damn reason."

"That's not how the court of public opinion will see it," Jon shoots back.

"It's how the law sees it!" Keene barks, jabbing a pointed finger in my direction. "Declan was merely walking through a lobby—a state building, mind you. He ran into your cousin, my daughter, who decided to disconnect her brain. Then she swung at him—"

"Still don't get how that's on me," Jon grumbles, head dropping in defeat as if carrying the weight of his imagined culpability.

"Because you ought to have predicted her reaction," Caleb interjects in a level, cold tone.

Jon's slump makes it painfully clear he's accepting blame for something that wasn't his fault. It forces a single burning question out of me: "How?"

All eyes zero in. I press, "How? He de-escalated the situation the best he could. We had our cover. So, how on earth was Jon supposed to do anything more?"

Keene's lips press into a tight, angry line, "Because she vocalized her displeasure about anyone involved in Laura's case—including and up to causing bodily harm if given the chance."

"When did this happen?" Cal questions.

"Not long after Laura's involvement. Why?"

"The timelines don't add up on my end," Cal declares bluntly.

But I'm stuck on Kalie's intentions. "She's that unpredictable?" I'm aghast.

Before Keene can finish the job his daughter started, Caleb relents enough to explain, "When you know people's triggers, you avoid them. We all share the same one." Seeing my bafflement, he continues, "Family first. There's nothing any of us wouldn't do for our own blood."

"Still...," I murmur, caught between disbelief and frustration.

Cal chimes in, "Enough, all of you. Kalie's safe. We have a bigger problem."

"What now?" I snap, exasperation lacing my voice.

There's the frantic clicking of keys on Cal's side before our phones erupt in pings. "Sam found a way to put a speed bump on their human trafficking highway because of the contracts Dec's been having them sign. Their newest target is an enormous problem."

This is exactly why I went undercover all those grueling years—this plus the desperate need to hunt down Tanya's killers. The tantalizing taste of a big payout is nearly palpable. I process Cal's words fully before demanding, "Who is it?"

"Open the file I just sent you. It's a catalog of who they're targeting for their next order. From what Sam discovered, the list has been in the works for months," Cal growls.

That's when I uncover an acquisition order for the firebrand who tried to demolish my face earlier today. Caleb inhales sharply, even as Keene's virulent curses slice through the air.

"This doesn't make sense," Jon growls, a raw blend of confusion and fury. "Why in the hell would they want someone like Kalie?"

Cal remains icy and pragmatic. "Two reasons. The first is because the Byrnes suspect we've somehow got someone on the inside. They're trying to make a statement."

"Al went after my fiancée, Cal. Of course we're going to try," Liam reminds him. Alfredo Tiberi, once a trusted member of Hudson Investigations, was taken out when Laura Lockwood was kidnapped. He let blood overrule his loyalty to this organization and has paid for those crimes. Now, he spends umpteen hours of the week begging me to rescue him from the festering cesspool of his own rotting mind and criminal incompetence.

I listen to him bitch before billing the Tiberis for the waste of my time.

Cal coolly counters, "They expected us to retaliate. But that's not the real reason they're going after Kalie. It's because of who she belongs to."

Then a picture flashes on the screen. It's the reason I contacted Hudson Investigations all those years ago—the man who's been well-fed from illegal coffers since his son cut him off from the family ones when he assumed conservatorship of them many years ago when he ran after his implied complicity in setting his daughter up for a nightmare. After all, Jack Marshall still needed a source of income.

Now, we're working to bring him down as part of the sweep targeting the Byrnes—his second cousins. Cal's voice penetrates. "Keep the intel to the list of people I send to you. They're the ones I've vetted and who you can trust. No one else."

His words hit hard, like a ruthless sucker punch. Every risk we've taken now compounds. A heavy silence smothers the room, quashing our tempers like a raging inferno doused by a torrent. Keene finally asks, "So, what do we do?"

"First, you find a way to keep Kalie safe."

"Because now she's not just Keene's; she humiliated someone under their protection," Liam surmises.

"Exactly that," Cal declares, nodding in my direction.

I immediately grasp the gravity of his words. The Byrnes don't give a damn about the Tiberis. What they care about is their immaculate reputation and how it reflects on them. They could not care less if the family who called in a marker for legal defense ends up rotting in prison —though the intel I'm gathering is going to set both their houses on fire. No, what they care about is the appearance of control and prestige.

Kalie, despite her perfect pedigree, defiled that.

With a sigh, I ask, "How do we do that?"

Jon doesn't hesitate. "We tell her the truth. No bullshit, no secrets."

Caleb winces. "Yeah. Learn from my mistakes."

I can hardly conceive Caleb acted that recklessly. "You didn't tell your daughter she was being stalked?"

Liam flings him a look of utter disgust. "Tell me about it."

"In my defense, I thought I was shielding her." His voice carries the weight of a man who almost lost everything and is doing what he can to repair his relationship all these months later.

I'd call him out for his severe lack of rationality, but here I am in a more convoluted mess for a person who's already gone. Liam shoots me a look of frustrated understanding. He knows about Tanya, about our relationship, about what she meant to me.

And what a fucking waste it was to lose her.

Cal's voice breaks into our internal monologues. "We're running out of time. Every passing hour, the trail gets colder. And every second, more women vanish."

His undeniable words suppress Tanya's ghost from taking over my thoughts. Instead, it's the knowledge of having to come clean to Kalie Marshall that has guilt churning in my stomach. Turning to Keene, I state my demands. "Despite what your daughter thinks of me, I should be the one to explain things to her," I state evenly, steely determination in every syllable.

"I don't give a damn about your opinion nor Kalie's right now. I only care about catching those sons of bitches before we end up trying to bring back my daughter's corpse. Or is basic comprehension something you forgot somewhere between Quantico and working for the Byrnes?" he sneers.

Jon grabs his phone and begins making plans. "Kalie is booked solid the next few days."

"You can't track her every moment of the day," Keene worries.

"I can." Silence descends on the room. Jon goes on, "While you all have been bickering, I sent her a link to a calendar invite that had an embedded tracker in it."

Cal mutters, "Thank God someone in that room is thinking straight. Good job, Jon."

"Thanks, boss."

Caleb wraps up with Cal before pivoting back to me. "Jon will shadow you as much as possible, but you know there are going to be moments when you're blind in the field. Your prime directive is still to take down the human trafficking ring. Not to protect Kalie, not to dismantle the Byrnes' empire."

I protest, "But..."

"Leave that to us," Liam placates me. "She won't be alone. She'll have her own detail."

"Still..." I hesitate.

"Still, nothing," Keene snaps with surgical ruthlessness. "You have a job to do. Now do it."

I'm aware that my intimate knowledge of this criminal enterprise is a prized weapon. I'm well-versed in the seedy underworld and its revolting inhabitants—having dwelled in their cesspool of twisted ambitions.

Now this family expects me to ignore that expertise while they guard their own. They're not asking me to sideline my personal vendetta. No, in fact, they're telling me the exact opposite.

Stay the course.

It's easier to concede to their decision and if it so happens I'm in a position to protect Kalie, I'll take my chances. "I'm in."

Jon claps me on the shoulder, his grip firm. "Then let's get to work—starting with figuring out how you're going to spin not pressing charges."

The deathly look Keene fixes on me makes my insides clench. "May God rest your soul if you can't figure that out," he mutters with a venomous finality.

CHAPTER TEN

After I was released with all charges dropped and I was made to feel like I should genuflect to not only the Darien Police but to Declan, my godfather waited approximately two minutes inside his limousine before he demanded, "Tell me what really happened today, Kalie. Why do I sense there's more to the story than what your father told me?"

Jared Dalton, not just my godfather but also a partner at Watson, Rubenstein, and Dalton, is a man to be feared in most legal circles. The fact that he's discussing Declan in hushed tones causes tingles to quiver along my skin. I waste no time divulging every sordid detail from my law school graduation until I saw him earlier today. I hesitate before finally adding, "There's just one thing, Uncle Jared."

"What's that?"

"You might not believe me—"

He cuts me off. "You know better than that."

That's when I let out what I held back to my father over the phone. "Jon was there. He...helped him."

His eyes narrow as he reaches into the mini fridge, its interior aglow with soft blue light, and pulls out two cold bottles of water. He hands one to me with deliberate care. "Care to repeat that?" he asked, uncapping his own bottle and taking a long, deliberate sip as if steeling himself for the next revelation.

"You heard me."

Jared pauses mid-sip, lowering the bottle slowly. "Was he just trying to smooth things over? Keep you protected?"

"That's what you'd think," I reply, my brows knitting into a sharp *V* as memory surged back. I remember, in painstaking detail, phones held high, recording every second. "Hold on." I yank my phone from my jacket pocket and frantically enter search terms into the engine, recalling every surveillance detail from earlier that day. I know they were focused on three distinct faces amid the clusterfuck at the courthouse.

Still, despite looking up my name, Jon's, hell, even Declan's, I find nothing.

Not a single video.

"What the hell?" I murmur, my voice barely above a whisper as disbelief mingled with dread courses through my body.

"What's the problem?" Jared asks, peering over at my screen with furrowed brows.

"Uncle Jared, at least forty people were recording us using their phones. I set the search parameters to capture everything, but nothing is showing up: no trace of me and nothing of the case. It's as if today never happened. Nada," I explain, tapping the screen to highlight the empty results.

He retrieves his own phone in a brisk yet measured motion. Within moments, he too was deep in a search, his thumb scrolling relentlessly. Every article and clip dissipated into digital ash. With each flick, confusion deepened in his eyes.

"Even StellaNova doesn't have this," I note, referring to the prestigious news outlet where Chuck works, my voice tight with incredulity.

"Kalie, that's impossible," Jared insists, his expression mirroring my own dismay.

"Not if someone is scrubbing this," I counter. My voice is laced with suspicion.

"But why?" he demands, leaning in. "If he wanted to press charges, hell, even if he wanted sympathy during *voir dire*, Conian needs positive media spin. It portrays him as less of a villain. There should be no reason why he wants what happened to vanish."

"But who has the pull to—" My voice fades as ominous connections begin to form in my mind.

"It's not necessarily what you're thinking," Jared warns, his tone a cautious blend of certainty and unease.

"What am I thinking?" I challenge, my eyes narrowing as I wait for him to articulate the inevitable.

"Just because it involves you doesn't mean your family is involved. It could be anyone the Byrnes are entangled with."

"You're right."

Jared leans back, considering. "I mean, a corporate giant? Political favor? Plenty of people owe the Byrnes a debt," he muses aloud.

"But which of those people has the clout to erase every digital footprint of damning evidence?" I press, feeling the pressure intensify with each syllable.

"Admittedly, that narrows the list quite a bit," he concedes. For a long moment, the hum of the limousine and the swirling autumn hues outside seemed to underscore our grave discussion.

As we wind through tree-lined streets, the landscape unfolding like a painting in rich detail, our destination looms ahead—the estate where my family's wedding and event planning business is headquartered. Crossing into the town of Collyer, I murmur, "Funny, I left this morning thinking I was just going to back Aunt Em over a minor issue."

"Now look—you're back as the first official family felon," Jared retorts with a wry twist of his lips.

"If what I'm thinking is correct, maybe I'm not the first. Maybe I'm merely the first to get caught," I counter, images of countless smartphone screens replaying in my mind like a broken reel. In this hyper-connected age, there should be some digital residue—the slightest trace of those videos—unless, of course, you had one or more of the world's most skilled hackers on the payroll.

Jared's eyes darken in agreement. "This isn't a media blackout."

"No," I say, voice low and certain, "it was a deliberate wipeout of the entire event." As our car slows and the trees yield to reveal the sprawling mansion where I spent many hours of my childhood, a shiver races down my spine, and I spot my father's car in the lot.

"Something tells me we're about to find out," I say, tilting my chin in the direction of the vehicle with a mix of dread and defiance.

Jared runs a hand over his brow, shaking his head. "What kind of shit storm has this family gotten into now?"

"Now you appreciate my reaction," I retort, a note of smug satisfaction creeping into my voice.

Before our banter has a chance to settle my nerves, the car door is abruptly yanked open from the outside. My mother's fear causes her lips to tremble. But before she can lay into me for scaring her senseless, Jared tries to alleviate the moment with a burst of humor. "Violence is never the answer as I've been educating your daughter." Jared winks at me, because he's been doing anything but that.

"Oh, I don't know about that, Jared." Without a word to me, my mother pulls me into her arms. I seek comfort in her indomitable spirit—the kind that could command a hurricane-like force with a mere look. She steps back before shaking me gently. "Why wasn't I your first call? Why did you call your father?"

"Mama," I try to interject, reaching out as if to calm her, but she is already too far gone.

Then her voice rises in a bellow that sends chills down my spine. "Before any of that, tell me why I'm being told to play nice when all I want to do is find that bastard, Conian, and throw my own punch in his face—not discuss him in my conference room!"

At that, both Jared and I blurt out, "What?" in unison, our voices echoing in the suddenly charged air.

"Don't tell me you weren't aware," my mother snaps, eyes narrowing. "Your father said we were all meeting here to discuss Declan Conian." She spits his name like a curse. "Keene said that's why he wanted to meet here after you were released."

Jared's eyebrows went shooting straight up to his hairline. "All I was informed was to bring Kalie here. Neither of us was aware that was Keene's intent."

I knew it was true and said so.

"Keene claims he said you requested this." My mother's confusion is evident. "In fact, he brought Caleb and Jon with him."

I feel the blood drain from my face. This is going from bad to worse. I won't have the opportunity to speak my truth. Jared and I exchange a glance as we hurry toward the entrance. My pulse races. Since this morning, I feel like my life is a movie on fast forward just before it skips to the end, and you miss the crucial parts.

The interior of the mansion is bustling with nervous energy as the various teams that make Amaryllis Events flit about. A new intern passes by, diligently replacing a floral arrangement Uncle Phil pieced together with a new one. The smell of cake permeates the air as Aunt Corinna and her team craft another masterpiece of edible art. As we walk toward the grand staircase, I note the door to Aunt Emily's studio is closed, but who knows if that's due to her having a client or to avoid the tension thickening the air.

After we ascend to the second level, it's easy to understand where the core of the tension is coming from. My father is pacing back and forth, cell glued to his ear. Caleb and Jon are off to the side, trying to remain invisible while locked in a hushed conversation.

Even as I want to walk by them without a word, Jon turns his head and catches my eye. His face holds so many emotions, I can't separate them. Is it relief? Regret? Or worse, complicity? I steel myself against the urge to confront him, knowing full well that whatever game was unraveling needed careful maneuvering.

"Glad you made it," Caleb calls out, waving us over with a grim expression.

"What's the point of doing this here?" I demand as we approach, skipping any of the typical family banality until I get the answers I need. My eyes lock in on my cousin's face. Every ounce of disgust I feel is aimed directly at him.

Jon opens his mouth to speak, but Caleb interrupts, "Conian claims he wants to let bygones be bygones. Says it's in everyone's best interest." His tone is caustic, but I know better than to think he isn't aware of every player, every moving piece. Even the one they have the least control over.

Me.

A sardonic smile twists my lips. "Peace, huh? How noble." My gaze never leaving Jon's face. "But peace requires trust, and trust requires loyalty. We all know that's something that's not in my playbook right now, Uncle Caleb."

Jon shifts uncomfortably, feeling the weight of my words. That's when I hear a snort from the top of the stairs. My mother and Aunt Cassidy are standing on the landing, watching the scene play out. Drawling, I tack on, "For being a master of manipulation, I think you overplayed your hand, cousin."

Jon flushes. "You might not trust me now, but trust this. Cooperating with Declan Conian is imperative."

"Imperative? Interesting, Jon." What he clearly realizes is I don't trust him, not after today. For a man who treated me my whole life as if I were his second sister, he didn't put my welfare first.

Before any of us can utter another word, my father barks out, "Conference room. Now."

As the members of my family continue to spar with words, the tension in the room thickens. Observing all of them, I realize I'm not just a player in their game, but a pawn. Somehow, someway, I got caught in the crossfire of something I don't quite understand.

But I will.

CHAPTER ELEVEN

If I were in the room with them, I suspect the killer looks Kalie is aiming at her cousin would be aimed in my direction instead. I much prefer watching it all unfold from the prime seat in Hudson's secure space, as Kalie verbally decimates her cousin with icy precision for not prioritizing their family.

Then poor Jon is blasted with a searing wall of disdain by her fiercely protective mother and *his* mother before their husbands cut them off. "You don't appreciate the delicacy of the situation."

Kalie leans forward. "Would you say I'm smart, Dad?"

Scrambling to make up points, Keene doesn't recognize the trap he's about to fall into. "Of course. You're brilliant, sweetheart."

"Then stop insulting my intelligence by patronizing me. You're knee deep in something, aren't you?"

Keene doesn't reply. Instead, Jon jumps into the fray. "I was just trying to protect you from him, Kalie."

She dismisses him with a single glance. Through the hidden camera Caleb apparently planted in the room years ago to monitor the coming and goings of strangers into his wife's domain, I can see how her actions cut him to the quick. Instead of addressing Jon directly, she turns to the refined older man at her side. "Did I tell you what Jon did when they arrested me?"

"No."

"That's because the answer is nothing. He stood back and tried to blend into the crowd." Her voice is glacial.

"That's not true, Kalie," Jon protests. He's cut off by Keene. "That's not how you explained it, Jon."

Kalie lifts her phone, then lets it clatter to the table. "Oh, it's too bad someone had all the footage of today's events wiped already, or I could show you exactly how he had my back. I mean, with family like this, who needs enemies."

"That's quite the harsh judgment, Kalie," Caleb interjects.

"Really, Uncle Caleb? Because I'm just calling it like I lived it. A few hours in a holding tends to clarify things."

"Jonathan," Kalie's mother hisses before she turns on her nephew like a viper ready to strike. "You knew your cousin had been arrested, and you left her there to...do what?"

He firms his lips, not answering. Not because he doesn't want to, but because he can't. Not without endangering all of them. Every man in that room except for one knows that.

Bickering ensues between the family members about the definition of loyalty. I could provide them a whole new perspective on it if I was allowed in this meeting, but Keene said now wasn't the time to bring me into the equation. "Like my wife, Kalie's fierce about those she cares about," Keene explained.

"I have the bruise to prove that. Thanks for the intel."

"She's not ready to listen to what we have to tell her about you."

"But she will," Liam tacked on. "The women in this family are incredibly resilient. Honesty is the best way to handle them."

After the shit show I'm watching, I'm beginning to think Liam has the right answer. Yet, without the correct information, they're priming my body for a quick burial. "Hey. Did you know you can get a body bag online? We can have it delivered overnight," Alison calls out in the Amaryllis conference room.

Kalie's eyes light, causing my dick to go rock hard, despite the fact she's talking about plotting my murder with ease. Christ, a single smile from her, and I'm solid. What would I ever do if it were aimed directly at me?

Next to Kalie, the refined older man referenced as her godfather—renowned lawyer Jared Dalton—sits with an unnerving calm before he shuts down the idea. "I'm good for bail, not murder charges."

All the women pout at him, easing some of the tension in the room before Kalie decrees, "You're no fun, Uncle Jared."

"Shall we get on with this?" Jared's cool, measured voice shreds through the tension that clings to the room like a noxious mist. With deliberate calm, he places a hand on Kalie's shoulder. When she turns and offers him a smile, my breath catches. This is the woman who managed to slip past every defense mechanism I erected and strike me down.

Why the fuck am I so drawn to her? I've been surrounded by beautiful women before. None of them have the same impact to my senses the way Kalie does.

Kalie isn't holding any of her vitriol back. She casts venomous glares at every male member of her family and then abruptly cuts the tension with, "I agree. Let's get this show on the road. I have plans tonight."

"Want to catch dinner?" Jon ventures hopefully, as if the simple act of sharing a meal could atone for what she perceives as his sins.

Her mother and aunt share mocking snickers, and even her father rolls his eyes in anticipation of the verbal storm about to break. With a deceptive sweetness, she announces, "I wouldn't be caught dead sharing a meal with you. No, tonight I have a pressing appointment to remove the dirt I collected between my toes in that sorry excuse for a room." Then her tone hardens, weaponized steel clearly inherited from her father. "So, can we finally get down to why I was forced to come here rather than go home?"

Her father lets out a sigh, which I know he's forcing out. But during our brainstorming session earlier, we decided this was the best course of action for Kalie to take, hopefully lifting the target she doesn't know is on her. "He dropped the charges because we assured him you would offer a formal apology."

Her response drips with mocking pity. "Bless your heart."

The urge to burst into laughter at the southern fuck you nearly makes me drop the tablet I'm holding—if only I didn't know how utterly necessary it was to try to tame the Byrne family from acting on their threats.

And making me burn the entire operation to the ground for a woman I barely know instead of for the one I shared every day with for years.

Unaware I can hear her, Kalie verbally dissects me, my lineage, and ridicules every future creation spawned by my sperm. Yet, I'm fascinated by the woman whose strength borders on fearless. On the surface, she embodies the high life, rich and untouchable—but as I've painfully learned, there's so much more beneath the dazzling veneer shown to the world.

What else would I find out about her if I were free to do so? From the moment I first saw her all those years ago, no other woman sparked my interest in quite the same way. Now, since Tanya, my life has been riddled with regrets while trying to stay alive.

But if I hadn't made a vow as strong as hers...

Keene is clearly across the table from Kalie. I can tell from the sound of his voice he's teetering on the precipice of control. Meanwhile, Caleb stands by his son's side. His face is unreadable. Jon's expression is a shattered wreck. It's painfully obvious this family shares a unique bond, but for Kalie to cut into Jon the way she has means he's done more damage than a simple conversation can repair.

No, not damage. Something. Someone. Me.

Taking the offensive, Kalie snaps, "When do you want this to happen?"

Jon's eyes bore into hers. "Soon."

"Will you be writing me a statement?" Before he can reply, she sneers, "Because that's the only way I'll get through it sounding in any way authentic."

"Damn it, Kalie. Can't you meet us halfway?"

"Who, Dad?"

"Who, what?"

"Meet who halfway?"

"Your family."

Not an ounce of reaction crosses Kalie's exquisite features. Then, shockingly, she tosses her head back and laughs—a low, incredulous sound that echoes in the charged air. When her laughter dwindles to choked chuckles, she jerks her thumb in her godfather's direction. "You hearing this, Uncle Jared? I'm being thrown under the proverbial bus and I'm being asked to meet them halfway."

"Kalie, trust us," Caleb begins.

"Trust you? Right." Her laugh is full of bitterness, not the melodic sound I pictured it being.

"Mr. Conian approached your cousin," he nods at Jon, who feigns a neutral expression. "With information."

"About?"

"That, I can't share."

Her frustration practically seeps through her pores. Instead, she tries a different tactic. "When?"

"Today, at the courthouse. Before your little altercation. That's why Mr. Conian allowed you to be booked, even though he had no intent of pressing charges."

Dalton jumps into the fray. "I know it was said at the station, but I want to hear you say it. He dropped them?"

I murmur, "Before she ever left the station." There's no trace that Katherine Laura Marshall was brought in for booking. Rachel took care of that for us.

Her resolve falters. Her gaze flicks toward her cousin. "Jon? Is this the truth?"

"Yes." He's able to meet her gaze without flinching because that's the truth. I was meeting with him to give him intel on the pipeline. I had no idea until later how much more Cal had uncovered—or how cold and calculated the Byrnes' moves really were.

Keene interjects sharply, "Kalie, I'm not comfortable with any of this. This is the kind of shit that gets you noticed in the wrong circles."

"Especially right now," Jon tacks on for good measure.

As I glimpse at the faces around the room, even her mother is wavering in her anger. "Kalie, sweetheart. Maybe listen to your father."

"Mama!" she shouts.

"Please."

She fumes but doesn't say another word. Keene continues, "For the time being, if you step out of your home or office, you're going to have a shadow."

She scoffs with icy disdain. "I can protect myself."

Caleb's voice drops, heavy with resignation. "We're being open and honest with you, Kalie. I didn't give those same choices to Laura. Don't make us regret it."

Her fingers lace together, her only outward sign of nervousness as Jon's twin is mentioned.

Caleb speaks even softer, "Give us the opportunity to do our jobs, Kalie."

Once more, she repeats with quiet fury, "You all trained me to fend for myself."

Stubborn woman. "Not if you're blindsided by the real threat."

That's when Jon takes matters into his own hands and snarls, "If you had any kind of self-control, we wouldn't be in this predicament in the first place."

In an instant, she lunges—impossibly fast, fury personified—vaulting atop the table and storming across it like an unleashed tempest. Her eyes blaze a surreal, iridescent blue as they lock onto her cousin. My jaw falls open at how fast the firebrand can move. I see her poise for attack when my camera view goes blurry. Keene hauls her off the table, shouting, "Enough, Kalie!"

Shoving him away, she spins and fires at him, "What the hell was that for?"

"You'd think punching one person today didn't cause enough problems?"

A sneer curls her plump lip. "Then stop your damn family from insulting people if you know what's good for them."

"They're your family too, Kalie," her father points out logically.

She shakes her head. "Not if they don't know the meaning of loyalty, they aren't." With that statement, she strides toward the door.

Before she can open it, her mother pleads, "Kalie." Just her name, but it holds a lifetime of love.

Kalie's head twists and she meets her mother's eyes—an unspoken, weighty conversation passing between them. I find my gaze locking onto Dalton. His eyes dissect the men in the room, as if he can see every hidden cavern beneath their carefully crafted facade.

Fuck.

The two women bow their heads together before Alison beckons Dalton to join them. After a few minutes of muffled conversation, Dalton announces, "My client agrees to your terms."

All of the men let out a relieved sigh, as do I from miles away.

He holds up his hand. "However, if we even get a hint you are using her for some kind of alternate agenda, all deals are off."

"What deal, Jared?" Keene asks warily.

Silence descends upon the room. I find myself holding my breath right along with the men when Kalie announces, "If I find out any of you are lying to me, I reserve the right to walk away."

I release my breath. "That's not so bad."

But when I focus back in on the screen, I realize, if anything, the tension in the room is higher than ever. It might be explained by the burning defiance in Kalie's eyes when she demands, "When is this debacle of a press conference taking place?"

That's when her father pulls out the drafted press release and extends it to her. "As soon as you approve it."

She snatches it away, muttering about self-righteous pricks.

The problem? I'm not certain if she's talking about her father or me.

Though, if the look on her face is anything to go by, it's anyone's guess. Certain her muttering is actually an ancient incantation designed to hurl me straight into hell's depths, I decide now's a good time to get ready for the press statement I'm going to have to release after Kalie reads her own.

CHAPTER TWELVE

DECLAN

THE ROOM IS SHROUDED IN SMOKE AND SHADOW DESPITE ITS floor-to-ceiling windows on the fortieth floor. It offers a glittering nighttime view of the city. Inside, the room is carved out of ice—the kind of cold that isn't about the number on the thermostat.

I stand at the far end of the table wearing exactly what they expect me to —an expensive suit and a sharper expression. I don't take my seat. Not yet. Not until I'm advised to.

Doing so before I'm told could earn me a bullet from either side of the table splitting representatives from the largest crime families in the United States.

Three men from the Italian side occupy one side of the long table. Salt-and-pepper hair. Black suits. Hands too still. They haven't touched the espresso in front of them. The silence between them is practiced. Tense.

The Irish contingent is sprawled across the other half. I almost did a double take when I sauntered in to find Keene's biological father—Jack Marshall—as one of the men included on behalf of the Byrnes. My intel didn't let me know he'd moved up in their ranks far enough to be attending a strategy meeting of this caliber. Instead, the bastard leans back like this is a poker night, one boot kicked up on the leg of another chair. In the background, Sid Tiberi's aligned with the other lower ranked officers, quiet yet watchful.

"Should I be offended no one offered me a drink?" I mock as I lay my briefcase on the table.

The Italians immediately launch in. Vito Spiori, middle-aged, sharp-nosed. "You made a decision last week regarding the Barresi seizure. The paperwork delayed funds moving out of Florence. That interruption cost us."

"It protected you," I return evenly. "There was a tip-off in play—quiet, but close. My contact in the Rome courts confirmed a clerical eyes-on. You were about to be exposed."

"We could've handled it our way," Vito snaps. "You stopped the transfer. You disrupted operations without clearing it through us."

"I stopped a collapse. You'd rather have the Guardia freezing your assets in real time?"

A cold beat of silence followed.

Then, from the Irish side, Jack chuckles. "Always the savior, aren't you, counselor?"

I don't blink. "Saviors preach. I read the fine print."

That draws a soft laugh out of Sid. Even Jack's lip curls with mild amusement.

But the Italians' faces don't change.

"Your judgment has always been... disciplined," says the eldest Italian, a man named Bellini, his voice smooth and slow. "But lately, there's been chatter."

"What chatter?"

Vito reaches into a leather portfolio and slides a glossy photo across the table.

My pulse hitches. I don't let it show.

The photo was grainy. Black and white. The courthouse. My face is fully visible. Her face turned away, likely out of embarrassment.

Kalie.

"You've been...preoccupied," Bellini says, steepling his fingers. "That's not like you."

"I have a personal life but she doesn't factor into it. She's a nuisance. One I've taken care of. I had her arrested to teach her a lesson. It won't touch the business."

"Everything touches the business," Jack says, finally sitting forward. "You know that. Hell, you taught that to Sid here when he was still slinging coke out of the shop office."

"True story," Sid grins.

I don't look away from the Italians. "What are your concerns?"

"That you are giving your all to our *famiglias* case."

"I am," I say with conviction.

"Maybe," Vito says. "Or maybe we should help you keep your mind where it's supposed to be."

Jack pulls the photo toward himself and examines it like a bored teenager. "She's got good legs," he murmurs. "Wonder what her face looks like?" He pushes it aside.

I have to force myself not to rise to his bait. *If he only knew...*

"We have always reported to our friends," Bellini nods across the table in deference to the Byrnes, and Jack returns the gesture with a firm nod. "You have our best interest at heart. It's part of why we trust you. But we can't help but be concerned when you do not consult us, Declan. We're smart men but cautious ones. Wary, even."

"Especially of ones who think they can play both sides," Vito adds, a little too loudly for my liking. His warning hangs in the air there, palpable. Tangible.

I slowly reach forward and tug the photo in my direction. "I protect this family's interests. That doesn't change."

"Let's hope not," Bellini says. "For everyone's sake."

"Women," Jack mutters with a grin, already losing interest, "put on this planet for one reason."

Vito can't help himself. "What is that, Jack?"

"To service us or to serve us up on a platter."

There's a scattering of laughter around the room, which cuts off when I snap my briefcase closed. "Is this meeting over?"

Bellini nods. "For now."

I turn, walking out with the photograph tucked into my briefcase. I don't let them see the burning desire to cap each and every one of them behind my calm facade.

Not yet.

Not until it is time to burn their entire world down.

After that meeting—after the veiled threats and cheap laughter by men who would be better off offering their organs to feed daisies—I don't head home. I drive fast. Faster than I should. As fast as I can to outrun the ghosts of my past. These same men are the ones who took out Tanya. I'm certain of it.

Instead of going home to plan my next strategy, I need to feel free so I can get the sick images out of my mind.

Kalie.

She's in their sights.

I yank my tie loose as I try to outrun the city lights that dim as I abandon the high rises in search of something else.

Something pure. Something untainted.

Knowing they deliberately pulled a photo with Kalie's back to the camera means they know exactly who she is. But still, they made me aware of what could happen to her if I didn't take care of their problems myself. Is that what's really the issue?

Then, I face my reality. No, that's not what's bothering me.

It's the idea of her appearing back in my life at absolutely the worst time.

To avoid killing myself or someone else, I whip my car off the Merritt and pull into an underground garage six blocks from my condo. Not my usual spot. I switch the Ferrari I drove into the city for the Lamborghini —one registered to a dead man in Kentucky who's been under Hudson's guard.

I've taken as many precautions as I can, always have. But tonight, I almost crumbled when I saw the photo.

Fifteen minutes later, I pull up to a nondescript storage unit—one of my off-the-books safe spots. From a steel box bolted into the floor beneath a crate of rusted engine parts, I pull out a phone.

Not a real one.

A burner I only use for my handler.

I dial.

One ring.

Two.

Then Jon's voice comes on the line. "Talk."

"They're piecing things together," I say. "Not everything. Enough to make veiled threats."

"Who?"

"The Italians. Possibly Jack. They implied that I'm deliberately bungling legal jobs. Used a photo of Kalie to try to smoke me out."

A beat of silence. Then, "Do you think you need to walk?"

My bark of laughter is hollow. "Do you really think I can walk now and live?"

"If they know what you're doing—"

"They don't. Not really. But they're circling."

"What do you want to do?"

"Move up the timeline. Have Cal hunt the next trafficking route and go to the Feds to see if it's enough. We prove Jack's alive and has been using the Byrnes to cover his ass. Not to mention helping them launder side deals that the Italians don't know about. If we split them—"

"You'll be expected to testify."

"I was always going to have to," I say. "But if we do it fast, I can do my best to keep your cousin out of it. Cal's intel is accurate. They're looking at her, Jon. It's the last thing I want."

He doesn't speak for a while as he considers everything. "You sure about their interest in her?"

"I've never been more sure about anything in my goddamn life."

Another pause. "Then it's time to finish it. We have to bring in the family. Then we start to burn it down."

The line clicks dead.

I bury the phone again before leaning back against the concrete wall, breathing like I just ran ten miles in dress shoes.

Kalie didn't sign up for this but because of her own brand of family loyalty, she's in it now.

Still, if I get a whiff, if they so much as breathe her name again, I'll go to war for her.

CHAPTER THIRTEEN

Every morning since I was forced to meet Declan's eyes across the parking lot at Amaryllis Events as I read out my apology for my "emotionally charged behavior that was not as a result of Mr. Conian's direct behavior but as a residual trauma from my own experience with his clients," my morning run has become more than a training exercise—it's become my salvation.

Especially since I can't sleep for thoughts of Declan's intense stare. It wasn't fury but something else burning in the depths of his eyes. A part of me wants to sweep the memory under the rug, but the part that was compelled by him all those years ago? Well, that part of me can't let it go.

So, even if I weren't already training for three upcoming marathons, I'd be out here relishing every mile, punishing my body for betraying my mind. This time of day, when I'm pushing myself in a way so few can, is the only time when my mind isn't complicated by that silent stare.

Without breaking my stride, a smug smirk tugs at my lips. Today's ten miles are brutalizing my newest trainee, Jon. Every agonized, wretched moment of my cousin's torment tastes far sweeter than any angry girl playlist I could listen to as I hone in on each precise, pounding step and measure every single breath I take.

Sure, there are agents who'd have killed to swap places with Jon—agents I've spent months with in the past fine tuning their training to conquer the New York City Marathon. But no. Today, retribution drives my pace. It isn't practical, but the feverish burn to punish Jon for his behavior in such a small fashion eases some of the humiliation of seeing my face on every gossip rag apologizing.

To him.

After a few hours, I leave my cousin in a sweaty heap before bounding up the stairs to our Craftsman. With a wiggle of my fingers, I call out, "Send someone with a little more stamina to follow me to work."

His response is a one fingered salute.

Hours later, as I make my way through the back path between Amaryllis Events and my reward for putting in ten miles, I try to untangle my feelings. On one hand, nothing should ever override the sacred bonds of love and loyalty our family holds.

Still, I know I'll eventually forgive Jon because he's family. His willingness to even form a loose-knit alliance with Declan has to do with business. I'm not certain why I still need to be protected like I'm the Hope Diamond, but if it eases the tension in the family, I'll deal.

But my guilt? I have to be honest with myself. It chafes knowing a man I've fantasized about is so completely out of bounds. It's time to admit it's myself I can't forgive. How can I trust my instincts when they wanted to lead me to Declan all those years ago and here he is now—someone who is willing to strike out at the heart of those I love?

My judgment sucks, plain and simple.

Barging into The Coffee Shop, not even the lure of a mocha can force the thoughts of Declan from my mind. Maybe it's because over the weekend when we got together at her new place, Laura said, "He's doing his job, Kalie. Just like you do. Isn't that justice?"

"But what if...?" I choked on the rest of my question before it fully formed.

Laura's no idiot. She laid my fears out brutally. "What if something happens to me? Again?"

"Yes."

"Then it happens. This time, we'll confront it. Together."

"Together. Right," I spat. My words laced with venom.

Her face froze. "You're still angry with Jon."

In that instant, my rage erupted like a volcano. "What made him leave me like that, Laura? He stood there and watched me get arrested before helping Declan—" I swallowed hard, unable to shake the feeling of disappointment and disdain that emanated from him.

Laura exhaled a long-held breath. "I have no idea. But I have to trust Jon. We're family, Kalie."

Yet my mind swirls with unspeakable possibilities. What hold do the Byrnes have over Jon? Is it more than just an alliance?

After hurling a curt "Thanks" to Zane—resident hermit, culinary genius, and the man Reggie has the hots for—I snake my way through the alley back toward Amaryllis Events. A swig of the sweetened caffeine calms me as I murmur, "Jon deserves every excruciating mile of his punishment."

"What punishment is that?" A voice deep and dark, as smooth as the melted chocolate on my tongue, startles me.

Spinning around to face him, a dangerous feeling rises deep inside. Sheer indignation flows through me at how criminally good he looks.

How can a man with so few morals saunter about society with no warning sign flashing "Danger"? And damn, I hate to admit, even if the man represents every newsworthy felon, Declan is no slouch in the looks department.

With every step I take in his direction, I check out his windswept black hair, towering six-foot-two frame, and the glint on his thousand-dollar wingtips before drawling, "Came to do your dirty work yourself? Consider me impressed."

Before he can retort verbally, or I can insult him further, I'm slammed hard enough against the nearest wall to have my back scrape against the brick. Declan's predatory hand constricts around my throat, trapping me in a steel cage of his body. In the next heartbeat, a screeching car roars past. Somehow. I twist my head, desperate to catch a glimpse of its plates.

There are none.

When I rotate my head in his direction to demand answers, I meet a pair of searing brown eyes locked onto mine. His voice, a low rumble barely audible over my frantic heart, carries a furious warning. "I thought you were protected by guards whenever you stepped out, Kalie?"

"I just ran out for coffee," I retort, voice strained due to the increasing tension of the hand at my throat.

He mutters something under his breath. I don't catch much but I hear the word "cousin" distinctly. I snap, "I'll deal with my own cousin. Thank you not so much."

He leans forward, his hand releasing. Now, he uses his forearm to crush against my windpipe, causing me to struggle for air for a split second. "Does any of this strike you as a joke? A car almost ran you down. You have bodyguards for a reason. Your. Life. Is. In. Danger."

Despite the narrow cut of my skirt, I manage to lift my leg high enough to get leverage so I can slam my heel against his instep. He staggers backward, shocked. Wrenching free of his vice-like grip, I clutch my throat as I rasp, "My life is endangered because of you."

He bellows, "No! It's because of you! Don't you get the Byrnes are tracking your every move?"

I've always prided myself on my razor-sharp mind, my relentless athleticism, and my unyielding determination. Never before had I felt such consuming passion and fury, but now it's all that fuels me. "Then call your damn clients off!"

He seizes my shoulders and drags me up against his body. I'm momentarily stunned by the fierce thump of his heart against my ear, and then his hoarse whisper shatters the silence. "It isn't that simple, firebrand. God, I wish it were."

He releases me, but not before ordering, "Run. Now. Back to your office. I'll have someone tailing you until you get there."

He doesn't have to tell me twice. I tear out of the alley, not daring to look back.

But what does it mean when, an hour later, Jon shows up at my door, offering a fresh mocha with a troubled expression? Gone is the infuriating arrogance I once adored. Instead, his presence reignites the lingering panic from the alley, even as my heart solidifies my bitter resolve. I stand behind my desk and cross my arms, trying to leash the storm raging within.

"A mocha? Really? Did Conian pick up the tab too?" I spit, venom dripping from every syllable.

"Thought you'd like it," he replies, his tone annoyingly calm. "And I paid for it."

"Wow," I snap back, eyes rolling in disbelief. "Look at you, Mr. Benevolence. Seems to me you're just covering all your damned bases lately."

"Even the ones you refuse to admit threaten you?" His voice is a low, controlled counterpoint to my seething rage. "Kalie, what the hell happened?"

"What happened? Your pal tried to choke me, and I nearly got flattened by a car."

His eyes narrow as he wrestles with the gravity of what he hears. "Choke you?" he echoes, as if to verify the truth in my words. Not that I've lied to him. Ever.

"Yeah, Jon. After a car almost ran me down."

His nonchalant facade crumbles. "You're sure?"

"No. I'm lying. If you doubt me, ask your new bestie. As much as I hate to admit it, Conian saved me."

Dropping the pretense, his voice vibrates with raw emotion. "You're not playing around. You're serious?"

"Deadly." I savor the word, letting its weight land like a crushing blow. "Didn't expect your new friend to become my knight in tarnished armor."

"That's not—Kalie, he's not what you think."

"Oh, spare me! Then what is he? A criminal misfit toy? Was he left behind instead of being delivered at Christmas because he's a mob lawyer with a heart of gold?"

"Just listen for once!" Jon snaps, his eyes blazing with urgency. He slams my door behind him, trapping the two of us together.

My anger temporarily abates as I react to his panic versus my own. He snarls, "We're in this together now. Me and you."

"We're nothing together right now, Jon." I watch as my words strike deep.

He flinches before he continues, "Hudson is chasing something huge—bigger than you can imagine. But one false move, and it all falls apart."

"Falls apart?" I repeat softly, my fury about to boil over at the idea me and my loved ones are in danger because of a case—a fucking case.

"I've got informants, placements. Declan is our in. One miscalculation and everything collapses."

"So, you're gambling with everything? With our damn family?"

His silence hollows the room with unspoken dread.

"All for some vague promise of an in?" I demand, incredulous.

"Yes. No!" He rakes his hand through his hair, frustration raw in his tone. "This is so far beyond anything you can possibly imagine."

Disbelief mingles with the adrenaline still pumping through my veins. "And that means trusting him?"

"It means trusting *me*," he insists fervently. "Stop making mistakes, Kalie."

"Trust you?" My laugh is brittle and riddled with scorn. "Right."

He steps closer, and for a fleeting moment, the cousin I once cherished flickers in his eyes. "Kalie, you are what I'm fighting for."

My anger falters, but only just. "Then why does it feel like you've gone over to the other side?"

Before he can say more, my phone shatters the tension with its ringing clamor. My father's number flashes on the screen to AWOLNATION. Jon's eyes dart from the phone to mine, urgency and dread coalescing on his face. "Answer it."

I lift my chin, defiant. "Get out."

"Kalie—"

"Out!" My command cracks like a whip, leaving no room for negotiation. He retreats, his eyes a swirling tempest of emotions I can't untangle. Alone now, I snatch up the phone and bark into it, "Dad?"

His voice is an anchor in the chaos, steady yet laced with worry. "Kalie! Are you all right?"

"I'm fine," I insist, though each word feels like I'm stretching the truth so thin you can see through it. "Someone tried to run me over."

"We know," he replies grimly. "I just got word. They're getting desperate."

"They?" My heart sinks as dread seizes me.

"Conian called Jon, who called me before he came to see you. You didn't take your protection with you." His tone is a mix of disappointment, fear, and something unspoken. Something I can't quite put my finger on.

"He saved me," I admit, reluctant but truthful.

My father mutters to himself, "They're more unstable than we feared."

"Who?" I snap back, bitterness seeping into my voice.

"Kalie," Dad's tone softens, "please listen to everything we tell you to do. Don't act out because you're angry. We cannot afford to lose—"

"I wouldn't give someone the satisfaction of dying."

"They'll do whatever it takes. You know that."

"Yeah," I murmur, images of that speeding car and Declan's choking warning flaring in my mind. "I do."

"We need to talk about this," Dad insists gravely.

"Fine. But nothing will change my mind." I hear the resignation even as I seethe.

"I'm sending a car to get you."

"Like hell you are!" I retort, voice raw with defiance and fury. But there's no one on the line any longer.

My father disconnects, assuming his will is stronger than mine.

I swear to myself if I didn't want answers, I wouldn't go based on his beck and call, but I do want answers.

No, I need them.

CHAPTER FOURTEEN

Sitting across from Caleb, Keene, and Liam, once Keene's office is locked down, feels like I'm poised on the edge of a knife. One wrong move either way and the edge can cause your death. In this case, we're dealing with something so powerful the fallout could be catastrophic to all of us—leaving these three men cast adrift from their loved ones.

The kind of world we're trying to protect their loved ones from isn't just from bad men who come up and steal candy from kids in strollers.

No, we're talking about a world where women vanish to places that leave them lost in an unknown hell. That's only slightly worse than the alternative, which is what I came here to tell them about—a farm located not too far from here where members of the Tiberis and Byrnes have mercilessly dolled out retribution for daring to cross them.

The kind of retribution that leaves a woman headless.

So, it's no surprise Keene checked us all for listening devices. Right now, he trusts no one. He's terrified of what could happen to his family as a result of the information I'm about to share with him. Hell, he even made me drop trou to ensure my dick piercings have been checked for listening devices.

As I adjust my slacks, he gives me a rueful grin. "Sorry. I can't take too many precautions."

"I don't blame you. Still, I think I'd remember if someone got near my cock lately."

"You think you'd remember." Liam mocks me. As a former agent himself, I appreciate that we have that bond between us. He knows the training I went through and although my name was bandied about as a traitor, he had Hudson do their own digging. I'm grateful for their intervention, even if the weight of what I have to share with them presses down on my chest like a sledgehammer. "It's not good," I preface. Then I tell them about the files.

The women.

The slaughterhouse on the farm owned by an associate on the outskirts of Schenectady.

The airstrip near Albany.

It's then I drop the bomb. "He didn't go deep enough for me to confirm it entirely, but there are links to other locations."

"Where?" Keene's voice is rough even as Caleb asks, "Who?"

This is the first time I hesitate. When I explain the details I was able to gather after I slipped the key logger onto Sal's computer, their muscles tighten with the urge to go after these men outside the law.

Caleb's eyes are stormy as he weighs every brutal possibility. "And Kalie?"

This is where my own stomach churns. "They want to make an example of her."

Keene surges to his feet and grabs my shirt front. "You did nothing to divert their attention, you bastard."

"Fuck you and fuck that, Keene!" I shove him back.

Liam pipes up, "Dec did everything possible to demonstrate he was in control of the situation. Even going so far as to have her arrested."

Caleb's eyes gleam. "But he didn't go through with it."

A cold wash of awareness hits me. "They have someone at the station."

Keene snarls, whether in frustration they hadn't figured it out before now or in ingrained parental defense, I don't know. Before I can speak, Caleb does. "Thanks for the intel."

"So, that's it? You're just going to take what I told you and sit on it?" I shout.

Keene snaps his head up, leveling his piercing green stare at me. "No. Now we do something with it. There's nothing for you to concern yourself with."

Caleb mocks, "Let's just say Keene has plans. Kalie inherited her deadly aim from her father."

"Nobody threatens my little girl," he snarls.

Glancing at my watch, I ask, "Isn't she supposed to show up any second now?"

"You're right." Even as Keene lifts the lockdown order, he circles back to the heart of our discussion. "Let's focus—what do we tell my daughter?"

"The truth," Caleb answers with an unflinching certainty that rattles me.

"How can you be sure that's the right move?" I question.

"Because Caleb ended up screwing over a number of people by keeping them in the dark, not to mention nearly getting them killed," Liam replies grimly. "If we bring Kalie in and explain who you really are, she'll be infuriated—especially after learning you're one of us."

"Not to mention Jon's been holding back on the details," Caleb tacks on.

"They're really that tight?" I feel like an outsider in a world of fierce family bonds I never really understood until I became an agent before everything went to hell.

Caleb nods solemnly. "Every single cousin shares that bond."

"It won't stop her from helping you," Keene agrees. "Even after her explosive outburst at the courthouse."

"Is that what you're calling it now?" Caleb jabs.

I press my lips together, suppressing a smile. It's likely their kids have inherited the same unbreakable camaraderie that their parents share. Keene, though, isn't letting up on the subject of his daughter. "Kalie's loyal, driven, and smart. She's fucking brilliant."

"Hell, Keene. You don't have to sell her to me like she's a pedigree dog."

"Shut your fucking mouth, Conian," he snaps.

"You forget, I know her finer qualities. I just fear placing a more appealing price tag on her." *Like the one that Tanya paid.*

Something in my expression must have given away my thoughts. "You did what you had to do—then and now," Keene asserts, his voice low and unyielding.

"Did I? Because from where I'm sitting, I lost a woman I cared for. For what? A case that dried up the minute she disappeared?"

Keene's tone is ruthless. "It wasn't for nothing, Dec. We took out the Tiberis involved in the hostage attempt. Then Jon nabbed some of them to give enough dirt to the FBI for racketeering statutes against the Byrnes. That's got to count for something. With that, you were able to slide into place as their damn attorney because we had the leverage to make some of their charges disappear."

A bitter laugh escapes me. "But what about the people at the top—the kings who call the shots on hits, kidnappings, drugs, gunrunning, and trafficking? You know—like your damn father? He's still out there raking in the dough." *And I'm still fumbling around, trying to keep my sanity while I struggle to make sense out of more questions than answers.*

Liam argues, "You can't think like that. You've been giving intel to us for years to bring down Jack Marshall."

Keene agrees. "It's been invaluable. We're closer than ever to locking up the motherfucker I'd like to deny gave me half my genes."

"Plus, if it wasn't for you, we would never have found our mole," Caleb confirms.

Before I can speak, Liam goes on, "You've been living neck deep in a cesspool of shit without selling out or losing your moral compass. Who else could have done it?"

Memories claw at the edge of my mind. Memories of being invited to parties where the Byrnes' hosted events filled with booze and drugs, of witnessing beatings delivered before sitting down across from the filth of the earth as the leaders of different scions within the same diseased family tree went shot for shot with matching cruelty instead of booze.

I shake my head to clear it from the reminders of orders I followed for the sake of getting closer instead of running as far away as possible. "I'll never be clean of what I did."

Keene's tone turns arctic. "That's what undercover work is. You have to make it believable or you're dead."

"Is that the explanation you plan to give her?" I demand. Before any of them can answer, I run my hands through my hair in frustration. "Kalie believes I'm their lawyer—that I'm as corrupt as they are. That I got Sal off scot-free on some fucking technicality."

"I know the story, Dec. I'm the one who crafted it," Keene snaps.

"We knew eventually we'd have to come clean about you," Caleb reasons. "We just never imagined it would be because Kalie can pack one mean right hook."

Keene smirks. "If anything, I'll deflect everyone to place the blame on Caleb."

"Hey now..." Caleb protests.

Then, as if on cue, a voice slices through our conversation. "Well, well, well. So Jon was telling the truth after all. For the record, I'm not apologizing to him." Kalie steps out of the hallway, her glare scorching every one of us. "Don't expect any apologies for what I'm about to say or do to any of you."

I rub my aching chin, letting the brutal weight of her words hang in the charged air.

CHAPTER FIFTEEN

I feel sick. Not puke my guts out ill, but the kind of nauseous you can't dissipate with pink liquid, ginger ale, or saltines. No, this is born of disappointment from being let down by people who swore they'd always protect me.

As I approached my father's office, I didn't hear anything. Assuming he had engaged his security measures, I waited patiently knowing the kind of clients he dealt with often meant he couldn't discuss certain cases with our family.

But never did I expect when the soundproofing lifted Declan's rising voice from inside. Nor did I expect the calculated way my family intended to keep information from me—us—about what was circling around us like sharks in the water.

Maybe I should have.

It's a betrayal on so many levels I'm not quite certain what to do other than trust the only person I can in this moment—myself. I shove open the door to my father's office, as a throbbing heat of fury and disgust surges through my veins, letting my instincts take over. When they realize I heard some of their conversation, my family's faces flinch.

Good. They deserve the agony I've just suffered.

But Declan? His eyes meet mine head on. Of all of them, he has the least to be shamed for. He didn't hold my hand growing up. He didn't make vows in ink. He didn't promise fidelity in truth.

No, all he did was smile at me and make me wonder and want.

"They say that if you eavesdrop on whispered conversations, you're likely to only hear insults. But I can't help but think the shadows reveal secrets that strip away any illusion of decency," I declare. My pulse pounds in my ears as my eyes clash with Declan's—a silent exchange that nearly strips the air from my lungs as his burn into mine with an intensity I last saw at my law school graduation.

Need.

Want.

Desire.

I try to steady my trembling hands, already assembling the words for a tirade well overdue. "How could you allow such a clusterfuck to happen?" My father, Uncle Caleb, and Liam wince. "The sheer gall of egoism and duplicity in this room burns through my very core."

"Kalie...," my father pleads.

Ignoring him, I step further into the room—a room my father built during my mother's pregnancy so that he wouldn't be too far away from us—and fix him with a look that reeks of contempt. "Tell me I misunderstood what I overheard. My—your—Jack Marshall is still alive?" I demand, my voice cracking like shattered glass.

Their silence speaks volumes. In my mind's eye, I replay every syllable I overheard in the corridor once the soundproofing was lifted—a twisted conversation that at first made me believe my family was making deals with the devil. That is, until the devil was revealed to be the hero.

Declan is nothing more than an accessory to a hidden agenda. My anger flares and my stare shifts, aiming toward Declan, whose face is coolly impassive. I tilt my head and sneer, "Since you seem to be at the center of this, you get to explain."

When he hesitates, I can't control myself. "Now!" I bellow so loud and sudden, all four men start.

Finally, he speaks—his voice measured. "I'm not who you think I am."

I let out a bitter laugh. "You mean the willful lawyer to kidnapping psychopaths?"

For just a heartbeat, his deep chocolate brown eyes flicker with regret—a flash of something vulnerable before he resumes his controlled composure. "Not in the way you believe me to be." His gaze darts then to my father, who hesitates a heartbeat before offering a slow, weary nod.

"Tell her, Dec. We have to trust her," my father finally murmurs.

"Gee, thanks, Dad. Trust me with what?"

Declan shifts his weight. That's when the man I thought I knew seems to melt away, discarded like a wrinkled suit. The man standing before me straightens abruptly, shoulders squared. Declan's posture suddenly radiates authority. In that moment, a chill runs through me as I'm reminded of my father and my uncles. He mirrors the same exact power they command.

My eyes dart to the other three men in the room. "Who is he?" I demand. Then, without giving them the slightest chance to respond, I turn to Declan. "Who are you?"

Leaning casually against the small conference table fashioned from polished mahogany—the very table my father insisted on because it reminds him of the one at Amaryllis Events—I notice the ease of his stance. Raking a hand through his tousled hair, he meets my glare head on. His low warning vibrates in the charged air. "I can't tell you more than the bare bones, Kalie."

The ease at which he addresses me should alarm me. Instead, it causes that annoying quiver to run up my spine. To tamper it down, I tap an impatient rhythm with my toe on the hardwood and cross my arms, my chest tight with indignation. "Why not?"

His jaw sets, and he grits out, "Because I don't need another woman's blood on my conscience."

Instinctively, I lean forward in fear. "My cousin?"

"No—my partner's." The words hang in the air like a cruel twist. My lips snap open in shock before he exhales a steep, bitter sigh. "My name is Declan Conian and I'm an attorney—"

"I know that." Even as I bite out the words, a litany of emotions cross his face—steely determination, a simmering rage, and something elusive I can't quite name.

He answers, "Before that, I worked for the FBI."

My gaze darts away toward Liam, who ducks his head. Something rotten settles inside my stomach before I ask, "And who, exactly, do you work for now?"

"For the last three years, undercover with Hudson Investigations. I've been working to take down the Byrne family's entire stronghold."

A low, bitter laugh escapes me as I turn my gaze away from Declan to stare into my father's eyes. "Of course you have."

"Kalie, sweetheart," my father pleads.

I slice my hand in the air. "Stop. You couldn't be bothered to tell me the truth before."

"I was trying to—"

"So help me God, Dad. If you finish that sentence with 'protect me,' I won't be responsible for my actions. You, all of you"—I let my gaze sweep around the room encompassing every member of my family—"have lied to us. Now, I want someone who hasn't to tell me the truth."

At first, no one speaks. "Well, that answers a lot. Let's start with you, Declan." I lean closer, voice low and probing. "You said you *were* FBI. How did this band of misfits recruit you?"

Tension fills the space as his jaw clenches visibly. "It happened a few years after I saw you graduate from law school."

His answer clearly shocks my father. "Wait? What? You two know each other?"

My eyes narrow. "We crossed paths prior to our—interlude—at the courthouse."

"Kalie." My father's voice holds a note of warning. "Tell me everything."

"No. Right now, I'm the one asking the questions." My tone is absolute.

"I need to know everything about how you and Declan met."

"Funny, you've had years to ask him that very question. Right now, it's my turn. Why were you at Harvard that day?"

"I went to hear Director Skorniak speak. My boss at the time—Holder— suggested it would be enlightening."

"And was it?" I challenge.

To my surprise, Declan quotes, "'*Judge carefully. Rule righteously. Ensure your heart, your mind, your expertise, and above all, the law will ensure future generations can live the life they deserve.*'"

I give him credit for remembering what I consider to be the best part of the commencement speech, which leads me to ask, "Did you know who I was before that day?"

"I had no idea the woman who captivated me across the tent as she enthusiastically applauded was going to end up being the daughter of my future employer."

I study him—the subtle bruise on his chin peeking from beneath a shadow of stubble. Declan's breath shudders out. "It wasn't until a few years later Liam contacted me." He nods at the man in question.

I glance in Liam's direction, who jerks up his chin in confirmation. Anger resurfaces. "Then why are you working to get the Tiberis released?" The words fall from my lips before I can restrain them. "If you stand for truth, justice, and the good ole Hudson way, why would you inadvertently harm our family?"

A mocking smile curves his lips. "You believe I'm actually working to help them?"

"Wouldn't you?" I retort. Before he can muster a response, I whirl around to confront my father and uncle. "Do you really trust him?"

Uncle Caleb speaks, his tone edged with exasperation. "Before he left the FBI, Declan was part of a task force where he worked as a handler..." My uncle's voice trails off before he picks up with his more recent history with Hudson. "Since he joined our team, he's worked exclusively providing intelligence to Jon and Liam."

"Excuse me?" My heart pounds against my ribs.

"He's not a criminal, Kalie," Caleb defends.

Declan crosses his arms tightly over his chest, his voice a murmur laced with defiance and more than a touch of regret. "I can't exactly say my hands are clean, Caleb. Not anymore."

Liam's patience snaps. "Doing what you've done undercover has been documented as necessary to maintain your cover." With that, the two bicker in a heated back-and-forth, debating whether Declan will face prison time for turning a blind eye to burglary, carjacking, and a litany of other nonviolent offenses—crimes committed in the murky shadows while utilizing his apparently clever mind to bring down the Byrne family.

My mind whirls with the revelations. "Why didn't anyone correct my assumptions right after the courthouse incident?" My question slices through the bickering like a knife.

Silence falls until my father strides forward, seizing both my arms in a grip meant to calm yet is undermined by his quavering tone. "Kalie, sweetheart, we had to let the lie play out."

A pained admission follows from Declan. "Because you're right, I got one of the bastard's out who hurt your cousin." Every word of his honesty stabs at me. He continues, and despite the turmoil he's churning up, I find my heart twisting with reluctant empathy. "I willingly combed through every piece of evidence, searching for a reason to get Sal Tiberi out. Do you know why?"

"You tell me," I challenge, voice cracking.

A heavy pause precedes his confession. "I did it for love." His admission halts me in my tracks.

"You see," he presses, his gaze dropping to his shoes. He scuffs them against the floor, uncaring of scuffing them as he's lost in regret, "not long after, my partner—a woman with a husband and two children who I loved as much as you love your family—vanished. That is until her bare head was delivered to the FBI office." He lifts his eyes once more, only this time they're devastated by something only his mind's eye can see. "The forensic pathologists said her skin was peeled from her face while she was still alive."

His words root me in place, my eyes never leaving his. "It's been years, and I can still dredge up the memory of the agony on her face before someone did her a favor and severed her head from her shoulders. That's what was on her face when they pulled her head from that box."

"Oh God." My whisper is as loud as a shout in the silenced room.

"So, yes. In trying to get justice for Tanya, I've shaken lives, broken trust, crushed innocent hearts—and until you threw a punch at my face, I was no closer to figuring out what happened."

Then, like a mask slipping back into place, Declan transforms once more into the feared Mafia lawyer. Slowly, he steps forward until our shoulders align, his presence imposing. Without turning to face me, he murmurs coolly, "I'm sorry what I did in the line of duty harmed you, Ms. Marshall, but frankly, I don't give a shit. I'm a little busy trying to hunt down murderers."

In one swift motion, he strides to the door and hurls it wide open, storming out and leaving me flanked by men I'd loved and worshipped my whole life and another I'd grown to respect just as fully . Trusted implicitly with everything from family squabbles to broken hearts to celebrations. But now, after overhearing their whispered conversation and learning the raw truth behind Declan's actions, I feel betrayed. "You both are the problem, not him," I accuse sharply.

"Kalie," my father snaps, his voice laced with exasperation and hurt.

I shake my head, stepping back. "No. It boils down to trust."

"We trust—"

"But you didn't. You didn't trust us, and here I am, caught right in the middle of your operation. Hell, Dad, before I was born, you didn't trust Mama with the truth about your own stalker and you nearly lost both of us." His face turns chalky with shame. "When are you going to understand that sharing your struggles doesn't make you weak? It only gives us more reason to stand by you." With that final proclamation hanging heavy in the air, I hurry out the door just as Declan had minutes earlier.

I decide against returning to work that day. Instead, I inform the agent assigned to me to tail me once I leave Hudson. I need to be away from probing looks and eyes that see too deeply for my own good. I know that if I were to cross paths with my mother or her sisters now, my face would announce that the world has gone mad. I'm now a custodian of secrets that push down on my chest like an unyielding weight.

Declan Conian is so much more than a gorgeous face in the crowd.

What he is to me is yet to be determined.

CHAPTER SIXTEEN

Storming out of Hudson, I slide into the seat behind the stolen Maserati Sal's "boys" gifted me not too long ago once I got their *consigliere* released. I have the Hudson team fully inspect it for bugs or trackers on a regular basis.

For a few moments, I do nothing but breathe before I jerk my fist back and pound the steering wheel over and over until the side of my hand throbs in agony. "What the fuck was I thinking?" I shout into the silence of the vehicle. Why did I admit everything to Kalie? I could have played it off—let her father absorb the fallout for me being in his office. I've gotten myself out of worse situations in the last few years.

But the lost look in her blue eyes as she stared at her father and uncle unraveled something deep inside me. It made something shift back in my chest I hadn't felt in too long.

My heart.

From the first moment I spotted her across the tent, Kalie's been an enigma, I admit. Starting the car, I put it in gear and peel out of the Hudson lot. Quick tempered and dangerous one moment, the look of open understanding on her gorgeous face the next almost brought me to my knees. I murmur, "It's like she was absolving my sins."

As if anyone can. I've long accepted my blame in Tanya's death. If he had his way, her husband, Ben, would have had "murderer" carved into every inch of my skin with a scalpel he happily wielded for "getting my wife, the mother of my children killed. You pathetic bastard. You can't even figure out who did this to her."

No, instead, I've dedicated my soul to it.

Gunning the engine, I give myself a few minutes of borrowed sanity before someone from what remains of the Tiberi's Connecticut outfit panics when I'm not where I said I would be. Although I don't have an official title other than being their attorney of record, I've been given more and more responsibilities as of late. Which is great as it pertains to the investigation.

But when it comes to finding what's left of my sanity after regurgitating my past to Kalie? Yeah. I need the few precious moments where I know there's no bug. I'm not being watched or monitored. I can have a reaction to something and not have to choke down what I really feel.

Right now, the most overwhelming emotion surging through me is weariness.

I thought I'd have solved Tanya's case long before now. Hell, I was so certain I could bribe one of the Tiberis or Byrnes rotting in the state penitentiary, but none will talk. Pressing down on the gas, I sneak through a yellow light just as it's about to turn red. There's no question of who did it anymore. The question becomes, is it time to let it go?

Once I help Keene, Caleb, and Liam break this trafficking ring, will I have paid enough penance to absolve myself from not being able to stop Tanya's death?

Is there a way to wash my soul clean?

The roads twist and turn, my car taking them with ridiculous ease. Reaching over to the rearview mirror, I yank the small pink frosted doughnut keychain off the string I have it hanging from. A tiny replica of the one from the Simpsons. Tanya's youngest bought it for me on their family vacation to Universal at the Lard Lad. The tiny keepsake was to remind me, "Don't eat too many doughnuts while on shift, Unca Dec."

I'd picked Emmitt up, thrown him in the air before making him a promise I wouldn't. I'd also promised to keep his mama safe.

I'm certain he gives more of a fuck that I failed at that.

Clenching it tight in my fist for just a second, I punch open the sunroof and let it fly away, along with my belief in absolution. Instead, I swear one more time, "I'll get justice for you, T," I choke out. "I'll make them all bleed for what they did to you."

The wind blows through the car, but I can practically hear her saying, "Good." With that, I whip the car back in the direction of Darien so I can finish the next stage of the plan.

⁂

I lean back in my chair, fingers drumming against the scarred wood table in the chop house's back room. Sparks flew once I sauntered in earlier, and not just because of the diamond plated angle grinders hard at work. There's something fueling the air, and it isn't the stench of motor oil—a scent I've long accustomed to associating with this off-the-books location where mistakes used to mean death until I took over the back room a few months ago to use for the Tiberi's legal dealings for the business.

The men in front of me are anxiously shifting back and forth, from side to side, waiting for my next proclamation. They don't want to be the one I call out, let alone force to defend their position. Despite the differences in our roles, there's one rule we live by—no mistakes.

Yet, they just made a huge one.

"I've been patient, waiting for the answers I need to represent you and get the rest of your derelict family members out of prison." I pause, letting my words penetrate. Leaning back, my jacket falls open, revealing my weapon. They practically swallow their tongues when I growl, "I don't like being patient with nothing to show for it."

Tony, Sal's second—or is it third?—cousin clears his throat. He's older than I am and should be smart enough to know that speaking now might seal his fate. Either he's showing incredible bravery, or he's so fucking stupid he'd never make it if a real Tiberi was sitting in this chair instead of just their lawyer. "We're still working on it, Declan. The shipments—it's like our pipeline to get them moved from each location has had a major malfunction."

Good. I nod like I'm considering his excuses, when in reality, I want to jump up and give the air a fist pump. All the information I've passed along to Jon has made it so these dumb motherfuckers can't go stealing babies from daycares or kidnap prominent women from exclusive social events where too many exits are left unprotected. Instead of showing my pleasure, I narrow my eyes at him. "Someone inside must be feeding them intel."

Tony's face blanches before he stutters, "Im-im-pos-sible."

Sal backs him up. "No one would dare."

I nod like I'm considering their words. "Let's see how that plays out on the stand."

They both relax. "Gentlemen, you're both criminals."

Sal pipes up, "You had mine thrown out."

I want to facepalm myself. "This one time, Sal. The rest still remain."

"Oh." He and Tony exchange a look of—Christ, is that despair? With his lower lip jutted out, he mumbles, "I thought you'd made it so I didn't have any past crimes."

"I'm a lawyer, not a god."

"We pay you like you are," Tony gripes.

Ignoring him for the moment, I narrow my eyes at two criminals who give zero fucks if the parents they've tormented thus far ever recover. "So, you're saying you have no idea who it could be?"

Silence. Not a peep from either of them.

I lean forward, bracing my forearms on the desk. I begin to tick off a list. "You two can't think of a single person who might want to fuck with what the *famiglia's* got going? Because let me tell you, when I call Mr. Byrne, he will not appreciate that answer."

"No, Declan. No one..."

I slash my hand in a "silence" motion. Shoving to my feet, my chair slides back so hard it slams against the wall. My fist comes down on the desk three times in hard succession. "If you can't be honest, you're going to get eliminated, you dumb shits."

Tony holds up his hands placatingly. "Now, just a minute—"

"You don't have a minute. Not on the stand," I cut him off. My chest heaving, I point out the office window to the chop house floor. "You think those men have loyalty? They're loyal because of money. They know nothing about being loyal because of blood, because of family." Sliding around the desk, I snarl, "Those shits would think nothing of capping me, you, hell—the DoorDash delivery person for some extra cash."

They both eye me like I'm a lethal cobra, not the attorney paid four figures an hour to keep them from toppling a centuries old empire. "Need I mention the cops who would love to throw your asses in the slammer?"

The appalled expression on their faces is my only answer. "But what really chafes me? Watching two dumb fuckers who think they can outthink me." With that, I jerk my chin up.

The next moment, my door flies open. Two men, enforcers for the Byrnes who have come down from Boston to "keep an eye on their investment," come in and lurk behind them. "Here's what you two are going to do. You're going to get the fuck out of here. You're going to find out who's involved with the logistics behind the fucking pipeline and you're gonna do it fast. Then, you bring the information to me. Do you think you can do that?"

Sal swallows hard. "Yeah."

"Understood," Tony whispers.

My head tilts. "Well, that didn't sound very convincing." I reach under my jacket and pull out my gun. Firing it above their heads, I can't say I don't enjoy the terror on their faces as the ceiling tiles disintegrate and land on their heads.

"We got you!" Tony shouts. "Just don't kill us."

"Better," I approve. "But let me warn you, if I don't have answers by the end of this week, I'll know where to start looking for the problem."

On my way out the door, I order, "Get to work."

As I storm out of the chop shop, I spy the team stripping a bright blue convertible. For just a second, I'm given a reprieve from the suffocating world I've submerged myself in for answers I know I'll never get as I'm reminded of the fire in Kalie's eyes both times I've been up close to see them.

And what I might need to do to see them again.

CHAPTER SEVENTEEN

ALL MY LIFE I'VE WORN MY FAMILY LIKE A BADGE OF HONOR—
proud of the sacrifices and the love that fueled our legacy. It was that
deep pride, the fire to make our parents proud, that drove every decision
I made from college to law school. Hell, even from my decision to defer
school for a year to train for the five rings few can achieve. But thirty
minutes ago, the pride that held me in its embrace over the course of my
life shattered when I saw my father, my family, and Declan conspiring
together.

In that moment, a crushing wave of disappointment hit me, making every breath a struggle, not as if my lungs hadn't trained to run marathons with speeds that had been likened to those of gazelles. This is the problem when people put humans on pedestals as heroes; inevitably, they topple off because they can't maintain the facade.

Today, it was my family's turn to crash to the ground.

There are days I wish I could see inside the twisted logic that makes up my father's brain so I could appreciate what he believes is so dire that there should be no comeuppance to lying to his family. From what it sounded like, Declan was already willing to help them bring down the Byrnes.

Walking in on that scene wasn't even close to what I was expecting when I went to my father's today. But part of me wonders if I should have. It was all too obvious after Declan laid it all out to me at Hudson, explaining in hushed, venomous tones how he planned to dismantle the families who took out his partner.

I can't say I blame him. If it were me...hell. It was me. I mumble to myself, "And if I'm not the poster child for things not to do when you're furious, I don't know who is."

I desperately wanted someone in the room to contradict him, that he hadn't lived through that kind of agony. But they didn't. He laid his truth bare, even as brutal as it was to accept. He isn't a monster, the enemy. He was a wounded warrior compelled to finish the battle, regardless of whether he was left standing.

Now, I'm left with the feelings he triggered in me the day of my graduation overlaid with this image. I find myself wanting to know more, wanting to know everything. Declan stirs something in the shadows of my heart that I can't turn away from.

The one thing I know is it isn't fear of him or what he could do to us.

Not anymore.

But what does this mean?

My hands are shaking so damn bad between anger and uncertainty they can hardly grip the steering wheel as I pull into my driveway. My SUV skids on loose gravel before halting to a stop in front of the garage. I stare blankly at the dashboard for a moment, feeling as if, for the first time in my life, I have no clear course ahead. But somehow I'm stuck in a race I neither trained nor signed up for.

Just then, my front door swings open. A flutter of hope skims through me at the sight of who's there. Is it crazy to think—or maybe just desperately want—the person sprinting at me can explain this whole mess away? Instead, Grace waves as she leaps down the steps.

I force myself out of the car. I know I'll need to share something with her despite the warning pinging around my head like a ticking time bomb. Just as I'm about to spill my guts, she fills the space with excitement. "Kalie! What are you doing home so early? Not that I'm complaining." She gives a quick look around as if she's expecting someone else with me.

I step into her embrace and stand there stiffly for a moment before relaxing into it.

Her arms tighten around me briefly before letting go. She studies my face with a look that tells me she knows I'm holding back on her. "What's going on?"

"Declan Conian." His name comes out barely above a whisper.

Her eyes widen like saucers. "You saw him? Again?"

I nod, licking my lips.

Her happiness dissipates as if it was never there to begin with. It's then I realize I can't tell her who else I saw him with—our cousin, our uncle. My father. My lips hold back the words deep down in my gut. The warning at Hudson is setting off alarm bells too loud to ignore.

Grace's shock shifts to immediate concern. "Did he threaten you? Are you okay?"

"I'm fine," I say quickly, too quickly. "He hardly spoke to me." I'm not sure if she buys my exaggeration of the truth or not, but it's close enough. He didn't need to speak—even though he said plenty.

Just his presence in my father's office said enough.

I expect her to offer some words of comfort, but instead, she fixes me with a piercing look and demands, "What did your dad say about it?"

That question cuts through me. Every member of our extended family believes in my father and trusts that he'll make the worst wrongs right. But with my trust in him crumbled to specks of doubt after what I overheard, I have to force down my resentment. "He says we're safe— that we're not targets. Claims there's a team working on taking them out." My voice hopefully doesn't betray the storm of anger I'm forcing aside for her benefit.

Grace draws in a long, steadying breath. I look into her eyes as she tries to process the tangled mess I've gotten us all into when I decided to play judge and jury with one single punch. "I hope he's right."

Then she grips my hand, giving it a quick, reassuring squeeze—as if to remind me that at least one person will always be in my corner. "You'd tell me if something was really wrong, wouldn't you?"

"Of course," I lie as smoothly as my father. As Uncle Caleb. As Jon. With that realization, my stomach churns.

She pulls back and gives me a firm look. "Then let's go inside and you can help me pack."

"Pack? For what?" My voice is tinged with disbelief. Did my father get Grace to move out? Get her out of the way.

She lopes an arm around my waist before guiding me up to our front porch. "I have the International Anaplastology Association conference in Belgium in like a week."

I slap my hand against my forehead. "God, Gracie. I think I left my brain somewhere."

"Jail?" she teases in a sarcastic tone to make light of that now infamous day.

"Ha, ha." I chuckle, deciding to play along. If I confess that it's not just my sanity but my faith that has decided to take a long run off a short course since visiting my father's office, she'd never leave. Plus, Grace deserves this. She's so excited to reestablish a relationship with her mentor, Dr. Amato, from the Center for Craniofacial Epithetics. Changing the subject, I grin slyly. "So, are you excited about the trip?"

Her eyes spark in a way I haven't seen in years. "So much, Kalie."

I can't resist teasing, "Any plans to see if there are any sparks left between you two, Surgeon?" I grin when she growls at her old lacrosse nickname due to her stick skills and passing capabilities on the field. Grace, once a lacrosse star at UCONN with a full scholarship, shifted her ambitions from kinesiology while on a summer internship. During her junior year, studying advanced anaplastology overseas with Dr. Amato, she hadn't just learned techniques—she'd rediscovered her own resilience as a woman.

She rolls her eyes, a small smile playing at the corners of her lips. "None whatsoever."

I shake my head, laughing softly. "Only you could end things while living up to your name—Grace."

Her smile falters for just a moment. "Not all my relationships end that way, as you well know," she reminds me quietly.

Between us hangs an unspoken secret, carefully hidden from the rest of our family—the kind of secret shared only between us and Laura. Yet now I carry on my back something even more dangerous, a truth that could hurt everyone if it comes to light.

The danger found in lies.

I draw in a deep breath, plastering on a smile. "Well, just in case, it's up to me to ensure you pack not only your latest silicone developments, but also the pieces that turn heads for an entirely different reason."

Hand in hand, we climb the stairs. As we round the corner, my eyes catch sight of my office—a stark reminder of the day I endured and the work I still have to do as a result of it. Muttering under my breath, I remark, "Maybe it's better if I work from home for the next few days."

Grace's concerned gaze fixes on me. "Is everything okay?"

"Absolutely," I force a laugh. "I just have a mountain of work to do. You know how the office can be—chaos should be the next tattoo we get."

Her smile blooms. "Especially during wedding season."

"When is it not wedding season?" I retort, and soon we're laughing together—a small moment of levity amid the turmoil.

For the next hour, I offer unfiltered opinions on every outfit, critiquing each choice. But as the laughter subsides, a heavier urge claims me. I need to escape this overwhelming storm.

> UNKNOWN:
>
> Today was a lot.
>
> You okay?

My fingers hesitate. I want to ask who this is, but in my heart of hearts, I already know the answer. I consider the many ways I could respond to his unexpected care and concern, but then my brain kicks in and I realize the danger he just placed himself in if I do.

So, I don't.

It's better for his safety if I put Declan out of my mind. As for me, the only way I can do that is to run.

Even if I have little hope of that working.

CHAPTER EIGHTEEN

I HADN'T PLANNED ON JOINING THE BRAVE STEPS FORWARD running group tonight. One minute, I was reading Declan's text and the next, I had to leave. Driven by a wild necessity—haunted by echoes of words, both verbal and written. One pervasive thought is on repeat over and over as each footfall lands and my legs churn while I lead the pack of runners on a heavily wooded trail.

Declan.

Declan.

Declan

My lungs burn as my footfalls synchronize with those of the other runners who are seeking to find their new narrative amid the chaos of their former lives. As powerful and hopeful as its name, it's a way to combine my love of running plus my legal expertise in helping survivors of domestic abuse move forward with new lives.

Donating money is easy for people. But what I've learned through my work with the organization is people carry trauma differently. Some get on with it, lying with every word that falls from their mouths. Others fracture, unable to make space for the pain. Our mission isn't to typecast anyone. All we ask is you take a step forward to try to live in spite of it.

The steady pounding of feet against the ground gives me something to focus on instead of the way Declan consumes my senses more than my breath. Even as sweat dampens my forehead and stings my eyes, I feel the tension I've endured since this morning slowly dissipate as I realize our nighttime running group that we'd been lucky to have half a dozen just a few years ago, is now more than forty strong tonight.

If it weren't for two broken parents who realized they needed each other to heal, I'd never have thought to create an escape for others who just might need someone—even if it's a stranger who will encourage them to go one more mile. Take one extra breath.

After all, the next thing could be the biggest challenge of your life.

Picking up my pace, I recall fondly how it was my mother who encouraged us to embrace running. My earliest memories include when she bribed my father to join our first 5K, clad in a bright pink tutu. Crazy as it was, that little bit of encouragement got my sisters and me away from screens and into a world of endorphin-fueled escapism. That long ago race—an Amaryllis Event, naturally—ignited a passion that soon ruled every spare moment of my life.

Mama extolled the virtues of running, claiming it was her first love—well before my father. I remember, in my early teens, asking her how she got started. With a tender kiss on my forehead, she would murmur, "Someday, I'll explain. Just know this."

"What's that, Mama?"

"True love is precious. It's a gift beyond any other. Like love, running isn't solitary or cowardly. Sometimes, it's the only way to get clarity and perspective. It allows you the time and grace to salvage parts of yourself that could be damaged otherwise. Just don't run without someone knowing where you're going," she advised me wisely.

Which is the exact reason I sent my cousin a voice text after I'd left the house to meet the running group.

KALIE:

Out for a run

GRACE:

Building an eyeball. I'm thinking sushi for dinner.

I can't help but snort as I recall her message while negotiating the incline. I lean into the pain, shortening my stride and balancing on the balls of my feet.

My mind wanders to Declan's lean legs encased in his custom-made suits making me wonder if he's a runner. He has an incredible build—arms and legs are rippled with sinewy strength. The memory of him towering over my not insubstantial height at Dad's office threatens to overwhelm me even as I push forward.

Picking up the pace, my breaths increase, trying to drown out the relentlessly intrusive images of a man on a mission—one I've somehow managed to get myself entangled with.

With the burst of energy from the group pushing me, I surge ahead trying to outrace my inner demons. I groan as I reach the dense pine cluster ahead—a sensory overload of Declan's cologne I inhaled earlier when he stood so close to me. It was warm pine and raw masculinity that enveloped me in a way I knew I'd be safe with him.

Damn him. Damn all of them for lying to me.

"Damn this secret they want me to keep," I mutter under my breath, anger battling desperation. The men in our family claim they want to protect us, to shield us from the sordid parts of the lives they lead. But when will they accept that this darkness is as much a part of us all as anything else?

The darkness in our family began long ago, long before my parents ever met. It started because my father grew up with the kind of wealth most people only dream of. Yet, when it counted, money couldn't save his family from true heartache—not after his sister was kidnapped.

For twenty-five agonizing years, his family didn't just fracture—it imploded. That was until Aunt Cassidy rediscovered her past after blocking it out due to traumatic selective amnesia long after she built a found family from those whose experiences were just like hers. One of whom included my mother.

After I turned eighteen, I learned Mama was the victim of human traffickers, sold by her own father. She was rescued alongside two of my aunts.

Fate, or some cosmic unholiness, placed my mother and father in each other's paths. But it wasn't until he was reunited with his missing sister that the stars somehow realigned their destinies, allowing my mother to come back into his orbit. Even then, my father—always a sanctimonious ball of snark—expected her to capitulate to his will.

My mother, fiercely independent, never did.

I can't help but smile at the memory, recalling Uncle Phil's playful recounting of their legendary bickering during my childhood. "Your mama and father used to have epic battles." He'd crow about how Daddy's attitude would always spark conflict.

I always endured his overbearing tendencies since I knew them to be a coping mechanism—a way to shield us from the ugliness he'd endured all those horrible years. My smile fades when I realize he hasn't changed. Is he still driven by those same protective instincts or by something else?

Something less altruistic?

I don't realize I'm so lost in my thoughts until a hand grabs my arm, steadying me. Layla Wheeling—a friend from law school—asks, "Are you okay, Kalie?"

I exhale sharply, fighting to steady my voice. "Just lost in thought."

She juts a finger toward the precipitous drop in the trail. "Bad idea so close to the edge," she warns, a teasing smile tugging at her lips. "Besides, that's not why we're here."

I push aside the churning of my gut as memories of storming out of my father's office at Hudson Investigations makes my stomach roil. Instead, I challenge Layla over my shoulder, "Race you," and feel a spark of defiance amid the inner turmoil.

Her eyes narrow, and with a burst, she sprints ahead, shouting over her shoulder, "You're on!"

Slowing my pace, I give her a head start—fully aware I can overtake her in seconds. But my soul needs a race, the fiery burst of adrenaline, to eclipse the tangled feelings coursing through me momentarily.

Surging forward, weaving between trees as the path narrows, I surrender to the familiar burn in my legs and the dull throb in my heart. Spotting Layla ahead, I can't help but call out, "You'd better run, my friend!" Her laugh, honest and unburdened, momentarily eases the ache within me.

Running, after all, is a choice—a raw act of participation in life, untainted by manipulation, much like the love I long to understand.

Just like love should be. Just like family should.

I push harder, taking a less traveled parallel path until I pull ahead of Layla. My focus narrows to each controlled, instinctive stride, every footfall a small reclamation of control amid chaos.

Neck and neck with Layla, sweat dripping as I pour every ounce of determination into the run, I finally burst into the parking lot—barely ahead despite her head start. I slow, linking my fingers behind my head, elbows flung wide as if to physically open my lungs to the night's cool air. Even as everything around me seems to be spinning out of control, this moment is mine.

Even if the rest of my life is out of control, I still have this, I think to myself.

Layla and I exchange a sweaty high-five, our eyes locking in a silent understanding. I've known her—and her secrets—since law school, and while the world has devoured almost all of mine thanks to the paparazzi that persist in following my family around, this latest revelation remains hidden—at least for now. "You okay, Kalie?" she asks with a squeeze of her hand before letting mine go.

Forcing a smile, I reply, "Yeah. I just didn't realize how much I needed this." Then, as if my very thoughts conjured his appearance, I spot the man who has been consuming my thoughts leaning against a sleek black Maserati farther back in the lot.

What is Declan doing here? How did he find me? And how much can I lie to myself that the pounding of my heart against my ribs has everything to do with my last burst of speed and not the man giving me the once over like he's a hungry panther?

And I'm his prey.

CHAPTER NINETEEN

DECLAN

I'VE BEEN HERE LONG ENOUGH TO WONDER IF THIS WAS A GOOD idea.

Leaning back against the hood of my car, I replay Jon's earlier call in my head. He explained he wasn't with his cousin but with someone who works with her on, "—her special project. I have to meet this doctor in the city."

"What for?"

His words echo in the recesses of my mind. "Kalie's admired for a lot of reasons by a lot of people, but it's her story to tell."

It's understandable, really. Kalie is the epitome of the word "fantasy" with her long, dark hair and deep blue eyes, not to mention legs that seem to go on endlessly. Still, it's not her looks that have me waiting for her and her trailing agent to finish the run her cousin suspects she took. It's the quiet worry something she learned is going to put her in mortal danger.

I remind myself of the grim side of what could happen to her after the incident at the chop shop. I need to ensure she never repeats what she uncovered, not even to her family.

Still, I'm completely unprepared for the frantic slap of sneakers. Immediately, my hand snakes beneath my jacket for my gun. That's when I see her charging into the parking lot with the surefooted speed of a cheetah locking onto a prize, every muscle visible beneath her skin. In that moment, she is all focus, all fierce energy—a presence that demands attention.

She abruptly slows near another woman—a tall, leggy blond in athletic gear—whose arrival is marked by a quick high-five and a burst of laughter that momentarily dissipates the tension I felt earlier. For a moment, her walls are down. I see the real Kalie, the one who enchanted me, captivated me, from the moment I spotted her all those years ago.

In the last few weeks, I thought that woman was merely a figment of my imagination. Instead, I've been confronted by the woman who would sooner have set me on fire if she'd had the chance instead of just letting her fist connect with my face.

Worse than an infuriated Kalie was the heartbreak I saw on her face when I told her what caused our paths to cross the way they did. Compassion bled from her pores inside her father's office.

I couldn't handle it. At least, not then.

I murmur to myself, "No wonder her cousin knew where she'd be." As if I summoned her attention by whispering in the wind, her head whips around. Regret and apprehension collide in a tight, burning knot in my stomach. My presence slams her defenses up faster than a shield. Bitter regret surges through me at her obvious tension. Muscles that were loose just seconds ago lock up as our eyes meet across the distance of the parking lot.

Even as she moves to where I'm partially hidden in the shadows. I straighten, bracing for confrontation as she approaches. Despite the earlier breakthrough we had in her father's office, her knowing who I really am, her eyes are still guarded. I can practically feel her walls going up.

"Kalie," I greet her.

"Declan," she returns cautiously. "Do you mind if we talk while I stretch?"

I mistakenly presume she's going to drop to the ground or cross one leg over the other. I wince as she casually throws her leg on top of the hood of my quarter-million-dollar car—even if it's one I have all intentions of handing over the very second I have enough evidence to topple the Byrne empire. Still, I can't help but respect the fact she gives zero fucks over the fact the car costs as much as most people's home, instead flexing her thigh on the sleek hood as if it were a park bench. "Yeah, not a problem. Happy to sacrifice the paint job." The words come out with a sardonic edge.

"I assume there are minions around who wouldn't mind buffing that out for fear they'll end up rotting in the big house." There's an amused tilt of her lips I can't help but respond to.

There's no way to prevent my lips twitching back at her. Her wit might kill me before the Byrnes do.

With a quick wink and a graceful hop, Kalie switches legs. I can't help the way my body betrays me—her sculpted calves and the line of muscle beneath her skin spark a reaction below my waist. Christ, I wasn't certain my cock even knew what it was supposed to do besides take a piss. Still, it's nice to know it's not dead, as it can't help but respond to the perfect view in front of it.

My tongue feels thick in my mouth, like the air has become too dense to breathe. What am I doing? She's Jon's cousin, Keene's daughter—and I'm supposed to be chasing down the people who killed my former partner. I vowed I'd take them down.

Then, slicing through the haze of my conflicted thoughts, Kalie's amused voice wonders, "Is there a point for you tracking me down other than checking me out?"

I lift my eyes slowly from the temptation of her sleek curves to the wild storm brewing on her face. Beneath the façade, there's a desperate plea for answers I can't give her. "You didn't respond to my text."

She shrugs. "I wasn't certain if I should."

Good girl. "Understandable, but I need you to listen to me."

"Declan," my name slips from her mouth on a sigh. Great. Now I know what I'll be hearing in my dreams later. "Why did you really reach out?"

I step closer. To anyone spying on us, it would appear as if we were about to embrace. "I need you to listen to me, Kalie."

Straightening to her full height, she glances from side to side before shifting forward just a bit. Each muscle tenses, as if to prepare her for battle. "About?"

"Your family."

I realize my mistake and poor choice of words immediately. Kalie may be furious with them, but she won't tolerate an outsider's slight. Her cheeks bloom a deeper red than even her run caused while her blue eyes crystallize in defiance. "Like hell."

"I'm just trying to...," I go to explain, but the hissing sound she makes causes my balls to draw up between my legs sharply. "Right. Let me rephrase."

"Be very careful about the next words out of your mouth," she warns.

"Got it." Judging from the way my nut sack is hiding behind my dick, I'll never forget the lesson. Not going to lie, as much as she's caused something inside me to sit up and take notice, I'm more than a little scared she'll shred me apart like she did her family. I lift my hands in supplication. *I should have thought about whose daughter she is and chosen my words more carefully.*

The banked fury in her eyes explodes like a star going supernova. I pinch the bridge of my nose. "I said that out loud, didn't I?"

She taps her toe on the ground. "Declan, what do you want from me?"

"To talk to you."

"About?"

"What you overheard today."

"What about it?"

"I need you to keep it to yourself. Don't say anything. Not to anyone."

Her expression twists in disbelief before it turns mocking. "Well, damn. Here I was going to call my cousin who works for StellaNova and let him know all about my new bestie, Lawyer Dec and his fake ass clients, right after we went shopping for the next charity ball together and I get a lollipop to suck on."

My jaw tenses. "I'm being serious."

All humor evaporates. "So am I. It's none of your business whether I scream at my family..."

"Please don't. You don't know if the wrong ears might be listening." I hope my words of caution come off as a plea for protection for me but they're really for her.

God, if something happens to her...I can't fathom the thought.

My concern must show on my face because she frowns. "Tell me why," she whispers. She moves so close until our noses almost touch. It forces me to inhale her scent of sweat and expensive perfume. The two smells mixed remind me of sex—a cocktail that stirs raw images of intense, uninhibited passion. Mind blowing, middle of the night release. Something I haven't had in so long, I can't remember what it feels like to slide into a woman's warm slickness.

Only, I don't just want it with anyone. I want it with her.

My body reacts, defiant and debased, and I silently pray she doesn't catch sight of my arousal.

I deliberately run through the catalog of crimes the Tiberis and Byrnes have admitted to with me as their defense attorney. Then, I feel it.

Her hand clasping mine.

It's an innocuous touch, yet once her skin brushes against mine, all I feel is the electric leap of her touch.

She gasps softly. Involuntarily, I cant my body forward ready to capture her lips beneath my own. My brain switches off as my mind forgets about why I'm even there as my imagination forms the lucid thought of Kalie sprawled in my bed, her hair fanned out like a dark, shimmering fan. A groan of conflicting desire escapes me.

"Declan? Declan? Declan!"

Her voice adds to my fantasy. "Yes?"

That's when the sharp burst of pain transmits through my foot. "Ow! Shit! What the hell was that?"

"I called your name four times! If we were being shot at, what good would you have been?"

Like a bucket of ice water, her words drag me from my sexual haze like nothing else possibly could. I don't blame her for snapping and finally resorting to something physical to get my attention—even though my dick wishes it was something more hands-on and my foot is cursing me for being a stupid fool.

"Your family—especially your father—they're my only lifeline, Kalie. I don't have a team backing me on this op, just them. There's nothing standing in between when I confront the Irish or the Italians except my brain and the knowledge that if something goes wrong, they know who I am and what I was doing." I raise my hand when she starts to argue. "I need the anonymity they maintain for me to operate in the field, to bring down the rest of these organizations."

Her breath shudders out. In the dim light, I recognize a glimmer of agony dulling the brightness of her eyes—a pain that twists something deep inside me. Something I thought long dead after Tanya disappeared. "I figured that out on my own, Declan. Still, don't tell me my family can or cannot be trusted. You don't get to decide that."

"I never said they couldn't. Just, what you heard is part of something much bigger."

"How big?"

I don't answer immediately but let our eyes lock in silence for a heavy moment. Finally, I murmur, "Look, this isn't the right place. But we need to talk about everything so you understand how to protect yourself."

Laden with bitterness, she retorts, "According to my father, I already heard too much."

My voice is steeped in regret. "You need the whole picture."

"Why are you telling me this, not my father?" she challenges quietly.

Is it even possible to make a daughter appreciate her father's outdated creed of protecting the women in his life at all costs? "I can't answer that. This is about more than your cousin's ordeal, Kalie. It's bigger than even what happened to my partner."

"I'm getting that. When and where?"

Relief surges through me at her willingness to listen. "When is the next time you can guarantee being by yourself?"

She stares off into the distance. "Friday. My cousin is flying to a conference and will be gone for a month."

"Friday night then. I'll come to you." My voice trails off as her eyes meet mine.

Her expression immediately turns serious. "If you do anything to betray my family, there won't be anything I won't do to annihilate you." As her words hang in the charged air, a piercing whistle crackles overhead—a call from her friend. In response, she blows a soft whistle of her own before she walks away from me. Over her shoulder she calls, "Don't make me regret this."

I let out a slow breath as she jogs away. Determination to keep this woman safe turns my guts into a knot even as I acquiesce silently, accepting her terms.

For now.

CHAPTER TWENTY

Since the night Declan confronted me after running, I've dodged any in-person encounters with the family—except for Grace. I haven't avoided the morning and evening texts I've been receiving from Declan though. I respond because he's assured me he's using a burner phone.

DECLAN:
Morning. Everything okay on your end?

KALIE:

Yes.

DECLAN:

Night. Hope today was successful.

KALIE:

A-OK.

While not overtly personal, each gambit between us grounds me like that perfect sip of coffee first thing in the morning. They let me know I had an ally in the emotional turmoil I was experiencing.

Finally, it's Friday. The day Grace leaves and Declan and I get to talk in person. As she departs for her trip in a whirlwind of frenzied hugs and fierce kisses, I tease, "Keep away from men who are just out for your body parts, Gracie. You know how sketchy they can be."

Grace rolls her eyes, scoffing as she grabs a case of silicone eyeballs and noses before jumping in the back of the car to catch a ride to Teterboro, where our uncle's jet is primed to shoot her across the Atlantic.

Earlier that week, she groused about hijacking the Lockwood Industries jet for herself until I pointed out her hyper-realistic silicone body parts might have Homeland Security suspecting her of a serial killing. "It's okay to accept help, Gracie." I chided.

She shot me a baleful glare—then reluctantly accepted our uncle's offer to whisk her off to Belgium.

Other than mild drama, the days have passed by with no eruption of a storm and a distinct lack of drama. With Declan's warning still echoing in my head, I'm hell-bent on wrangling my natural impulse to share information with my family. So, I feign a cold as a flimsy shield to work from home for the week.

Cough, cough.

Meanwhile, despite juggling all my work—hell, I even made a dent in the backlog—I end the week ahead. I grumble, "So, all I need to do to catch up is fake an illness?"

Or lie to them. With that reminder, guilt surges through my system. "Christ. How the hell does Declan live his life constantly undercover?"

He's been on my mind every minute I'm not buried in contracts, counter signatures, and conference calls. Truth be told, if I'm honest with myself, I've done more than think about him.

Seriously, I'd be terrified about what my internet searches would reveal if it weren't for that nifty piece of tech my cousin Mike engineered for Hunt Industries and subsequently leases to the DoD he's had me testing for the last year because as he said, "I know you'll adhere to the ethics of using it, Kalie. That Harvard Law degree has to come in handy sometime."

The info I uncovered about Declan's career with the FBI isn't just shocking, it's an earth-shattering bombshell. He wasn't just a special agent—he was a highly decorated one. After staying up all night reading about some of the higher profile cases he worked on, I'm still reeling from it.

It was an understatement to call me distracted when I wished Grace a safe trip to Bulgaria before she reminded me, "Belgium, not Bulgaria. Home of chocolate, beer, and waffles."

"Right. Belgium."

"Is your cold getting worse? Do I need to delay my flight? Call Laura?"

"No!" To distract her from my vehemence, I whined. "I just need to rest."

She cast me a sidelong glance. "If you say so."

"Bring me home top tier chocolate. I'll be just fine."

Still, nothing but a large glass of wine is going to ease my anxiety about how tonight with Declan is going to go. I gulp a large swallow recalling the news articles I found after Declan left the FBI and his former colleagues accused Declan of succumbing to greed. Of losing his honor. "What utter crap."

For a moment, I consider if I should let someone know about my impending visitor, before shrewdly guessing, "He's probably told them he's coming."

"I let Jon know when I asked him for your address, yes. Still, next time tell your detail so they don't walk in and find you dead. Be smarter about what you're up against."

Lifting the stemless goblet to my lips, I enjoy the way the wine's peach flavor shimmers down my throat before turning to find Declan already inside my space. He's dressed in all black—jeans, button-down, boots. Instead of making him look harsh, the lack of color in what he chose to wear makes his natural coloring pop more dramatically. Even the shoulder holster he sports fails to unsettle me. He's not the first man to wear one in my presence.

No, it's his expression that screams "danger" louder than any words, eyes shadowed, jaw clenched like a coiled spring. I tilt my head, scrutinizing him. The desperation in his eyes dredges up faint memories of my childhood—ways my father would look at my mother with a vulnerability he couldn't hide.

Not even from me.

What is this man so afraid of? That fleeting thought burns at the forefront of my mind as I offer. "Drink?"

He jerks his chin up. "I wouldn't mind some of that."

Carrying my glass with me, I make my way into the kitchen. He calls out, "Smart move, Kalie."

"What's that?" I spin around only to find he's followed me on silent feet despite the heaviness of his footwear. Instead of being in the family room, he's positioned at my back. He braces his arms on either side of me before leaning into my back.

For just a moment, I close my eyes and pretend this is any first date—giving myself permission to soak up the scent of pine mixed with his natural masculine scent. My lips part when his head ducks down and his nose nuzzles against the knot of hair I have twisted up against the back of my head.

This has to stop before we both cross a line we're nowhere ready to step close to.

Spinning in the cage of his arms, I press my hand against his chest and push him back a step. His lips form a pout that's both seductive and boyish at the same time. I want to grin at it but, "It's far too soon for this, buddy. Try again."

Declan's eyes hold a little less weight in them when he jokes, "I was simply about to compliment you on taking your glass with you."

"And it was a moral imperative to get this close to me to do it?"

Amusement and admiration flash in the depths of his fathomless brown eyes. "That is simply a perk."

Shoving him back, I reach for the wine and pour him a glass before topping off my own. Gesturing for him to retreat back into the family room, I follow him from a safe distance. What I didn't expect was that I'd be treated to a delicious view of his rear. *Christ. Now, I get why all the bad boys in movies always had all the girls drooling over them.* Then a sound of amusement escapes me. *Not to mention Uncle Phil.*

Once we're both seated, I ask him questions, to set the tone for the evening. "Would it be easier for you if I just ask questions and you can say yes or no?"

His lips twitch. "You think you know what to ask?"

"Only one way to find out."

He takes a sip of wine and makes a circular gesture. "Go ahead."

"You were born Declan Sean Conian."

His brow furrows. "Yes."

"Raised in the suburbs of Boston, you excelled in languages—graduating high school speaking three. Impressive."

"How—"

I trample right over him. "Went to BC. Majored in languages and pre-law. Dual bachelors. Approached by an FBI recruiter on campus who recommended you get your pesky law degree even while preparing to go straight into Quantico."

Oh, to have a camera trained on him to capture the shock on his face when I throw that information at him. He leans forward and sets his glass down carefully. "How did you unearth that information?"

"How am I doing so far?" I flip my hand. "Answering with a question is still an answer in this case."

"No, Kalie. How did you uncover that information? Did your father tell you?" he demands.

My brow furrows. "No. Of course not. I haven't spoken with him since that day at Hudson...what the hell are you doing?" I yelp as he towers over me.

"Then tell me how you found out all that when that information is supposed to be erased!" he roars directly in my face like a wounded bear with a knife jammed through its paw.

I hold up both hands in front of me, almost touching his broad chest. "I... used a program my cousin gave me."

"Which cousin? What program?" he snaps, intensity morphing into outright threat.

My eyes narrow. "What's it to you? That information is publicly available."

"It's not, and if you could find all that out after the tech team at Hudson did their damndest to bury it, there's going to be hell to pay. My mother may be gone, but some of her relatives are still alive. Tanya's family is still here. Hudson buried my past so her family wouldn't be in jeopardy from the Tiberis or the Byrnes. If you could get to it, who knows what other information could be found out about me they can hold over my head?"

"Shit." Understanding finally, my hand lands on his heaving chest.

He reaches up to hold my fingers in place. At first, I thought it was just a surface attraction between us, something I had a chance of beating. But when he speaks, something shifts inside me. Something I've never come close to experiencing. "We're not close like your family, not anymore. But I don't want their blood on my hands."

"Calm down. Let me call Jon."

"On speaker," Declan commands.

"Aye, aye, captain," I mutter as I connect the call.

It rings once before Jon picks up. Immediately, Jon asks, "What's wrong?"

"Tell him, Kalie," Declan orders.

I do so in a way that won't ignite Declan's temper but will give Jon the information he needs on an open line. "Mike's been testing new toys. I found information that might be problematic for someone who enjoys my right hook. Understood?"

There's a long pause before he says, "Got it. Have a good night."

Now Declan's expression has turned baffled. "What just happened?"

"He'll handle it."

"By doing what?"

"By calling my cousin."

"What does that mean, exactly?"

I don't explain Jon will likely badger Mike for the new tech to use at Hudson before it goes to the DoD to make Hunt Industries more money than it could possibly need. "It's being handled."

He gives me a look riddled with doubt before he asks, "Now what?"

I cross my arms akimbo. "Now, be honest with me. Can you do that?"

CHAPTER TWENTY-ONE

Kalie

DECLAN NODS. NO PROTEST, NO ARGUMENTS. JUST A HEAVY weight he wears on a chain around his neck. "There's no point in lying to you. You're too smart." Then his lips quirk into a wry smile. "Then again, you'd probably search the web and find the right answers anyway."

"Not anymore. Not that I know what's truly at stake."

His eyes widen imperceptibly when he realizes what I'm saying. Still, that doesn't alleviate the danger emanating off of him. As alluring as it is, it's the kind of dangerous that could place my loved ones at risk. I jerk my chin toward the other end of my couch before ordering, "What do you want me to know that my family isn't telling me?"

When he really lets me see the unguarded version of himself, the wounds I spy almost bring me to tears. The pain Declan's weighed down with causes a ripple to travel across my heart and tears to prick my eyes. I reach out and brush my hand over his arm to offer some relief to his pain. "Oh, Declan."

"Tanya was my partner. For this case, they only needed a woman to go in. I was to act as her handler." His eyes fly up to mine to see if I understand.

"Were they trying to trap the Byrnes using a honeypot?"

He nods. "It wasn't ideal. Tanya is—was—happily married. But the man she was targeting—Cian Byrne—was impotent. Had peripheral artery disease." He scrubs his hands over his face. "Hell, even tiny blue pills couldn't help him get it up. She wasn't worried about...that."

I didn't respond. Just waited for him to speak his truth. At this point, it was more about him unburdening himself than anything.

"She overplayed her hand with the old man. I found out through back channels there were some of the family who were suspicious and warned her about it at our last meet up." His eyes drift shut in memory. "God, that place was a dump. It was a run-down coffee shop in South Boston. Hell, we came up with a fucking backstory that should have stuck—telling old man Byrne her brother was having emergency surgery. That's all we needed—a reason to deviate from her schedule."

"But she didn't want to," I probe gently.

"So damn stubborn." He sniffles, swiping tears from his cheeks. "Said she was on the cusp of the big payout. Three more days. Pleaded with me to wait."

"But something went wrong."

"Exactly." He exhales. "Despite their criminal ties, the Byrnes are considered old money. Old power. Not the good kind. They're the kind of people who never appear in headlines because the ink printing is done so with blood."

My pulse quickens. Yes, I'd grown up with substantial influence and enormous secrets, but Declan's secrets are more painful. And he hasn't got to the worst part of his story.

"They own people all over the damn state—police, politicians, judges. While waiting for the high sign from Tanya, I gave an update to my agent-in-charge."

A sick feeling starts to churn the wine in my stomach. He continues, voice low. "The next thing I know, I'm being called back to the station by the director...something went wrong. Everything unraveled. People were frantic. Tanya couldn't be found. Gone. Like she'd never existed."

"Kidnapping?" I ask gently.

Declan's eyes flickered. "Yes," he said. "Then after a few days, Tanya's head was sent to us. It was a warning—a huge one." His voice chokes up. He slugs back a drink of wine before managing to continue. "I was the one to go notify her husband. He smiled when he opened the door to me. Led me to the living room. Their wedding photo was above the mantel. His screams brought the kids into the room..." He sniffs. "I can still see their faces in my sleep."

I don't have words. Instead, I just offer him the solace of silence so he can regroup. "Now, it's all jumbled in my nightmares. She's headless trying to get back to a blood-soaked wedding dress. Instead of joy, it's a fucking massacre. It's all my fault, Kalie. It's all my fault. If I hadn't checked in, if—"

"Declan, stop it."

He runs his hand beneath his eyes to mop up the tears. I reach over for the tissues and offer them to him. He takes one, murmuring his thanks. I probe, "Have you spoken to anyone else about this?"

He shakes his head. "I went right from the bureau to Hudson. I dove right into finding Tanya's killers. I have to do whatever it takes to bring them to justice. I have to for Tanya, for her husband Ben, for her kids."

"And for yourself."

"I don't deserve forgiveness." His laugh is bitter. "That much was made evident to me by the way I was persecuted by everyone at my job, investigations into Tanya's death, fingers being pointed."

"Let me ask you a question," I begin.

"No, I don't send them Christmas cards every year," he snaps.

"Wow. So not what I was going to ask, but good to know."

"Sorry. You were asking?"

"If you *were* the one undercover, would Tanya—your partner—have executed the same protocols if you'd had the same meeting with her?" The question is brutal but necessary.

It takes a while, but his barely audible, "Yes," sounds like a shout in the quiet of my living room.

I feel the sting of the guilt Declan still carries twist my gut, but I don't let it dissuade me from getting my answers. "How did my family get involved?"

"Your family has their own vendetta against the Byrnes."

"Why?"

"Your father has been working to shut them down from a multitude of angles. Quietly. Legally. The problem is that these people are smart. They have connections that go back decades—business, politics, people you wouldn't expect."

"They can't catch them?"

"They can in other ways but that could take years. They have too many favors owed to them. But since they placed me in a position to have access to their records, we're getting close." His eye twitches in the corner. There's something he's not telling me.

"What are you hiding?" My voice is crackling with uncertainty.

He doesn't answer my question directly. "My position at Hudson initially started because your father wanted me to give him every last detail about the individual. He wants this person annihilated—no, I think even that's too soft of a word."

The shudder that ripples up my spine at his words is the kind you get when someone dances on your grave. I already know the answer based on what I overheard, but I need for him to confirm it. "Who?"

He lets out a deep breath. "Your paternal grandfather—Jack Marshall. He's their right-hand man."

His words steal the breath from my lungs as the fear my father must be experiencing comes full circle. My dad's biological father hasn't been heard from in years, but no one worries about it because he hasn't brought it up. I'm certain most of the family assumes he is dead.

Instead, my father's been hunting him. "What does he want with him?"

Declan stares at me. "The same thing I want with Tanya's murder —justice."

CHAPTER TWENTY-TWO

THE NEXT MORNING, I RECEIVE A NEW TEXT FROM DECLAN THAT sets my heart fluttering. I try to disregard my physical reaction but it's no use. Instead, I'm left with wondering what's going to happen later in the night to come.

DECLAN:

Did you sleep after I left?

KALIE:

Let's just say I'm grateful it's the weekend.

DECLAN:

Again tonight?

KALIE:

Sure.

"How are you holding up after discussing what happened to Tanya last night?"

"Honesty?"

"Absolutely."

"It's the first time in four years I've slept without headless brides chasing me in my nightmares." He lays a hand on my arm, and either I'm the only one who feels the electrical arc or there's a damn short circuit in my home. His eyes bore into mine and the steadiness of his gaze takes my breath away. His thumb rubs up and down on my bare arm, his touch leaving goosebumps in the wake. Forget words. It's in our silence that lays the foundation for what could be more between us. I'm certain of it.

Finally, after moments of quiet, he breaks it. "Thank you. Thank you for letting me grieve, Kalie."

"You don't have to thank me for that." I hesitate before saying, "Can I ask some questions about Jack Marshall?"

The hesitant smile he had on his face fades away. Now, in its place is the cold mask he had on his face at the courthouse. It's cold and unbreakable. "Now you're asking questions I can't answer, Kalie. That's something you have to broach with your father. I can't betray their trust by telling you what I know about him."

Silence settled over the room like dust. "I see."

He relents, before reaching for my hand to hold, causing my heart to flutter. "I will tell you this. He's not focused on your family."

A sigh of relief escapes me. But it's too soon when Declan informs me, "He is, however, asking questions about you."

I squeeze his fingers so tight, he winces. "Christ. Why didn't my father tell me?"

"I can't answer that."

"Not helping." I glare at him.

"I know," he said.

"Why me?"

"The working theory is you've been on their watch for years. But they're taking action because of you hitting me at the courthouse."

I curse myself, but he stops my diatribe by lifting his free hand in my direction. "Would you have acted any differently? Remember, you still wouldn't have known who I was."

Begrudgingly, I admit, "Unlikely."

"Then stop beating yourself up about it."

"If I endangered the people I love because of being reckless..." My voice is pained at the idea.

But Declan stops me. "I've been living undercover with this scum for a long time, Kalie. If it wasn't this, it would have been something else that brought you to their attention."

"That's both terrifying and encouraging."

"Happy to help." I still don't know what I feel when he leans forward and removes my wine glass. Turning to face me, he clasps both my freezing hands between his, staring deep into my eyes. My breath hitches. "Kalie, I need you to trust me. I know what it's like to lose someone I love to the Byrnes. I won't let your family go through the same."

My heart stutters even as my head falls forward. "Declan..."

"I know you may have a right to be frustrated, but I need you to believe me when I say give up whatever feelings of right or wrong you're harboring against your father right now. He's working in survival mode. He's not thinking clearly since you inadvertently brought yourself into this op. You have to be smart. Careful. But you have to trust the people with the most experience and right now, that's your dad. Hell, let *me* protect you, even if you think I'm a worthless piece of shit."

"You know I don't think that about you."

His eyes drift shut. When he opens them, they're bright with moisture. "Thank you. That means a lot."

Declan's passionate plea on behalf of my own family hangs between us. I'd already decided to let my family back in. Oh, there will be punishment, but not the kind to detract them from the job they're doing. Not that he needs to know that. Still, I feel compelled to help him with his own demons. I clear my throat. "What made Tanya a good partner?"

"What?" His tone is riddled with disbelief. "That's what you want to ask me?"

I lean forward and press a hand against his wrist. "Declan, most of what you told me I either found out or I could have asked my family. You went from tragedy to persecution to op. Have you really talked about the good you learned from your partner?"

His eyes drop to the floor. "No."

"She deserves to be remembered," I press. "Doesn't she?"

Declan looks up. Unrestrained pain in his face shows how much he hides when he's in full operational mode. "Yeah. She went through the classes at Quantico a few years before me. Right off the bat, she told me she didn't do probie partners."

My smile is tentative. "So how did she react to being partnered with you?"

His smile turned rueful. "About as well as you'd expect. She was brash, arrogant, made fun of my accent every time I spoke in a different language."

Tears well up in my eyes at the filial fondness in his voice.

"She was lethal and vicious but had this calm way of watching people— seeing them without letting them know she was watching. She was supposed to be my partner. But she became more than that."

"She became your family," I whisper.

His eyes meet mine. "What amazes me about you and your family is you can see that yet people I worked with, people I spent years with, people who knew us both whispered openly that I must have had her murdered to get in with the Byrnes."

I don't flinch at what Declan is saying. However, an overriding urge is compelling me to do something that, a week ago, I never would have imagined I could be capable of. Standing, I reach for his hand and tug him upright. Removing his glass from his hand, I give him a solemn look.

He frowns down at me. "What is it? Do you want me to leave?"

Without a word, I wrap my arms around his waist and hold on. I feel a tremor of shock run through him before he steadies himself and he clutches me tightly. He doesn't release the storm of emotions I know are still locked inside him, but I can tell something settles within him.

"What do we do? What do you need from me?"

He pulls back. The same intensity is in his eyes but the storm is banked. For now. "I don't make the same mistakes. This time, no one will get hurt."

Stepping back, I pick up my glass and toast him. "That's a plan I can drink to."

Later that night, as I am getting ready for bed, I receive a text that cracks my heart wide open.

> DECLAN:
> You keep surprising me.
>
> DECLAN:
> Tonight...I have no words.

> KALIE:
> Whenever.

> DECLAN:
> Soon.

I crawl into my bed, feeling safe. Knowing that I'm protected.

CHAPTER TWENTY-THREE

DECLAN

After spending so long undercover, I believed my emotions had been tampered with—hibernated before they could betray me. Yet tonight, after spending time with Kalie, the more I feel about everything.

Especially her.

I never could have imagined someone like her entering my life—so fierce, so full of fire.

So perfect.

Sinking back in my desk chair in my home office, I catch a glimpse of my face reflected back at me in the mirror on the opposite wall. I can't help but wonder how Director Holder would react if he could see what I've become. Would he berate me for blurring the boundaries he demands his agents maintain—for feeling something for a woman who should never have been involved in the op to begin with?

Then again, I've been under for years. How long is a person expected to live without feeling something? Anything?

A raw chuckle escapes me as I imagine his dressing down. Likely he'd threaten to pull me from the op. But maybe he'd listen about why I'd insist on staying. This isn't solely about taking down the people who hurt Tanya—though it started that way. It's now about bringing down two seemingly untouchable empires.

The Byrnes—they're not just legends. They're fact. People think the Irish Mafia is some half-forgotten legend. A few whiskey-drinking men running card games out of a snug, while the world's moving past them.

They're wrong.

The Irish haven't just survived—they adapted.

They fold themselves into corporations, into politics, into unions and real estate. They take over trucking routes and railroads. In some places, you can't tell where a town ends and they begin. It's no longer about bar brawls and glasses shattering. No, they wear suits and shake hands in boardrooms.

But I've learned not to fool myself. The rules are still the same. Their credo is still the same—loyalty or blood.

Still, while I'm undercover, I'm the guy they call when they want it to look legal. When they want it invisible. When they want to flaunt their redemption. Gloat they're legitimate even as they wag their fingers and bare their necks encased in blood diamonds. Because nothing sells the appearance of acceptance more than money.

Even if that money was made selling other humans.

How is it Kalie seeks to understand my motivation the way no one else has? How could she take in the pain as if it was her own? It was obvious in the way her countenance softened. Then there was the empathy in her tone.

How is it someone who should have been damning me as being their greatest enemy turned into something I never thought to contemplate having again in my life? As a friend? As more? Sure, Jon's been by my side at Hudson. But tonight, Kalie touched a part of me I wasn't sure existed any longer.

My heart.

When she asked about Tanya and insisted I talk about who she was, she broke down the barricades I wasn't even aware were still up. I thought the man who had those emotions died the same day his partner's head was delivered to the field office.

Maybe he did. Maybe I hoped he had. If I didn't let anyone get too close then I wouldn't be able to be hurt again.

Then, Kalie surprised me by landing punches that never should have happened—the first to my face, the second to my heart. That hasn't happened in years. She didn't judge, nor did she condemn my decision to avenge Tanya.

Instead, she just wrapped her arms around me and held on.

The feel of my lips curving makes my muscles in my cheeks ache. But as fast as it occurs, it fades as a chill surges through me. What if she ends up being the next casualty, like Tanya? Her father is pulling every string, baiting every trap, desperate to ward off another impending tragedy.

The Byrnes want Kalie's blood for being such an upstart to insult their family. Hell, I'm surprised they didn't put an outright hit on her, considering they believe I'm their life raft trying to keep afloat their precious pipeline to traffic women and children when, in reality, I'm doing everything possible to destroy it with my own two hands.

I'm terrified that I'm running out of chances to keep another innocent woman safe.

Fumbling in a drawer, I retrieve an old photo of Tanya, me, and her family, its edges worn. Even now, it's hard to look at. To know my actions—even though they were unintentional—led to her demise.

Had I known, I'd have dragged her off that damn op instead of basking in the moment and reporting that we were ready to wrap things up with a slam dunk believing in the power of our chain of command.

Our division.

Our organization.

That night, my life shattered.

I should have known better. By the time I was back from making the call, Tanya wasn't responding. There was no way to pull up her tracker. Weeks later, the dress it was sewn into would be found in a four-alarm fire—a haunting reminder of the brutal way she had been severed from it.

In the wake of her death, vengeance became my sole companion. I became consumed with taking down the Byrne family, burning with a resolve that I had never known.

I began laying the groundwork for my cover with the Byrnes, faking fury over Tanya's betrayal with certain people—the only individuals I knew I spoke with at the FBI.

When Ben heard about it, he almost killed me himself—his emotions were completely out of control. I know a part of my soul died inside as he barred me from his home, from seeing his kids. Those truths were damn real and helped my backstory.

But then, more stories arose from a corner I never imagined they'd come from—my fellow officers and Internal Affairs. With some nudging by Hudson, files went conveniently missing. Years of dedicated service forgotten. And then permanently forgotten after the Hudson team ensured all files were truly removed. Instead, drawing a picture of me as someone ready for a sighted scope, they put a different kind of target on my back—a man ready to be recruited.

I was willing, if not resentful.

My law degree came in handy as I quickly worked my way through the grunt work piled on me by the family. Within the organization, I found errors made by other firms—errors I set them up for. I solidified my position as I uncovered mistakes, and they began to trust me when I presented them with paperwork for additional security protocols.

Security my ass, I had them sign away their rights for open surveillance.

One night, my legal mind saved me from being taken out by Jack Marshall himself. I tried to get him to admit to selling his child for profit and leaving Mildred Lockwood holding the bag. He raised a gun to my head, demanding, "Why should that matter to you?"

I lifted my hands in the air and lied. "I just want to know who to go to if I need...assistance...in the future."

The tension in the room dropped when Jack pulled the gun back. "Don't worry about it, *boyo*. If there are problems in your future, we'll be well ahead of them."

Christ, no wonder Keene wants to eliminate his father once and for all.

After the ease at which Jack held a gun to the center of my head, my senses told me he knew more about Tanya's disappearance than I could prove. I became more dedicated than ever to taking the Byrnes out.

Still, they threw a wrench in the works when they loaned me to the Tiberis for the purpose of getting key members of their family out of jail. I have to find out the truth about why, even as I utilize the weaknesses in our court system to delay their trials. A part of me welcomes the finality, where I no longer have to be this person. I can't imagine who I'll be after this nightmare is all over, but living the life of anyone else has to be preferable to standing in the shoes I'm in right now.

A flash of Kalie's gorgeous face comes to mind. My heart thumps once. Painfully. I'm terrified to let myself feel anything for her—especially while I'm entangled with people who are targeting her. Besides, letting anyone close isn't a good choice right now.

It leaves me with a vulnerable spot for the Byrnes to strike.

But how can I resist a woman who has no qualms about standing up for...how did she put it? "Truth, justice, and the Hudson way?" I chuckle, the sound rusty in the empty room. Kalie hit me, both literally and figuratively. She's fiery, fearless, and stronger than most men I know. She grew up wrapped in resilience and honor.

Still, it's the compassion she offers me that terrifies me the most. She already has me questioning if I'm truly so irreparably damaged I can't change.

No, I can't let her end up like Tanya.

In the end, I'll do anything to protect her. I won't let the Byrnes harm Kalie. I slip the photo back inside the desk drawer and close my eyes. "I just wish I could have saved you."

I can't have another woman's death on my conscience. My jaw clenches, knuckles white on the glass. For a woman who grew up with a family like hers, her lack of self-awareness when it comes to danger is infuriating. Her actions have already drawn the wrong attention.

I wonder what made her so fearless. I wonder what gave her that confidence.

These questions are the bare minimum of what I want to know about her. Still, I cannot, will not, let what I'm beginning to feel for Kalie derail me from my objective—taking down the people who killed my partner. Nobody will stop me.

As much as I yearn for answers and a potential glimpse into the future, I need to tamper my urges about Kalie down. It may be next to impossible since it feels like the barn door's already been shut and Kalie's trapped inside.

Right next to me.

Which scares me to no end.

CHAPTER TWENTY-FOUR

I DREAMT FOR THE FIRST TIME IN LONGER THAN I CAN REMEMBER. A true dream, not one of the nightmares I've suffered of Tanya's headless bride ghoul-like impression.

I wrap Kalie in my warm embrace, resting my head against her shoulder, nuzzling her soft hair. Then, I pull back and stare down into her exquisite face.

She cocks her head to the side. I lean down while my heart thunders. My cock aches. Every part of me calls out to her, no pleads.

Don't leave me.

In the trancelike way dreams have, every moment was sluggish as I lifted my hands and cupped her chin to hold it in place. Even as I fell headlong into pools of dark blue instead of drowning in a sea of regret, I knew this was where I was meant to be—with her.

That's when my traitorous alarm blasted me awake by playing the theme song to the Sopranos.

I shudder in agony as the song's blues and grittiness screamed through my bedroom. My dick is hard as a spike. I roll onto my stomach to ease the agony of my morning wood and bemoan fate. "I was about to fucking kiss her. You couldn't even let me have that?" I rail at God.

After a few moments where I question a god who decided men should have an appendage that causes more agony than pleasure, I swing my legs over the side of the bed and pad naked into the shower. As much as I want to sink back into the pillows and give my dick the desperate release it needs, there are more important things to do that morning other than mooning over Kalie.

Like ensuring she's safe by guaranteeing her protection detail is topnotch.

Under the spray of the shower, I curse my weakness. I want to fall back into my dreams so I can meet her where there's no enemies chasing us, where no barriers exist to keep us apart.

Maybe if we'd had that chance all those years ago before my life changed, when we first bumped up against each other, maybe things would have been different. This heat between us could have fully ignited. Before I can follow the water down the drain in a puddle of regret, an alarm beeps on my phone. Blindly, I reach my hand out of the shower and drag it in.

Cursing, I scrub off quickly before turning the tap off. The little firebrand is on the move. Judging by the speed, she's on foot.

What I don't know is if she took an agent with her and I can't leave her unprotected.

Not when she's somehow buried herself in something I thought long dead—my heart.

Showing up in Kalie's neighborhood isn't the brightest of ideas in the light of day. Still, I know I need to lay eyes on her—to make certain she's safe. *Damn, Declan. You should take your own advice before you arbitrarily endanger her by showing up at her home,* I curse myself.

Still, my heart pounds in fear when I realize she hasn't returned to her home. I've already reconned her property and there's no sign of life inside. Fear and anger swirl together in my brain.

I'm going to give her a tongue lashing for worrying me.

Please let her just be out with her agent.

God, what if something happened to her after I offloaded all my crap onto her shoulders? I'm not certain I could live with myself. But Kalie did more than listen; she asked. She lanced out the pain I didn't even realize was still festering beneath scabbed over wounds.

The engine of my car throbs through the steering wheel beneath my fingers as if it too understands the problem.

I know I shouldn't be here. I have places to be, things to do. But there's no way I'll be able to focus until I know she's safe. Just then, my Bluetooth rings. My heart leaps but crashes when I realize it's not her, but Sal. I answer with a snap, "What?"

"Declan, we have problems." That's when Sal launches into the litany of issues that have already gone to shit this morning. Some of his crew were arrested overnight after being caught booting a shipment of cars. There was a brawl at the strip club in the wee hours of the morning. The worst part is that he wants me to come with him and the enforcer whose job it is to collect from a string of mom-and-pop shops in Bridgeport because they haven't paid on time for protection.

Scrubbing a hand over my face, I growl, "I get why you're calling me about the first two, but what the hell does the third have to do with me?"

Sal's confusion is evident. "Well, they signed a contract."

"Is it an enforceable one?" I demand coldly. Before he can answer, I interject, "That means there are no clauses for physical retribution in the event of failure to pay, no interest rate hikes that fall outside federal guidelines. So help me God, if you've done either of those and expect me to defend it in court, you will lose. Tell me right now if you can lose any more of your crew to concrete cages before you ask me to go with you to Bridgeport."

He's silent for a minute. "Right. Why don't you focus on the first two issues?"

"That sounds like a better idea. Christ, I'm not your Don, not anywhere close. What the fuck do you expect me to do?"

That's when he floors me by saying, "Well, since you, the boys and I were talkin' bout how things are really lookin' up. Maybe we want you to step in—just until you get the bosses cleared."

"Right. And even if I wanted to entertain that idea, you know the second they did, they'd chop off my head," I reply.

"No job is without risks. In fact, did you hear bomb threats have been called in to credit card agencies?"

At this point, I'm rocking myself back and forth in the car in anticipation. "For the love of all that's holy, please tell me if it was any of you who did that?" He may think I'm desperate for him to say "no," but in my head, I'm pleading for him to give me an affirmative response.

"Nah, it was posted as something that happened on the Mafia Reddit channel."

Hearing that, my mind short circuits. I literally can't form words. When my brain resets, I shout, "There's a channel on Reddit for the mob and you idiots are on it sharing...no. Don't tell me. I want plausible deniability."

Sal chuckles. "Gotcha."

I glare up at the speaker. "This isn't funny."

"Lighten up a little, Declan. You need to get laid."

With those words, an image of Kalie floats through my mind. Smart, sassy, intelligent—exactly the kind of woman who does it for me. Vaguely, I make a non-committal response.

We talk for a few more minutes about the fuck ups from yesterday's work and I promise I'll see if anything can be done. After hanging up on him with a grunt, I reach out to the Darien Police Department. Since it's the weekend, I'm not surprised Sal's guys won't be arraigned until Monday. Which frees up my time to go back to what I was doing previously—staring up Kalie's street.

I have hundreds of hours of work to plow through before Monday. Numerous cases to look at. Motions to tweak to be just off enough to be thrown out by a judge. Discovery filings that are accurate but filed just past their deadline. Instead, none of that seems to matter as I keep staring up the street at Kalie's home, wondering where the hell she took off to.

I lean my head back against the headrest, closing my eyes for a brief second. Her reaction to what I told her about Tanya is at the forefront of it all. The pure emotions that flickered across her face for a woman she didn't know. The way her natural compassion shone through before she offered me a safe place to grieve without judgment.

It forces me to take an uncomfortable look at what I'm doing and if it's for the right reasons. If I had someone like Kalie in my life back then, would I have walked this path of vengeance? Would I have quit the bureau and joined Hudson?

Truthfully, the answer to both is I don't know. But something tells me it would have been different.

My life wouldn't be the same because she would have been there to help me deal with my grief the same way she is right now. After all, depending on who helps you heal, no two scars are identical.

Last night, something fundamentally changed between Kalie and me. I'd felt it when she listened without judgment as I exposed parts of myself I had to bury deep to function every day. When she didn't flinch at the worst of it, merely looked at me like she could see past the mask I always wore.

Now, seeing Kalie isn't just a want. It's a need I have to have just to survive another day in this fucked up life I'm living.

That alone terrifies me.

My eyes flicker open when I hear a dog bark in the distance. Focusing on the front of Kalie's home, I don't see any sign of movement. Sunlight blinds me from seeing in through the front windows, but other than that one sound, it's peaceful here. Serene.

Which is why I jump when there's a knock on my passenger side window.

My hand shifts beneath my jacket instinctively before I get a good look at who it is. Then I release the tension-riddled breath when I recognize the woman in form fitting jogging gear and the man standing down the street—Kalie and Jon. Turning on the ignition, I roll down the window.

Her first words make my lips twitch. "Tell me you didn't spend the night out here. I would have at least let you sleep on the couch."

"No, firebrand. I went home."

She makes a thoughtful humming sound, whether at the nickname I've bestowed upon her or my response. "Yet, you're back."

Jon calls out something I can't quite make out. She rolls her eyes. "Give me a sec." Then, she leans forward and into the window so I'm enveloped in her scent and paralyzed by her blue eyes. "Next time, bring a different car. Even in my neighborhood, this one's kind of noticeable, Declan."

I blurt out exactly what I'm thinking. "I just needed to see you."

She's quiet for a moment, studying my face, not saying a word.

The words come from a place deep inside of me before I can stop them. "I think I just needed to make sure you were okay with everything."

"Oh." Her expression softens. "I'm fine. What about you?"

Even now, she's putting me first. It warms something that's been cold and dead around my heart for a long time. "I'm okay."

She studies me before offering. "Do you want to come back later when you're not quite so...noticeable...to talk?"

I should say no. I should drive away from the openness shining on her face. Instead, "Yeah. I'd like that."

"Text me to let me know what time you'll be here." Then she leans back and jogs over to her cousin.

Something settles inside of me. Before I have a chance to process it, a text comes through on the screen of my car.

SAL:

Christ, Declan. It's a shit show.

Need you down at Velvet Vice.

I voice text back, "I'm on my way." Then, after ensuring Kalie and Jon are safely inside her house, I wheel the car in the direction of the strip club but my mind's not there.

It's thinking ahead to the many hours until I can get back to Kalie's.

CHAPTER TWENTY-FIVE

THE HEAVY VELVET CURTAIN TO VELVET VICE SWINGS CLOSED behind me, muffling the bass thumping through the club's cheap speakers. Red light bleeds across the cracked leather booths and makes the battered chrome on the poles more visible. The air is stale with sweat, perfume, and the sharp bite of cheap whiskey.

I'd rather be bailing out criminals than be anywhere close to where the Tiberis conduct most of their messier operations. My only role is to act in a legal capacity for the club's owner—drafting employment contracts, burying the bodies on paper, and keeping the heat off Sal's back.

Not the guy who gets the bottom of his shoes sticky walking across a strip club floor.

But Sal wanted me here because he claimed he needed a legal presence. In other words, the strippers were about to make things messy and they knew if I were there, any bullshit excuses for starting a fight would be documented and looked into. Then I'd spend the next few days giving him all the information he needed to "throw the fuckin' trash out."

I spy Sal near the back, lounging in a booth like a king surveying his kingdom. His current lieutenants, Tony and Frankie, flank him, sneering over a crumpled envelope tossed on the table.

Across from them, three of the daytime dancers who want nothing more than to fuck their way to the evening shift—Chrissi, Tammy, and Nerissa—stand half-dressed and visibly furious.

"I told you, I'll do anything for it!" Chrissi hollers.

"Obviously, not your job," Sal riles her up.

Chrissi stamps her foot. "That's all the money I've made in the last week. Either put me on nights or give me a little more time!" Chrissi's whole demeanor changes as she saunters toward Sal. "That is, unless you'd rather work it off me in a different way."

Christ, I might be sick. I can't prevent the curl of my lip. After having just come from Kalie's, the machinations of this bitch make my stomach churn.

Tammy shoves Chrissi's arm. "You're not the only one who wants to make that deal!"

"You shut up! I'm not the one who blew her cash on her cokehead boyfriend!" Chrissi spills Tammy's secrets.

The two women shove each other hard enough that a nearby table collapses when they bump into it. Beers crash to the floor, spilling all over two unassuming patrons. Fucking fantastic. Then someone in the crowd hoots, "Naked catfight!" and wouldn't you know? That sets the two women off like they're exhibition stars in the porn version of the women's WWE Championship.

Is this really my life?

Within minutes, the bouncer has shoved his way through the circle and I want to choke the fuck out of Sal, who waves him off with an easy flick of his wrist.

"Let 'em," Sal says, voice low and amused as he sees the flying dollar bills punctuate the air. "Maybe I'll make back the money they owe me this way."

Frankie and Tony chuckle. I don't.

Instead, I take note of all the patron's lifting their cell phones to get some shots of the girl-on-girl brawl occurring without an additional admission fee. I manage to keep a somber face but wonder how long it will take for this new video to go viral. Is it any wonder the Tiberi's case is getting so much media coverage when every other day there's new footage like this being released?

I was dragged away from Kalie to protect Sal's interests, not watch this catastrophe that'll make my job ten times harder when I have to prove the Tiberis are able to be released on their own recognizance. Sal pauses when I warn him of that. But like a child who is given too many toys, his attention is diverted when Chrissi swings an open hand against Tammy's cheek—a slap so vicious it echoes over the music.

Tammy screeches and launches herself back at Chrissi, nails extended.

Nerissa tries to reason with them both and pull them apart. She gets mule kicked in the gut for her trouble. She taps out, limping over to the corner. Frankie makes his way over to her with a frown when he realizes she's not breathing properly. He shouts, "Do I gotta call 9-1-1 or somethin'?"

"Fucking hell!" I bellow. The whole thing is turning into a full-blown brawl.

Sal, bastard he is, grins at me. "You gonna step in, counselor, before you end up as a witness to murder?"

I clench my jaw and step in to do just that with the realization that Hudson doesn't pay me enough for this shit. A raise is the first thing on my agenda for Monday—even before heading to the station to bail out the Tiberis.

Wading into the chaos, I grab Chrissi by the hair just as she's winding up for another hit. She twists, snarling, until she sees my face—and her body rolls into mine like a sinuous cat. She knows exactly who I am and she's made no bones about the fact she wants a piece of me. Her voice tries to imitate a breathy schoolgirl when she redirects her hand, choosing to slide it up my thigh. "Hey, Declan. Come to save me?"

I push her away. "Thanks, but no thanks. I don't relish having scabies."

Her passably pretty face twists, making her look like a Botoxed mummy. She takes a swipe at me. Before she makes contact, I shout, "Enough!"

My voice cuts through the noise better than a gunshot. The women stumble apart, panting, battered and glaring. I raise my voice loud enough to include Nerissa, who appears to be gasping for air. "You signed a contract. No fights. It's that simple."

Chrissi attempts to touch me again, "But, Dec, baby—"

I cut her off. "First, I'm not your anything. Second, let me lay it out in terms you'll understand." I jerk my thumb toward Sal's booth. "You don't strip, you don't get paid. You don't strip, he doesn't get his cut. He doesn't get his cut, he deals with you. Real simple."

Nerissa speaks up from the corner where her back is against the wall. "I can get the money to you by Friday, Sal."

Sal leans forward, lazy and dangerous. "I don't like getting stiffed, sweetheart."

I step in before he says something I'll have to defend when I know I'll be putting in an eighty-hour week over the stupidity he already dropped in my lap earlier. My eyes convey that to him, and he merely shrugs without a hint of regret. "They pay with interest by Friday. The full amount, no games. Or the club starts docking their tips."

Chrissi sneers. "You think you scare us, Declan?"

I smile coldly. "I don't need to scare you. I just need to make one phone call to my boss. We all know that isn't Sal, don't we?"

Her face pales the moment I remind her of that.

Nerissa, obviously smarter than the others, acquiesces. "We'll have it by Friday."

Sal's smile widens, satisfied. "Good girls," he says. "Now get outta my sight before I change my mind."

The three stagger off toward the dressing rooms, still muttering under their breath.

Sal claps me on the shoulder as I turn back toward him. "See? You do have a use outside of a courtroom, counselor."

I don't bother answering.

Instead, I wish I could trust even a glass of goddamn water in this place to try to rinse the sour taste out of my mouth. Because no matter how many contracts I alter to permit surveillance crews in places they never should be, no matter how many pipelines I get shut down, no matter how many criminals I've helped put away, or how much I've dismantled from the inside, this reminds me that I'm not a good guy.

I'm a part of this world.

Until something happens where I'm not.

CHAPTER TWENTY-SIX

I'd given up on the idea of Declan coming over until close to eleven when I received a text from him.

DECLAN:
If you're still awake, I could use somebody.

KALIE:
Meet you in the same place.

Twenty minutes later, I was in my family room waiting for him as I sipped from a steaming cup of tea. I'm not certain what I'm expecting, but it isn't the worn-out man who magically appears in front of me. "Well, you look like your day went to shit after I saw you."

"I'm supposed to be a lawyer."

"I take it that's not what today was about?"

"If you equate lawyering to threatening multiple people, then yes." He drops down onto the couch in the same space he was in last night. His eyes search mine before he admits, "I almost didn't come over."

"I figured that out myself." I take another sip before lifting it to him as an offer.

He wrinkles his nose. "If you have something much stronger, I'll gladly take that."

"There's a bottle of Lagavulin in my office." I don't tell him it's a bottle I share when my godfather comes over to argue contractual law with me. Tonight, there's a weariness on Declan's face that wasn't there when we spoke earlier. Something happened and he reached out. He needed me and I'm here for him. It's as simple as that.

"Yet you're drinking scented flowers?"

I roll my eyes at him, place the mug down, and order, "Follow me."

I'm on the fourth stair before I hear him falter. Without turning around, I address the sudden elephant between us. "My office is at the top of the stairs, Declan. I'm not luring you up here for some nefarious reason." *Not yet anyway.*

"I didn't want to make any presumptions."

I turn to face him and find him right at eye level. His dark eyes bore into mine when I graze my fingers against the scruff of his beard. "Declan, when it's time for us, you won't have to guess."

Leaving him sputtering, I turn around and continue to climb the stairs. After a few seconds, his footfalls pick up the pace behind me. In unison, we hit the landing, before I take the lead and head into the room I've made into my home office. Striding over to the cabinet that holds a tray of liquor, I'm curious about Declan's opinion as he inspects the space. I smirk, as whisky splashes into two heavy crystal tumblers, hearing his occasional huff of laughter or a mutter of "impressive" depending on where he is in the room.

His sharp intake of breath tells me where his eyes just landed in the room.

Turning, I hand him the glass before I remark, "You're treating it like it's more important than the other items I hung up in my office."

His head swivels in my direction, eyes bulging. "Maybe because it is?"

"I guess that's a matter of perspective. Personally, I'm more impressed by the fact I still managed to graduate law school only a year behind since I needed to train." I lift the scotch to my lips and relish the smoky caramel texture burning down my throat.

"I never expected to see anything like this up close."

"It's shiny, for sure," I remark drolly.

He slugs back part of his own drink. "I mean, Jon talked about you being a runner."

"I think the term you're looking for is he bitched about it." It's clear to me Declan considers Jon a friend. Despite my previous irritation, I'm grateful he has that in the murky world he lives in, and Jon? Well, my cousin is buried in his own shades of gray despite our very blue-blood childhood. "Was it along the lines of me being obsessed?"

"That's putting it mildly, but this?" Declan waves his glass at the medal, which showcases the pinnacle of my running career, carefully framed by Uncle Phil along with preserved flowers, all laid out on top of an American flag. "Kalie, you won a gold medal at the Olympic Games."

I lift a foot and point to the infamous five rings on the foot that doesn't have my amaryllis tattoo emblazoned on it. "Got some pretty ink afterward too."

"Seriously? That's all you have to say about it?"

I think about how to put this into perspective for him. "Declan, what is the most defining moment of your FBI career?"

He answers immediately, "When I finished Quantico. When I knew I was off my probationary period."

"Not when you made Special Agent?"

"No," he answers slowly.

"Do you know what mine is as a runner?"

"You wouldn't say that?" He jerks his chin toward my medal.

I shake my head and move toward my desk. Picking up a photo, I hold it out to him. "It's this."

He takes it, looks down, and immediately bursts into laughter. I can't prevent the grin that crosses my face as the rusty sound echoes in my office. He takes a drink and snickers before he exclaims, "The great Keene Marshall in a tutu?"

I step next to him. Resting my head against his shoulder, I glance down at the photo of my dad wearing the bright pink abomination right along with me, my mom, and my twin sisters in our first race. "He made a promise."

"Was this your first race?" At my nod, he surmises, "That's why this photo is more important than that medal?"

"Exactly. Just like when you finished training was more important than any other milestone." I lift my glass to salute his excellent deductions.

He hands me my photo back. After placing it back on my desk, Declan's agitated once again. I place my drink down and slide my hands up his forearms stilling his motion. "Talk. Tell me what happened."

"You want the sprint or the marathon edition?"

"Whichever you need. Actually, do you have a dollar?"

"Yeah, why?"

"Give it to me," I demand. While he fishes out his wallet, I spin around before yanking a piece of stationery closer and scribbling out a contract that permits Declan to disclose what he needs to, as per attorney-client privilege. When I'm done, I sign it before straightening. When I do, he's crowding me—his front to my back. My heart leaps, not out of fear, but the sheer thrill of feeling his body press against mine so fully.

Breathlessly, I hand him the pen and paper. "Fork over the money and sign this."

Intrigued, he scans it before doing what I asked—first slapping money in my hand. Scrawling his signature on the bottom of the page, he murmurs, "Okay, so maybe the most impressive item on your wall is that law degree."

"If we were defined by a single moment in time, most of us wouldn't exist." His face turns thoughtful as he considers my words. "The world doesn't revolve around one defining instance, but by the hard work that goes into who we are and what we do if things don't work out the way we expect them to."

I can tell I've caught him on the raw. Giving him a break, I ask, "Now, do you want to tell me what really happened today?"

When he does, I feel something shift inside me—a quiet victory. It settles deep in my chest, something I don't have a name for yet. But if it offers this complex man a reprieve against the relentless fight he's up against, I'm happy to offer it.

CHAPTER TWENTY-SEVEN

Is it odd how I can accept Declan under the justification of love, yet my father's overbearing nature still requires forgiveness? Perhaps it's because I have no expectations of Declan? Maybe it's because Dad's always been a hero in my eyes? Maybe it's because I've never been directly caught in the crossfire of one of his machinations?

Regardless of the why, I need to meet with him before I return to the office. He needs to understand where my disappointment and anger are coming from. I texted him directly.

KALIE:

I'd like to meet with you to talk.

DAD:

Name the place, baby.

KALIE:

Daniela Trattoria.

DAD:

I'll make reservations.

I drive into the city and park in the Hudson Investigation parking lot at their Rockefeller Center office, then walk over to the restaurant on 8th Avenue. Immediately after stepping inside, I am greeted with the clink of silverware and the low hum of conversation that filled the tiny Italian bistro. Without bothering to stop at the hostess station, I head toward the back stairs.

Intuitively, I know where my father reserved a table for us.

Every memorable event we've shared as a family has been experienced here. Dating back to my uncle's engagement, my mother's law school graduation, my parent's mutual proposal and subsequent marriage. Now, we come to the restaurant much more frequently as our family expands. When my honorary uncle, country musician Brendan Blake, had his last concert at Madison Square Garden, we rented out the entire restaurant. When our close family friend Kee Long hit number one on *The New York Times* best-seller list, we celebrated here. Engagements, birthdays—I can't remember not doing so here.

But this is the first time I recall coming here full of uncertainty.

It makes me hesitant to climb the last bend in the stairs to face my father. But when I reach the top, I realize I should have known better. The tables have been pushed aside, and there's a table for two—just like the way he had it set up when he told me Mama was pregnant with my twin sisters.

He stands the moment he sees me. With the smile he reserves just for family, he leans down to kiss my cheek. "You look tired. Still recovering?"

I pull back and let him seat me before I reply. "I wasn't sick."

"That's what you told your mother."

"It was better than me telling her the truth at that point." I flick my napkin open before laying it in my lap. When the waiter appears, I request, "Just a club soda today. I'm driving."

He doesn't ask why I stayed away. Instead, he lifts his coffee to his lips and takes a drink. "You're angry with me."

"Of course I am." I pause once my drink is delivered. I hold my tongue while we're asked what we want for our meal. After placing my order, my father orders for himself and we're again given the solitude for our conversation. "Dad, you've been hiding things. Important things. Not just from me, but Mama. The whole family."

He levels his gaze on me. "I have."

"Why?"

"That's a much more difficult question to answer, Kalie." He sighs but doesn't try to get out of it. "There are things I need to do, protect you from, not just in the line of work we do but because of our family's past. Things that could bring about unnecessary harm. I've always done things with everyone's best interest at heart, sweetheart."

"Have you?" I retort. "Because I don't see how keeping the fact you have Declan working for you is protecting us."

His eyes soften on me but don't lose their edge. "If I had my way, you'd never have found out, Kalie."

"This is exactly what I mean, Dad!"

"But then again, you'd never have confronted him the way you did either. Jon says it's made a difference in him. He's healing."

"If that's because of me, it's because I'm asking," I retort.

He nods thoughtfully before admonishing me. "Still, if he was as bad as we built his reputation to be, you could have been hurt, died...or worse."

"W-what?"

"Kalie," he lets out a broken sigh. "I need to tell you the full story about your grandfather."

So he does. He tells me about how his father and Uncle Caleb's mother had a torrid affair. How his father broke it off, and when they did, placed my Aunt Cassidy's life—my father's sister—in jeopardy. "I never stopped looking for the people who took her."

"Excuse me?"

"In what world would you contemplate I would have?" His words are mild, but his eyes are turbulent. His hand clenches on the table. He's coiled tighter than I've ever seen him—even when I went out on my first date. "It wasn't until I hired Declan that I found the piece I couldn't locate."

Declan's words from the other night spring to mind. "Jack Marshall."

He nods. "My father. The man who started it all. The person who is in bed with the Byrnes. I have...so many questions."

"I imagine you do."

"But more than answers, I need to know you all are safe." Before the shriek that wants to leave my lips can bring a member of the waitstaff scurrying toward us, he leans over and covers my mouth. His voice lowers to a whisper, "Kalie, we found out the Byrnes are part of the pipeline that traffics women and children."

Ripping his hand away, I hiss, "Tell me you're going after them."

He nods. "But carefully."

"I'd have thought you'd have shot first and cleaned up later."

A faint smile crosses his lips. "Maybe. If it weren't for one thing."

"What's that?"

He tucks a piece of my hair behind my ear. "You knocking Dec on his ass."

Crap. "I wasn't exactly thinking."

His voice is quiet but firm. "I understand, Kalie. It's just made things... difficult. There have been...threats...made."

"Against who, Dad?"

His gaze skitters away from mine. Even if that's telling enough, I need the words. "Dad?"

"I swore from the moment I held you for the first time I'd protect you with my life, Katherine Laura. I'll never ever let up on that vow."

"Daddy?" Tears clog my throat as I push him to answer my question.

He cups my cheek before he leans over the table to kiss it. "Don't worry about the threat, sweetheart. I'll always protect you."

With that, I push away from the table. My father sits back as I hurry around the table. When he realizes what I'm about to do, he slides his chair back to make room for me on his lap.

While he's hugging me close, he lets his love and protection wash over me.

The same way he did my whole childhood.

After spending most of our meal catching him up on the unusual friendship I have established with Declan, I take a bite of my food before laying something else on his shoulders. "I'm not gonna lie to Mama, the aunts, the uncles."

He leans forward, fury leaping into his eyes. It almost causes me to recoil. Almost. "You don't get to decide that—"

"You don't either. We're smarter than you give us credit for, Dad. You think you're keeping us safe, but what you're doing by lying to us every single day is not giving us the tools to protect ourselves. What would Jack Marshall walking into Amaryllis Events do to Aunt Cass? To Mama knowing you knew?" I meet his fury head on before his brain catches up to his emotions.

He opens his mouth and snaps it shut. "She'd castrate me."

"She would," I agree. "If it's about one of her children or her family, she demands to know everything you're doing behind closed doors. It would be an all-out war in our family. Do you want to be responsible for it?"

"You don't know the kind of emotional turmoil you're about to stir up," he warns me.

"No, I don't. But if I've learned one thing, it's that we're stronger together." Lifting my chin, I challenge him. "Isn't that what you all raised us to believe?"

"Fair response, counselor. We are."

My father looks away, out the window at the street traffic beyond. For a moment, he looks older than I've ever seen him. Maybe it's because the weight he's been carrying finally has a name and it's the same as ours.

"Do you think your mother will forgive me?" he asks, almost too softly to hear.

I swallow the lump in my throat. "That depends. Are you going to tell her the truth? Or wait for it to come out in trickles?"

He accepts the challenge in my voice. Despite the worry in his eyes, the resolution in them makes me sigh inside. "I'll tell her the truth, the whole truth, and nothing but the truth."

"Tonight."

"Determined little thing, aren't you? Tonight." He releases a heavy sigh. "This was much easier when you were nine."

"When all you had to do to appease me was wear a tutu?" My lips quirk fondly, thinking of the laughter Declan enjoyed at his expense.

"Yes," he grumbles. He takes my hand, gripping it in between his own. "I just want to say something, Kalie."

"What's that?"

"I'm proud of the woman you've become—someone who would stand up for her family regardless of the circumstance."

"Thanks, Dad."

For the rest of the meal, I let him know my opinions about Declan with him without breaking our attorney-client privilege. "Dad, he needs some sense of normalcy. No one can be undercover as long as he has without it."

His face is thoughtful before he nods. "Let me think about it."

Point made, I return to my food and embrace having my father back in my life where he belongs.

CHAPTER TWENTY-EIGHT

TODAY, WHILE I KNOW KALIE'S PROTECTED BY THE BEST—HER father—I decide to snoop around to locate some more dirt tying the Italian and Irish marriage made in hell. With that in mind, I hit the chop shop, assuming no one would be around on a Sunday.

It's far from my lucky day when I walk in and find one of the newer members of the Tiberi outfit stripping down a BMW. Ciro jumps when the metal door clangs shut behind me, echoing through the stripped-down garage like a warning. The BMW on jacks in the center of the room is picked clean—headlights out, guts exposed, doors pried off like ribs.

A sneer rushes across his face. He straightens from where he was leaning against a workbench, cigarette dangling from his lip. Next to him is Vin—a young, nervous kid strapped to a plastic chair. Even from this distance, I can see his lip is bloodied and his hands zip-tied so he can't fight back.

Ciro looks up and grins. "Sure you want to be here, Mr. Law and Order?"

Despite the churning in my gut, I manage, "What have you got?"

"Caught the kid stealing from us." He cracks his knuckles and Vin pales even more, if that's possible. "Now it's time to get even. But this isn't something you want to know about. Right?"

I roll my shoulders and step further into the room to get a good look at the kid, mind whirling. Is there any way I can get him out of his certain death sentence? "Something like that."

"What are you doing here anyway?"

"I bailed early the other day. Have to catch up on some paperwork," I gesture vaguely to the back office.

Ciro snickers. "And here I thought you spent your weekends draped in tits and ass from Velvet Vice. At least that's what Sal reports back."

I ignore the implication because there's nothing there. The strippers drape themselves over anyone in the VIP section at Velvet Vice as they try to amp up their tips—nothing more, nothing less. They're not the woman who interests me.

They're not Kalie.

Kalie, who walks around her home barefoot in the kitchen, hair tied up. Pouring a glass of wine as she listens with understanding and offers thoughtful insight. The way she welcomed me into her home for a few hours with hardly any hesitation increases the blood flow to my dick.

Ciro chuckles. "Yeah. You got a hard-on for one of them, for sure. What's her name?"

I smirk just enough to sell it, eyes flicking toward the kid in the chair. "Don't ask."

If I had my way, I'd speak it reverently, like a prayer. I'd moan it into her mouth in the dark, feel what it's like as I say it against her lips.

I crouch down to get a better look at Vin. "What was he stealing?"

"Leather from inside the BMW. Saw it in his pockets."

"Got proof?"

Ciro reaches into his own pocket and yanks out the leather in question. Tosses it onto the floor. My lip curls. "If I go into the office, am I going to see a clear shot of him stealing this on the cameras?"

Ciro rears back as if he's mortally offended I'm challenging his word. He works up enough phlegm and spits at my polished shoes. "How dare you question me?"

Straightening to my full height, I move at a lethal speed. Shoving him up against the lift with my forearm. "If you end up along with the rest of your feckin' clan behind bars because this kid can ID you, I'm not doing dick to save your ass."

He narrows his eyes. "You're our lawyer."

My smile turns lazy with malice. "I'm not *your* lawyer. Get that straight. I was hired for a specific purpose. Dealing with shit like your fuckin' hard-on for some fresh little boy meat? Nah, I'm not defending that." It's exactly what the Byrnes want me to do—protect their precious pipeline —but some two-bit Tiberi soldier helping himself to the merchandise? Not happening.

I step back and recommend, "I suggest you disappear."

Ciro comes at me, fist cocked. "You..."

I catch it in midair before it can connect with my face. "Stop playing games. If you want, we can make a call to discuss what I just walked in on." I bare my teeth. "Who do you think they're going to believe—me or some sick fuck who isn't paying the going rate?"

Ciro snarls, "Someone woke up with morals today."

I bark out a laugh. "I woke up with my hand stroking my dick, thinking about the next pussy I plan on fucking, not the family I plan on fucking over." The reality is that I woke up thinking about Kalie. I couldn't stop thinking about her, the warmth and steadiness in her actions. The way her husky voice says my name causes vibrations to dance up my spine.

For just a few minutes, it was enough to be just me—not the me who had to roll around in slime and use a burner phone to call her so I don't make a mistake and lead them right to her.

Ciro's fists clench and unclench at his side, torn between his denied treat and knowing he now has a witness. Finally, I say, "Cut him loose. If he really did what you say he did, scare him. But no more."

Ciro doesn't say a word, just ensures he slams against my shoulder to throw me off balance before he storms out the door. I wait a full five minutes before I turn toward the kid. Leaning in close, I murmur loud enough for Vin to hear, but not loud enough for the microphones I surreptitiously planted to pick up. "You were damn lucky tonight. Don't forget it."

He nods fast, breath catching. When I release the final ankle tie, he leaps to his feet and falls back a few steps. "Wa-was he really go-gonna...?"

I nod once as I monitor Vin's breathing. If I need to knock the kid out to keep his mouth from running, I will. Before I can decide, Vin takes off at a sprint. The metal door bangs open as he escapes.

I fling the information off to Cal to have him dig a little deeper for me while I head toward the back office so I can be seen working even as I'm digging into files on my end. Sliding my phone from my pocket, I check it for the information I need to look up—sales manufacturing slips for companies that don't exist. Incoming vehicles that were reported stolen. Oddities that, while in the overall picture of a shop might not raise any red flags, definitely do so when you're dealing with the sale and transportation of humans.

I can't help but check my texts before I get down to work. There's nothing from Kalie, not that I really expected there to be while she's with her father. Still, just thinking about her makes me want to reach out to her.

DECLAN:

Hoping things are going well today.

After sending her the text, I dive into the mountains of paperwork, trying to get ahead. As I do, I slip in the occasional search, as if the files I brush up against are being accessed accidentally.

It's after ten before I come up for air.

She is probably already asleep by now. Lights off. Bare shoulders against clean sheets, dreaming the dreams of the unburdened. Meanwhile, I have blood on my hands and vengeance in my heart, but, God, I want to see her, touch her, be with her anyway.

Even if I didn't deserve it.

Still, I check my phone.

KALIE:

Come over if it's before midnight. I'll stay up for you.

I walk out of the garage without another word, the cloying scent of evil clinging to my skin. The cool night air hits like a reset, but it doesn't clear my head.

The drive to Kalie's is almost muscle memory—twenty minutes of silent streets being guided by a beacon of hope. I don't turn on the radio as I want to hear nothing but her voice in my head on my way there. I don't want anything but her to fill the spaces I'm already carving out for her.

I park down the street, turn off the engine, and just sit there.

In another life, I'd have pulled directly into her driveway. Knocked on her door. Hoped she answered it in a little bit of nothing. Pushed her inside, kissing her as I did. I would've urged her onto her bed, and ensured I had the right to press my mouth to her lips, the curve of her shoulder, and beyond.

Instead, the fact is, I can't. I'm tied to the very people who want to hurt her—fuck, I'm their goddamn lawyer. At least for now—the best way for me to protect her is to resist what my heart already knows.

She's mine.

Still, I scrub a hand down my face and whisper to the night air, "You make me want out. For this to be over and done with so I can move on."

I don't know if this makes Kalie a liability, a further danger, or a chance for hope.

Then my phone rings, and after I listen to what Keene has to say, my fury at the woman waiting for me inside ignites.

CHAPTER TWENTY-NINE

Kalie

He appears inside my home without warning. I'm curled up on the couch working on a brief I need to file in Connecticut Superior Court to protect Amaryllis Events against a bride who is trying to sue us over the fact she walked in on her fiancé cheating on her with her maid of honor.

Really, it takes all kinds.

When I look up, Declan's there with his hands fisted at his side. I press my hand against my heart. "Jesus. You scared the crap out of me!"

"You should be scared." His voice is low and tight like he's holding back from shouting. "You told your father you were planning on telling your mother if he didn't? What the hell, Kalie? Are you trying to get your family hurt?"

I fling my laptop aside and surge to my feet. "You don't get it, do you? You may be buried up to your eyeballs in this op. You may be able to snap your fingers and have people's sentences set aside in a second. You may be able to dictate law and order between chop houses, strip clubs, bodegas or whatever the hell else the Byrnes and Tiberis have you drafting up legal documentation for this week, but you don't get to control me. Nor do you get a say when it pertains to my family."

He sends an infuriated glare in my direction before wearing a path back and forth in my carpet. "You don't appreciate who your father's dealing with."

"He explained it to me."

Ignoring my response, he plows on, "The minute your mother starts asking questions, the moment anyone in your family does—"

"They're smarter than that. I'm smarter than that. You think keeping all of this a secret is the best way to handle this?"

"It isn't your choice!"

"It's my life! And that's what I told my father to talk to my mother about."

"You can't do that without..."

"I can."

He walks over to my couch and grabs a pillow. Holding it to his face, he screams into it, releasing days, months, years of fury. When he finally pulls it away, his face is awash with tears. I approach him, but he steps back. "No."

I refuse to let him wound me. "Then walk away, Declan. Walk away from me if you don't want me to care. As for me? It's too late for that."

He completely misunderstands. "You're damn right I want to get away from them!"

"Why?" I challenge.

"I don't want them near you!" he shouts.

"You don't want them near me? Why is that so important to you?"

He freezes mid-pace. His head turns slowly, as if it's about to start spiraling counterclockwise like *The Exorcist*. Then, without warning, his shoulders slump in defeat. "Kalie, what will I do if something happens to you?"

I open my mouth, but no sound comes out.

Nothing, because what can I say?

Instead, it's Declan's words that cause a seismic rift to open between us when he declares, "I can't do this between us right now."

Stepping back, I clench my fingers into a fist. "What? This? Us?"

"Yes. To all of it." His jaw clenches. "I can't have a bunch of civilians screwing up what I've worked so hard for."

His words infuriate me. "I'm giving you some grace. Despite knowing *some* of my family, you don't know all of us."

"I know enough from the stories I've heard."

I try to explain differently "You don't get it. If the family finds out I knew and didn't say anything, they'll never forgive me. That's not who we are. We shoulder burdens together."

"This isn't just about your family. This is about drawing a line with people who don't have a need to know."

"They do."

"They don't."

My voice doesn't waver. "We really do. Why? So that this time, instead of being caught off guard, we'll be prepared. This time we won't be blindsided, and we'll have people we trust at our backs."

He stares deep into my eyes, then finally admits, "I don't know how to protect you from this."

"You don't have to," I whisper, my throat tight. "That's not your job."

He steps closer, our bodies brushing against one another. "Then why does it feel like it is?"

I don't back away. Neither does he. Silence stretches between us again, heavy and thick. When Declan finally speaks, his voice is like gravel—worn down, stripped bare. "Why am I dreaming of you?"

His words cause my lips to part on a gasp. But he's not done. "I dream of you, and when I do, for the first time in years, I sleep."

My chest feels like it does when I'm entering the stadium after a medal race—like I'm sucking in air because I'm in an emotional chokehold. I can't say anything because I'm afraid anything I'll say will be wrong.

He lifts his hand and brushes his fingers against my cheek. "If you got hurt..."

"I won't."

"You don't know that." His voice rasps against my nerve endings. He shakes his head. "The man I've needed to become isn't worthy of someone like you."

"Isn't that for me to decide?"

His fingers tangle in my hair even as his eyes bore into mine. In them I see regret, guilt, want. Then, his lids droop and when he lifts his gaze to mine, there's something else there.

Surrender.

I lift my chin, my pulse hammering, and lay my free hand against his chest. "Declan. Are you yelling at me because you're angry or because you're scared?"

"Both," he rasps. His hands slide out of my hair before they come up to cup my face. His fingers brush under my cheekbones until they rest gently against my jaw.

I lean in. Our breath mingles together.

"You're not the only one scared."

With that admission, he slides one hand into my hair and wraps the other around my waist. Pulling me up, he stares deep into my eyes as his head dips. My heart goes into overdrive. My breathing becomes ragged as I determine if he wants this—me.

When his lips touch mine, I willingly accept them. It isn't soft. It isn't slow. It's raw, desperate, and consuming. It's every emotion Declan's been holding inside. They reveal the inner storm that Declan has been fighting. His lips are proof that the gods want us to absorb the strength of lightning and thunder and remain standing.

I return his kiss with a hunger I never expected existed. I wrap my arms around his neck, drowning with the pleasure he floods my system with. Declan's energy is overwhelming and the thought of resistance is nonexistent.

Not that I would. I've never wanted a man like this. His kiss causes a flood of lust to rush through my body, causing liquid heat to pool at the apex of my legs. It's taking everything inside of me not to climb him like a tree and demand he give me more.

That he gives me everything.

His hands roam my back, pressing my hips against his rock hardness. I let out a low moan that I can't keep in.

Which turns out to be a mistake. A huge one.

He freezes, his lips still pressed against mine. Slowly, almost reverently, he releases me. Then he steps back—one, two, three steps. I'm not certain if it's the silence or the physical distance Declan places between us that makes my soul ache.

Then I realize it's neither when he takes a sledgehammer to my heart. "This can't happen again."

My body stiffens. "No? It sure felt like it could when you had your tongue..."

"Kalie!" he snaps.

I back away before flopping back on the couch. Giving him the once-over, I notice his dick is impressive behind his dress slacks. Licking my lips to keep the drool in place, I murmur, "I wasn't the one who kissed you first."

"Let's just chalk it up to bad judgment."

I snort out a laugh. "Every girl's dream."

His brow scrunches together in confusion, so I educate him. "To be called someone's 'bad judgment' after the single hottest kiss of their life."

His countenance softens. *Yeah, buddy. I don't think so.* I look down and pick at my nail polish. "But don't worry about it. I'll do a true comparison after my next date."

Ooh, he doesn't like that. That is if the way the flash of heat in his cheekbones is any indicator. *Too bad, so sad.* I fake a yawn. "If you're done lecturing me about my family and my ability to kiss, you can see yourself out."

He glares at me. "This isn't a game, Kalie. I shouldn't have gone there."

"Maybe. But since you didn't break a law, I don't need to report either of us. After all, there's no sanction against two consenting adults kissing."

"I'm leaving."

I wiggle my fingers at him. He starts to slip out the back slider when I call out, "Let's see who initiates our second kiss before you call it a mistake."

It isn't until after he slams the slider that I let out a frustrated sigh. My world seems to be tilting on its axis. But while the lawyer in me wants to dot every *I* and cross every *T*, the woman in me knows I don't need all the answers right now.

I just need a chance.

Hopefully, he's willing to give us one of those.

CHAPTER THIRTY

Kalie

IF LOVE IS A BATTLEFIELD, THEN AMARYLLIS EVENTS MUST HAVE been declared by the State Department as an official war zone sometime between yesterday and today. The thought pings through my head as I reach my office door Monday morning. I enter the mansion and everything seems perfectly normal at first.

From the depths of the mansion, Aunt Corinna is shouting at Uncle Phil to get out of her kitchen—to stop trying to steal scraps from cakes she's carving. Aunt Holly is changing the art in the main foyer to some of her summer inspired prints. Aunt Em is in her office on the phone with an Irish lace distributor, arguing about how an increase in import tax is going to bankrupt us.

In other words, it feels like it's going to be just another Monday. Still, I'm cautious as I make my way upstairs. I've yet to confront the two people who will be directly impacted by any lies I may have to tell them— Mama and Aunt Cassidy. Having not heard from my mother since lunch with my father, I have no idea if he kept his word. If he didn't, I don't know how I'll be able to face them.

Once I reach my office, there's a note pinned to the bulletin board just below my nameplate. Plucking it down, I read:

We're in the conference room with breakfast. Join us. Not a request.

"Well, I guess the cat's out of the bag," I mutter. Quickly opening my office, I dump my bags inside before I head to the conference room either to be fattened up for slaughter or to be told no harm was done in the communicating of Declan's employment by Hudson Investigations.

Mama and Aunt Cassidy are sitting on the same side of the long mahogany table with a platter of doughnuts. They both look up when I walk in. My heart punches my ribs like a boxer warming up for a match at the calculating look in their eyes.

"There she is," Cassidy says, waving me over. Her tone is deceptively sweet, which makes all my red flags wave like they're being twirled in a parade down Main Street. She gestures for me to take a seat at the head of the table.

I frown as I slide into the chair, wondering why, if I'm about to be interrogated, I'm not across from them. Neither of them says anything, they just stare at me.

"So... how was everyone's weekend?" I ask, trying to sound casual but failing miserably.

"Interesting," Mama says, quirking an eyebrow. "I had an unexpected dinner...date with your father last night."

Well, that's that. He kept his word. I brace myself for the fallout, leaning forward and snagging a doughnut as if carbohydrates might shield me from the emotional explosion I'm anticipating. "That must have been... nice." I try not to sound too eager or too terrified.

"It was certainly illuminating," Mama replies, gauging my reaction.

I plow through the first doughnut, have the second shoved in my mouth, and stretch for a third before my mother reaches over and gently slaps my hand, admonishing me. "Those aren't for you to avoid answering our questions. They're for our guests."

"Whaa goosts?" I chew and swallow before trying again. "What guests?"

"You'll find out soon enough," Cassidy says airily.

"I don't have my laptop." I stand to make a break to hide in the sanctuary of my office, but my mother's stare pins me in place.

"You won't need it." Just then, the conference door opens, and my father slips inside. His eyes seek out my mother first. He makes a beeline for her, kissing her warmly. Well, she didn't nut him. That's a good sign. A sigh of relief escapes me.

Maybe things won't be so bad after all. I cross my fingers beneath the table even as I knock on the underside of the wood.

Then my father proceeds to walk over to me, pressing his lips to my forehead and murmuring, "It will be okay. You were right, this needs to happen," before making his way around to do the same with Aunt Cassidy, before returning to sit next to my mother. By the time he's seated, Uncle Caleb is in the room, greeting us all in much the same manner. He takes his place next to my father.

I'm about to ask what's happening when the door opens again. Two men enter. Both of them are dressed casually in ball caps, worn T-shirts, and faded jeans. I immediately recognize Jon, but I do a double take when I realize the second man is Declan. I'm not certain if I'm more knocked off balance because he's not in a suit or because the casual clothing he's wearing isn't black. In fact, I think the worn Harvard Law T-shirt and jeans he has on belong to Jon. Both men sit next to Caleb.

I'm so stunned they're here I almost fail to acknowledge the door opening and another couple entering the room—my cousin Laura and Liam.

Tension ratchets up when they sit across the conference room table from her twin and Declan. My gaze swings from person to person like I'm a spectator at Wimbledon. Cassidy and Mama are watching their husbands closely, waiting for them to crack under the pressure. Caleb's jaw is clenched, his eyes locked on his daughter. Liam glares at my father. Laura, in turn, is calm as her eyes shift between her twin and the man who she may or may not remember from the broadcast during girls night.

And Declan...well, his eyes are locked on me.

The doughnut I swallowed suddenly feels like a rock in my stomach. "Well," I start, "this is... unexpected."

Cassidy praises her sister. "Ali thought I should understand what was going on."

"You were right to encourage your father to speak with me, Kalie." My mother's voice holds an edge as she scowls at the man beside her. My father's expression doesn't flicker in the slightest.

Jon starts to open his mouth, but a withering glare from his mother has him snapping it shut. I can't prevent the snicker that escapes. Even now that Jon's some fearless special agent for Hudson, one look from his mama causes him to crumble like a dry cookie.

Declan turns on me, snarling, "This isn't funny, Kalie."

"Declan," I warn him only to have my mother leap in to shield me.

"I do believe, Mr. Conian, she was laughing at her cousin being scolded by his mother. Not you, nor the situation we all find ourselves in. You don't have to protect us from each other," she tries to soften the reprimand.

"I obviously do. None of you should have the kind of knowledge you do. It's for your own good. I'm doing my damndest to keep you all safe."

"Are you? By doing what?" Laura's question silences the room. I suspect if she had a scalpel in her hands just then, she would have shanked

Declan. "Was it considered helping when you got one of the men who held me hostage released on a technicality?"

Well, that answers that. Laura definitely recognizes Declan.

Liam sighs. "Sweetheart, listen to them."

Her head twists on Liam slowly. She hisses, "As you were aware of this, hush your mouth if you know what's good for you, Liam."

His eyes plead for mercy—as if he doesn't know better than to expect any. "I knew Dec when we worked together at the agency. I recommended him for the job at Hudson. Yes, I knew he was working undercover inside the Byrnes' organization."

Uncle Caleb clears his throat. "Right. Laura, I might have forgotten to mention that."

Laura and her mother both track Uncle Caleb with their eyes with equally lethal glares. Even as Aunt Cass inhales sharply, Laura blasts her father. "You seem to forget quite a bit these days, Father. Perhaps we should look into getting you some occupational therapy at the hospital to assist you with your defects."

Jon shakes his head before his gaze lands on Declan. "Yeah, you're on your own, buddy, for whatever they dish out."

Declan's jaw drops, flabbergasted. "Are you for real?"

He points at his twin and then his mother. "They scare me."

Declan points at me. "Well, your cousin frustrates and scares the ever-loving hell out of me, but you don't see me backing down when it comes to her safety, do you?"

Jon's eyes narrow. "What's that supposed to mean?"

"It means I'd rather ask for forgiveness than beg for permission if I know I can keep her alive for one more damn minute." His palms slap down on the polished mahogany. The sound echoes around the room.

Silence reigns in the room at his declaration. That's when Uncle Caleb speaks up. "Does everybody appreciate the seriousness of this discussion?"

Dad steeples his fingers together. "Everyone needs to listen to the real story of what Declan's doing." Methodically, he recounts every moment of how he never gave up looking for his and Aunt Cassidy's father. That Jack Marshall, as a distant relative, was accepted as a member of the Irish Mob. "The Byrnes aren't a wannabe group, Cass. They control most of the northeast. It wouldn't surprise me if at least a quarter of your clients are in some way related to them."

"Do you think he knows who I am?" Cassidy asks with a calmness I envy.

"No. He might speculate, but he doesn't know."

She relaxes marginally at that. Mama wraps her arm around her shoulder. But their relief is short-lived when my father drops a bomb in the center of the conference room table. "I'm absolutely certain he knows who Kalie is and has been entertaining the idea of going after her, which is why I've upped her protection."

If someone were to hook the room up to a Holter monitor, it would send off alarms due to the way emotions in the room are spiking and plummeting with each new revelation. Dad swings his gaze in my direction before jerking up his chin. "I promised you—complete transparency."

"You knew?" Mama shouts at me.

"Only for the last few days." My eyes find Declan's. His swirl with a dichotomy of emotion—fury and support. "Declan told me the truth after a confrontation at Hudson. At first, I thought Dad was just being his natural autocratic self because I'd slugged Declan at court."

He grumbles, "I wouldn't say you slugged me, Kalie. Punched me, sure."

My mother's voice could re-freeze the polar ice caps. "I heard she landed you on your ass with a single hook, Mr. Conian. Considering you're a trained agent and my daughter isn't, I'd give the round to her."

"Personally, I'd have preferred if she'd landed a second swing at my brother—but there's still time." Laura bares her teeth at Jon in a facsimile of a smile.

"I didn't do anything," Jon argues.

"There you go making the point for your sister," Aunt Cassidy interjects before her son can say another word. "What's our motto?"

He mumbles it under his breath.

"I'm sorry. Can you repeat that?" She holds her hand to her ear.

"Family first."

Mama slams her fist on the table. "Now, from every bonded member of our family."

The men hang their heads. They mumble, "Family first."

"Exactly." Mama's eyes are daggers, but she's fisting the necklace she's worn my entire life—my grandmother's diamond. It's her signal to my father they can work anything out together. "Fix this. I want my daughter out of the line of fire."

There's a murmur of assent in the room.

Aunt Cassidy's tone is monotone when she asks Declan, "You've met him. What did you think of him?"

"Jack Marshall?"

"Yes."

"Considering he had a gun pressed in between my eyebrows at the time, not much." It's the calmest Declan's been since he came into the room. "I also am under the working theory he killed my former partner."

Cassidy's chin jerks up. "I see. Thank you for your honesty. It's a refreshing attribute around here." Her glare encompasses her husband, brother, son, and Liam. Ouch. Laura's wince mirrors my own.

I try to soothe flaring tempers by leaping into the fray. "Everyone calm down. We're all on the same side."

Declan's fury returns. "A side which wouldn't be this aggravated if you hadn't forced your father to loop in your mother."

Mama snaps her fingers. "Poof. Just like that, all your bonus points just evaporated. You see, Declan—you don't mind if I call you Declan, do you?—all the women in this family are forged from strength. There isn't a single one of us who can't handle what the world tries to throw at us."

"Don't underestimate us," Aunt Cassidy agrees.

"Don't underestimate them," he snaps back. His eyes dart to meet mine, and I read the fear in them.

There's a part of me that wants to curl up and purr in satisfaction, particularly after the way he left last night. *Well, well, well. Isn't his reaction interesting.* Instead, I maintain a stoic demeanor while the battle rages on.

Ultimately, we leave the men in the conference room to argue strategy about what to do now that we all know. On our way down to the kitchen, Mama's hand falls to my shoulder. I turn my head to the side and find myself meeting her determined eyes. "Nothing is going to happen to you."

"You can't promise that."

She leans forward and presses her lips against my forehead. I breathe in her scent and halt our descent. I've needed a hug from her for days. When I mention as much, she mutters, "Another thing to be pissed at your father about."

I let out a watery laugh.

Then she probes carefully. "This Declan. Who is he to you?"

"Honesty?"

"Always."

"I think he could be my downfall."

She rears back, appalled. "Good lord, Kalie. Tell me you're not falling into something with a man just like your father."

I hook my arm through hers and wait until we make it down the back steps before I admit, "He's like a ticking time bomb, Mama. I'm just waiting for things to explode in my face."

CHAPTER THIRTY-ONE

I'M STUNNED. FLABBERGASTED. AND, NOT A LITTLE HURT.

I thought what Kalie and I shared was under attorney-client privilege, but here, it was being discussed by her family. I figured eventually my cover would be shared with her family, but now, they're openly aware of why I'm undercover, my op, and the reason I went under in the first place.

Jon lays a hand on my shoulder, in support which I appreciate but I shrug off. I need to feel angry and him trying to placate me isn't helping. Especially when he says, "She did what she needed to."

"Let all my secrets out in the wind? Got it."

Jon frowns. "Kalie didn't share anything with anyone."

"Right. First Kalie meets with her father. Then, Keene calls and tells me he plans on looping in his wife because his baby girl demanded it. Now, we're here and everyone's spilling their guts—and blowing my cover?" Before Jon can give a rose-colored glass version of what just went down, I plow on with my own. "Someone broke a promise to me, and I sincerely doubt it's been the men covering my fucking ass the last few years."

Jon's mouth opens and shuts without sound.

"She convinced your uncle to tell them, Jon. She broke my trust even as she swore she wouldn't due to attorney-client privilege."

He rubs his hand over his chin while I pace around the now empty conference room like a caged animal. Finally, he suggests, "Why don't you talk with her? Find out what really happened?"

I stop in my tracks, the idea holding all kinds of appeal. "Yeah. That's a good idea. Which office is hers?"

Jon gives me directions and I exit the room, heading down the corridor. Glancing to confirm I'm at the correct door, I shove it open without knocking.

Kalie looks up from where she's unpacking her briefcase. "Declan. What's wrong?"

My lip curls as I slam the door. "Like you don't already know what I'm here for."

Her eyes widen comically. "What are you talking about?"

"Kalie, why the hell did you betray me like that?" Before she can speak, I launch into my diatribe. "Your cousin calls me this morning telling me to meet him, and what do I walk into? A coffee klatch where my undercover op is the main topic. What the fuck is all that about?"

Her mouth falls open, then shuts again. "I didn't tell them. All I did was encourage my father not to lie to my mother."

"Look at what the hell that did!" I shout.

"How in the hell is that my fault?" she yells back.

My pulse is throbbing through my veins so hard, I'm afraid my head is going to explode. "What did he do? Have lunch with his little princess then sit down and tell her mother every detail he's been hiding from her for almost a decade?"

Kalie's face pales but I ignore her reaction. "So, because you're worried about lying to your precious little family, Daddy spoke to your uncle and called a damn family meeting about who I really am? I mean, Christ! Now, one mistake, one slip up and I'm compromised. Dead. Is that what you want?"

"No! Of course not. I didn't know he was going to—"

"Bullshit. You wanted your mother to know. You said it last night that they had a right to the truth."

She recoils at my words like I slapped her, and while part of me hates that for her, the truth hurts more. I despise being the one to hurt her, but it's also better than either of us winding up on the wrong side of a bullet and that's if the Byrnes are feeling generous. But despite the way she wraps her arms around herself protectively, I don't retract a single word. "What the hell kind of lawyer are you? What I told you was in confidence and you sat there while your father told everyone in that room what was happening," I sneer. "You just let it happen."

Her voice cracks. "You think I planned this? I was just as blindsided as you were. I walked into that conference room a few minutes before you."

"That whole thinking on your feet thing must have been a class you skipped during your Olympic training."

"Enough," comes a harsh voice from the door.

Both Kalie and I turn and find her mother standing in the doorway. If I'm being honest, Alison Freeman-Marshall scares me a little with the way her cold blue eyes lock onto my face. "My daughter had no say in what my husband chose to tell me about you, Mr. Conian. I haven't spoken with my daughter since Friday afternoon."

I whip around and find Kalie won't look at me.

Crap.

God, she didn't sell me out.

Keene's the one who shared the intimate details of the case with his wife. "Mrs. Marshall—"

She cuts me off. "Also, you should be reassured I'm one of *his* attorneys of record, so nothing discussed in that conference room can leave it."

I thought I couldn't feel even worse than I did until I hear the huskiness of Kalie's voice as she addresses her mother. "Thank you, Mama. However, I was just about to explain to Mr. Conian that I didn't, in fact, discuss or share any privileged information without his consent. However, if he'd like to retain you or Uncle Jared to pursue a suit if he feels he was wronged, perhaps that would be best."

Alison steps up next to her daughter and slides her arm around her shoulder. "I think your godfather would be an excellent resource for him." She shoots me a filthy look. "If you feel the need to make a complaint, Mr. Conian, we'll provide you with the contact information for the American Bar Association. They take all ethical complaints seriously and will certainly send someone to investigate the claims you are making against my daughter."

I feel about as gross as dog crap that's stuck to the bottom of a shoe that has a tread filled with old gum. "Let me offer my apology," I grit out.

"Fine," Kalie manages.

"Now, please leave," her mother tacks on.

I want to rant that as awful as I feel about my baseless accusations, these people are still in danger. It doesn't negate the fact that my life is now in more danger than ever. Whispers in back alleys raise questions in places where there should be none, and that's what gets you killed. I make my way to the door when Kalie calls my name. I pause and look over my shoulder at her, "Yeah?"

"Good luck on your hunt. I hope you and the rest of the team find what you're looking for." Kalie's voice is excessively polite. However, her eyes burn with something I can't name.

Or maybe I'm afraid to because if I do, I don't know how I'm going to live with myself for putting it there.

CHAPTER THIRTY-TWO

FOR THE NEXT FEW WEEKS, LIFE RETURNS TO THE NORMAL I LIVED prior to Declan sneaking into my house. If only it was that easy for my heart to evict him, the only oddity would be the guards following me around as I go about my life. I choose to ignore them much the same way I do the paparazzi.

I spend most of my days in the office, focusing on our team executing successful spring weddings, knowing that the next few months will be nothing but chaos once May hits. I also ignore every unknown message that pops up randomly on my phone.

> UNKNOWN:
>
> I'm sorry.
>
> I should have done my homework before I flew off the handle.

A few days later, from a different burner phone.

> UNKNOWN:
>
> I'd really like to talk to you.
>
> Can we meet in the same place?
>
> Listen, firebrand. I was wrong.
>
> I've kept my ear to the ground and I've heard no rumblings.
>
> You should be safe.

Does he think it's that easy to make up to me? That I'll capitulate at his feet because I'm not in danger? I'm not some weak-willed woman. I'm not a puppy to roll over at the first sign of praise from its master. Still, I replied to that text string, knowing that if I didn't, Declan would show up inside my home despite my having changed the locks. Grace, who decided to extend her stay in Europe, gave me a curious look when I explained why she would need new keys when she returned home. After a blithe, "Dad said we needed to upgrade security," she let it drop.

I just wish Declan would let the conversation drop as easily or that I could forget the power of that kiss.

> KALIE:
>
> No.

Just one word. Two letters. Direct. Clear cut.

> UNKNOWN:
>
> Talk to me.
>
> Please don't shut me out—I really want to make this right.

I tap my nails against the screen for a second before considering how to reply. Then I decide on a clear answer that lets him know where my emotions stand.

KALIE:

I'm late for my current coffee klatch about my subpar lawyer skills and remedial Olympic training. Perhaps we could schedule a time to discuss this on the second Sunday after never?

I haven't heard from him since. Nor has Jon reached out since I asked my father to have him removed from my detail with the logic that Declan needs him more and, "There's no need to punish Jon, Dad."

"Jon feels horrible about what happened in your office, Kalie."

"It wasn't his fault your employee is a jackass."

My father's lips twitch, but he holds his tongue. "Besides, I'm training for this summer's races."

"Oh? What's in the lineup?"

"Maine, Boston, and New York Marathons. I'm at the point of training where I need someone who can keep up. We both know that isn't Jon."

My father chuckled over my logic before agreeing to send over an agent willing to run fifteen miles with me each morning before I leave for the office. "Theo has run full marathons, sweetheart. He'll keep up."

"Thanks, Dad."

I'm surprised to find Jon lounging in my desk chair when I arrive this morning. He's immaculately dressed in a Tom Ford suit, vastly different from the last time I saw him sporting his old Harvard regalia. Not even bothering to be polite, I say, "Get out from behind my desk."

"Are you always so cheerful in the morning?"

"Only when I have nowhere to put my crap. Move, Jon."

He divests me of my bags and my coffee. Standing behind my desk, I snatch my coffee back and demand, "What new sunshine and joy brings you to my doorstep?"

"This isn't like you, Kalie. You don't hold grudges."

"Why, Jon? Whatever do you mean?"

"De—"

I lift my cup back up and threaten, "Say that name in my office and you'll be wearing my drink."

His lips quirk. "Your former client."

"Right. Speaking of that." I flick open my briefcase—a gift from my parents when I passed the bar. Pulling out the file that contains Declan's handwritten contract, I write V-O-I-D on it and dig around in my purse for the dollar bill I've been carrying around like a talisman. "When you have a moment, can you give this back to him?"

Jon gives me a penetrating look. "He was wrong. He knows it."

"He called my capability as a lawyer into question."

Jon holds out his hands in supplication. "I know."

"Do you?" I shout. "Do you understand what that's like?"

"Do you appreciate waking up knowing that day could be your last, and you do it every single day for weeks? Then those weeks turn into months? Then years?" His words stop me in my tracks. My head cocks to the side as he muses, "I imagine Dec would get along with our mothers—hell, even Uncle Phil. They have that in common. The knowledge that life is so fucking precious and it can be taken away at any moment."

"You think I didn't understand that part of him?" I snap.

"I think if you did, you wouldn't be holding a grudge against a man who could eat a bullet tomorrow," he says quietly.

I flinch at that, the image of Declan dead due to a bullet now prevalent in the forefront of my brain. "Do you really believe I'm in the wrong here?"

"Not wrong." Jon's voice is low and soothing. "Just stubborn."

I sink into my chair before massaging my temples. Jon doesn't say anything else. He doesn't have to. The targeted words he's aimed at me since I walked into my office bounce around my head. I recall Declan's texts on my phone.

Maybe I am stubborn, but so is he. "Couldn't he see I was trying to do the right thing for all of us? I wasn't trying to place him in danger. That's why I went to Dad."

Jon stands and adjusts his tie, a clear signal he knows our conversation has reached its conclusion. "I'll let you get to work."

I nod absently as he walks out.

My eyes drift to the mountain of paperwork on my desk, but instead of getting lost in disputes regarding seating charts and color palettes, I'm lost somewhere else entirely—in thoughts of Declan. I reach into my purse for my cell and pull up the last text, hoping he still has the phone. That I'm not inviting trouble by sending the message I'm about to.

KALIE:

Tonight. Same place. Same time.

Laying my phone face up, I unpack my briefcase and dock my laptop. A few minutes later, a message pops up.

DECLAN:

I'll be there, firebrand. Thank you.

Something unclenches in the region around my heart. Tonight, Declan and I will have a much needed heart to heart. I just hope it's enough to cut through the space we inserted between us.

CHAPTER THIRTY-THREE

SITTING IN A CORNER BOOTH OF A DINER A COUPLE OF BLOCKS away from Kalie's, I'm repeatedly tapping the face of my burner to check the time. I've been here since nine o'clock, nursing a cup of coffee that's long gone cold. She said same time, but there was no way I wasn't going to be nearby earlier to make certain I was spitting distance away in the event she needed me for anything.

Over and over, I replayed Jon's words in my head since he cornered me after leaving Kalie's office. He accused us both of being stubborn. Her text came through in the middle of our conversation. I yielded to his degradation, ceding the point when I added on, "So long as she's not done with me."

"You have a chance. Don't blow it."

I suppose I shouldn't be surprised when the bell above the door jingles and he saunters in. Striding over, he slides into the booth and drawls, "So, you're going to make up with Kalie or I might shoot you myself."

I grumble, "I really regret giving you the ability to monitor my burner phones."

He flicks his hand dismissively. "That's for your protection. The side benefit of being able to spy on your personal life is just an added bonus."

"Another coffee over here?" the waitress interrupts, eyeing Jon up and down appreciatively.

Jon smirks at me before he flashes her a smile. "Please."

After she recovers enough to leave, I lean back in the booth and cross my arms. "You're here to babysit me until it's time for me to head over to Kalie's?"

"I'm here to make sure you don't do something stupid like bail."

"You think I'd do that?" I challenge, but I already know his answer. He's not too far off the mark. Since she'd texted me, the idea crossed my mind a thousand times. Maybe it would be better for me to walk out of her life now than risk hurting her again.

"Listen, man," Jon says, his voice dropping to a tone he reserves only for his family. "She's giving you a chance. Get your head out of your ass long enough to appreciate what that means."

I nod because what else is there to do? He's right. That alone pisses me off.

"So, when do you head out?" Jon asks.

I glance at my phone face down on the table. "About an hour."

"Good. What are you going to say?"

"Everything she needs to hear," I say, not entirely sure what that means. It's been just a few weeks, but the words haven't formed the way they should. The only thing clear is my need to see her in person, and hope they come together when I do.

Jon pins me with a look like he knows every thought running through my head. "Make sure she says everything you need to hear too," he says, then gets up and walks out.

I watch him leave, still as annoying as ever, and try not to think about how long an hour really is when you're waiting for it to pass. The waitress watches his departure with a longing in her eyes. She returns to my table and tops off my cup. "Your friend's cute."

I grunt in response, not wanting to fuel any more fantasies about Jonathan Lockwood than social media already perpetrates. Digging a ten out of my wallet, I toss it on the table and make my way out onto the street lit by the diner's neon sign. I've got time to burn, but I can't sit still. Not when everything's so close to falling apart or coming back together.

Darien's barely alive at this time of night, with only a few cars driving by as commuters make their way from working late to their multi-million-dollar homes. Despite Jon's nagging, despite knowing better, I'm tempted to disappear into it all and let Kalie forget about my troubled life.

But I'm too fucking selfish for all that, despite knowing the trouble I'm certain to bring to her door if I walk through it again.

I pull out the burner phone I've reserved for texting her and scroll through messages. We each are so careful in how we speak to one another. It's just another reminder of how dangerous it is to be near her.

The problem now is since I've been exposed to her, I can't stay away. That is what makes this the worst decision. I'm a threat, and she doesn't even realize it simply because I can drag blood to her doorstep just by breathing her same air.

CHAPTER THIRTY-FOUR

Kalie

WHY I'M NERVOUS ABOUT HIM COMING OVER THIS TIME WHEN HE'S basically committed B&E every other time, I'm uncertain. Maybe it's because this time, I'm the one who has extended the invitation. Me. Not him intruding on my space.

If I'm being honest with myself, I've known we'd end up right back here hashing things out since he took a sledgehammer to my heart in the middle of my office. A pulse of anger burns inside of me. See? That's right. You've been waiting for this confrontation for weeks.

So, game on, girlfriend.

Maybe it's because, now that it's here, I'm second guessing myself since Jon came to my office. All day I've been considering his words and the life Declan has been leading for the last however many years. I'm flip-flopping between wrapping my hands around his neck and choking him for his detour to the town of assholery and wrapping my arms around him and just holding him as close as I can.

Jon's words sobered me in a way I didn't want to look at because they forced me to consider how much Declan has slipped under my skin without my noticing.

Sitting down on the couch, I lean forward and place my head in my hands when I consider what kind of impact the life he's leading could have on mine. It's terrifying in a way I've never really considered. When my father met my mother, he was past the hands-on aspect of the undercover agent game, but Declan is neck-deep in it.

Am I strong enough to stand by his side as he dives into the murky depths, risking his life again and again?

What Jon may not realize is that my feelings for Declan have never been clear—not since that first meeting all those years ago. There are so many questions I have to ask myself.

What does he want?

What do I want knowing I could lose him?

All these questions float through my head, but they're answered with one I can't quite push aside—should I even try if my heart's going to end up broken?

It takes less than a nanosecond for the answer. Even if the answer to that is yes, I have to see where this goes.

When I sent him the text earlier, something inside me broke that I hadn't heard from him for weeks. But when I saw how quickly he replied, my heart flipped in my chest. "Damn you, Declan Conian."

I hear his voice at the same time I hear the soft tap of his knuckles against the drywall, causing my head to snap up. "Not sure if you meant for me to hear that."

My breath catches in my throat as he greets me with a cautious smile. "Hey, firebrand."

"Hey, yourself." I stand and gesture for him to join me. "Take a seat."

He does so hesitantly, like he's waiting for me to attack him—either verbally or physically. Which, if I'm being honest with myself, is a pretty realistic expectation on his part. I remain standing, staring down at him while gathering my thoughts when he speaks. "I was wrong. I'm sorry."

I blink.

"For not giving you the benefit of the doubt."

"What else are you sorry for?"

"For not letting you speak?"

"That sounds like a question, counselor. Rephrase."

His luscious lips curve. "I acted like a jackass."

"Damn right, you did." I cross my arms, but my resolve softens at his words.

"Should the court object to foul language," he teases me back.

I blink in shock. "Declan, did you just make a joke?"

He scrubs the back of his neck. "Maybe?"

"You're not sure?" My heart breaks inside my chest for this man.

"It's been so long since I let anyone in, Kalie. I don't know how to." His voice is low, almost as if he expects me to interrupt him, but I stay silent. "You're the first person I even considered letting close. When I thought you sold me out—"

"I didn't." My argumentative nature fires, but I fight it. He's here; he's trying.

"I know that now." He looks up at me with something unguarded and raw in his eyes. "But I'm terrified."

"Of what?"

"Of losing you." He swallows before pushing the next words out of his mouth. "I won't put you at risk. I'll do anything to protect you."

"You have to start by trusting me."

He holds his hand out, palm up. "That's what I'm trying to say."

I lay mine on his. "What?"

"I do trust you."

My eyes narrow. "Sure didn't seem like it."

He absorbs my condemnation. "I feel like I have to keep pushing you away to keep you safe."

My fingers tighten on his. "Stop pushing. Trust me to come to you if I think there's a problem or if I believe my family is in danger. Start there."

The words hang in the air between us. He's weighing them, fighting against the part of himself that's been closed off for so long. Finally, he gives me a part of himself I never expected he'd hand over.

His trust.

"When I'm with you, everything is real—every word, every emotion. Nothing is a lie."

The flutter in my chest increases. I interlace our fingers. "Is that so?"

"It is." He lifts my hand to his mouth and brushes his lips across my knuckles back and forth. "How does that make you feel?"

"Excited. Anxious?"

He huffs out a laugh. "At least I'm not alone."

"In what you're feeling?"

"Yeah, firebrand."

I tilt my head to the side. "Why do you call me that?"

"Because a firebrand is someone who is provocative, passionate, and disruptive." He quirks a brow. "Sound like anyone in this room?"

I feel my cheeks warm even as Declan pulls me closer. His forehead rests against mine. For a long moment we don't say anything. I whisper, "What do you want?"

"Now or long term?"

"Both."

"Long term, I want to stop pretending I'm something I'm not."

"Then stop." My cheek nuzzles against his.

He turns into my touch, his lips grazing the sensitive skin of my neck. The sensation sends a jolt of electricity through me. His voice drops low, like a promise. "I don't know when that's going to be possible."

I lean forward and brush my lips across his. "We'll figure it out."

This time, he doesn't hesitate. This time, it's not a mistake. He pulls me to him, burying his fingers in my hair. My body melts into his. I grip his shoulders, holding on as if I'm afraid he'll disappear.

But he doesn't. He deepens the kiss, breathing life into my very core. It's a kiss that tells me everything I need to know about how he feels. It tells me he wants to be with me, a fact I didn't know if we'd ever reach or if I'd ever know. The fact he's here now is as clear as any words he could say.

But he's just as scared.

I get it. Because I do, I pull back, my lips tingling and my heart beating like mad.

"Wow," I murmur.

He leans his forehead against mine, the sweetest smile on his face. "Firebrand," he says, like it's the highest praise he can give.

We stay like that, an eternity packed into a few brief seconds. I'm the one who pulls back, afraid if I don't, I'll never have the strength to tell him the next part. "Declan, I'm willing to see where this goes. I want to. But I need to know, do you want this too?"

He brushes my hair from my face, tucking it behind my ear. The intimacy of the gesture causes my heart to skip a beat. He kisses my forehead before he replies, "I want to. I'm not sure how good I'll be at it."

I can't stop the grin that breaks across my face. "I'll take that. Just don't wig out on me again, okay?"

He lets out a choked laugh. "You're the only person who would dare call me out like that and have me coming back for more."

"Does that mean you're not going to run?"

"Not unless I need to sweep you off your feet and carry you somewhere safe."

"Let's hope there's no need for that."

"I won't let there be." His words are as much a promise to me as they are to himself. "Kalie, I'm—"

This time, I cut him off with my own mouth before he could apologize again. He doesn't resist, instead pulling me closer still.

I let him. For now.

Later that night, I explore some of the selfies we took together on my phone while we were snuggled together on the couch.

He didn't protest, just turned his face into my hair and buried his lips into it.

The fact he didn't gave my heart hope that we're more. We're building something together. Still, when he snuck out earlier, there's a small part of me that wonders what we are and where we're going. Mentally shrugging, I give up control.

We'll figure it out when we get there.

CHAPTER THIRTY-FIVE

Our night starts with an argument over pizza toppings.

"Mushrooms are not a topping," she declares, curling her dainty bare foot on her kitchen stool with a glass of cabernet in one hand. "They're fungus. Fungus is not conducive to romance. Thus, while I don't have a problem with the bride and groom wanting an individual pizza party buffet, I vehemently disagree with the inclusion of fungus. It's wrong."

I raise a brow as I watch her prepare a large thin crust pizza smothered with sauce, cheese, and pepperoni, which she insisted on cooking for us from scratch when I arrived—late, per usual. "Neither is pineapple, but you're not banning that."

"Because pineapple is a fruit. It's tropical. Joyful."

I lean over the counter. "It's offensive. Like putting tie-dye on the Constitution."

She laughs, the sound light and unguarded—something I'm fighting a war to protect. "Wow. You really went full 1L with that analogy."

"I did not go first-year Harvard Law. All I did was protect human rights to not ruin a pizza."

I didn't tell her this was the first time I'd ever made a meal with a woman. Not takeout. Not half a cup of coffee so it didn't seem like I was escaping like a dire wolf. Just this. The simple enjoyment of banter and good food.

She twirls her wineglass, watching the deep red swirl. "I bet you were insufferable in Con Law."

"I dominated Constitutional Law." I can't help but brag.

"Why does that not surprise me?"

I flick my hands down my arms. "Because I'm your specimen of perfection?"

She rolls her eyes. "Let me guess, you quote Justice Scalia at parties?"

"Only when severely provoked."

She slides the pizza into the oven, wipes her hands, and leans next to me against the counter. She's dressed casually in a ratty Brendan Blake T-shirt that has seen better days. It hangs off her delicate shoulders, making me too aware of her smooth, creamy skin and the casualness of us being together, alone without any pretense. I want to reach for her, but instead, I take a drink from my wineglass.

It's getting harder and harder to resist her.

She looks up at me over the rim of her glass. "So...why Harvard Law?"

I tilt my head. "Is this your version of twenty questions?"

She shrugs, twirling the stemless glass in her hand. "I remember you at my graduation, but never really asked if you went there. I figure now's as good a time as any."

I could lie. Say what I always do: "Because it was the best," but her eyes are too sharp, too knowing. She wouldn't settle for less than the truth.

So, I give it to her. "Growing up was a challenge. My parents? Well, Dad was gone long before I was born and Ma? She was amazing until she got sick when I was in college. Couldn't figure out how to work the system to get more assistance." I look down into the ruby red liquid and take another drink before continuing. "Then she was gone, but she told me I could help more people than just her."

"And then?"

"Then, I spoke with my next-door neighbor. He was a special agent with the FBI." A pang hits my heart when I think about Director Holder. Times like this, I want to reach out to him. "As my world was falling apart, he was there. He explained my options. Law felt like order. Like if I understood it well enough, maybe I could stop things from happening."

"So, you got your law degree?"

I nod. "Took the bar as a backup. Then, trained physically and mentally before my time at Quantico."

"Were you a good agent?"

"I was...until I wasn't." Tanya's head arriving at the office slashes through my memory. I shudder in revulsion.

Kalie, for her part, doesn't press. Instead, she squeezes my arm, leaving her hand there for a brief moment before she moves away and faces the oven where our pizzas are cooking away.

Then, she opens up and gives me a gift I wasn't expecting. Her voice is softer than I've ever heard it. "I wanted to speak for people who were hurt. That's what I went to school for—criminal justice and psychology."

"What changed your path?"

"Living it. I did my internship at a battered women and children's shelter. I wasn't assigned to work with women who never had a shot. Women like

my family. Who were dismissed before they even opened their mouths."
She takes a deep breath. "Instead, I was assigned—as an intern, mind you
—to teach the batterer's intervention program at the local jail."

My whole body stills. "You've got to be kidding me."

"No. They were underfunded, and there I was—smart, free labor."

My spine tingles with awareness. "What happened?" Because I know
something did.

She wraps her arms around her chest. "It wasn't a big deal."

Liar. I coax, "Let me be the judge of that."

She bites her lip before admitting, "One night, I was teaching a class
about anger management. Overall, my class was made up of guys who
were in for bar fights, B&E, things like that. But there was one..."

"One what?"

"One who was in for sexual assault." She shivers. "The others built a
human wall to keep him away from me after he tried to corner me."

I grit my teeth together. "Where were the guards?"

Her head lifts and her eyes meet mine. "Outside the room."

I want to howl at the desolate expression on her face. "What did
you do?"

Her mouth kicks up in a self-deprecating smile. "Exactly what you think
I did. I told my father."

"Good." The word is ripped out of me savagely. "Tell me Keene went
after the bastards?"

"Actually, I think he first got sentences reduced or thrown out for
everyone who protected me. *Then* he went after the inmate, guards, the
shelter—anyone who thought it was a good idea to send an intern into
that situation." Her expression morphs into one of regret. "Turns out it
wasn't the first time."

Before I crush the delicate wineglass in my fingers, she plucks it from my
hands and entwines her fingers with mine. "Something good came from
it, Declan. I started my own charity."

I look down at our hands—hers, smaller but no less strong. Squeezing gently, I ask, "What charity is that?"

"Brave Steps Forward." Kalie goes on to explain how she personally healed from the trauma by taking a new step every single day. She used a good portion of her trust fund to help others to do so in a healthy way.

"That's what you were doing the night I saw you? Running with your charity group?"

She smiles tremulously. "Though those are people who are now back on their own. They just support one another by getting together and running. My law school roommate, Layla, helps coordinate the efforts both here and in her hometown of Seven Virtues, North Carolina."

"Have I mentioned," I shift so she can slip into my arms, "you're amazing?"

"No, you haven't."

"You are."

Her smile is bashful. "You're trying to charm me."

"Is it working?" I want nothing more than to pull her toward me and kiss her, but the timing isn't right.

As if to prove my point, the timer beeps on our pizzas.

She makes a show of fanning herself even as she pulls away. "Right on time. Plus, it smells terrific. Be still, my starving stomach."

I stand up. Even though Kalie is taller than the average woman, she's dainty compared to me. I lift her onto the stool and place her wine in her hand. "Let me. Just give me directions."

Kalie takes great relish in ordering me around her kitchen. I pull the pizza out, letting it rest while accumulating napkins and cutlery. Then, I plate it with a flourish—making her roll her eyes before I take my seat on the stool next to her, our knees casually bumping into one another.

We spend the rest of the night comparing our Harvard professors, the ridiculousness of some of our assignments, and the worst oral arguments we've ever had to give in court. I feel like I won a prize when I made her crack up over the Byrnes wanting to sue a gun manufacturer over bullets not being released fast enough so they sustained injuries in a shootout. She, meanwhile, explains her daily duties at Amaryllis Events. "I might be willing to trade you mobsters for bridezillas."

I hold up my hands and give her a horror-stricken face. "No damn way. Those people are insane."

That line made her laugh so hard she chokes on her wine.

But our discussion reminds her that she needs to send a file to her mother about a client. We wander up to her office. While she accesses her computer, I trace the spines of her legal texts with their gilded edges. When she finishes, she leans against her desk, studying me. "Do you miss it?"

"The FBI?"

She nods. "The mission."

I walk over to her and slide my arms around her waist. My head rests on top of hers before I admit, "Sometimes. But they didn't believe in me."

She pulls back and her brow furrows. My lips curve sadly when I remind her, "About Tanya."

I think I fall a little more when the light of battle illuminates her gorgeous blue eyes. She tugs me closer against her before declaring, "Then you're better here with people who believe in you and in what you're doing."

Her words strike something deep inside of me. She's right and suddenly everything before her feels like a different life that belonged to a different man. "You're right."

Kalie's hand smooths up my chest. "That's a very good line, Counselor."

"You're right? That's the line you're talking about?"

"Most women would agree with me."

I throw my head back and laugh. "It's not a line if it's true."

"Use it a lot. It's a turn on." Kalie rises on the ball of her feet and kisses me—soft, slow, unhurried.

For that moment, in her office full of pizza and wine, everything else falls away as I deepen the kiss. No threats are being made against this incredible woman. No mobsters, no shadows, no revenge.

It's just us—two people who once saw each other in the crowd at Harvard Law graduation. Now, we're clinging to something much more important than our once treasured degrees.

Each other.

CHAPTER THIRTY-SIX

ONE NIGHT, WHEN WE'RE CUDDLING, I PUSH DECLAN TO TELL ME more about Tanya. He stiffens. "Why?"

"She was important to you—important enough to put your whole life on hold." I lay my head against his shoulder. "Have you talked to anyone about her and what she meant to you?"

He shakes his head.

"Not even my father? My uncle?"

He hesitates. "Jon and Liam...a bit. Your father and uncle were more interested in the logistics of what we found out about the Byrnes, your grandfather, and the Tiberi connection." He releases a harsh breath. "To be honest, what I said to you that day was probably the most I've said about her since I walked out of my former director's office to go undercover."

I twist so I can lay my head against his shoulder. "I'll listen."

The late spring night shimmers through the patio doors lit up by the string of lights Grace had insisted on installing around our pool. The surrounding property is quiet—at least as quiet as it can be with the insects happily frolicking about.

In other words, it's just the two of us and the kind of night where emotions have the space to fill it without regret.

He just stares out at the night, lost in memories he hasn't let go of but has no place to rest them. "Pain's a heavy weight to bear alone."

He turns his head and places his lips on my forehead. For a long while, that's all he does. I'm not certain if he's gathering strength to speak or just absorbing mine until finally he says, "Tanya was by my side for years. She was the one person who relied on me." He pauses and takes a long sip from the water I placed by his side earlier.

I didn't dare speak. I wouldn't interrupt now that he was opening up. I just let him relieve himself of some of this pain.

"I told you about her kids," he continues, his voice lower now. "Little boys. They were four and six when she died. Great kids—Bryan and Emmitt. They used to call me Uncle Dec. I remember every one of their birthday parties. I held them both the day they were born. Tanya's husband, Ben, is a doctor. He is a good guy. Incredible father. Better husband.

"For a while, they considered me family. Tanya insisted if we weren't working, I was to come for Sunday dinner. She had no problem picking up the phone and telling me to come get one of her boys because she needed to run an errand. It was the kind of friendship where I'd crash on their couch after a Sox game and drank a few too many beers.

"Then they assigned her to a case here. Demanded I was her handler. That way I could not only look out for her but for 'her guys' too. It was supposed to be just a few weeks. Then those few weeks extended to a few months."

"What did her husband think about that?"

"It was hell, but not just for him. Her kids were so young they didn't understand why Mommy wasn't coming home, but Uncle Dec was there. Every night, same kind of hell—'Mommy home?' Emmitt would ask. When I'd say no, he'd shove his thumb back in his mouth. Every time, Bryan would get more angry. And Ben? He was just lost without her."

I am barely breathing. I just study the way his eyes glass over as the memories come rushing back.

For long moments, silence permeates the air between us. Then he shocks me when he tells me about the investigation and how people tried to tie him to it. How Ben pushed him away. "He wouldn't let me go to the funeral," he manages.

"That's cruel."

"Was it? If I hadn't done my job by the book..."

"She still might not be alive. We both know it." I hope that all these years later, he can see that, but it might be asking too much.

I'm somewhat relieved when he gives the smallest nod.

"What made you go undercover to take down the Byrnes and Tiberis?" *My grandfather.* The idea my biological grandfather is a part of this is still something impossible to wrap my head around. Then again, it also supports the theory behind the debate between nature and nurture. Hell, my whole family is a case study for it.

"I couldn't not do anything. I had to avenge her."

"You loved her."

"I did. I do," he says honestly. "But never in a romantic sense. From the day we met, Tanya was my sister in every sense of the word. Somehow, I have to make up for letting her down."

"She'd say you never did."

He looked at me. "I've been trying not to drown in the guilt."

"She'd be proud of you."

"That's what Holder used to try to convince me of."

"Who is that?"

"My former director."

We sit in silence again, the kind that didn't need to be filled.

"She didn't get to see them grow up," he said finally. "But I still keep tabs. Quietly. I know what school they go to. I know Emmitt's a great little artist and Bry's got his mom's determination. I just wish—"

"You were still a part of their lives," I conclude.

He nodded. "Every damn day."

I lean in and kiss his temple and hope he doesn't disappear into the darkness so deeply he can't find his way back to being the man Tanya's boys loved.

Back to a place he once called home.

CHAPTER THIRTY-SEVEN

Finding time to get together is difficult between his duties to take down the Tiberis and Byrnes, not to mention my responsibilities and my family. Then there's the fact Grace doesn't have a clue the same way Laura does. I never thought I'd resent having a roommate, but in the month since Declan and I started being whatever the hell we are, we've seen each other four times alone.

Every other time, someone else has been around like an overbearing chaperone—namely, Jon.

Tonight is the first night we have more than a few hours alone. Grace was invited back overseas—this time to consult on an ear. Everyone in my family plans to get together for a family dinner, and I've warned them I'll be leaving early.

My body feels as taut as a stretched tightrope, every muscle quivering with sharp tension. I roll my shoulders repeatedly, trying in vain to shake off the almost unbearable tingling of adrenaline coursing through me—a sensation rivaling the electrifying start line moments of an unforgettable race in my storied career.

Tonight is a different kind of anticipation—a charged readiness pounding through me that has nothing to do with competition and everything to do with wanting a certain stubborn man's hands on me.

I change clothes three times before deciding on yoga pants and a camisole topped with a jean jacket. Every part of me is alive, every cell humming, and I've never wanted anyone as much as I want him.

Or worse, been so afraid to hope for what we might become.

I know he wants what I do. He just can't see beyond the horizon of his mission, and I'm terrified he'll retreat into the undercover world, leaving me behind.

He's never done this and doesn't know if he can. But he told me he wants to. Told me he wants to try.

I do too.

I shake my head, trying to clear the "hope for the best but prepare for the worst" attitude. I've never been like that. I've always been balls to the wall and letting things play out.

I need to stop acting like I'm a different person because he's in my life.

I need to be me.

A knock sounds at the door and a frown mars my brow. "I'm supposed to be meeting everyone at the farm." Curious as to who it could be, I pull it open.

Declan braces one arm on the jamb, eyes raking over me like a man starved. His hungry gaze lingers on my body, making me feel like I'm wearing nothing at all.

He's here.

He's not backing out.

He's braving a family dinner.

The relief that floods my system is intense and overwhelming. "Damn, Kalie." His voice rumbles with a raw, aching need.

A slow smile crosses my face as I step back to let him in. "What are you doing here? I thought you were just going to meet me there."

He brushes his lips across mine in greeting, setting my blood on fire before I capture the hint of vulnerability he tries to hide. "I hoped you wouldn't mind company on the car ride."

"I'm glad you came. I could use fortification before facing the family." I pull him in, my heart flipping. He cups my face, kisses me again, and I swear my bones liquefy.

He pulls back, his eyes dark and heated. "It's getting harder to leave you."

I savor his words, trying to memorize the way they feel inside of me. "Then don't."

His chuckle is low, sending a jolt of arousal through me. "You're dangerous."

"You have no idea," I tease.

He follows me into the kitchen, leaning against the counter as I grab my keys. His lips twitch. "I'm not going to be skinned alive once I walk through the door?"

"Not now." I step closer to him. "You've been invited by how many members of my family?"

"Eight," he answers unhesitatingly. "Including your mother, aunt, and cousin."

"Then, you're fine." I pause. "Wait. There's a very important question I have to ask you."

His face pales. "What?"

"Did anyone warn you about the dancing?"

His face relaxes in amusement. "Jon mentioned something sounded funny when he told me about it. All the women in your family dancing on tables? As if."

My smile is slow as I pick up the keys. "Oh, you'll see."

"Check the group chat. Uncle Phil tried to insist on having a light meal tonight once he got his cholesterol results back," Laura's voice explodes in laughter over my Bluetooth. Fortunately, Declan insisted on driving my vehicle so I can do just that.

I frown, wondering why she's laughing so hard. "Is there a problem?"

"No, Uncle Phil just ate like garbage the week leading up to his test. He openly admitted to having no self-control. Mama said that's his problem, and she's not going to be subjected to crap food because he can't control himself. Uncle Jason agreed."

"Ohh, this should be good." I unlock my phone just as it chimes with more messages. The screen floods with texts:

> **MAMA:**
> Apparently, Phil's basic comprehension of fasting for bloodwork is worse than his understanding of scheduling.

> **AUNT CASS:**
> I'm not going without because you can't follow directions. That's where I draw the line.

> **AUNT EM:**
> Don't make me spit on you on purpose.

> **AUNT CORI:**
> It's either that or the women are eating somewhere else—in protest.

> **UNCLE PHIL:**
> RED ALERT! JASON! HELP!

AUNT CASS:

Don't know why you bother asking for Jason to intervene. You know he doesn't respond to these texts.

NIC:

Don't worry, I've already placed everyone's take-home orders from the bakery.

MAMA:

You can forget mine. Keene doesn't deserve anything that tastes good.

ME:

Mama, are you still punishing Dad?

AUNT CORI:

Oh, the places I can take that comment.

UNCLE PHIL:

I want to escape this chat. La, la, la.

AUNT EM:

We can make that happen, Phil.

AUNT CASS:

Be careful what you wish for, brother.

UNCLE PHIL:

I'll take Keene's portion of goodies as therapy, Nic.

ME:

Now, now, Uncle Phil, don't be rude. We have guests coming.

So, I claim dibs on Grace's portion.

UNCLE PHIL:

I guess that's fair.

WAIT. WHAT GUEST?

MAMA:

I love how you get to the salient part AFTER you worry about your stomach.

That's fine, sweetheart. I'll save them. Cori baked brownies.

LAURA:

You. Will. Share, Kalie.

These Hudson men eat a lot.

ME:

Truth.

UNCLE PHIL:

Noooo! Not another Hudson man.

AUNT CASS:

Shut up, Phil.

AUNT EM:

Can it, Phil.

MAMA:

FFS, Phil.

AUNT CORI:

And I was going to make you caramel for your suffering.

GRACE:

I'm missing home so much.

AUNT HOLLY:

Miss you, too, baby. Hope you're having a blast.

GRACE:

I am. Someone take lots of pics for me.

UNCLE PHIL:

Umm, Gracie. You do know who your mama is. Right?

AUNT HOLLY:

#lesigh

AUNT CORI:

Phil, if you don't stop, I'm going to make you help me in the kitchen.

UNCLE PHIL:

See you all soon! I'm going to walk on the treadmill now.

After a flourish of XOXOs, I'm cackling like a hyena as I read the text to Declan. He noticeably relaxes. "Think they'll be like that in person?"

"Are you kidding? It will be worse."

"How could it be worse?"

"Do you remember me mentioning the dancing?"

CHAPTER THIRTY-EIGHT

I LEAN OVER TO JON AS WE SIT AT THE TABLE, SHAKING MY HEAD IN disbelief. "I know you said your family had world-class cooks," I say in a low, incredulous tone. "But this is Food Network worthy."

"It should be." His voice is tinged with amusement.

"Do you guys have it catered or something?"

Jon shrugs sheepishly. "Nothing quite like that."

"Then what?"

"Check out who is in the kitchen."

I twist around and catch sight of Kalie's Aunt Corinna, who I was introduced to earlier. Next to her is a man who the world knows for his incredible country hits. Both are wearing aprons and having a fight with leftover caramel in front of a man with silvery-blond hair who has an outraged expression on his face—Kalie's Uncle Phil.

I arch a brow and lean forward. "Is Brendan Blake cooking in your kitchen a regular occurrence?" I ask, my words edged with shock and awe. "If it is, I swear, I'll take up a rotation. Something, anything. Side dishes, salad. You name it." I can't help but think of the past few years when, under the guise of my undercover persona, I've been feasting like royalty, yet this family, who is the epitome of the American dream, is having a damn food fight.

I yearn to be a part of it.

Jon slips his hand into his pocket and yanks out his cell. "There's nothing about Uncle B on rotation in the guy's group chat."

I tear off a bite of the only thing left on my plate and chew slowly, my eyes never leaving him. "You all have a group chat too?" I ask, incredulous.

"Yeah. There are a few. First one, the whole family participates. You get added when your parents decide you're mature enough for the conversation to go completely off the rails." He gestures vaguely, as though the chaotic process of his family's decision-making is somehow perfectly logical.

Recalling what Kalie read to me in the car, I can completely understand why addition is at parental discretion. Before I can question Jon any further about the other chats, I'm completely derailed when Rhianna's voice blasts over the speakers. The bass reverberates through the walls, and even outside the steady hum of the party, you can feel the vibrations in your chest. It completely drowns out any chance of a conversation.

Jon rolls his eyes heavenward. "Here we go again."

Soon, several men stop what they were doing and head inside, drawn by some kind of secret male bonding. Caleb, Keene, Colby, and Liam practically cause a traffic jam trying to push their way past one another.

"What's happening?" I ask, trying to seek out Kalie but unable to spot her.

He hesitates, eyes darting around at the departing figures before he speaks. "Well..."

I cut him off, voice firm, "Spill it." Before I can move to get inside, Jon steps in front of me.

His next words are both apologetic and wickedly amused, even for him. "You know how some families force a karaoke session?"

My eyes widen, and I instinctively take a step back. "That's not what's happening inside, is it?" I ask, my mind racing. If they're dragging relatives into some impromptu, off-key madness, I wonder if I can make it to Kalie's car before anyone notices I've disappeared.

"Not quite," Jon continues, his voice trailing off, "The women in my family—and my Uncle Phil—they..." His sentence trails off.

"They what?" When he doesn't answer, I snap impatiently, "Jon, Kalie's told me stories about your Uncle Phil and on the way here, read me selections from her chat. It can't be any worse."

"Depends on what you consider worse," he mutters.

"Spill it." I press.

"I told you they all like to dance on tables," Jon reminds me with a combination of mortification, love, and amusement.

"All?" My head snaps in the direction of the door. The image of my fiery, irreverent woman—and it strikes me in the chest that I just claimed her as mine—takes my breath away. Suddenly, I'm painfully aware of the stir in my groin—a reaction that keeps getting worse every time we're together.

She is going to dance on a table?

Fuck my life.

"All of them. It's like they—" he starts, but his explanation evaporates as I catch sight of Kalie through a nearby window.

Holy. Shit. All the blood in my body has made its way to my dick. I'm not even certain if my heart's pumping blood anywhere else.

One of her impossibly long legs is drawn up gracefully against the side of her body. Then she trails her fingers deliberately, tantalizingly down a path over her thigh.

I recall nearly having a heart attack earlier when Kalie stepped into the room wearing her yoga pants, and now I understand exactly why. Each and every move pulls the thin material taut against her ass, proving she's either bare beneath or the scrap of nothing is so small I can rip it off with my teeth.

I'm not certain which I'm hoping for.

With a fluid spin, she presses her hand against the wall. Her hips sway as though every movement were a deliberate challenge to gravity itself. Throughout this shockingly sensual display, she's nonchalantly munching on a decadent brownie as if it were the most natural thing in the world.

Uncertain of how my feet are able to move, I stumble toward the door.

I vaguely hear Jon call out, "Just remember, it's your funeral." His smartass voice is swallowed by Rhianna as she drowns out everything else in the room.

Inside, chaos reigns. The living room has transformed into a bizarre dance floor. It's not just Kalie but all the women—and, Christ, Uncle Phil—are dancing on tables. Laughter overrides the pulsating music. If their partners are on a table, the men are beneath it. But what stops me in my tracks is catching sight of Keene—Mr. Stick Permanently Glued Up My Ass—spinning his delighted wife around on the dance floor when the song changes to one by Kelsea Ballerini.

I'd wonder what was baked in those brownies but then, as if by magnetic force, my eyes lock with Kalie's again. Up on a table, she glows with the kind of happiness I could never imagine being able to give her. Her spirit challenges the universe with every step, her presence defiant and intoxicating. In that moment, every guarded part of me softens; I can't tear my eyes away.

I never want to.

She might be a firebrand, but she's the fire my soul needs to burn.

Jon's voice comes over the cacophony, his tone rough but enthusiastic. "I told you it gets crazy!"

I just nod, unable to tear my eyes away from Kalie.

"You keep an eye on her."

I never want to move them away. The thought is as truthful as it is terrifying. I force my way through the crowd, each step drawing me closer to her. I know this is a train wreck waiting to happen, but I can't slow my movement down.

A part of me doesn't want to.

With her arm draped casually around Laura's shoulder and another of their cousins by her side, Kalie tilts her head back as she erupts into a wild, joyous whoop. She spins gracefully, each movement exuding the same recklessness that leaves no trace of regret or restraint. My heart hammers in my chest as I shorten the distance between us.

The moment our eyes meet, she leaps down from her perch recklessly— a mix of trust and daring that makes me want to give her everything and take off in the opposite direction because I'm terrified of what will happen to her.

What will I do if something happens to her? The weight of the potential scenario slams into me even as she drags me closer to her parents. For now, for this moment, I'll let her have her way and just be free.

Even if I know nothing is.

CHAPTER THIRTY-NINE

Kalie

Returning to my home after family dinner, I'm still dancing around the living room, high on the energy of the night. The echo of my own laughter fills the empty house as I float from room to room, glancing at my phone every other second.

Declan hadn't stayed long once we'd gotten back to my place, and part of me wonders if I scared him off by being a little too much, a little too demanding, a little too Marshall. I pause and rest my head against the wall, letting out a soft groan of frustration. The moment we walked in the door, I'd looped my arms around his neck and pressed my lips to his. He returned my kiss with the same fervor that matched the night until I surged against him, so damn ready for him to take it further.

That's when he stiffened. I immediately pulled back. When he brushed a lock of hair off my forehead, I knew he was going to bail. His eyes had a haunted look. "Kalie. Tonight was...overwhelming."

At least he hadn't lied. Maybe that's why I hadn't asked him to stay. I knew he needed time to process the chaos of the evening. I didn't want to push him, so I let him go. But now, alone, I can't help but wonder if I gave up too easily. I run my fingers through my hair, restless, feeling like I'm coming down from the world's most intense adrenaline rush.

It was a good night.

I can't shake the fear that I've blown it by letting him in too much. Too fast.

That I'd gotten under his skin in a way he wasn't ready for. I'm not sure how much I can ask of a man who hasn't had any kind of normalcy in years. But the fact that he came to the farm tonight, that he was willing to be part of my family—even just for an evening—has to mean something.

I tug on my bottom lip. It has to mean something, right? Even if he's not willing to admit it to me yet. Even if he's not willing to admit it to himself. I draw a breath and anchor myself against the wall.

He hasn't texted since he left, and that leaves me more unbalanced than I'd care to admit. I'm torn between reaching out and letting him come to me. It's like waiting for the gun to go off at the start of a race, adrenaline and anticipation pumping through my veins. I feel the need to move, to run, to—

My phone buzzes, and I nearly drop it in my haste to grab it off the counter. My eyes scan the message, and I flush at the words that are on the screen.

DECLAN:

Open your door.

Now.

The text from Declan sends a shiver of excitement darting down my spine. Without thinking, I move to unlock the door and fling it open. He steps inside without waiting to be asked, his eyes raking over me from head to toe.

My heart races as I wait for his next move.

"All night, I've fought this," he growls, pulling me into his arms before crushing his lips against mine. His tongue delves deep, tasting and claiming me as his own. His hands roam over my body, teasing and taunting me with his touch. One hand finds its way under the fabric of my camisole, the other down the back of my pants teasing at my G-string.

I arch into him, needing more contact. Needing him to touch me where I ache with longing.

He deepens our kiss. The taste of him makes me wild, the feel of his rough hands sending shivers down my spine.

"Turn around," he commands softly, his voice a low rumble in my ear. I hesitate for just a moment, then slowly turn and brace myself against the wall.

He steps forward, kicking the door closed behind him. Once it's just the two of us, he presses closer, his body aligning against mine from behind. His body is like a furnace pressed against mine and pure, sensuous energy.

One hand grips my hair tightly as the other slides down my stomach to tease at the dampness between my legs.

"You're so wet for me," he murmurs, nibbling my earlobe. "You want this, don't you?"

I moan softly, bobbing my head up and down. I'm unable to form words as he continues to nibble up and down my neck, increasing the excitement pulsing through my veins. Declan nips at my bare shoulder, then eases the sting with his tongue. A shiver of pleasure rips through me. I moan his name, "Declan..."

His hand slides under my camisole and up. Snagging my bandeau bra along the way, he sweeps both over my head—exposing my breasts to the cool evening air. One hand cups the weight of one breast—tugging, twisting my nipple. I arch into his fingers, wanting more.

Wanting him.

I'm babbling about how I want his mouth to surround my nipples, how I want him to get me off with his tongue. He snarls, "Next time."

Then I feel the fingers of his other hand catch along my waistband, and he tugs them down below my hips. His primitive growl erupts before he traces his index finger along the solitary line of my G-string. "You mean to tell me this is all you were wearing when you were dancing tonight?"

"Yes," I whisper, my voice barely audible. "Please, Declan."

"Please, what?"

"I need more."

He chuckles darkly, his breath tickling my ear. "You're going to get more."

With one swift movement, he pulls his hand away from my breast. I whimper at the loss. That is until he uses both hands to yank my pants and undergarments down to my ankles. "Step out." Once I do, I feel exposed and vulnerable.

Looking over my shoulder, those nerves settle when I see the intensity on his face. For just a second, time stands still. Until he drags a finger from the nape of my neck down my spine, in between the cleft of my cheeks, in between my thighs. He rims my dripping entrance. "Is this where you want me, firebrand?"

My legs, strong legs that have carried me thousands of miles, quiver.

He slides his finger in one thrust. "Ahh!" My body clutches at his digit, throbbing. My eyes roll back, and I'm afraid I'm about to come. When I tell him that, he smirks before adding a second and thrusting lazily. "I always wanted to feel fire. Burn on me, Kalie."

So I do. I detonate, squeezing his fingers as I explode. My world rightens when I feel his body press against my back, even as my slickness slides down my thighs. Before I can ramp up for a second round, he pulls away.

I let out a mew of disappointment. That is until I see him reach for the buckle of his belt.

Twisting until I can admire the striptease in front of me, I bite my lip at the thick arousal he reveals. "Let me touch you."

"Not this time, firebrand. I need to be inside you." Before he shucks his slacks completely off, he reaches inside his wallet for protection. After sliding the condom on his cock—a cock that has a barbell right behind the head which causes my juices to leak even more—he pulls me forward against him. His hand slides beneath my thigh to align us.

I wrap it around his hip before he nudges the other to encase his waist. Bracing me back against the wall, he positions himself at my entrance, slowly pushing inside until he's fully sheathed within me.

I gasp at the feeling of being so full, so owned, with the extra pressure of the metal nudging my walls. I can't help but beg for more. "Please..."

His hands grip my hips tightly as he begins to move, thrusting into me with a rough rhythm that sends waves of pleasure crashing through me.

"You're mine," he growls, grips my hips tighter, pulling me on and off him.

"Fuck," I cry out, my voice echoing in the silence of my living room. "More, Declan."

He grunts in approval, increasing the pace of his thrusts. His free hand braces against the wall as he controls the pace of our movements.

I'm about to fall off the edge. I gasp, "So...so close. Please..."

Then I fall over, every muscle inside me desperate to pull him over with me. I wrap my arms around his shoulders as shudders of completion rip through my body. Turning my head, I run my tongue up the side of his neck.

"God...Love...More...Kalie...," he grunts. A few final thrusts, then Declan drives in deep, holding still as he empties himself inside me.

We're barely standing, panting heavily. Sweat trickles down from the corner of his temple. My hand comes up to brush it aside. Despite the primitiveness of it, our coming together was perfect. It was us. It was ripping open our souls.

"You're mine," he repeats softly, leaning forward to press a kiss against my sweaty forehead. "Always."

"And you're mine." It comes out breathless, like I've run a marathon.

But why am I worried I won't be able to hold on to the prize at the end of the race?

CHAPTER FORTY

I'VE NEVER BEEN SO AFRAID IN MY LIFE AS I AM WAKING UP NEXT to Kalie the next morning. I've never been filled with this kind of fear before—one that has nothing to do with violence, death, or betrayal, but everything to do with her.

What she makes me feel.

My heart is overflowing with emotions I haven't ever allowed myself to feel for a woman. Even tangled in the sheets, her face relaxed and peaceful, she's the most beautiful thing I've woken up to. Her breathing is soft and steady, her chest rising and falling with each inhale and exhale. Her features are serene, an expression of absolute trust that makes my heart clench.

I need to ensure it stays that way.

After last night, I know I will never be without her in my life. For the first time, I truly understand what I'm risking. I'm not just selfish for wanting her so much, for thinking I can have it all before getting closure on the bastard who killed Tanya. I'm endangering her more than she already is.

Now, after waking up tangled in her, my resolve is even stronger.

Still, I need these few moments. I need to store them away in a sacred place no one can touch so I know what it's like to live with Kalie by my side for those dark days to come when she can't be next to me as I finish the job I was set out to do. It's not that I don't want her there, it's that I refuse to endanger her. Having Kalie by my side is everything I could possibly dream of. She's perfect—someone brave enough to put her heart in my hands even after everything I've done.

Without thinking, I reach out and brush my fingers gently across her cheek. Her nose twitches, but her eyes stay closed. She shifts slightly, tucking herself closer to me in a way that's so trusting and pure I'm afraid it's going to destroy me. Then her lips part, and she breathes three little words that crush my soul.

"I love you."

I hold my breath, my heart collapsing at the same time it's trying to beat its way out of my chest. Internally, I'm now fighting a war within myself. Should I wait for her to wake up? Should I let her sleep? I push a strand of hair threatening to tickle her away from her face as I decide I should let her sleep.

I should let myself enjoy these few quiet moments of peace before I leave.

I'm not certain how long I stare at the woman I'm hopelessly in love with. Every part of me rebels at the idea of leaving her bed. The sun starts to rise higher in the sky and I still can't let her go.

Nor can I return the sentiment. I'm terrified it will place a larger target on her back than the one that's already there.

Finally, I know it's time. I nuzzle her ear and whisper, "Firebrand." She lets out a small noise, her breath warm against my neck. The trust she places in me becomes another burden I have to balance because it's born out of love —ours. The one we created in the long nights we spent here in her home, getting to know one another without the rest of the world interfering.

But as I drag her from her sleep, I realize she's everything I've ever wanted but didn't know what I was missing. The problem is, I have no idea how to go about keeping her—let alone keeping her safe.

Since she's apparently dead to the world, I slip out of bed and move over to stand by the window. The sun's warm against my bare skin, but in the few hours since Kalie whispered those words, my whole life has shifted off its axis.

I don't know which direction is right. I only know I'm terrified because I want to just be with her, being me, not under the constant pressure of living the life of someone else—someone she's supposed to despise. That's who I want to be for her.

But I can't.

Not yet.

Kalie rolls over in her sleep and murmurs my name. The sound of it, the vulnerability of it, tugs at my heart and my guilt in equal measure. I run a hand through my hair and pace the room.

Goddamn it. I have to do this, but I'm not sure how. I'm out of practice with being honest. I don't want to hurt her. I want to be everything she wants, everything she needs. The only person she looks at with love in her eyes for the rest of her life.

I'm not able to tell her any of that.

Not yet.

I squeeze my eyes shut, trying to erase the self-doubt and hesitation. Now, I'm stalling. When I open them again, the sun's higher in the morning sky. Kalie's still asleep, but I won't leave her without a word.

I lean over to brush a kiss against her lips. They're soft and warm, and I feel them move when I pull away. Her eyes flutter open, sleepy and confused.

"Declan?" she asks, her voice rough but happy.

"Hey, firebrand."

She reaches for me, and it takes everything I have to take her hand instead of lying back down with her.

"Where are you going?" she asks.

I sit on the edge of the bed. I open my mouth, wanting to say something she deserves to hear—like I'm just running out for breakfast or I'm going to get a drink. But I can't do that.

What she needs is the truth and yet when the words come out of my mouth, they feel so mediocre in comparison to what she made me feel last night, I regret them almost immediately. "I need to know you're safe before we can be together."

Her eyes narrow. "What do you mean?"

I reach for her hand, but she yanks it away. "Talk."

Tucking a stray lock of hair away from her face, I murmur, "I made a promise, Kalie. And between that and us, you're now in more danger. I have to let you go."

Her breathing accelerates, but she doesn't say a word. I try to make her understand again, "I have to believe if I walk away, nothing will happen to you."

"You do, do you?"

I wince. Her tone is as cold as it was that day in the courthouse rotunda. Still, I try to break through. I reach for her hand. After fighting with her for possession, I clasp it between both of mine. "I swear, Kalie. Once this job is done, I'm yours."

She's silent. Emotions chase one another through her eyes before resignation settles over her face. Then a look of resignation darkens her gaze. "Right." She pulls her hand back.

The panic that lands in my chest causes me to frantically reach for hers again. When I try, she slaps my hands away. "Just go."

"It's not forever."

"Go."

"Kalie, I have a meeting—"

"Just. Go."

I can't deny the pain I see in her eyes. Not when I know I'm the cause. Not when realizing I'm in love with her gave me the push to end this once and for all. But if I'm going to protect her, truly protect her, this is the only way. I retreat, knowing anything I say now will make things worse.

But I hate that this feels so much like goodbye.

By the time I get out to my car, there's already a call from Jon. I answer with a gruff, "Yeah?"

"I've been monitoring your burner cells. You received three calls from Sal. He's freaking out."

I start the engine. "About what?"

"You name it. Does the man have a sixth sense?"

"Why are you asking?"

"Because our bug picked up on him freaking out about the Byrnes having someone working with the Feds. Now he's getting antsy. He's contacting everyone he knows in the pipeline. Guess whose name is at the top of their target list?"

"Fuck." I cast a backward glance toward Kalie's home and then gun my car down the street. "How long do I have?"

"Why?"

"I need to go home—shower, change."

"You didn't go home last night." It's a statement, not a question.

"No." I say no more, but I don't have to. He knows where I was yesterday, and he knows who I left with.

"Now you're leaving her unprotected?"

"Agents are there."

"Agents aren't you!" he shouts.

There's an imposing silence on the other end of the line before his voice comes out harsher than I've ever heard it. "Do not put my cousin in danger for a vendetta you can't let go of."

His words cut deeper than he'll ever know.

I pray to God Jon will never understand the conflicting need to make sure Kalie's safe before wrapping up my past so I can become the man she needs. Once I do, I can let this go. I'll never have to go down this dark path ever again.

But we agree on one thing. Kalie's in more danger the longer we all take part in this clusterfuck. The longer I'm out of touch, the riskier it is for everyone.

I have to shut the pipeline down.

Now.

Ignoring his bitching, I disconnect the call. Less than half an hour later, I'm at my apartment. Shoving my keys into the lock, I curse when they scrape the door instead.

I hadn't realized how badly my hands were shaking.

I can't let it all fall apart when I'm this close. If it does, she'll be in danger regardless of what everyone wants to believe.

Inside, I shower quickly—even as water splashes off my body, I can still feel the touch of Kalie's skin against mine. I can hear her voice in my head, a haunting reminder of the night before.

But now I have to focus. I have to shove the sharp pain aside. I have to shove her aside. I have to shove everything aside other than this final push to ensure Sal hasn't figured out who I am.

Because knowing they're coming for Kalie makes this mission even more critical than it was before.

Now, I'm not just tying up my past. I'm trying to save my future.

CHAPTER FORTY-ONE

THE VIP ROOM OF VELVET VICE REEKS OF SWEAT, EXPENSIVE whiskey, and something I can't quite pinpoint. The moment I sat down, a glass of whiskey in my hand before I could order it. That alone tells me I've spent way too much time here.

Dim red lighting pulses against the mirrored walls while the bass from the main floor throbs louder than normal—or so it seems to me. What shocks me as I step through the curtains is Jack Marshall—legs spread wide apart, coat open, the tip of his cane resting on the floor between his shoes—holding court with the strippers around him like a king.

Sid lounges beside him, already two drinks in and absolutely playing the part of the court jester. If this is supposed to be a normal business meeting, he's making a mockery of it with his shirt unbuttoned halfway to his navel. He meets Jack's gaze before laughing too loud at what appears to be nothing.

All it makes me wish is the whiskey I'm holding could be arsenic and I could pin one or both of the men and pour it down their throats. Affecting a bored tone, I yell, "Can someone tell me what the fuck I'm doing here?

"Loyalty, boys," Jack swirls the dark liquid in his glass. "It's the only real currency we've got left. Money fades. Influence wanes. But loyalty—that's priceless."

"Tell that to your dead wife," Sid cackles before bursting into another wheezing laugh.

Jack only smiles.

Nerissa moves past us—clearly shaken. Her heels shuffle across the floor. Her left arm is clutched tight to her stomach, as if hiding something broken.

Chrissi isn't as discreet. "Listen, Dec," she says, voice sharp, mouth slick with gloss. "Nerissa's milking it. It was barely a shove—"

Jack doesn't even blink.

He stands. Lumbers slowly over to Chrissi and pulls a blade from the inside of his jacket.

"No," I protest. But my warning comes too late.

Jack already has his arm wrapped around her neck—fast and sudden. The redhead's scream is cut short as the blade slices across her throat. A spray of red hits the mirrored wall. She drops, body still twitching. Tammy stumbles backward, appalled her partner in crime is dead before she hit the carpet.

Nerissa shrieks, unable to hide her fear.

Sid's enjoyment is a nightmare unto itself. "Bloody hell, Jack. That's better than the damn floor show!"

I force myself to breathe. To not react. I can't blow my cover, not now. Not when I have to report a fucking murder. The line I wasn't supposed to cross—the one Holder warned me about? It's now in my rearview due to Jack Marshall. That and the knowledge that I can't have Kalie end up like this are the only coherent thoughts running through my head.

Kalie.

Christ. I sit up straighter. Now, I'm more grateful than ever I pulled back. I can't have her be in this maniac's line of fire.

"Clean that up," Jack bellows to no one in particular, wiping the bloody blade against Chrissi's hair before sliding it back into its sheath. "Mouthing off in front of gentlemen? Trash."

Nerissa trembles, her mascara already running.

Jack glances at her, then back to me. "I thought I wanted her, but she's too skittish for what I need. Use her for the next half hour. Try not to break her. She still belongs to the club."

Everything inside of me screams this is wrong, but I can't back down now. I swallow the bile threatening to rise as Nerissa's pleading eyes meet mine. "Thanks."

Jack and Sid meander toward the bar in the back, laughing, but I know they have a sharp eye on the two of us despite giving the illusion they're moving on.

Nerissa turns to me with wide eyes and a face too pale under the lights. "Help me," she whispers.

I think quickly before ordering her, "Just act normal."

She moves behind me, stumbling. Her arm drapes across my shoulder. I murmur, "How much pain are you in?"

"They wouldn't let me see a doctor."

A furious rush of breath escapes. Her head drops down as she tries to inhale before gasping, "I need to tell you."

"About?"

"About the girls."

"What do you mean?"

"They're using the club as a hub."

My body stills as she straddles my legs—whether that's because she knows I'm not one of them or the intelligence she's passing along, I'm not entirely certain. But Nerissa's fingers don't roam over my chest. Her hips don't grind down. She leans closer so her breath brushes against my ear.

"There's a door below the dressing room," she whispers. "Leads to a basement. They keep girls and their kids there sometimes. Not just the ones who try to get out of Velvet Vice, but ones I've never seen before."

Nerissa looks down quickly before tossing her head back in supposed pleasure. When she leans forward again, she murmurs, "They think I'm deaf in one ear, blind in one eye. I'm not. I can hear and see everything."

I slip a bill between her fingers—cover—before asking, "How many have gone through?"

"Two tonight. But there's no set rotation. Some come through just to be cleaned up. Some stay a few days before being sold." Her head twists, and she lets her hands rest on my shoulders. "It's worse when *he* comes in."

"Him who? Sid?"

She shakes her head.

"Jack." My voice is grim.

"Yes." Her voice shakes, but she keeps up the act—moving just enough to pass for a show. Just then, she lets out a pained gasp. Her face turns chalk white. She starts to slide off my lap.

My hands reach out to steady her. "What's wrong? Is this from the last time I was here?"

"No. Chrissi had a turn at me the other day. Said I stole her client." She twists her head and glares at the body still on the floor. "I'm not sorry she's dead."

Just then, the lights catch Sid and Jack looking our way. To play into what's happening, I lean back on the Chesterfield. "Why are you telling me all this?"

"Because you're not like them, are you?"

I shake my head imperceptibly.

"Didn't think so."

"You took a huge gamble, Nerissa."

"I'd rather be dead than let one of them touch me again." My jaw clenches at that pronouncement. I hand her some more money. She slips it into her bra, pulling something out at the same time. "You think no one notices you're different? That's why they're testing you tonight."

My jaw is a rock from how hard I've been grinding my teeth. "They'll kill you if they find out."

"They going to kill me anyway," she says. "Just make the info I gave you count."

Her fingers graze the back of my neck. I catch the tips and whatever she's passing to me. It's an innocent touch, but I'll still wait to look at it later, lest Jack or Sid see it. "What is it?"

"Names. Places. Things I've overheard they think I can't."

I suck in a breath and offer her a radiant smile. Finally, some goddamn proof. I murmur, "You did good." Quickly, I slide the coaster—the proof —inside my jacket pocket where it won't be visible.

She nods, trembling, and slides off my lap with practiced grace.

As she disappears into the shadows, Jack claps his hands once. "Well?" the old man asks. "She loosen your morals or just your belt?"

My smile is dangerous knowing I have him and Sid. And quite possibly, depending on what Nerissa gave to me, the ability to topple the Byrnes and Tiberis. Finally, "Both."

Jack's eyes narrow, but he only says, "Loyalty, Declan. That's what makes you valuable."

I give a curt nod, the coaster burning a hole in my jacket pocket. If I'm lucky, my loyalty will give me the ability to burn this place and most of the people in it to the ground.

Soon.

I don't go straight back to my condo. I take the long way so I can stop off to use the burner assigned to Jon to give him the good news. He tells me to head to the pre-arranged meeting place. The one we hoped to use years ago.

Now, it's time.

Then I drive to an industrial park after being extra cautious and switching to an SUV at the storage unit—a car I've never driven.

My eyes sweep for tails and the coaster is still lodged next to my heart. Right where I hold Kalie's sleep filled words.

Soon, I promise her silently. Soon I'll be able to respond to those words with everything inside me. Pulling off behind an abandoned schoolyard, I cut the lights and kill the engine.

Now, I have nothing to do but wait.

Exactly five minutes later, a plain black SUV slides up beside me. Windows tinted far beyond legal limits. No headlights. The driver doesn't get out.

I roll my window down just a crack.

A long pause.

Then a voice sounds through the dark.

"Report."

"VIP room. Stripper passed me a list. Names. Transfer location. Said two girls are downstairs now, with a rotation expected by morning."

"Reliable source?"

"Risking her life for it. Saw Jack kill one of her coworkers for talking back tonight. So did I. Still came to me."

"Was she marked?"

"Injured. No visible tags. Ribs messed up. Limping. Might need an assist out."

A rustle. A click of a pen.

"Where's the list?"

I slide the folded coaster through the two-inch gap. A gloved hand plucks it from my fingers.

"You do anything to draw attention?"

"I did what was expected. She danced as she gave me the intel. They watched from the bar. Pretended like it was the best thing since I last got my rocks off."

Silence stretches between us then, "You got them. Finally."

"And I'll finish them."

A pause. Then he says, "Tell me about the lawyer."

I blink at the unexpected question. "What about her?"

"She knows about what you're doing?"

"Yeah. She knows everything."

"And she didn't walk?" Now the voice sounds incredulous.

"No." Then I think about our conversation this morning and swear. "I don't know."

"She think you walked away from the mission?"

I look out my windshield, heart aching.

"I told her I'd be back when this is all done."

"Well, aren't you the dumb little shit," the voice I haven't heard in years lectures me, much like he used to when I'd get caught raiding his wife's flower bed for Mother's Day flowers for my ma.

"She's Jack Marshall's granddaughter," I explain, as if that says it all.

"So? Right now, you're technically a criminal."

"Gee, thanks, Holder," I snarl.

"Keeping it real, Dec. Why'd you fuck it up so bad?"

"She's perfect."

"The problem being?" Ace waits for my answer.

"What if I can't protect her? What if I can't stop what Jack keeps threatening? If I walk away, maybe that's another way to keep her out of it." Then I hasten to add, "Not that it means I'll stop protecting her. I'll just do it from the shadows."

Holder's voice softens just slightly. "You're in deeper than I've seen you before."

"She's the one."

Another pause. Then he informs me, "The intel checked out. We'll move on the club tonight. Quietly. We'll get the girls out."

"And me?"

"You're out. Get to Hudson and wait for debrief. Jack's going to try to retaliate."

My grip tightens on the steering wheel turning my knuckles white. "I need to keep Jack away from Kalie."

"Then focus on that." He rolls down his window, and for the first time in years, I see Holder's full face. The pride on it is unmistakable. "You did it, Dec. You swore you'd pick up the lead after Tanya was killed. You found out what she did and you likely just found her killer."

"Let's confirm that before we celebrate."

"When we do, we're reinstating every fucking accolade you had Hudson delete from your file." Before I can protest, he holds up a hand. "This time, I refuse to give in to you. Great job."

A minute later, his SUV rolls away.

I sit in silence long after Holder's taillights vanish. I think of Nerissa, of Chrissi's blood on the carpet. I recall the way Tanya's head was delivered to the office—each piece of skin pulled from her face. Of Jack Marshall's talent with a knife and his remarks about loyalty.

"This was for you, Tanya. Now it's time to reclaim my future." With that, I turn on my engine and head back toward the Hudson office to finish what I started.

CHAPTER FORTY-TWO

Kalie

EVEN IF I'M NOT ONE OF THE PEOPLE DAMNED BY CIRCUMSTANCE who run in Brave Steps, it's taking everything inside me to put one foot in front of the other after that photo came up on my newsfeed. On several newsfeeds. All I wanted to do was crawl into bed and feed off the pain, but I know what I'd share with the others—reclaim your sense of self.

Still, I can't help but recall the words he left me with this morning as he was trying to sneak out of my bed—nothing but sweet little lies. At least

I know them for what they are now. Anguish fuels my muscles as each footfall lands.

He told me it was a business meeting. He said it right there in my bedroom. Lied right to my face. *"Kalie, I have a meeting—"*

"Just. Go."

I watched him walk out the door. Despite everything, a small part of me let myself believe him.

That was a mistake that will never happen again.

I was halfway through reviewing a file I needed for the office when my phone buzzed on the counter. A message from Jon—a news link to Sexy & Social with no explanation. It isn't like him to drop a link without calling first.

Then, I get his text.

> JON:
>
> Kalie, I just didn't want you seeing this and thinking the wrong thing.
>
> I'm certain you guys discussed his cover.

My stomach churned before I even clicked. The link opened to a trending post. An article. A flood of photos.

It's Declan in all his glory. Apparently, his little speech to me this morning had nothing to do with keeping away in order to keep me safe but being free to sit back and absorb the perks of being part of the mob. After all, what did I have in comparison to the VIP section of a high-end gentleman's club? Hand trembling, I zoom in on the grin the paparazzi captured like he hadn't spent last night deep inside of me, moaning my name over and over.

Tears well up in my eyes as I swipe through the photos. There's a knockout woman trailing her fingers across his broad shoulders. In another, her face is buried against his shoulder from behind. I keep going, swiping through the slideshow of my heartbreak.

She straddled his lap, lips pressed to his ear.

His arm is slung casually around her waist.

Fingers splayed around her hip—the same fingers that traced their way over every inch of my bare skin. Like they had every right to touch her.

Next, his hand grips her hip.

But it's the final photo that crushes me. Declan's head rests back against the Chesterfield. Her hand rests against the side of his jaw. He isn't pushing her away. No, instead, he's smiling up at her.

Eyes at half-mast, lips pursed. It's sexy as fuck, that smile.

I should know. It's the way he smiled at me last night every time he wanted inside my body.

Still gripping the phone, it's the fastest race of my life as I dash toward the bathroom. I barely make it in time to vomit everything in my stomach. Over and over my stomach heaves and I try to breathe through tears, snot, and bile. Once I finish, I collapse in the small space.

I need to finish this. Hands trembling, I scroll down until I see the headline.

Declan Conian Caught Blowing Off Steam After High-Stakes Business Meeting!

A gurgle of a sound is ripped from me. "Some meeting." I text Jon back.

KALIE:

You're sure this was today?

JON:

You didn't know?

I can't disillusion him. My heart pounds as hard as the tears that fall out of my eyes. Over and over, I hit refresh somehow hoping the images will disappear. That Sexy & Social will print a retraction. They'll admit it was a mistake. A misunderstanding.

Something.

Instead, I'm unable to string together a coherent thought other than the knowledge of one thing.

I need to get out of here.

I text Jon,

KALIE:

Who's my watchdog tonight?

JON:

Why?

KALIE:

I'm going for a run. If they can't keep up, that's not my problem.

Little dots flash then...

JON:

I'll let them know.

I run straight to the closet and head for the only place I can feel peace.

It's on the run I come up with the plan of what to do next.

By the time I get home, Declan is blowing up my phone like a malfunctioning gun.

DECLAN:

Hey, firebrand.

Sorry for running out this morning.

Meeting's done.

Want me to come over?

Kalie? You okay?

Out running?

Text me. Your phone is showing you're home.

Each ping assaults my phone one after another, each one hammering into me, making my anger surge as the betrayal from earlier screams through my veins. It takes everything in me to not reply but to plan.

As I shower, every heartbeat pounds like a war drum as I prepare for the true battle to occur—the one between me and Declan. I close my eyes to rinse my hair and the images pop into my mind. Her hands on his body, his hands on hers. The way he leaned back and his smile.

That fucking smile.

That smile that isn't just mine anymore.

It belongs to the world thanks to Sexy & Social's significant following.

Shaking the spray out of my face, I mutter, "At least the world doesn't know he played you, Kalie."

No, all I had to deal with is the brutality of his deception.

Bitter and enraged, I mutter aloud in the steamy room. "What does this show you that you are to him, Kalie?" I swallow a mouthful of water and spit it out just before the truth falls from my lips. "A ruse. A blind. Of course he took advantage of what was being offered."

Before I could drown in despair, I turn off the taps. Towel drying my hair, I slide into my worn Harvard Law T-shirt and sleep pants before I strip the bed. It might be midday, but I can't bear to be in the same space his scent lives in.

I can't let him be that close to me.

Not ever again.

Clenching my jaw, I make my way to my laundry room and drop in my contaminated sheets. After punching every button enough to strip the color off them when combined with the amount of bleach I pour in, I spin around to the linen closet and remake my bed.

Once that's done, I pull out all the cleaning supplies and scrub down every inch of my home. Anything and everything Declan could have touched, I scrub it within an inch of its life. From the top of the end table to the bottom of the stairwell, there isn't a surface left untouched.

I'm not just cleaning, I'm scrubbing his presence from my home.

Next, I do something I haven't felt the need to do since our new alarm system was installed after our home was invaded. I drop the bar into the sliding glass door.

Short of breaking a window or a door—which will have both the police and Hudson agents inside my home in under ten minutes—there's no way Declan's getting in if he comes over.

Hours later, I'm taking small sips of water. I'm exhausted, but I'm finally ready to confront him. I sit down on the bench in our hallway with nothing but the painted wall as my background. My hair is swept away from my face. He doesn't get to come back into my home. Not in any way.

Not again.

KALIE:

Fine. FaceTime if you're available.

DECLAN:

Whenever you're ready.

I press the video icon. It *bleep-bleeps* once. Twice. Then his gorgeous smiling face greets mine. That smile fades when concern takes over. "Firebrand—" he starts, but before he can finish, I jump in.

My voice is dead when I ask, "How was your meeting?"

"Good. We got a lot accomplished."

"So I saw."

His brow furrows. I'd prepared my text to him before I started this call. I send him the link to Sexy & Social. His face pales.

"You bastard," I say in the same monotone. I refuse to give this man a single moment of my heartache when he's already stolen a piece of my heart.

Declan exhales raggedly, words failing him until, with a hollow tremor, he finally manages, "It isn't what it looks like."

My chest tightens. I crave confrontation—a fight, a justification, even a sham denial. "All I get is a pathetic excuse? Wow. I guess you skipped the thinking on your feet class at law school too." His own words being flung back at him cause him to recoil. "I'm surprised you haven't been killed yet with your inability to think on your feet better than that."

His mouth opens and closes, but I shift into lawyer mode. I get my raging emotions under control so I eviscerate him for the right reasons.

"You claimed this morning you wanted to wait on us until this was done. Fact."

"Firebrand—"

I keep going. "You claimed you had a business meeting. Fact."

Despite my initial reticence about Declan, I'd never thought him anything but honorable. Wasn't I the stupid one. I tick off another box. "The 'meeting' occurred at a strip club. Fact."

"Kalie. You know my cover—"

I cut him off. "You were caught by the paparazzi. Fact." Before he can even attempt to wedge in some half-assed response, I continue, "You know, if just her hands were on you, I might believe this bullshit you're trying to shovel in my direction. But the fact your hands were on her? The fact—" I swallow hard so I can maintain the same icy courtroom armor I've worn for our entire call. "You gave her the same damn look you gave me last night? That's what we call slam dunk evidence."

"Slam dunk evidence of what?" His voice is raw and that ignites my fury.

"Of the fact last night meant nothing to you. Which is fine. That's on me to deal with."

His eyes widen, panic etching every line on his face. "No. Kalie. The pictures aren't—"

"Don't!" I choke out, each word laced with seething pain. "Don't you dare tell me it wasn't what I saw." Clenching my eyes shut to gather the fragments of my fading composure, I demand, "You have one chance. Why?"

He remains mute—exactly as I had feared. He stays still until I finally scream, "Say something!"

His eyes brim with sorrow and regret, nearly crushing me with their weight, but his next words drive the knife of betrayal deeper still. "I had to. I didn't have a choice."

All my heartbreak and anguish come out when I ask, "Why not let me go before demolishing me entirely by sleeping with me?"

A sound of mortal anguish escapes his lips. "What the hell does he have the right to be broken about?"

I don't realize I've spoken aloud until he's moaning my name, "Kalie. Firebrand. Please..."

My head whips sideways, as if I've taken a full slap to the face. Swallowing past the lump in my throat to respond, I open and close my lips, but nothing comes out. Not a sound.

I can tell my pain is washing over him despite the distance between us. Finally, a bitter laughter erupts from me, filling the air between us. "In my family, we believe nothing is worth more than a sacrifice for love. I just wish I wasn't the only one in love and wasn't anything more than the collateral damage you used on your path for revenge."

"No, Kalie. I lo—"

I cut him off. I don't want to hear the words I should have heard at any time but never because of Declan's desperation. "Life's about the damned choices we make, Declan. You picked the one that suits you. I hope you're fine living with that regret."

With that, I press *End*.

Emotionally drained, I mentally make a list of everything I need to do before I leave. Then, only then, will I allow myself to address Declan's betrayal. Then, when I feel safe enough, I'll crumble in the embrace of those who truly love me.

CHAPTER FORTY-THREE

Kalie

ONCE I REGAIN MY WITS, I HEAD UPSTAIRS TO MY OFFICE. THE first thing I do is request two weeks off. I abhor the feeling I'm abandoning my mother and the rest of my family at the start of our wedding season rush, but I can't stay here. I can't barricade myself in my home if Declan is going to be pounding at my door every single moment when he thinks he can break through my shell, nor can I leave if he's going to try to ambush me.

I keep it short and sweet, requesting leave for "an unexpected personal reason to begin immediately. I plan to have my laptop with me for any emergencies."

Within moments, my time off has been approved by Aunt Cassidy who writes, *Leave the laptop at home. Just take care of whatever you need to.* Since she CCs every member of the executive team, this opens the floodgate on a new wave of texts asking if I'm okay.

I'm obviously not.

I'm trying to figure out what to say when my mother replies with the news link to Sexy & Social in the family chat.

Enough said.

If I thought my phone blew up because of Declan before, it's nothing in comparison to the way texts are coming in fast and furious in our chat.

LAURA:

What the actual hell?

Aunt Ali, tell me this is BS.

MAMA:

Wish I could, sweetie.

LAURA:

I'm not reading this.

KALIE:

Do you want me to share how I reacted?

MAMA:

Your father and I are on our way.

ME:

LAURA:

Liam is furious.

AUNT CASS:

So's Caleb.

KALIE:

Tell them to get in line.

I feel so cheap.

At that, a bunch of protests, "NOs," and threats from my family erupt. I read them through a film of tears.

KALIE:

He took what he wanted and played me.

GRACE:

I swear if he comes to the house, I'm going to take off an actual body part.

AUNT EM:

Choice. Pinking shears or scissors?

AUNT CASS:

Like our book club, I'm going to ask, why choose?

VAL:

Own your smut, Aunt Cass.

REGGIE:

Have any other weapons of choice, Aunt Em?

AUNT EM:

MAMA:

For the love.

MAMA:

Look at your elders.

AUNT CORI:

Who are you calling elder?

AUNT HOLLY:

Exactly.

MAMA:

#lesigh

Can you keep threats vague enough I don't need to bleed bail money?

UNCLE PHIL:

Hell no. Let me have a go at him.

UNCLE JASON:

For once, I'm letting Phil off the leash.

AUNT CORI:

Say WHAT?!?!?!

AUNT HOLLY:

Whoa. Jason spoke in the chat.

LAURA:

This is epic.

GRACE:

Mark the date and time.

VAL:

This might require theme music.

REGGIE:

Angry girl playlist?

AUNT CORI:

Is there any other kind?

MAMA:

I give up. Fine. I want to tear his limbs off.

KALIE:

I love you all.

A flood of "I love you's" hit my phone within milliseconds of each other.

I can't reply. I'm too emotional. I carry my phone to my bedroom, tossing it on my mattress. It's time to get ready to leave. Declan can judge me all he wants—I know how to win, I know how to lose. But without respect or love to build off of, there's nothing worth fighting for. Nothing worth sticking around for. The pain isn't worth the agony.

I'm going to be gone for at least a few weeks to lick my wounds and recalibrate my world without the presence of a man who stormed into my life and left me standing here devastated. We were friends—at least I thought so. We had a solid foundation before he touched me with intent.

Clutching a running shirt to my breast, I bow my head. "How did we go from making love to him giving away parts of himself to random strangers?" I would have sworn he was like the other men at Hudson. A man like my father—a man of honor and integrity despite spending his life in the shadows.

A bitter laugh escapes. That was my first mistake. Thinking he was like any of them.

My second mistake was believing he gave me the parts of himself he'd never shared with anyone else.

I head into my closet and yank down one of my larger suitcases. Throwing clothes onto my bed, my mind is set on one goal—distance. I need to figure out how to get space and time to process the ruin Declan left in his wake without him knowing where I am or, worse, following me.

Considering he might have more burner phones than I do pairs of running sneakers, I want to make one thing explicitly clear. I text him one final time.

KALIE:

Don't contact me again. I'm done. We're done.

As I stuff my suitcase to the brim with clothes, my phone rings from where it lays. The sight of his name flashing on the screen causes a pulse of anxiety to shoot through me. There's no way I'm picking up. After his little speech this morning and our FaceTime, what more is there to say?

How's he going to explain to my heart what happened?

No, I can't hear his excuses. Not right now. If it's something important about my protection, he'll contact one of the agents or my father. If I have to hear his voice, it will crack open my chest and set all of my emotions loose.

I ignore the persistent ringing until it finally stops. My heart pounds in my chest, a mix of anger and hurt that I'm not sure I'll ever escape. Then, all at once, everything explodes. My phone, my door, and my heart.

I pray to God it isn't him. I'm not ready to face him. Not now, not yet. I inch my way to the door just as it swings open.

"Sweetheart," my mother greets me. Her eyes flick from the bag to my face, and she comes to a resolve in a single second. She beckons to someone in the hallway. "She's in here, Keene." Before I can so much as draw breath, my father is in the room, wrapping me in his arms.

"It's okay, sweetheart," he soothes.

I shake my head against his chest. "No. No, it's not."

"It will be," he reassures.

"Why would he hurt me like this, Dad?"

His arms tighten around me. "Because he's the same as I was. He's trying to keep you out of the line of fire to protect you."

"No, he's not. He's not you, Dad. He doesn't love me. He walked out of here this morning and said we needed to cool off until his case was through. Then, he went *there*." I spit the last word.

He pulls back slightly, his eyes searching my face. "He went where?"

"To a stripper, Dad. In public. Caught on camera." I scrub my face to wipe away wasted tears. "I guess I should be grateful it was caught, so I know what he's really like, huh?"

"Let me see."

My bitterness is tinged with the wetness of my tears. "It's not hard to find. Just go to Sexy & Social's site. Hope they haven't crashed with the number of hits."

Carefully, he probes, "What did he tell you before he went there?"

"That he had to go to a meeting. That he'd come back to me after this job is over."

His face is a stony mask before he finally says, "That's it?"

"Yes!"

"Nothing else?"

"Nothing! He didn't have to. I mean, obviously, he has other entertainment to keep him busy. He doesn't need me." I feel a fresh wave of tears threaten to overwhelm me.

My mother's hand falls to my shoulder. "Sweetheart, I didn't want to say this in the chat, but you know better than to trust what you see on those sites. You should talk to him."

Meeting her eyes, I tell her flatly, "I did."

Her lips part. No words escape. Her head swings in my father's direction. An uncomfortable silence descends on the room.

My father runs a frustrated hand through his hair. "You don't know the entire story."

"Then tell me!" I shout.

"I can't." My father's jaw clenches.

"Keene," my mother warns.

I'm too emotionally wrung out to care about the threat in her tone.

He sighs. "Where are you planning to go?"

"Away." The word is choked out. "I need to get away until I can face everyone and not break down."

My mother crouches down. "Why don't you come home tonight? Spend the night with us?"

Needing her more than I ever thought possible, I bury my head in my mother's shoulder and nod. Heartbreak isn't something you should go through without your people at your back.

My father gestures to the door. "Let's get you out of here."

Soon, I'm in the back of their car while my father secures my home. My mother sits beside me, cradling me next to her heart. It isn't long before my father has a quick word with my guards before he slides into the driver's seat.

I take note when they don't follow, but I don't have the energy to care. Not when my heart hurts as badly as it does.

I just wish I'd told them to keep Declan out to begin with.

CHAPTER FORTY-FOUR

THE SECOND I HEARD HER VOICE, I KNEW SOMETHING WAS WRONG.

The moment the web page opened, life as I prayed it could be was reduced to nothing but ashes.

I'm not certain who whipped out their cell this time, but of course, they couldn't snap a picture of the dead body on the floor. No. Instead, they sold Sexy & Social just enough of a scandal to publish about me.

Out of a one-hour meeting, someone captured the moment Nerissa whispers in my ear, grabbing my shoulder.

Her collapsing, using my body to remain upright as she gasped in pain.

Me grabbing hold so she didn't land on her ass in front of the very unexpected presence of Jack Marshall and look weak. Because weak would have got us killed.

Did it show later when the mother fucker kicked Chrissi's lifeless body aside before Jack ordered the body to be cleaned up? Instead of going for his fucking throat, like I wanted to, I had to restrain myself.

None of that ended up on Sexy & Social. Of course not. No, only the pictures of Nerissa's fake lap dance were front and center instead.

Now, due to my panic this morning, Kalie thinks she means less than nothing to me.

Pacing back and forth, I don't think. Don't take time to plan. Just drive from my condo to Kalie's like a man possessed, engine screaming. My heart slams so hard I'm certain it shakes my ribs as I take corners at a speed I shouldn't as I grip the steering wheel with one thought on repeat.

If I can just get to her—if she will just see me—she'll understand. She'll know I was telling the truth.

She'll believe me.

She has to.

When I pull up to her street, there's very little sign of life. Saying screw it to the security protocols I had put into place for me to see her, I drive directly into her driveway, taking note of the very prevalent agents in her driveway.

Dashing up her front porch, my movement sets her security lights ablaze, flooding the property in harsh, sterile white even as none of the interior lights glow.

No movement from inside.

I try ringing the bell, pressing my face up against her doorbell camera.

Nothing. Not a sound.

I try the handle. Try to slam my shoulder against the door. It won't budge. All the locks have been engaged. That's when it comes to me. The house is merely reflecting the owner's wishes.

Both are rejecting me.

My heart trembles in my chest. No. This can't be the way we end. "It's not possible."

A sick, hollow feeling rips through my gut at the thought, but I don't give it a chance to slow me down. I race around to the backyard like I have every other time I've snuck in through the back slider. When Kalie would be waiting on her couch drinking a glass of wine or tea after a long day.

Not tonight.

Tonight, everything is sealed tight. I try to jimmy open the sliders, only to glance down and find metal bars bracing the doors closed. Keeping the threats out.

Including me.

I stumble backward, hope diminishing every second inside me.

That's when I spot it.

Yes! There's a single light on inside on the second floor! She must be home! Deciding that making a spectacle of myself is absolutely justified in this instance, I race back around to the front. Leaping up to the porch, I shimmy up the Craftsman columns, not caring if the cops are called on me. Hell, at this point, my actions will just give me credence to the damn motherfuckers I still technically work for.

But when I get close enough to spy in her bedroom window, I fall to my knees against the roof. The room looks like a hurricane tore through it. Clothes are tossed every which way. "No," the moan escapes my mouth.

Crawling on my hands and knees to the next set of windows, I peek into her office. Her computer's gone. So's her favorite photo—the one of her family.

Part of me feels relief—she wasn't taken. The other part of me feels absolute fear. Where is she? It's obvious she's planning on leaving and taking her most cherished item—her family.

But she intends on leaving me behind.

"No! Kalie, no! Come on, firebrand! Please, please, let me in!" I sob. My hand hits the side of the window so hard I know I'm rattling the frame. My brain is calculating everything that happened at warp speed. I shout, "Please, trust me. It's not what you think!"

Nothing. No sound. No footsteps. No sign she's even there to listen—or that anyone is other than the agents below.

Terror coils tight in my chest.

Where is she? What is she doing? Is she barricaded alone in there, heart breaking because of a cover? Doesn't she understand?

"Don't judge me by those photos," I choke out. "Don't—don't judge us by one fucking lie. You know me better than that. Please, firebrand."

Still nothing.

I slide down from the extended roofline and make my way around the side of the house. I try every door and window again, praying for a miracle. Denied. Kitchen door—deadbolt. A peek in the window shows the alarm set. Any attempt to break in will trigger a massive onslaught arriving from Hudson's security team beyond the two in the driveway.

Running around to the garage places me directly in front of the agent's car. I bend down and try to lift the white door.

Nothing budges.

The two men step out of the car and watch. One blatantly has his camera out and is filming me.

I don't care.

Let Keene, Caleb, Jon, who the fuck ever get the show of their life. All I want is a chance to talk to Kalie face-to-face.

I continue to call Kalie's name until my throat turns raw, until my heart feels bruised from over exertion. I can't think properly. I know I'm not able to breathe properly. The one thing I know for certain is every second I can't give her a full explanation, I'm losing her. The second thing I know is there isn't a goddamn thing I can do to stop it.

Stumbling back to the front porch, I land on my ass. My head falls against the column. Maybe if I stay here, if I stay close enough, someone will take mercy on me. Either that or she'll feel my presence and return. "I love you. I swear to God, I love you. I would never betray you. Please —don't give up on me. Don't give up on us."

The two agents return to their car, obviously sensing I'm fresh out of entertainment and am not a threat to the house. Inside, Kalie's lights stay consistent. There's no trace of movement. I rest my head in my hands, feeling the night crush me from all sides.

I stay until the sun rises, chasing the last light in her house away. Until the sky turns the color of light blush meeting midnight.

Until I know there is nothing to gain by my being here.

She's gone.

I never got a chance to apologize. Then again, did I deserve it? What reassurance did I give to her that I would mean it?

On shaking legs, I drag myself back to my car. Sliding inside, I grip the steering wheel until my knuckles turn white from the lack of blood. That's when tears flood my eyes and I can't see. It takes a long while for me to blink them from my vision before I feel safe putting my car in gear.

After I regain a semblance of control, I drive away.

But I promise myself I'll be back because there's no way I'm giving up on her.

Or us.

Not ever.

CHAPTER FORTY-FIVE

THAT NIGHT, I DON'T KNOW HOW I MADE IT THROUGH. BUT I'M fairly certain it was being held by my father and being tucked in by my mother. Lying amid my old bedroom, it was an email I received from my mother in the middle of the night that both brought me comfort and shattered my composure.

My darling, Kalie.

I know exactly how you feel right now, and I won't push you to talk about it.

When you're ready, know that both your father and I are here for you. In my case, I'm not just able to speak as your mother, but as a woman who has endured a similar agony and heartbreak.

There was a time when I wasn't sure I'd ever find my way back to our life here. As you know, I was convinced I wouldn't. On my worst days, while you grew inside me, you became the only light that kept me going.

Let me be there for you when you need that voice to get you through the rough days. When you think you're ready to come home—like your godfather was for me.

No matter where you go, we'll always be your home. We'll be here waiting, armed with all the love you could ever need.

Now. Always. Forever.

I love you, my baby.

Love,

Mama

Her words touched something deep within me, temporarily stemming the bleed on my heart. Her words reminded me of the bond we share as a family and how I needed to not close mine out when they were obviously so stunned on my behalf.

I knew it wouldn't matter if it was the middle of the night. I pulled up our cousin's chat after several hours of locking away the initial agony and found the fortitude to FaceTime Grace, Laura, Nic, and my sisters. After some initial grumbles about the late hour, I explained to them what had happened with Declan. I also let them know I was trying to figure out where to go to get a break.

It was Nic who came up with the solution and set about getting the plan in motion. She dropped the call, promising, "I'll call him right now. I'm certain he's still on set."

Not long after, we wrapped with my solemn vow I'd have Mama let them know I was safe. All I really wanted was a few weeks of solitude to lick my wounds, but barring that, what I really needed was to pretend none of the last few months had ever occurred.

Not losing faith that Nic would get ahold of her brother, I forged ahead with my plans. Sometime after dawn, I called my godfather and his husband to stowaway on their corporate jet heading toward the Pacific Northwest that very day.

That's when I received a thumbs-up from Nic.

Pulling up a contact known only to a precious few, my heart calms and my hands cease trembling. Then, my cousin Peter's worldwide famous voice is a balm as it holds both fury and concern. "Kalie? What the fuck did this douche canoe do?"

Before I can answer, he asks me a second question. "More importantly, are you okay?" His loving concern in that simple question breaks the dam I built around my emotions. A raw sob escapes, one I hadn't permitted since I hung up on Declan or sent off emails tying my life in Connecticut to a close for the next few weeks.

I fight hard against another sob—until Peter's anxious tone at the lack of my speaking unravels my restraint completely. I press a palm hard against my chest, trying to push the anguish back inside long enough for my voice to emerge, but it fails. With the dam burst, I struggle past the relentless pain, unable to shift into the anger and betrayal I know should be roiling inside me. But I'm not there.

Not yet.

I barely catch a breath when Peter's voice and his words finally penetrate. "I'm on my way."

"No," I croak, my voice raspy with sorrow.

There is a pause, and then he asks, "Are you coming to me?"

"I want to, yes."

"I'm supposed to be filming in Banff for the next few weeks."

"All the better. Can you book my room under your name?" I plead, desperate to eliminate any trail for Declan to follow.

"Yes." He responds without a moment's hesitation. "What else do you need?"

"Mama and Dad will give me money. If I go through it, I won't be able to pull out any cash or use my cards."

He scoffs, "Please. As if that's an issue."

"Right." To me, Peter will always be my annoying younger cousin who attracts too many women for his own good—at least according to his mother, Aunt Corinna. To the rest of the world, he's celebrity chef Peter Freeman, poised to inherit billions.

"How are you getting here?"

"Uncle Ryan and Uncle Jared are flying to Singapore. They're refueling in Seattle," I explain.

"Good. Catch a ride with them. I'll meet you at the airport. Then we'll drive over the border, and you can vanish for a few weeks." Cheekily, because he knows it will bring a reluctant smile to my face, he asks, "Think I can get a ride on the plane home when you head back East?"

"S-sure." I inhale deeply, trying to keep the tears at bay, but it's not enough. Another sob rips through me, leaving room for an aching river of sorrow.

"Hey, no tears are to be shed for assholes," he admonishes softly.

"That's all he left me with, Pete," I confess.

After a brief silence, he growls, "When do you get in?"

I close my eyes and whisper, "Tomorrow."

"Good. Not enough time for me to fly my ass back home and commit homicide," he threatens half-heartedly.

"You don't even know what's going on."

His voice is as smooth as the Chantilly cream he often uses in his cooking. "But someone will text me soon enough, won't they? I'm certain of it."

I exhale a shaky breath. He's right—once my mother shares with her siblings where I'm headed and why, Peter will be provided with every detail they think can help mend my heart.

Before I give much more thought to logistics, Peter's next words remind me why I have to start healing from these sharp, brutal wounds. "You don't have to be anyone here, Kalie. Whatever you need—space, love, or even someone to let out all the hurt—I've got you."

My throat clenches tight, but I manage, "Thanks, Pete."

"Always. You'd do the same for me."

After the call ends, I stare down at my cell. My recently changed backdrop shows an image of me and Declan I took the night when I went selfie crazy on my couch. It was what I hoped was a glimpse into our future, even if it was only a sliver of our reality. In such a short time, I grew accustomed to having his presence in my life, yet now it feels completely wrong. A heavy weight settles over my chest.

Stop hesitating, I chide myself silently.

I switch the background to a cherished picture of me, Laura, and Grace from Laura's engagement party. With one last act of finality, I set an away message on my personal email explaining that I will be unreachable indefinitely, and then I move on to the most daunting of tasks.

Acceptance.

Though I had sworn to my godfather and his husband I'd nap in the rear cabin of the Lockwood Industries jet, my mind is relentlessly replaying the painful episode of seeing those photos. My fingers dig frantically into the soft, luxurious sheets, as if trying to anchor me against the storm raging inside.

Was I just someone to hold him tethered to this reality? Was I just a person to protect? Was sleeping with me a convenience?

I allow myself to replay every word of his whispered, honeyed lies and future promises. I let him weave a spell around me of fascination—leaving me open to whatever fabrication he wanted to ply me with. I shouldn't be surprised—he's a master. Then again, he never said anything to the contrary. It was me who convinced myself I meant something unique to him.

I was wrong.

A tear drips down my cheek despite my clenched jaw, a quiet betrayal of my personal strength. I let him in with a détente, but I have no one to blame for not resisting him. In the end, I still refuse to call love weak. After all, I stand as a testament to its strength and power.

Instead, I focus on the betrayal, the insult to who I am as a woman, a person.

How could he touch me as though I were a rare treasure when clearly his words, not mine, brought me to a place where I would assume he wanted more? Instead, I was treated as disposable—a fleeting placeholder in a life that was anything but genuine.

I listened to his journey—a story hard to endure because of how it affected him. I felt the first stirrings in my heart when I realized he was a man like my father—one who sought redemption for love—even if that person was a friend.

I wonder if he'd now walk the same path he did then with his investigation knowing how much he'd hurt someone who didn't deserve it. With the amount of time he'd been undercover, would he have become the man he swore he wouldn't?

My stomach churns violently. I yank the covers off and sprint to the tiny en suite before a surge of bile overtakes me, forcing me to heave over the sink. Gripping the counter, my eyes shut tight as I berate myself for believing Declan's words—merely seductive lies to drive us to the point his body would have the opportunity to thrust inside mine over and over as we made love. No, I correct myself bitterly, after he fucked me and I made love to him.

Because if a picture could speak a thousand words, then the image of him with a stripper all over him on Sexy & Social's website illuminates the fact I was nothing more than a fleeting moment. And I'm worth more than that.

Forcing myself upright, I realize that I'm not responsible for rebuilding the trust Declan shattered. He is, and not just with me. The only thing I'm responsible for is taking back control of what happens next in my life and moving on.

Digging deep for the strength of my amaryllis roots.

After rinsing my mouth and splashing cool water across my face, I crawl back into bed. As sleep slowly begins to claim me, a bittersweet truth unveils itself in the dark. I'm running toward something, just like I always do.

At the end of this finish line, there will be a new beginning where I choose to put myself first.

CHAPTER FORTY-SIX

TWO WEEKS LATER

Kalie

THE SECOND PETER AND I GET ON BOARD, MY GODFATHER HOLDS out his hand before making a "gimme" motion.

"Hand over all your electronic devices and dump them in this bag. This is your last chance for peace before you head back."

The bag in question is something I recognize as one of the little gadgets from my father's office—a black bag that will block all incoming and outgoing transmissions.

It also ensures tracking our return flight to New York City will be next to impossible unless someone hacks the flight's tracking devices. Knowing it's for my own good, I agree with only one caveat. "You get to tell Mama when we're expected to return."

His fingers fly before announcing, "Done."

His husband—my Uncle Ryan—steps forward to place a clean device in my hands. "For your inflight entertainment. It's a long flight."

Drawing my fingertip over the pristine screen, I raise a brow in challenge. "After two weeks of no outside communication, you're letting me have free rein? Dangerous." Though not quite as dangerous as what awaits me on the other end of this flight.

Picking up the scattered pieces of my soul and seeing if there's enough lifeblood to rejoin them back to my body.

He immediately squashes that inanity. "Do I look foolish?"

"No, never."

"We had the browser block app your cousin, Mike, developed installed. It's customizable so you won't be able to look up certain subject parameters. Damn thing has so much crypto protecting it, not even the best of Hudson can get hack through it."

"Baby bro's been busy," Peter says, impressed. "If that's the case, there's little chance of him tracking us before we get home."

Two words stand out beyond the mumbo jumbo he continues to prattle on about the kind of technology—home and him. Right now, both cause a rolling in different parts of my body—one in my head, the other in my heart. But because the "him" means the man who splintered my trust. The one man I let in.

Declan.

The last few weeks have allowed me to sort out my thoughts. I will always support what he was doing while undercover, despite becoming an inadvertent target. I don't despise him for that. No, the scars my heart bears stem from what he did to me personally—taking chunks from my heart and not cherishing it.

He didn't need to hurt me to get the job done, but by doing so, my heart hasn't healed from the devastating injury it sustained. Right now, I'm not certain it ever will be.

After two long weeks of considering everything that happened between us, I'm no more certain of what role Declan plays in my future than when I headed west to escape the twisted agony of knowing he was a few miles away. I'm still left with the burning question of what is better —being alive in his arms and sacrificing my soul or walking away knowing I love him.

Even now, on my way home, I can't answer that question despite his umpteen number of text messages begging, pleading with me to listen. To explain.

The part of me that gave my heart to him wonders, *Could there be an explanation?* The part of me that developed from roots of strength and courage silences her.

Often.

Understanding I'm still barely clutching onto the remaining threads of my soul, Uncle Jared plops down in the seat across from me to distract me with updates for Brave Steps Forward. Half listening, I think back to the clear air I inhaled as I ran for miles training in Banff, hoping and praying it would give me insight into my situation.

Every step I ran left me questioning every moment of our "relationship" —if it could be called that. I'm now stripped to the bone with more questions than answers. Why did he do this to me? How could he?

Peter reaches over and presses his hand against mine in silent support, giving me more strength to do what I know to be what I need right now —head home. The time I took to center myself again was necessary, but it's time to return to reality.

As the jet speeds up down the runway, I revisit the way my life has changed course over the last few months. How Declan changed the way I looked at myself, at him, so much. I not only accepted his reasons for rolling around in filth. I supported his reasons for vengeance. None of that shook my belief in who he was; in fact, it strengthened my resolve in the man beneath the public persona he had to wear. Declan appeared to appreciate the same sacred vow I did—family first.

I let him in and he imprinted himself indelibly into my pores, my heart, my very soul.

What soul there is left, I think in disgust.

There's just a flaw in my logic. Tragically, it's a catastrophic one.

Declan would have had to have considered my feelings the way I did his to not have hurt me the way he did that night.

As the jet hurls our small consortium from one coast to another, I stop trying to rationalize the damage that's already been caused. Over the last few weeks, I resolved my guilt about getting away—placing thousands of miles between us. Especially once I received his text telling me it was probably for the best.

But time and distance haven't mattered, so it's time to return home. Pain just follows you. If time and distance won't give my heart the break it so desperately needs to form a detachment from the man I fell too easily in love with, then it's time to stop shirking my responsibilities.

Still, my time away gave me one gift. It gave me a chance to develop an armor so when I inevitably run into him, I can function. By getting off the grid, it gave us a clean break. Let him return to working for my family while I...well, I'll do what I've been passionate about before—races, cases.

Declan thinks he knows who I am, but I'm stronger than even he has witnessed.

Still, in the part of me that hasn't quite scabbed over, it hurts to know I fell in love with a man who doesn't love me back. Tears leak from my eyes as I stare blindly into the sun as we reach cruising altitude. All that matters is that it's over.

A discreet flight attendant comes by to ask if I need anything. I shake my head wordlessly. What could she bring me, anyway? Unless my uncles somehow managed to figure out a way to replace emotions, I don't need anything. I don't want anything.

Right now, I'm not certain I ever will again.

Desperate for something to do, I tug the tablet toward me and pull up a national news site. A bitter laugh erupts when the lead headline shows the latest speaker at the Brookings Institute is the former Director of the National Counterterrorism Center—the same woman who spoke at my law school graduation.

The first place I laid eyes on Declan.

I don't know what it was about him that struck me so hard he never quite left my subconscious. What I do know is I have to do everything possible to erase him now so my heart can heal from the blow he just dealt it.

The plane bumps through some turbulence, but my stomach doesn't feel the funny twist it normally would. How can it when my heart has stopped beating inside my chest? I touch my fingers to the side of my neck to make sure I haven't slipped into some sort of catatonic stasis. Nope. There it is. Proof of life that I'm still alive.

Too bad I just don't feel it.

The repetitive thud of my pulse mocks me, reminding me I still have to endure the memory of what I saw for days? Weeks? Years? I'm not certain how long it takes for a heart to heal from a betrayal this strong, to be honest.

Despite the one hiccup, the air taking us back to the East Coast devolves into a mostly smooth glide through the sky. That alone should reassure me that life will go on. Instead, it just reiterates the very simple fact that a small glitch can cause this flying air trap to plummet to the ground at any second.

Right along with the shredded remains of my heart.

As we approach our final destination, the captain requests that we buckle up. Moments later, the plane glides into a smooth landing, but my head is still up in the clouds. Being back on terra firma doesn't mean anything more other than I can no longer escape the truth as my tablet goes crazy.

Declan is trending in the news. Again. Another one of his cases is about to come before a judge.

Good to see he's back to work. Nothing breaks his stride.

Not even losing me.

I click on one of them before I can stop myself. Funny, for a man who has been texting me non-stop for the last two weeks, he doesn't look any worse for the wear. In fact, there are an awful lot of shots to prove him as the professional liar I know him to be. The best feeling in the world is falling in love. The worst? Watching it unravel before your eyes, not knowing what you did to precipitate it.

If there was something you could have done differently.

Slamming the device into the open seat next to me, Peter looks up from the contract he's been reading. "You okay?"

The firming of my lips is answer enough. His hand captures my hand beneath his. "I got you, Kalie."

Tears prick my eyes as I stare into his familiar golden eyes. "I'm so grateful you were there for me."

"I hope to God you'll never have to do this for me. Falling in love sucks."

At his raw honesty, I scoff. "That's the truth."

"I think I'll put that off for the foreseeable future, thanks."

"Still, if you ever do, I've got your back."

Once we're safe to remove our seatbelts, he sweeps me into his arms for a hug. "I know."

Sniffling into his shoulder, I choke out, "Thank you." For a few minutes, nobody says anything. Finally, Uncle Jared murmurs, "If we're going to be on time tonight, we need to get going."

Right. The Fair Harvard Reunion. A party I've not missed since I graduated Harvard Law.

Snatching my carry-on with one hand, Peter guides me off the plane and into the waiting car. "Let's get out of here before I'm spotted."

I follow without protest. Once, I would have thrown out some snarky comment about the size of his ego matching the size of his dick—lacking. But right now, I don't have the energy to jump into going shot for shot with someone I'm as close with as a brother.

Once we're on the way toward Tribeca, my cousin demands, "Now that we're alone, do you think Declan is going to show up for the party tonight?"

I shake my head no.

His brow skyrockets. "You really think he's done with you?"

"No. I'm certain he's going to try to approach me there."

"Even if it means blowing his cover?"

I nod. Then I hold out the phone to show him Declan's latest message that appeared the moment I turned my phone back on.

> DECLAN:
>
> I'm coming for you, my firebrand. I won't let you go.

Peter doesn't say another word until we're safely ensconced in my parents' Tribeca condo. I tense, knowing what he's going to ask—knowing I've run out of time.

"This has gone on long enough. Are you in love with Declan?"

Collapsing on the sofa, I hug a pillow to my chest. Then I take a deep breath and answer him.

CHAPTER FORTY-SEVEN

Kalie

PETER AND I GO SILENT WHEN WE HEAR THE SQUEAK FROM THE front door opening. There's a murmur of voices before the door closes and a familiar tapping of heeled shoes on wood floors has my heart thundering in my chest. Surging to my feet, I bolt off the couch before Peter can shift to a standing position.

The warmth of my mother's arms surrounds me the second our bodies collide. I bury my head into her shoulder and inhale her familiar scents.

For long moments we stand like that. Having her here restores, if not my heart, my flailing spirit.

Even knowing she was coming so she and I could be dressed by my Aunt Emily for tonight's gala, where I'll likely have to confront Declan in a room filled with Harvard's elite, doesn't dampen the pleasure of having her arms around me as I nurse my broken heart.

She pulls back far enough to cup my cheeks before tsking me. "If your aunt has to do last-minute alterations on your dress because you've lost weight, she's going to lose her mind."

A ghost of a smile crosses my face. "She'll look at it as a challenge, just like she does when she has to fit models during Fashion Week."

My mother caresses my cheekbone with her thumb. "Too true." Over my shoulder, she meets Peter's eyes. Extending her hand to beckon him closer, she welcomes him warmly before offering in mock disgust, "If only you would stop being as gorgeous as your parents, maybe you wouldn't be followed by every member of the paparazzi. It's criminal to be this handsome."

Peter barks out a laugh before smacking a loud kiss on her cheek. "Good to see you too, Aunt Ali. How are my folks?"

She slaps him on his shoulder. "I hope you plan on sticking around long enough to find out, you reprobate."

He tugs me against his side. "It depends on if this one takes me out for real food after this snooty ass party we're all going to."

My mother rolls her eyes. "You're a world-famous chef, yet your food choice is deplorable—just like your father. This proves there are some things genetics wins out over. After every formal event, your father wants nachos. To this day, your mother indulges him."

Peter's eyes light up at the thought of a hot, cheesy mess. Before my mother can shoot him down, my phone pings with an incoming text. My body stiffens. Since that night two weeks ago, I assigned Declan his own ringtone so I'd know who was trying to contact me.

Mama frowns at the expression on my face. "Do I even need to hazard a guess at who that might be?"

I don't bother answering. Instead, I unlock my phone. I'd long turned off the feature that would alert Declan I was reading his text messages. I read his latest attempt and pretend to feel nothing, but what I feel is so enormous I can't prevent the solitary tear that tracks down my cheek.

> DECLAN:
>
> Kalie, I swear to you, it wasn't what it looked like.
>
> Just five minutes.
>
> Tonight. I'll explain everything. I promise.

Peter pulls my phone out of my hand. After scanning the message, he murmurs, "I guess it's a good thing we're going to an event where you'll be surrounded by people who won't let him near you."

My mother worries her lower lip in her teeth and I know why.

It's because she knows—as do I—that Declan, despite his present nefarious clients, is a Harvard Law graduate. He received the same invitation we did. He has every right to attend the reunion, just as we do.

He risks his cover being blown—a cover I almost blew apart when I slammed my fist into his face three months ago—just for the chance to set the record straight.

CHAPTER FORTY-EIGHT

After the makeup artist finishes painting my lower lip a deep crimson shade, I wait patiently while my face is spritzed with makeup setter. Next to me, my mother is in her final stages of transformation. Checking out my appearance, I nod, accepting the woman in the reflection.

"I just want to say this before the makeup people leave."

I brace, causing my mother to chuckle as she comes up behind me. "You are stronger than you are beautiful." My mother's hands land on my shoulders.

I turn around to face her. "I come by it naturally."

Her face softens in the same manner it used to whenever she used to tell me stories about her childhood, her escape from her personal nightmare, and finding and falling for my father. Speaking of which, "Where's Dad?"

She mumbles something I can't quite understand. "Excuse me?"

Her lips curve upward. "He's on his way."

My jaw flops open. "He's going to be late to the Fair Harvard Reunion?"

Her brow raises gracefully. "There are some things more important than a party."

"Yes. You," I retort firmly, indignant on my mother's behalf.

She doesn't appear to be half as disturbed as I am. Instead, she pats my cheek. "He promised to meet us there."

I'm still sputtering when she blithely continues, "I hope you don't mind sharing your 'date' long enough to get inside the Plaza."

The idea of sharing Peter causes my lips to curve as I think about the paparazzi shooting pictures of him with multiple women—almost always family—hanging off both arms in the past. *What's one more night?* I think with a touch of amusement. " Of course not, Mama,"

"Good. With the dress Em designed, I need to wear these killer heels or I'm going to trip in this dress." Our eyes connect and we burst into laughter.

Amid the moment of levity, Declan's ringtone interrupts us. Mama curses. "If I didn't know your father as well as I do, I'd swear the man has someone watching us. That foolish asshole is interrupting us at all our fun parts today."

Instead of comforting me, her words send a shiver of fear down my spine. "You don't think Dad has the place rigged, do you?"

Mama picks up my phone, reads the messages, before shaking her head confidently. "No. I think your young man—"

Bitterly, I interrupt, "He's not exclusively mine, remember?"

Her hand runs up my back, smoothing away the harsh edges. "Apparently *Declan* is determined you know he's ready to crawl to get back in your good graces." She hands me my phone.

Warily, I take it from her.

> DECLAN:
>
> I mean it, Kalie.
>
> I need you to know I'm not hiding how I feel about you.
>
> I'll crawl across that damn ballroom floor on my knees if that's what it takes to get five minutes with you.

"I don't think he's dramatizing his intentions, sweetheart. Prepare yourself." She wraps an arm around me until I'm steady enough to get ready.

CHAPTER FORTY-NINE

Kalie

Aunt Emily explodes into the room with two garment bags over her shoulders. Handing one to my mother, she sends her off to try it on before forcing Peter to act as a hook so she can unzip the bag long enough to display the masterpiece she'd created for me.

The second it pops into view, tears prick my eyes. I reach out for her hand and whisper, "Aunt Em, it's perfect."

She slides an arm around my waist and squeezes. "That's you, Kalie. I couldn't be more proud of the woman you've become than if you were one of my own."

I bury my head into her mass of curls and breathe deeply as the compliment washes over me. Pride is one of the cornerstones of our family benchmarks, much more so than wealth and fame.

Months ago, Aunt Em first asked me what I wanted my dress to convey as I descended the steps, knowing every eye would be on me. I rolled my eyes at her and said, "You're the designer. You tell me."

She took my hands in hers, explaining how the process worked. "You're my muse, Kalie. I'll design a dress that I feel represents you, but I need to know what message you want to send to the people in that room."

Just like that, the words popped into my head. One by one, I listed them for her. Instead of writing them down, as I expected, she leaned back in her chaise lounge and began sketching. Now, I was seeing the words alive because I gave them to her. I recall them as I shared them: beauty, blessed, determined, fearless, proud.

Then, a month ago, I added one more.

As I circle around my cousin, I find the dress far exceeds any expectations I ever could have. "I may be a bit biased, but this may be your most beautiful creation yet, Aunt Em."

She critically eyes the plunging neckline to the cinched waist to the multilayered tulle skirt, giving the impression of Harvard crimson even if the actual layers were of blood red and black. The high-low cut will show off my legs as I descend the stairs while giving me ease of movement around the dance floor.

Peter jokes, "I'm going to have to fend off the Secretaries of Defense and State, aren't I?"

I roll my eyes even as Aunt Em chortles. Just as I'm about to retort, my phone pings again. *Him.*

Peter's jaw tightens. "Do you want me to...?"

I shake my head. Staring at the dress, it's impossible for me now to not acknowledge the last criteria I asked Aunt Em to add—an amaryllis. It's in the tulle layers of the skirt, so carefully disguised that few would know it's there. But the few who do are the people closest to my heart, those who are bleeding right alongside me right now as I mentally shore myself up for tonight's events.

DECLAN:

You'll be the only woman in the room tonight.

I'll try not to whisk you away, but no promises.

You're mine.

If that was truly the case. My eyes sought out the last element I asked Aunt Em to add to the dress knowing I was feeling it for Declan.

Love.

Now seeing our family's symbol on the dress when my heart is cracked wide open hurts. I thought we were growing something together despite the agony of what he'd endured. My feeling grew, consuming me over the course of the month we were together.

Then he threw me away.

I couldn't, wouldn't do that to Aunt Em's exquisite creation. After all, love, even rejected, is a gift. My soul might feel like the world is ending, but my head knows it will persevere.

Eventually.

Even if tonight it might be damned knowing he's so close in a room filled with almost a thousand people.

CHAPTER FIFTY

As Aunt Em helps me dress, I recall the nights Declan and I spent getting to know one another.

We went from strangers to enemies to friends to...more.

My heart thuds in my chest so hard I'm certain it must be visible in the plunging V of the dress I'm in. Over the last two weeks, I've been trying to close the gap Declan punched in my chest first by pushing me away after we made love, then by being photographed with that stripper.

"Kalie," Aunt Em reprimands me. I glance at her reflection in the mirror. "Peter and your mother are already downstairs. Are you ready? You're running late."

"Sorry, Aunt Em." I smooth the fine material of my dress down and turn from the mirror to face her.

Something of my emotions must show on my face because hers softens. "The only thing you should be 'sorry' for is not letting us in when we knew you needed us. You were out of touch for two weeks too long, sweetheart."

She draws me into a hug. When she pulls away, her hands fall to my shoulders. "Don't make that mistake again, Kalie. Not with Declan. Not with anyone."

Shaking my head, I murmur, "I was willing to risk everything to stand up for him, be with him."

"And a photo changed that?" she questions.

"What changed was the fact he walked out on me. He didn't protect us by telling me something like that could be a possibility."

"Kalie, do you love him?"

"It isn't that I love him, Aunt Em. It's that I don't know how to stop." I make my way to the door, determined to get through tonight.

After that, I don't know what comes next.

CHAPTER FIFTY-ONE

Kalie

THE BALLROOM AT THE PLAZA HOTEL GLITTERS AS IF IT HAS BEEN dressed in formal wear—much like the attendees. Some years, I think the party organizers plan it that way. Holding on to Peter's arm, we make our way down the grand staircase after our names have been announced to the room at large, after Uncle Jared and Uncle Ryan, then my parents.

Every year since I became a graduate and officially received my invitation, I do a little happy dance inside knowing I'm attending the Fair Harvard Annual Reunion. There are faces in the crowd that people see on the news because they're former presidents, members of Congress, or military officers of such high rank that their dress uniforms look like they're wearing tiny, jumbled flags.

Still, it gives me a thrill to hear my name, "Katherine Laura Marshall, Harvard Law Class of 2018. Amaryllis Events. Escorted by Peter Freeman."

Partway down the stairs, my parents pause. They both turn their heads and beam up at me. Their smiles aren't because I followed in my father's footsteps and attended his alma mater. Nor are their smiles because of the fortitude it took me to get through law school. Tonight, their smiles are because I had the strength to show up.

I descend the stairs, my head held high. When we make it to the bottom, Uncle Jared stops a waiter who is carrying a tray of champagne. After getting a glass for everyone, he lifts his in a toast. "Thank you, Kalie. Tonight, you made me feel a couple of decades younger."

I grin. "What a lovely compliment, Uncle Jared. But nobody is intending on blowing anyone off tonight the way Mama did Daddy."

Uncle Ryan snickers and my father groans even as my mother laughs. Peter frowns. "I don't get it."

My mother takes pity on him and explains that her first time attending the party wasn't with my father but with Jared because Ryan was traveling. At the time, my father was less than her favorite person and Uncle Colby, his father, recognized it instantly.

Peter, never one to not toss crap at a family member, drawls, "So, Uncle Keene, you mean my dad was tossing woo at Aunt Ali and you let your famous temper get in the way?"

"Again," I tack on before my father can say anything. "The word missed in that statement is again."

My father takes a sip of his own drink before tugging my mother close to his side. "Listen, your father had eyes for no one but your mother. Your aunt was using him to keep me from sweeping her off her feet." His eyes narrow at Jared. "Come to think of it, you were involved with the great nacho debacle that night as well."

Peter perks up. "Nachos? There were nachos involved? Hell, why didn't anyone say anything."

My mother rolls her eyes. "Like your uncle implied, same genetics, different decade."

Just as I'm about to retort, another announcement is made. "Declan Sean Conian. Harvard Law, Class of 2010." There's a pause before the emcee slides the card into the champagne bucket, where he's placing all the invitations.

For that precious moment, my father tenses, and then his shoulders relax imperceptibly. He mutters, "If he'd have announced he was working for Hudson, I would have had to have killed him."

And if he announced he was a mob lawyer, then what? The thought causes a bubble of hysterical laughter to escape. Instead of saying who he worked for, Declan chose not to answer what is often the most crucial question when attending the Fair Harvard Annual Reunion—your employer.

As he descends the steps, his eyes lock onto mine. They don't leave even for a second. Peter steps closer and wraps his arm around my waist. I lean into his side, appreciating the support he offers. Declan eyes remain laser focused on our group before an eager waiter blocks his line of sight.

"Now would be an excellent time to mingle," my mother encourages.

I should have known she would have anticipated this and had a plan in place. I swallow the last of the champagne and pass it over. "Good idea."

Over the next hour, our small group mingles with friends and clients from Hudson as well as Amaryllis Events. Yet...I still feel like I'm being watched. Every few minutes, I turn around, expecting to find Declan.

"Do you really think he'll approach you here?" Peter asks me when we have a moment alone in the crowd.

"I don't know." I truly don't. He could be here undercover or he could be here for other reasons, none of which has anything to do with me.

That's when a hand brushes my elbow. Peter's eyes narrow and he practically snarls at the person behind me. Since this isn't the first time in the last hour I've seen that expression on his face as I've been approached by numerous leaches, I expect one more. I turn and find it so much worse.

I'm face-to-face with Declan.

His lips murmur, "Firebrand."

Before I can find the right words, Pete mutters, "I'm going to get your dad before I kill this guy here and now. Don't move, Kalie."

Seconds later, we're alone in the middle of the crowd.

I study him much the same way I imagine he's doing me. The other men in the room, with maybe the exception of my cousin, should cry at the way he looks so good in a tuxedo. The way it fits over his broad shoulders and nips in at his waist.

A waist I've traced with my hands, my mouth. Begrudgingly, I admit, "You look nice."

"You look exquisite, Kalie." He lifts my wrist to his lips and presses a kiss there.

I jerk my wrist away and glance around. "Are you insane?"

"It's over, firebrand. That's why I came tonight," he explains.

My curiosity gets the better of me. "What do you mean, 'it's over'?"

He steps closer, his voice dropping to a whisper before he shares, "The Feds took down the Tiberis. They're in the process of rounding up the remaining Byrnes."

I can't hide the relief that flows through my soul, knowing he'll be safe. Still, I step back. My voice is cool when I say, "Congratulations. Job well done."

His brows crease into a *V*. "Kalie, I came back to your house the moment I could the night you last FaceTimed me."

My heart thunders in my chest when I hear him refer to our night together as that. I affect a diffident expression. "I wasn't there."

"I know. I know you left. That was probably for the best. It freed me up to focus on doing my job."

"Did it?" *I fell in love with this sanctimonious ass?* The thought flits through my brain. Before I do something stupid like smack him in the face, I snatch up a glass of champagne and sip it.

Declan's earnest, I'll give him that. He cups my cheek. "I meant what I said that night, Kalie."

"Which part?"

"The part where I told you I'd come back for you." His voice rings with sincerity.

My mouth falls open. *Is he really this clueless?* The problem wasn't his job or the amount of time it took him away from me, but that he broke my trust. I'm about to blast him when he steps forward and stares down into my eyes. "I kept texting you because I wanted you to know I was thinking of you. I didn't beg you to come home the way I wanted to because I didn't want you getting caught in the crossfire."

My eyes close. It would be easy, too easy, to fall back into his waiting arms. I step back again.

He follows.

Then I give him the harsh truth. "It wasn't the danger that drove me away, Declan. You broke me. That day, you decided my heart wasn't worth caring for."

His face pales. "No. I mean, it was. I mean, I didn't intend…"

"Whether or not you intended to, that's what you did. Frankly, your argument sucks. You're predicating your whole case on two main arguments—the first is that I'd be waiting when you came crawling back. The second being I'd be willing to forgive you for your mighty list of transgressions since it was for the greater good. Right?"

"I was hoping the news would…"

"What? Make me so happy for you that it would make me want to talk with you?" I scoff. "Go back to law school, counselor. I think you've spent too long outside of a courtroom."

Spinning, I'm about to make my grand exit when his hand clasps my wrist. I twist around and glare at him. My frustration boils over. "What, Declan?"

"Is there really no hope for us, firebrand?" The rasp of his voice strikes a deep chord inside of me.

"I deserve more than to be ambushed, Declan. I deserve to be wooed all over again. I expect you to earn back my trust. Then I'll decide what happens next."

With that, I surge blindly into the crowd in an attempt to find Peter or my parents.

A few minutes later, I wish wholeheartedly I'd stayed and argued with Declan when another man approaches. Despite the fact that he's well-dressed and has a clean shave. His eyes are hard and cold when he slams against my chest.

"Apologies," he says smoothly. "Your husband sent us to bring you to him. Urgent matter."

I stiffen, automatically retreating. "I don't have a husband."

The stranger smiles. "My mistake."

Another man appears at my back. I barely notice until it's too late. Something cold presses in between the boning of my dress. Not a hand.

A knife.

"Don't make a scene," the first man murmurs, that same smile never leaving his face. "You want the press catching this? Photos of your death in a room where your daddy couldn't do a damn thing about this?"

My heart beats faster. "You're making a mistake."

"No, sweetheart," he says. "Dec did. Now, let's go."

They flank me—one gripping my elbow, the other behind me. Together, I'm unwillingly guided toward a shadowed exit—a side door near the caterers' hallway. The music keeps playing. Chatter rings out behind me.

No one notices.

Not yet.

As we pass through a dim service corridor, my heels scuff the tile. "If you hurt me—"

"Oh, we won't hurt you," the first man says cheerfully. "Not until he makes us."

"You're bait, darling," the second man adds, pressing the knife tighter to my side.

I try to memorize every corner, every door, every turn they make, hoping to be able to run back to safety. That is until the third man shows up.

"You should've kept your hands to yourself. Jack said you were never supposed to be part of this. But Dec made you part of it. That makes you his weakness and we plan on exploiting that."

A black van waits just outside the door. My hand brushes the amaryllis in my skirt. I squeeze it firmly. With a flash of bravery, I hiss out, "I'm not afraid of you."

The man holding the knife leans in close, breath hot against my ear. "Good," he says. "Fear's boring. But pain? Pain always gets his attention. At least it did that night at Velvet Vice."

Then, I'm tossed inside the van. Two of the three men jump into the back, sealing the darkness in.

Before we pull away from the curb, I feel the first lick of pain as one of their feet lands on my ribs.

I just hope the transmitter Aunt Em sews into all our formal clothes for just this reason is setting my father's receiver off like crazy.

CHAPTER FIFTY-TWO

DECLAN

Leaning against the balustrade overlooking the ballroom, my eyes scan the crowd waiting to be announced before they descend to the party. My eyes constantly seek her out. She's a beacon amid the crowd with her long dark locks carelessly swept up and a neckline plunging so deep, it's a wonder her dress is managing to hold in her ample cleavage.

More than one man has admired her, but she's oblivious to it. Then there's her escort—the infamous Peter Freeman. If I didn't know the man was her cousin, I'd be ready to commit murder at her being so at ease on his arm.

Still, my heart clenches at her radiance. I'm not certain what's brighter—the crystal chandeliers or her effervescent laugh. I can't prevent the smile that graces my lips as I watch her. Kalie is always beautiful, but when she smiles, it reminds me of how much brighter she has made my life.

The emcee announces her uncle, Jared Dalton—partner at Watson, Rubenstein, and Dalton—escorted by his husband, Ryan Lockwood. Then, he announces Keene, escorted by Alison.

Finally, I hear the words that take me back to the beginning of our journey, through the time we spent together, bringing us to where we are now.

"Katherine Laura Marshall, Harvard Law Class of 2018. Amaryllis Events. Escorted by Peter Freeman."

Kalie descends the steps confidently, my smile disintegrating when I recognize how carelessly I treated her. I was a fool not to fall on my knees begging for her forgiveness for my idiocy in trying to subdue my feelings before I ever left her home that morning. I should have let her know long before then about the intricacies of my cover—including the chop shop and meetings at Velvet Vice.

I should have given her a choice, and by failing to do so, I may have self-destructed the only thing that matters—our love. With that knowledge, I make my way over and hand my invitation to the announcer. He glances down, offering me a small frown. "Sir, you didn't indicate any employment."

"I know." I don't offer him any more or any less. Half the people in the room who haven't announced their employment are former presidents or heads of agencies who received boisterous rounds of applause. I won't receive the same, but many in the room will wonder if I'm a part of the intelligence community or if I'm in between jobs.

Right now, it might be a crap shoot if they're right.

He lifts his microphone to his lips before proclaiming, "Declan Sean Conian. Harvard Law, Class of 2010." He pauses a moment before sliding the card into the champagne bucket, where he's placing all the invitations. "Be cautious descending the stairs, Mr. Conian. Welcome to the Fair Harvard Annual Reunion."

"Thank you."

I find her eyes on me as I descend the steps. Then Keene mutters something, making me wish I had enhanced hearing, as her family chuckles before moving off in the opposite direction I'm in.

For the next hour or so, I trail her at a distance. I come close to ripping the eyeballs out of a few men who can't seem to meet her eyes instead of her plunging décolletage. When they manage to look away and meet my feral glare, they falter before stammering something—likely incoherent— and shuffling away.

That's right, fuckers. Get the hell away from her. She's taken.

After a while, she and her cousin separate from the rest of their group and I decide to make my approach. He tags me first. The second he does, his lip curls. I find it amusing he thinks it will have the same effect on me as it has on the other twenty or so men who have approached Kalie.

I let my fingertips graze against her elbow. When she turns around, the world stills.

Her dark red lips part as she sucks in a gasp of air. She must steal mine because I can't quite get my lungs to work. Then my brain reminds my organs to work. She pales even as I reach out and murmur, "Firebrand."

Peter mutters, "I'm going to get your dad before I kill this guy here and now. Don't move, Kalie." There must be a god because I'll take the small favor of my impending death if it means we're alone in the middle of the swarming crowd.

Up close, her dress is a work of art. Jeweled straps lead into a satin bodice with a black overlay that turns the sharp red into Harvard crimson. Her skirt isn't crimson as it appears from a distance, but a multitude of layers that reflect again the depth of not only the dress but the woman wearing it. I open my mouth to compliment her, but she beats me to it. "You look nice."

"You look exquisite, Kalie." Reaching out, I lift her wrist to my lips. I need to feel the pulse of her heart against my lips since the location I truly want to place them might be visible, but would be utterly scandalous to this crowd.

She jerks her wrist back before hissing, "Are you insane?"

Instead of answering the question about my sanity—since the fact I was a damn idiot about how I treated her is clear evidence I wasn't, I lean in to share with her the information I haven't even told Keene yet. "It's over, firebrand. That's why I came tonight."

While I was sitting at home, staring at the Fair Harvard invitation, knowing exactly where Kalie would be, I received a call from Ace. He informed me, "We swept up the rest of the Tiberis. Sal is back in jail after singing like a canary. You know he was at Velvet Vice the night you gave me the intel, and we raided it."

"I do." Fortunately, the team found Nerissa and immediately took her testimony before arranging witness protection, so she'll be around to testify in a few years. Her full story, shared with me by Holder, is nothing less than heartbreaking. I just hope she's able to reunite with the people who matter most to her.

Maybe someday.

"As for the Irish, Paul, James, and Thomas Byrne have all been taken into custody."

"And Marshall?" I asked. "What about him?"

"They're on their way to get him right now," he crowed. "It's over, Dec! You did it!"

Kalie drags me back to the present. "What do you mean, 'it's over'?"

My voice drops to a bare whisper as I brush my lips against her ear. "The Feds took down the Tiberis. They're in the process of rounding up the remaining Byrnes."

I should have known better. Kalie isn't the type of woman to have had a normal reaction. Instead of her body sagging in relief, she takes a step back and offers me congratulations on a job well done.

I inform her that I came to her the night we FaceTimed. Her cool, "I wasn't there," churns up acid in my stomach.

"I know. I know you left. That was probably for the best. It freed me up to focus on doing my job."

"Did it?"

Warning bells go off in my head. Still, I need her to know the truth. Daring much more than I should, I cup her cheek. "I meant what I said that night, Kalie."

"Which part?"

"The part where I told you I'd come back for you."

He cups my cheek. "I meant what I said that night, Kalie."

"Which part?"

"I kept texting you because I wanted you to know I was thinking of you. I didn't beg you to come home the way I wanted to because I didn't want you getting caught in the crossfire."

She moves further away. I step closer.

That's when she hits me with a reality check. "It wasn't the danger that drove me away, Declan. You broke me. That day, you decided my heart wasn't worth caring for."

I feel the blood leave my face. "No. I mean, that's not what I meant..."

"Whether or not you intended to, that's what you did. Frankly, your argument sucks. You're predicating your whole case on two main arguments—the first is that I'd be waiting when you came crawling back. The second being I'd be willing to forgive you for your mighty list of transgressions since it was for the greater good. Right?"

"I was hoping the news would..."

"What? Make me so happy for you that it would make me want to talk with you?" Bitterness is evident in every word she flings at me. "Go back to law school, counselor. I think you've spent too long outside of a courtroom."

I stop her just before she storms off. My chest is heaving. Her eyes are the color of the deepest part of the sea. "What, Declan?"

"Is there really no hope for us, firebrand?"

"I deserve more than to be ambushed, Declan. I deserve to be wooed all over again. I expect you to earn back my trust. Then I'll decide what happens next."

When she says that, I know I'll do whatever it takes to earn back her trust. Even if that means loving her from afar.

I watch her as she walks away, searching for her cousin or parents. I cringe when she's stopped by—not a shock—another man. This time though, she stiffens when another man approaches her from behind.

That's when I notice the glint caused by the chandelier off the object in his hand.

The hair on the back of my neck stands up. My heart skips a beat as panic slides through my veins, fast and furious. I take my eyes off her for a second as I scan the room for Keene, her uncles, her cousin, but I can't spot any of them.

When I turn my head back to where I last saw her, she's no longer there. Neither are the two men. The sudden realization has me on high alert. Where is she?

My instincts scream something is wrong.

Immediately, I begin pushing through the crowd, moving quickly. I finally lay eyes on her cousin, who is holding court with a gaggle of women. His smile falters and he immediately excuses himself. We meet at the edge of the buffet table. "Have you seen her?"

"The last time I saw her, she was with you," Peter snarls.

Seconds later, we're joined by Keene, who is holding his phone out like it's a tracking device. He jerks up his chin. "She's outside."

My stomach drops. "She...she was just here."

His voice is lower, clipped. "Now, she's moving."

"Oh God, Keene. She...she was just talking with me. Someone—someone took her."

"What happened?"

"I got the call from Holder. They were taking in your father tonight."

The blood drains from Keene's face. "This is his play. He's going to try... he took my..." Keene's free hand grips my lapel and jerks me forward. His voice is lethal as he pulls himself together. "We're going to get her out. In the meantime, you'll catch me up on everything."

Before I can agree, he spies someone over my shoulder. "Alison."

I turn, already preparing for the worst. Her hand reaches out and grasps my arm in a grip so tight, I'm certain there will be a bruise left with five small fingers. "Do whatever you have to. Bring my daughter home alive."

Then she grabs Keene's face and kisses him hard. "Go."

He shoves me forward toward the side door. "Move."

Neither of us stops until we're at street level. The moment we reach it, an unmarked SUV pulls up. A blond with cold blue eyes is driving; a black-haired man is next to him. "We dropped off our primary. Where are we headed?"

Keene looks down at his phone and snaps off coordinates before making introductions. "McCullough, Clifton, meet the jackass."

The dark-haired man shifts around, giving me a once-over. "I'm Clifton."

The driver weaving in and out of traffic like he's stolen the vehicle mutters, "McCullough. What did you do to get on Keene's shit list?"

"I fell in love with his daughter." Then I swallow before admitting, "Then I fucked everything up."

McCullough mutters, "Yeah. You'd better hope you bleed."

Clifton adds, "Because if not, Keene can still take you."

Keene barks, "Jon's meeting us there. What's our ETA?"

"Fifteen minutes if we don't get stuck on the bridge."

"Then don't get stuck on the bridge," Keene snaps. "Bastard has my girl."

Fortunately, we don't get stuck, and we manage to craft a plan using the computer in the slick vehicle McCullough and Clifton have access to, as well as the small armory they keep in the back. By the time we meet up with Jon, I have hope we'll be able to get her out alive.

CHAPTER FIFTY-THREE

Kalie

The dark tulle of my gown is shredded from the damp warehouse floor I was tossed onto before the brutes dragged me into one of the two chairs and zip-tied me in place. I twist and turn, trying to find some give. Fortunately, the voluminous skirts of my dress are able to shift even as they absorb the blood I've shed within the layers. Somewhere in my less than delicate transport, I've lost my heels. Besides that, I do a quick assessment. My worst injuries appear to be my ribs from when I was kicked in the van, a split lip, and an eye nearly swollen shut from the fist to the socket.

"The real question is are they bruised or cracked?" I try to breathe as deeply as I can without causing further injury. If they're cracked, I don't want to puncture a lung. The pain is agonizing, but I can breathe, so that's a good sign.

Keep breathing, Kalie. It will not only help you keep calm but avoid crying.

Meanwhile, do what Dad would have you do. Assess the situation.

Two of the three men who'd taken me pace back and forth. One sits across from me in a ladder-back chair. Cigarette smoke curls in the air above his head, mixing with dust and rot and motor oil.

"She's tougher than she looks," one of them mutters, wiping blood from his knuckles.

I glare at him. He's the one who threw the punch at my eye. "I hope it hurts, asshole."

"Enjoy that smart mouth for now," the seated one replies, voice lazy. "The boss hasn't got here yet."

My senses sharpen. The boss? Who's that?

The metal doors groan as they open.

There's a hitch in the footsteps, telling me it's not someone who is intending to rescue me from this hellhole. Instead, the thump and drag echoes. Sharp. Deliberate. There's no *pop-pop* of automatic gunfire. No shouted orders.

Just one man approaching, as if the whole world belongs to him.

I lift my head up, despite its pounding, and wish I hadn't when the man steps just inside the circle of light.

He's much older than the others. Tall. Straight-backed, despite the cane in his hand. Expensive coat. Irish wool. His silver hair is combed back from a face that is all too familiar. I should recognize it, as I've seen it every day of my life. Had this version of it not been etched with a lifetime of bad decisions and hard living, he'd be just as handsome as the son he sired and abandoned.

But by his own choices, my biological grandfather will never be half the man my father is.

He peruses me in much the same manner. It doesn't freak me out until he smiles. "My God. I always thought you were the spitting image of my baby girl, my Riley."

I shudder hearing that name out of this man's mouth. It's the birth name of my Aunt Cassidy. And hearing it from her birth father's mouth is like another full punch to the ribs. "Don't you mean Cassidy?" I sneer.

He spits on the floor. "I dare you to call her that again."

I keep my focus on breathing evenly. "Want to formally introduce yourself?"

"You know damn well who I am, lass."

"Oh, I know, *grandfather*. I was trying to be polite."

His smile deepens. "Such exquisite manners, young Katherine. We never truly had a chance to bond as family, did we?"

"Having me kidnapped and beaten doesn't exactly scream 'Grandpa's looking for some long-lost cuddles.'" *Then again, this isn't your everyday family reunion.*

"Blame that bastard who sired you. He tried to erase my very existence." He shuffles closer, letting the shadows fall behind him. "I'm your grandfather, Jack Marshall."

I hope my acting skills are up to par. It might buy me some time as I pray someone realizes I was taken. I flinch back as far as I can against the chair I'm bound to. "You're supposedly dead. My father said so years ago."

"I disappeared," he corrects, voice sharp. "Walked away from a worthless family. Found one that knows the value of loyalty."

I snarl, "You mean you abandoned your daughter to monsters. You let your son live with that agony."

He tilts his head, eyes glittering down at me. "Yet here you are. His child. He survived."

I jerk up my chin. "He did. Better without you in our lives."

My already bruised face receives brutal treatment from his punishing fingers as he slaps me across the cheek. "Watch your tone. You're worth more to me alive than dead—for now."

I don't say another word. He takes my silence as acceptance of his edict. Then a raw cackle escapes his withered throat. "Look at ye, lass. I just made you your father's biggest failure instead of his star."

My heart aches knowing he's probably right. Still, I don't speak. Jack boasts, "For me, you're a prize I'll always cherish. I should take a picture and send it to him, showing his perfect princess at my mercy. Brought straight to me by real men—not that pansy I beget. No, instead, you're mine by men I trained myself."

My breath catches. "This is insane."

"I watched you grow up, you know. From a distance." Jack kicks the back of the chair across from me, forcing one of my kidnappers to scramble to his feet. He lowers himself down across from me like we're two people settling in for a long chat. "Didn't dare get close. Suspect that mother of yours would've set me on fire with her bare hands. Wonder if she hates me more than she loves your father."

"Perhaps because her sister was sold to human traffickers? Ring a bell?"

His smile disappears. "They told you about that?"

It's with quiet pride I inform him, "My parents don't hide our family legacy. They told us everything about who we were and why we should be proud of who we became as a family." Never before had I ever felt such pride in being Katherine Laura Marshall than I did in this moment when I stared into the face of the man who set off the explosion that tried to destroy my family legacy.

He failed then. I just prayed he'd fail tonight as well.

He's quiet for a long moment. "I did what I needed to do to prove my loyalty to the Byrnes."

"And Uncle Caleb's mother," I taunt, reminding him of the story of the affair between him and my Uncle Caleb's mother—another winner in our family tree.

He dismisses Mildred Lockwood with a flick of his hand. "She was an easy lay who had the right connections. I used her to gain an introduction to the Byrnes."

"That isn't how she remembers it," recalling what my father told me about the years of pain he endured when Aunt Cassidy went missing.

"It's the truth." His eyes take on a distant focus before sharpening back on me. "You know, there was a reason I had you brought here."

"It wasn't because you thought I needed some facial work done? I'm touched."

His eyes scour my face. "My boys get a bit too enthusiastic with their work. I told them to leave you intact, if that helps."

"Am I supposed to be grateful?"

He lurches forward, causing me to rear back. "You could have had the same treatment as your aunt."

Thinking of the way Aunt Cassidy was brutalized as a young girl, I find myself eternally grateful, though I'll never admit it aloud. He doesn't seem to care much as he continues on in his half dreamlike, wholly unbalanced state. "Did ye know there was once a time when the Marshalls ruled half the docks in New York?"

"No."

"That kind of legacy doesn't last on sentiment. I wanted to restore us to that glory. The Byrnes needed proof that I'd do anything."

"And their price..." I can't bring myself to say the sentence.

"Was Riley." He shrugs his shoulders as if selling his daughter off was a simple business transaction.

"She was your daughter!" I shout. I hate giving him my tears, but I can't restrain them.

"Look at the life she now leads. Listen to me, lass. I coulda taken her out at any time over the years. Since she survived her little ordeal, I spared her in the end."

I'm revolted. "You're disgusting."

He chuckles low in his throat. "You're just like Riley. All fire. All judgment." He leans forward on the cane. "But I never stopped watching you from the time you were a little girl."

That sends shivers up my spine.

"Look at the life you lead because I left you alone—Harvard Law. The Olympics. I'm impressed."

"Don't say that like you hold any true affection for me."

"I thought about taking you," he says, ignoring my fury. "Back when you were Riley's age."

I still at the implication. "What?"

He gives me a cold smile. "You were valuable, even back then. Pretty. Smart. Determined. All things that make a girl desirable in our world. Fragile. Breakable."

Bile rises in my throat. "You sick bastard."

"I didn't take you," he snaps, voice hardening. "That has to count for something."

"Not much."

He stands, placing weight on his cane as he paces slowly.

"What do you want from me?" I finally work up the nerve to ask.

"Closure," he says simply. "You were going to be left alone. I'd negotiated it—until you stirred things up. Acting like your feckin' mother. Falling for that...*gobshite* who works for your old man."

My eyes snap to his, unable to hide my horror. *He knows who Declan really is.*

"Yeah," he says darkly. "I know all about Declan Conian. Thought he was clever. Thought no one would give a flying fig about the FBI agent turning to defense attorney for us less than savory types. I sat back. Watched. Waited. Decided to see how he'd handle our business." He strokes his chin. "Let's just say his work was...deliberate. Methodical."

"I'm asking purely as a lawyer. That's a bad thing?"

"No. Not always. I was just about comfortable with him until you blew up his house of cards."

I refuse to let my expression give this monster any more satisfaction. Then Jack—I refuse to acknowledge him as my grandfather—informs me, "My bet? He's gonna come here to save you. But he doesn't know what he's walking into."

I try to play off my hope. "Why would he bother? He used me. We're done."

His eyes narrow as if he's miscalculated something. "Well, if he doesn't, that doesn't bode well for your chances."

"I don't matter in the grand scheme of things."

He grins, showing off perfectly capped teeth. "Good to see ya know your place, lass."

"Besides, in a fair fight, Declan's stronger than you."

"Who said anythin' about it being fair?" He leans forward as if he's about to tell me the secret to the universe. "'Sides, he ain't nothing without you."

While I'd have loved hearing that even a few weeks ago, all it does is make my breathing heavier. "Maybe, maybe not. Either way, the jury concludes the same thing at the end of the day."

"Oh? What's that?"

"You're a murderer, aren't you, Jack? A coward. You couldn't even face the FBI after killing one of their agents." *Say it. Say it,* I urge him.

Jack turns, lips thin. "So, you figured that out?"

I shrug. "Wasn't hard. Declan mentioned you enjoy using knives. I'm surprised he hasn't."

He applauds slowly. "No one put the two together until now. I had to get rid of Tanya, though I let the boys have fun with her body before I sent it back through Uncle Sam's own postal service."

I never thought I'd appreciate the cold air in the warehouse, but if it were any warmer, I'd be puking over my grandfather's confession. Then, soft as a whisper, he says, "You remind me of her—Tanya."

I don't respond.

"The last time I saw her, she was hoping Declan would rescue her too. And here you are—doing the same, I bet."

I force myself to look at him. "She didn't survive you. I will. When I do, I'll enjoy testifying at your trial. Then, after I put you away, I'll have another thing in common with my Aunt *Cassidy*. I'll have survived you."

"Oh, if only you're alive to claim that win, lass."

A heavy beat passes. Then he admits, "I wasn't going to hurt you, you know. I planned to let you live your life."

"What changed your mind?"

"I decided you would be the one to teach them all about loyalty."

I laugh so hard at the irony that this bastard is going to teach the most loyal people in the world something he has no concept of that I don't see the blow coming. My face whips to the side when he backhands me a second time. He huffs, "See, Katherine, you strike out at one of ours, we strike back. Even if he is a *gobshite*."

"Here you are getting all worked up when you don't consider Declan yours? How does loyalty work for you, Jack?" I counter after spitting out a mouthful of blood.

His eyes dilate wildly as he sputters for an answer. "If you'd just accepted your place, you could have gone on with no repercussions. But that day, you struck out at the *Byrnes* when you lost your marbles in public." He thumps his chest. "My family."

"Ah, so it wasn't that I struck Declan, per se. It was *your* people who were humiliated."

He's pleased I appear to grasp what he's saying. "Exactly."

I nod before declaring, "It's official. You're unhinged."

I'm not ready for the blow to my already bruised ribs from his cane. He swings it around wildly, narrowly missing my head with a lethal shot. "I am *not* crazy!"

After he regains the narrow grasp he has on control, he leans against a nearby pillar, breath heaving before shouting, "See what you made me do?"

I can't prevent the wheezing from the renewed pain nor the tears streaming down my face forced out by agony. It takes everything in me to gasp. "Made you do?"

"Tough love, lass."

"Is—" I gasp. "Is...this how you raised my dad?"

His eyes water in some fucked up sense of love I hope my father never witnesses. "No. I love—loved—my son. It must have been Laura who turned him against me before she died."

I declare flatly, "You mean before she was murdered."

He whispers sinisterly, "What?"

"Mildred Lockwood admitted to murdering her. My father blames you for ruining his mother, for abandoning him, but not for her murder. He will," I pause to try to suck in some more air, "blame you for harming his daughter. Fear that."

Jack's warped mind is so wrapped up in his denials of the past he doesn't hear the small scrape of the warehouse door, but I do. I pray it's help and not more people to drag me into the depths of darkness my family pulled themselves up from. The steel door in the back groans again.

This time, Jack hears it too.

His gaze snaps to the dark corner. For the first time, I see something in him that isn't insanity or misplaced power. It's something delicious —fear.

I smile, even with my face bruised and bloodied. "Calvary's coming."

Then, because I can't take anymore, I let the darkness consume me.

CHAPTER FIFTY-FOUR

THE FOUR OF US SLIDE OUT OF THE SUV AS QUIETLY AS POSSIBLE. Jon's waiting—garbed in all black. His face is grim.

Keene snaps, "Status report."

"Four total. Three Byrne enforcers, one Marshall psychopath." His eyes hold mine. "The real question is whether you or Declan are going to take the kill shot on dear old Grandfather."

Keene stills before hissing, "My father's in there? Is Kalie hurt?"

Jon's nod tenses every muscle in my body. I snap, "How bad?"

"Face and ribs for certain. I can't tell much more from where I've been able to observe."

The air is rent with curses from four different directions. McCullough hands me a semi-automatic weapon and a web vest that's already kitted out with enough ammo to take down a small city block. "What's the plan?"

"To get my fucking daughter out of there alive and to kill my father. Preferably fast. It's not rocket science." Keene's on the razor's edge of sanity right now.

Jon holds up a hand. Brave man. I never knew how much until he says, "Uncle Keene, Kalie wants him alive."

Every muscle in my body tenses when he hisses, "What?"

"I recorded as much as I could." With that, he plays back the last few minutes before he got the signal to meet us.

The last time I saw her, she was hoping Declan would rescue her too. And here you are—doing the same, I bet.

She didn't survive you. I will. And when I do, I'll enjoy testifying at your trial. Then, when I put you away, I'll have another thing in common with my Aunt Cassidy. I'll have survived you.

Oh, if only you're alive to claim that win, lass.

"Then we give Kalie the choice—kill him or get Jack out alive," I growl. "She delivers his justice."

Keene turns on me like I'm fresh meat. "You're insane."

"No. I want to give your daughter the opportunity to regain her power. It's the only way she will."

Something like respect flickers in Keene's eyes for barely a second. Then malice returns to the forefront. "Take out anyone in the way of Kalie. Then, we take care of Jack."

I'm on board with that plan. I'm already planning my first moves once we get inside, ready to take out the enemy with razor-sharp movements. Use deadly force only if necessary. I slide on my tactical face mask and wait.

Keene gives the signal and we don't speak. We don't need to. All Hudson forward maneuvering agents are trained for this.

Don't think. Just act.

In the lead, Keene takes down the first guard swiftly—silent as death. It's a smooth single motion with his elbow that crushes the man's throat before he can even raise his gun. The next two are farther down the alley, near the entrance to the warehouse. McCullough and Clifton move like shadows, closing the distance without a sound. They take down one, dropping him like he's nothing. McCullough's brutal kick breaks the gunman's grip. Then Clifton kicks his throat before he can call out to the other.

Finally, Jon slides forward. He ruthlessly applies his steel knife across the throat of the final guard. I'm surprised his head is still attached when it's done. Still, Jon doesn't let him fall, giving Jack the advantage inside the warehouse.

Now, it's my turn. I slide up to the warehouse—wary of any alarms or tripwires. Closing the distance without any sound, I'm focused on one man.

One enemy.

One last obstacle before Kalie is safe.

When I reach the warehouse entrance, I do a final perimeter check, just in case more reinforcements arrived while Jon was coordinating with us. Shit. There are two more guards near the door. Fortunately, they're too distracted by one another, talking instead of keeping watch.

They deserve what they're about to get.

The first guard never sees me.

I deliver a sharp jab to the neck. With that, he crumples to the ground, unconscious. The other guard raises his weapon, but I'm already lifting mine beneath his chin. I sneer as the smell of urine permeates the air, showing his cowardice.

Instead of killing him., I grab the man's throat, cutting off his breath. His eyes widen in confusion before he tries to struggle. I keep the force up until his eyes roll back in his head and he slowly slides down the front of my body, utterly limp. I murmur, "Fuck, I hate when they pee on me."

Keene approaches out of nowhere. "That's the price you pay for shitting on my daughter. Now, let's go get her."

My heart thunders in my chest at the thought of Kalie being so close, but still in so much danger. Before I open the door, Keene lays his fingers across mine. "Whatever happens, I need you to know this wasn't your fault. It's Jack's."

Absolution. I don't deserve it, but I still nod to let Keene know I heard him. "On three?"

He jerks up his chin. "One, two..."

I pull back the door, cringing at the small squeak. I try to wedge myself inside, but there's not enough space to force myself through. Keene shoves me out of the way. "Let me try." He tries to wedge his leaner build through, but no joy.

We both take a step back and search for an easier entrance. "The windows are easily a good fifty feet off the ground, and we don't have the kind of equipment with us to repel down from the roof."

"Fuck," Keene curses. Then he holds up his hand. His whole body shudders.

I edge closer. "You hear her?"

"I hear *him*. He's berating her for saying I'm strong enough to hurt him." His eyes glow behind his mask. "I know he killed your partner, but now he's hurt my sister and my daughter. I owe him."

Just as I'm about to reply, the others join us. I nod at the two just beyond the entrance. "Both are still alive."

Clifton murmurs, "On it." Stepping away, he talks into his radio even as he trusses both of our hostages up like Thanksgiving turkeys.

"What are you two waiting for?" Jon asks.

"Door's stuck," I snarl.

McCullough then Jon put their hands on the rusted handle. Keene places his hands on either side of theirs. Finally mine go right next to

Keene's. We're all ready to rip off the warehouse door. I plant my feet and call, "One, two..."

On three, we all pull back as hard as we can.

This time, the door creaks open. The hinges protest under our brutality. Jon and McCullough take guard while Keene and I make our way inside.

That's when we hear a warbled, "Calvary's coming."

Then nothing at all.

The silence inside is palpable except for the scuffling sounds of our boots against the concrete floor. I creep forward, every sense on high alert, listening for any movement, any noise that would betray her location.

Finally, I step into the unprotected center and want to murder someone.

The cavernous room is empty except for two people and two chairs. I take little notice of the man standing. Instead, my focus is locked on Kalie. She's still breathing, though even from a distance, I can tell it's labored.

The urge to revoke my earlier statement about letting her exact her revenge surges through me when I see her strapped to a chair.

Jack standing over her, his cane raised over his head.

The sight nearly makes me snap, I'm not quite certain what the sound that emits from my throat is. But while I'm busy trying to control my inner animal, Keene lifts his Desert Eagle and fires.

The first .50 caliber round takes off his father's lower arm, causing the cane to go flying away from Kalie's limp body.

The second shoots off his father's leg.

The moment he's down, I race toward Kalie.

I take in the damage in one glance before shouting, "We need a medic!"

Keene's patented smirk makes an appearance before he calls, "We need two if you want this one-legged arse to appear in court."

At that, her lashes flutter. "You heard?"

I smooth her hair away from her battered and bruised face. "Jon did. He recorded most of what you said."

She takes a breath and groans before coughing. "Hurts."

Keene makes his way over to his daughter. "Baby, let me take care..."

"It'd be murder. Not like him." With that, her energy fails her and her body slumps to the side.

Jack wheezes in agony.

I shout, "Keene, stuff something in him to keep him alive, but shut him the fuck up."

His eyes glitter. "With pleasure. Give me your belt."

I quickly undo my utility belt one handed before whipping it out as I let Kalie's body rest on mine. I don't want to lay her down on the cold floor, not without the paramedics there. Nor do I want to disrupt the crime scene so I can't even release her from her restraints.

Instead, I bury my head into her neck and take stock as my tears soak her bare shoulder.

Her glorious ball gown is torn and stained with dirt and something darker. I run my hands up and down her ribs, noting when her breath catches. "I think her ribs are cracked."

"Is she still conscious?" Keene demands as he yanks as hard as he can on the stub of Jack's right arm. Jack's slipping into unconsciousness until Keene slaps him to rejoin the party. "Hello, Dad."

"K-Keene." Terror and pain riddle Jack's voice.

"After all these years, if you wanted my attention so bad, all you had to do was drop by the office on family day. Might have cost you a lot less." Keene slips the other belt beneath Jack's knee and yanks it as tight as he can.

Jack screams in agony before he passes out.

Just then, two teams of medics arrive, as well as the NYPD and the FBI. With the addition of the last, I'm in no way surprised to see Caleb and Holder bringing up the rear.

Keene immediately steps back when the medics reach Jack. After ordering, "Don't lose sight of him."

"I won't, Keene. Swear it," says Holder.

With that vow, Keene heads in my direction to crouch at my side as the medics document Kalie's condition. The FBI and NYPD both document her wrist ties being clipped. "Jack had better be grateful she's still breathing," I snarl as her chest rises and falls with shallow breaths.

Jon and his father approach. Jon hands Holder his phone with the recorded evidence. Then he smooths a hand over his cousin's head. "You made me proud, Kalie."

For just a moment, after hearing Jon's voice, Kalie's eyes flutter. Then they dart in my direction.

I think she relaxes when she sees me, but for now, I need to believe there was a flicker of recognition and a sigh before she passed out from the pain.

"Let's get them to the hospital. Stat," I order.

Holder says, "We'll follow you there. When they're ready, we want to be first on scene to get statements."

"The others?" Jon asks cooly.

"Already in the back of our shops," the NYPD chief assures us. "This is fairly open and shut for us."

If only it were that way for my relationship with Kalie.

CHAPTER FIFTY-FIVE

THE BEEPING OF HER HEART MONITOR IS THE ONLY SOUND IN THE room when I finally step inside.

Yet, Kalie is the most beautiful sight I've ever seen.

It doesn't matter that her face is a mottled backdrop of blues and purples overlayed with bandages. Her arm is tucked protectively to her side. While pale blue is definitely her color, the hospital gown hangs off her slender frame and is streaked with betadine and other substances I hope aren't blood.

Her hair, which was glossy and elegant for the Fair Harvard Annual Reunion earlier, is now tangled against the pillow. But none of that matters. She's conscious. Alive. Still, I'm certain I don't take a complete breath until her gaze flickers up.

Better still, she's as stubborn as ever. "I'm fine."

"Cracked ribs, concussion, and you call that fine?"

"It's a hell of a bruise to my ego since I was just told I can't run for the next three months. But I'm not dead."

I choke on tears and laughter. "Not funny."

"It is to me. I survived."

I can't move closer. Not yet. She's just a few feet away, but the distance between us makes it feel like miles. Especially when everything about her screams fragile.

"You scared the hell out of me," I finally manage.

Her head tips back before she admits, "I was scared too."

Just as I'm about to pour my heart out, the door opens behind me. A doctor—no, an intern—young and annoyingly confident, steps in holding a tablet.

"Ms. Marshall." He flashes Kalie a smile that lingers far too long. "I'm here to check your vitals."

She huffs, "I don't need babysitting."

"You're on a concussion watch. We babysit even the unwilling."

The intern reaches for her wrist. She gives it begrudgingly, amused.

Even as he checks the dial of his watch while holding her wrist, he tries to charm her. "Were you on a photoshoot gone wrong when they brought you in? That dress? Sexy."

My spine snaps so hard that I'm surprised the chiropractor on duty doesn't rush down to check on me.

"I try to make dramatic entrances," she says dryly, glancing toward me.

"You're something," he remarks appreciatively, eyeing her.

I want to wrap his stethoscope around his neck and hang him from the nearest air vent. I try to justify that it wouldn't be murder. After all, hospital staff shouldn't be hitting on patients.

Right?

Kalie encourages him with a small laugh before groaning and holding her ribs. I shoot forward, but she waves me back. "I get that a lot."

The intern gives her a wink even as he types in her vitals. "You need anything, just press your call button. I'll look for your signal. I'm here all night, just for you."

As the door closes behind him, I scowl, but that doesn't seem to bother her in the slightest.

"Now, that was fun."

"Watching me want to squeeze the life out of someone for seeing you flirt with them? If that's how you get off."

She lifts her good eyebrow. "Now you know how I felt when I saw that picture. And he didn't even touch me beyond taking my pulse."

I flinch. "You're right. You're absolutely right."

"I know."

"I deserve whatever you're planning to throw at me for everything. It doesn't matter how big or small, every hurt I caused I need to fix."

She nods carefully. It hurts me to watch that uncertainty, not knowing if that's due to her emotions or the physical pain she's in. "There's just one thing I need to say."

"Say it."

"I never touched Nerissa with intent. I swear on my life. It was a ruse to keep us both alive. That's all it was."

"I figured that out after tonight, but you still didn't talk to me. You pushed me away, Declan. That's what hurts."

"Yeah." I blow out my breath.

"Take how you're feeling about the flirty intern and amplify that by a thousand. That's what I was feeling."

Knowing the murderous thoughts I entertained just a few short moments ago, I can't imagine the pain I put her through. My eyes burn as I vow, "I would've burned that whole building to the ground to get to you tonight."

Her lips curve in the tiniest of smiles. "I hope I wouldn't have been inside."

Her eyes glance down at her visitor's chair. "Let's talk."

Making my way to her side, I pause. Then I drop to my knees. My fingers grasp the same wrist the intern touched—one of the few parts of her not battered and bruised. "I thought I lost you."

"But you didn't."

"I will if I don't say this right."

"Say what right?"

I open my mouth to get my apology out when the door opens again and a tall, broad-shouldered man in a white coat, green scrubs, and hospital badge enters while looking down at his tablet. "Ms. Marshall, I'm doc..." His body freezes.

"Declan," the man accuses. "What the fuck are you doing in my ER?"

Kalie's eyes flicker between us. "You know him?"

The doctor's eyes narrow on him. "Oh, I know him. He has a tendency of getting his partners killed—like my wife."

I rise slowly. "Ben."

Ben steps inside and closes the door behind him with a soft click. Tension fills the room like smoke. No one speaks until Ben breaks the silence. "She's my patient. Didn't expect you to be here."

"I didn't expect to be here either," I say. "Not like this."

"You have some fucking nerve—"

"Enough," Kalie snaps, cutting him off with what I suspect is her reserve strength. "You don't get to come in here and accuse him of anything—not after what he's done."

Ben's brow furrows. "What he's done? You mean other than leave a dead trail of answers surrounding my wife's death?"

"Your wife died in the line of duty. You don't get to walk in here acting like an ass."

"Excuse me?" Ben is shocked by Kalie.

"Declan did everything in his power to find out who was behind it. He went undercover for years. He risked his life a hundred times over. He wanted the answers for Tanya's death just as badly as you did—for you and your children."

Ben falters, clearly taken off guard.

"He infiltrated not one, but two criminal empires for her. He rescued me from one of the heads of them," she continues, gesturing toward herself. "As for your wife? If she's half the woman Declan's told me about, she'd be appalled at the way you're acting instead of honoring the women she died trying to save."

I look down, stunned by the way she's blasting Ben, how her belief in my mission never wavered, even if her trust in me did.

"Declan didn't betray anyone's memory," she finishes. "He honored it."

Ben looks from her to me, haunted emotion flashing behind his eyes. Then, with a stiff nod, he turns and walks out. The door closes behind him, cocooning us in silence once again.

Then, Kalie breaks. Her agony due to her injuries fills the room when she moans before reaching for the call button. "God, can someone get me some pain meds? I think I just tore into my only chance at getting any."

"You show up at a ball looking like the heiress you are, fought for your life and won, destroyed a man's illusions, and the only thing you're complaining about is a lack of narcotics?"

"I'm multifaceted."

I reach for her wrist again, this time not letting it go. "I don't deserve you."

Kalie's smile fades away. Instead, she stares at me with the kind of look that I'll remember a year from now and hopefully at our fiftieth anniversary. It's the kind of look that cracks a man's soul knowing you hurt your woman so deeply, the only thing that will repair it is time.

"No," she says quietly. "You don't. But you'll find a way. One day at a time."

"You mean that?"

"I wouldn't have said it if I didn't. I don't throw around forgiveness like Uncle Phil tosses around confetti or Aunt Cori throws frosting." Then she frowns. "Though either is an option depending on if I do or don't get some narcotics. Can you work on getting some for me?"

I kiss the inside of her wrist gently. "Whatever it takes."

"Thanks," she says, closing her eyes. Then they pop open. "Start with the intern. He seems to like me."

"Don't push it," I whisper.

She smiles before easing back while we wait for Ben to return with the good stuff.

※

Thanks to Ben, Kalie is well on her way to drifting. Her lashes flutter against her cheeks. I know I could step away, stretch. I don't dare move an inch.

The silence between us has shifted—no longer heavy with what hadn't been said, but filled with what could be. I look at the hand she trusts me to hold, the one with the IV. It's bandaged and bruised. Might be that way for a while, but she's safe.

Still warm. Still alive.

Leaning back slightly in the chair, my eyes roam over her face in the dimmed light. Right now, the powerhouse who threw a right hook at me isn't in sight. Nor is the glamorous woman who dazzled me earlier tonight. There's evidence of the strength of the woman who captured the hearts of the world when she crossed the finish line first, earning her gold. But even that's muted. Right now, she's just Kalie.

My Kalie.

My heart.

She shifts in her sleep, a soft sound escaping her lips.

I lean forward and whisper, "I'm here. Don't be afraid."

Because I wasn't certain she wanted to hear it before, I take the luxury of saying it now. "I love you. You saw me, you judged me, and you made me a better man for it."

Her hand flexes slightly in mine, even in sleep.

"This started for justice. Closure. Maybe even revenge. But I finished it for you. Because they hurt my firebrand. And I swear to you, not one of them will get away with that."

Sitting in Kalie's hospital room, the weight of everything she'd been through presses down on my chest. Tears trickle down my cheeks. I don't wipe them away as I need them to heal.

As much as I need her.

CHAPTER FIFTY-SIX

Kalie

THE ACHES OF MY BODY REMIND ME ALL TOO WELL OF LAST NIGHT, making me desperate for some more of Dr. Ben's magic narcotics. Even as I wage an internal war to waste what little energy I have to seek out the nurse call button, I find myself gasping in panic when I can't move my hand.

My eyes fly open and the fear in my heart immediately settles when my eyes rest on the ones I inherited—my mother's. Gripping my hand in between both of hers, she presses her lips against our folded fingers before murmuring, "I never wanted you to know this kind of pain, Kalie."

With her words, something inside of me shatters. The breath I didn't realize I was holding exhales before I rasp out, "Mama."

For a long while, she doesn't speak. Her actions do all the talking. My mother's touch is reverent—lips pressing against my hand clasped in between her own. It's a worship of gratitude, a humble thanks. I give her those quiet moments uncertain of the time that passes because my pain eases simply by her being next to me.

But my heart remembers Declan being by my side when I fell asleep and can't help but wonder where he is.

She dispatches that question before I can even ask it. "After I ensured your father was sane after last night."

"And vice versa?"

Her weary smile acknowledges I'm right on target. "I forced Declan to go get a shower and debriefed—not necessarily in that order." Her gaze softens. "He didn't leave your side once, Kalie."

My head tips upward so my eyes focus on the drop ceiling. "Love is never quite as simple as a love story makes it out to be."

"The memorable ones aren't."

"Like yours and Dad's?"

"I've never hid the fact your father came into my life flashing hazard signs—forget red flags."

A whimper of laughter escapes. I clutch my ribs. "Don't make me laugh, Mama. It hurts."

Her hand reaches up and smooths one of the bruises I can feel blooming on my skin. Moisture makes her eyes appear iridescent. "I had a lot of wishes when I knew I was pregnant with you, Kalie."

"Like what?"

"I prayed you'd grow up strong and smart. I hoped you'd love your family the way I do. I prayed you'd find love." A lone tear tracks down her cheek. "But never did I want you to experience the physical trauma behind our promise to remain loyal as a family."

I lift her hand and cup her fingers to the side of my battered face. "I don't think I would have endured it if I didn't have such a strong role model, Mama."

Her eyes close briefly. When they open, they're misted over with love. "I love you, Kalie."

"I love you too."

"Now, about Declan," she starts.

"Can I ask for more pain meds before we have this conversation?"

With a small smile, she presses the call button. After a nurse pops her head in and asks what we need, then reassures me my precious pain meds will be on their way shortly. Mama continues, "In the time I've loved your father, he's swung from being my lover to my worst enemy, the love of my life to the bane of my existence."

"What's your point, Mama?"

"Love isn't the law. Even when you have all the facts, there's always mitigating circumstances." She tucks a stray hair behind my ear.

"I know."

"Do you?"

"I never stopped loving him."

"That's good to know."

"And after last night, it's even harder to not forgive him when he's so hurt by what happened to me." I meet her eyes. "Still, deep down, our beginning wasn't normal. I need that for a while."

"Then take that time. I have a feeling Declan's not going anywhere." Her smile turns feral. "Besides, it will give me the opportunity to get to know him."

"Play nice, Mama." I blink up at the harsh lights. "How long am I stuck in here?"

"At least a week."

I frown. "My injuries aren't that bad, are they?"

"You won't be racing this season," she prepares me.

My nose scrunches up in displeasure. "Nothing? Not even a 5K?"

"Will it make you feel better to man a water station?"

"Only if Dad runs in a tutu again."

A voice from the door vows, "If it makes you feel better, firebrand, I'll make damn certain it happens."

I groan. "Declan. I don't suppose we could ask you to keep that from my father."

He strolls forward to the opposite side of the bed from my mother. Leaning forward, his aftershave floods my senses, overriding the antiseptic smell of my hospital room when he presses a lingering kiss to my forehead. "I heard nothing."

My mother mutters, "We'll see," under her breath.

Declan continues, "But that's because I plan on running right next to him, tutu and all."

My breath escapes on a small puff of air. "You do?"

His lips twist in self-depreciation before he turns to my mother to ask, "Alison, do you mind if I have a few moments alone with Kalie?"

She regards him thoroughly—her demeanor protective, not hostile—before nodding and squeezing my hand. "I'll go update the family. Your Uncle Phil was threatening to lay siege to the hospital later," she says, voice thick with emotion. She lingers a moment at the door until our eyes meet and hold. Finally, she gives me an imperceptible nod, as if reminding me what we talked about.

Nothing is simple when it comes to love.

After she leaves, Declan assumes her seat, scooting the guest chair closer. He doesn't sit. Instead, again looms over me, both hands gripping the steel rail at the side of my bed. His face is wary, exhausted, and tentative. Still, a radiant smile breaks the tension when he's done perusing my features and declares, "You look good, firebrand."

I raise my brows, amused but grateful. "You're a liar and a half, Conian."

He laughs, hangs his head, and when he looks up again, whatever defense he's built crumples. He's just Declan—no more masks. No Mafia lawyer suits to hide behind like armor. No Hudson agent. Just Declan laying himself in front of me to judge. Almost as if he can read my thoughts, he says, "Last night I said I wanted to start earning you back. That begins today."

"Why?" The question's out before I can stop it.

He doesn't flinch. "Because cutting you out emotionally before it almost became physically permanent was the stupidest thing I've ever done. You were right to walk—no run—as far as you could away from me. You deserved to be wooed, treasured. While you slept, I realized how little I did that."

"You're not making a good argument for trying again," I point out.

"Then how about this. I didn't leave because I didn't have feelings for you. I left because they were so overwhelming. I'd already lost one person close to me and..." His voice chokes up. "Well, you see how that turned out."

My natural compassion wins over his obvious pain. "For what it's worth, I think we gave Tanya's husband something to think about last night."

He corrects me. "No, you did because you care. You love and you love openly. Freely. I'm terrified the feelings I have for you are going to ruin you."

"Which are?" My heart is thudding in my chest.

"I love you. I'm in love with you. I'm not giving up on us. Not now, not ever." He pauses before he adds, "And what I said to your mother?"

I snicker. "I didn't take you seriously."

He shakes his head. "No, that was a serious offer. I want to run with your dad. I'd be honored to wear a goddamn tutu if it means ending up in a place of pride on your desk—of becoming so cherished in your life again."

I close my eyes. It would be so easy to soften. Too easy. But if the last twenty-four hours have shown me anything, it's that I need to be more cautious. I warn him, "You have to know, after everything, trust is going to take time."

"I know. That's why I'm going to be there by your side. I'm going to earn back your trust and your love."

I stare at the ceiling, blinking back tears. After a long moment, I turn my head. "Then you'd better make damn certain you can keep up, Conian. Dad's a fast runner."

The flash of his smile is almost as bright as the love he has for me that's visible in his eyes. Then, he looks down and seems to realize he's gripping the bed rail instead of my hand. Sitting down, he slips his fingers through mine as if testing how it feels to be touching me again.

My heart skips a beat when he lifts our joined hands to his mouth and presses a soft kiss to the top of it.

"I'll make certain you enjoy that water station, firebrand."

Three months later, at a 5K fundraiser in honor of Brave Steps Forward, every female in our family whoops and hollers at our men since they followed Declan and my father's lead wearing tutus and tiaras.

Including Ben and his sons, who all shot me a jaunty little wave when they passed by the water station I'm dutifully manning.

I still can't run, but both my body and heart are well on their way to recovery due to Declan's tender care.

Much to my surprise, Ben remained my primary doctor while I was in the hospital. "Declan and I can talk later. I want you to have the best care there is."

Once I was discharged, they did meet. What was said exactly, Declan never told me. But when he came back from that conversation, his soul was lighter.

Immensely.

After their talk and while I was recuperating at home, Ben brought his sons, Bryan and Emmitt, to see Declan for the first time since Tanya died. To say it was an emotional reunion is a complete understatement.

Ben pulled Declan in for a quick, manly hug. Though my view from the couch was slightly blocked, I watched as Declan returned Ben's grip—two men having moved into the next stage of grief.

Together.

When they broke apart, Emmett launched himself at Declan with the energy of a very young kangaroo, nearly knocking Declan off his feet. "Missed you, Uncle Dec!" Declan righted him, ruffled his hair, before Bryan almost took him down doing the same move from the other side. "Same!"

I'm not certain how he held his tears back, but he did. Still, he choked out, "I missed you both. I love you so much."

After they made it inside, Ben couldn't help but check on me. "Kalie, if you keep up with your PT, I see no reason you can't be running again by fall."

"That's good to hear. I'm going stir crazy."

"I bet." His eyes twinkled as his gaze wandered around my home.

I groaned. "Declan told you?"

"Actually, I knew who you were. That's why I was brought in to consult." His eyes were salacious. "Is it here?"

I rolled my eyes before I pointed toward the stairs. "Yes. It's in my office."

"What is?" Emmitt asked his father.

"A special medal Kalie won for running," he replied.

Bryan wondered, "Are you good?"

Declan grinned with pride. He grabbed each boy by hand and led them to my office. "Let me show you."

Ben scrambled to his feet. "I'm coming too!"

That's when they learned about the important artifact in my office and why it's not my Olympic medal.

It's family and love.

First.

Last.

Always.

Now, out of the corner of my eye, I see Aunt Holly frame a shot of Declan and my father just as Dad leaps onto Declan's back to be carried.

Declan's laughter rings out. "Old man, you know your ass is sticking out in those running shorts."

My father snarls, "Who are you calling old, punk?"

I shout, "Both of you are showing off the goods. Now get back on the course before I show you both up!"

Both their heads whip in my direction, sending me overprotective glares.

I think back to where I was when Declan entered into my life.

Now, we've fought wars and come out the other side stronger.

Together.

We still have so far to go, but this is a marathon, not a sprint. Every step we take is one step closer to our forever.

Finally, I think I'm ready.

Even if he is wearing a tutu.

EPILOGUE
TWO YEARS LATER

THE FEDERAL COURTHOUSE SMELLS LIKE LEMON-SCENTED CLEANER and has my nerves strung out as I sit on the witness stand. My suit itches and since I flat out told her father that I refuse to wear one to the office ever again, I haven't worn a tie in months—not since the last funeral we'd gone to together.

Even then, I'd torn it off the second we got back to the car and tossed it in the backseat like it offended me.

Today, though, it is necessary. Part of the armor I used to wear when I was an FBI agent. A part of a uniform I wore with pride.

I'd adjust it again, but I'm certain the federal prosecutor is contemplating wrapping it around my neck and yanking both ends tightly. She's trying to finish her questions with clinical precision, but her eyes dart up every time I fiddle with my stupid neck apparatus.

She wanted me to keep things neat for the jury. Keep it surgical. That just isn't possible. Not with what we're being forced to dig up.

"Thank you, Mr. Conian," she says, nodding before retreating to her seat.

I nod back, but don't look at her. My eyes find the jury. Seven women, five men. Mostly middle-aged. Some skeptical. A few sympathetic.

Then my eyes find the woman who was harangued by both the prosecution and the defense earlier in the trial. Sitting in the second row of the gallery. Dark blue blazer. Hair pulled back in a knot she only wears when she needs to look tough—depositions, confrontations, days when she was coming to Hudson Investigations to scold her father for keeping me too late at the office.

Her eyes are locked on mine.

God, she's the only reason why I can manage to make it through reliving this nightmare.

The judge turns to the defense. "Mr. Allister, your witness."

Victor Allister stands like he's preparing for his swan song. His suits throughout the trial have been multi-thousand-dollar shades of Quaker Oats. When Kalie's Uncle Phil first mentioned that at a family dinner, her Aunt Em spit out her drink across his chest.

For once, Phil didn't seem to mind. He pulled Emily close, kissed the top of her head, and said, "That one's a freebie."

Allister steps forward and presents a tight, civil smile to the jury before beginning his verbal warfare. "Mr. Conian. Let's get into it."

I lean back in the chair, rolling my shoulders. "Let's."

"You were with the FBI for—how long again?"

"Eight years. Last two, I was a handler while my partner went undercover at Velvet Vice."

"Velvet Vice," he repeats like he was tasting it. "A gentleman's club."

"If you want to call it that."

"Then you left the FBI?"

"Yes."

"And did what, exactly?"

"I went to work at Hudson Investigations."

Allister turns to the jury. "A private firm. Not affiliated with law enforcement. No jurisdiction. No oversight."

"We work with local PDs, state agencies, even federal when asked. We handle cases they can't. Or won't."

"Right. The noble mercenary." He flips a page in his notes. "You've testified before, haven't you? But not like this. Not against your former contacts."

I don't respond. Not yet. He wants me to fill the silence. "Why is that, exactly?"

"There were concerns about whether or not my partner was killed as a result of information I provided to my superiors." I pause. "For the record, an internal investigation by the agency has cleared that."

"But you still went rogue?"

"Yes. I wanted answers."

"What did you do, exactly?"

"I became a defense attorney for the Byrnes' family interests."

"Money?'

"Yes"

"Violence?"

"On occasion."

He leers at me. "Girls?"

"Never."

"Never? Never is an awfully long time." He pauses. "Did you or did you not have your photograph taken at Velvet Vice?"

I stare Kalie directly in the eyes when I lean into the microphone and admit, "Yes, I did."

The jury titters among themselves.

"Yet you say you were never involved with the girls?" he jeers.

"I never was. The VIP room was used for business meetings."

"Your honor, I would like to enter photographic evidence from Sexy & Social showing Mr. Conian receiving a lap dance at Velvet Vice."

"Objection!" shouts the prosecution. "Those photos are being taken out of context."

"I'll allow the evidence. You'll have the chance to challenge the context shortly."

Allister, the slime bucket he is, tries to get me to admit the dance Nerissa performed was more than just an information drop. But he fails. Spectacularly. Especially when I point at his client—Jack Marshall—and explain how he murdered one of the other strippers in cold blood that night.

Allister can't let it go. Won't let me go. "While you were undercover, you attended parties. Conducted legal transactions for my client's people. Were lent out to another crime organization to resolve their cases. Took part in legal transactions."

"While collecting evidence, yes."

Allister gives a casual shrug. "You admit, then, you lied."

I keep my voice calm, the way Keene grilled into me during witness prep. "You don't get to frame it like that."

"How should I frame it, Mr. Conian? You were in deep with my client and his network. You acted as their lawyer of record to stay under. Now you're breaking your oath to come clean."

I let the silence sit for a moment, then give him credit, "You're right about one thing."

The courtroom stills.

"I knew testifying would cost me. I have no doubt that the bar association is going to revoke my private license. Hell, I'll be lucky if the penny ante crap I actually prosecuted isn't overturned. Certainly, the Byrnes should be concerned whether the villas I purchased for them in Cork and Tuscany are legal. But I didn't come here to protect my career."

I glanced at Kalie again. She hasn't moved, but her eyes aren't as fierce as they were before. They're as warm as they were when we woke up in bed together this morning. "I came here because I will not sit by and let these men walk."

Allister scoffs. "So you claim you'll sacrifice everything. For justice."

"No. There's only one thing in the world I have worth protecting. It's not justice. Not anymore." I motion with my eyes toward my wife. "She's sitting right there. The woman I gained because she punched me in the face at the courthouse two years ago. She didn't know I wasn't just a two-bit attorney bent on protecting criminals. It was her sense of justice that led me to where I am today."

A couple of jurors exchange glances. The older woman in the back leans forward.

"She forgave me when I didn't deserve it for harming our relationship when I got scared over too many things related to her and this case. When I finally understood what being undercover meant. Not once did she ask me to give up justice for my partner. My wife just gave me a new purpose when it was all done—love."

Allister opens his mouth, but I don't stop.

"We bought a house together. Tons of bedrooms, creaky floors, a backyard with a stubborn pine tree. We painted the kitchen together, even though we fought over the cabinet color. We run together first thing in the morning, sometimes after dinner. She reads contracts on the couch while I work cases that still matter—finding missing persons. The people who have fallen through the cracks."

A lump lodges in my throat, but I push it down.

"My wife's not just my future. Kalie's my redemption."

Allister frowns. "Your Honor, I'm not sure how this is relevant—"

"It's relevant," I say, cutting him off, "because you keep trying to convince this jury your client's somehow not guilty of attacking my wife—his own granddaughter. That I'm here to save my own skin. That I'm betraying some sacred code by throwing away a career I give two shits about when the truth is, I already gave all that up. The only thing that matters to me if I ever lose it is her. Nothing else matters but that."

The judge studies me for a long second. Then nods. "Continue, Mr. Allister. But tread carefully."

Allister tightens his grip on the podium. "Mr. Conian, are you or are you not aware that testifying today could compromise ongoing investigations related to the Byrne family?"

"I cleared my testimony with federal oversight. Anything I've disclosed is admissible and isolated from classified operations."

Allister clicks his pen once. Twice.

"I have no further questions, Your Honor."

"You may step down." The judge gives me a nod.

I stand slowly. My legs feel heavier than they should. I turn and make my way down the steps from the witness stand, each footfall stronger than the last.

I don't glance at the jury. I didn't bother with Allister.

I have eyes only for Kalie.

Her gaze connects with mine with the look that wrecks me every time— equal parts love and pride. When I saw it in her eyes on our wedding day, I knew I'd do anything and everything to see it again.

A silent I see you.

I love you.

Always.

This is what matters. No courtroom in the world could take it away.

The courthouse doors swing shut behind me with a weighty thud, the ending of a chapter I never thought would be over. The cold hits first. Then air. Fresh air.

Much like it did when I was a defense attorney for the Byrnes, the press crowds the sidewalk. Questions are shouted. But they blur into white noise because off to the side, away from the hoopla, she's waiting for me.

God, I still don't deserve her, is all I can think.

I move toward Kalie like the moon circles the earth. No hesitation. No deliberation. She's my orbit, my anchor. When I reach her, I stop short of touching her. Not yet.

Her eyes probe mine before her lips curve upward. "You didn't have to say my name."

"I did."

She steps forward and lays her hand flat over my heart. I cover it with my own. "I meant what I said in there," I murmur. "I started this for justice. But I finished it for you."

Her throat moves as she swallows. "I know."

For a moment, we're caught in a bubble made of just the two of us. Nothing else exists. No mob. No crazy grandfathers. No bridezillas trying to sue her or hysterical families needing my help. It's just her hand over my heart and the love we've built between us.

"Is it really over?" she asks.

"Our part testifying is, yes. "

She nods slowly. "Good." Then, more softly, "Take me home."

The door clicks shut behind us.

She toes off her heels by the door. I watch her for a moment, admiring the way she moves in the space we built together—our home.

My jacket lands on the back of the sofa we spend every night snuggling on together. She shrugs off her blazer. I toe off my own shoes and peel off my socks before walking toward her in bare feet. Then, I tug her against me and just hold her against my chest—pressing a kiss to her head without a word.

Kalie nestles into me like she's been waiting all day for that one kiss. "You're quiet."

I relax my chin on her shoulder. "I don't remember the last time I felt this much at peace."

She smiles against my chest.

For a long time, we just stand there absorbing each other. Eventually, she pulls back and tugs my hand.

"Come on," she says. "Let's go to bed. You need to relax. I want—"

I don't let her finish.

Bending at the knees, I swoop her up into my arms before carrying her down the hall. We pass framed family photos, running medals we'd earned together and into our master bedroom. I carefully step over the pieces of our baby's bassinet. We have months until our "we" turns into "three," but we're ready for moments that smell less like stress and instead drown us in sweet scented baby powder.

Wrapped in Kalie's arms, after loving her to sleep, I hold on to my future with nothing left to hide. Our trials are over.

Finally.

WHERE TO GET HELP

DECLAN'S CHARACTER CAME TO ME WHEN I WAS WATCHING THE Rookie. There was an episode where Lucy went undercover as a nanny to reveal a money laundering scheme. I couldn't help but wonder how attached the soft-hearted officer would get to the children she was in charge of had she stayed any longer. Fortunately for Lucy, the episode was only around 44 minutes, plus commercials, so she escaped relatively unscathed.

Declan, however, did not. His emotional IQ suffered tremendously for the years of dedicated service he invested to avenge his partner's death.

As a criminal justice major, I studied the effects these types of assignments have on our law enforcement personnel. I even experienced some of it first hand. But as I researched Declan's character, I appreciated more the significant toll placed on individuals like him every day.

According to Psychology Today, undercover operatives are prone to more feelings of isolation and abandonment, as well as a lack of support from their chain of command. There are consequences due to long-term solitary operations including relationship damage at home, with family, and even at work. Some of the less obvious ones include interpreting neutral behavior as threats, depersonalization—loosing the parts of themselves they had before going undercover, not to mention aspects of their undercover life that continue after they return to "normal."

Their undercover assignments may also lead to threads of empathy growing for the people they are investigating

In the United States, COPLINE was established to remove the stigma associated with an officer's decision to keep his/her emotions inside for fear of retribution and/or retaliatory action if his/her personal information, feelings OR state of mind is revealed to his/her agency. For more information, visit their site here.

The undercover journey is one of great danger, psychological and emotional. For those who brave it, we thank you for your service.

BONUS SCENE

Want to read more about Kalie and Declan? Click here for an additional bonus scene!

FREE TO TASTE

If you started to fall in love with the way Peter Freeman lived by the "Family First" motto in Free to Fall, then were excited to see him again in Free to Judge, you'll be excited to know his story is coming next with Free to Taste.

Coming in 2026.

Keep reading for a sneak peek at Peter's deliciousness.

PETER

I CHECK MY GPS TO MAKE CERTAIN I'M NOT IN THE WRONG location because unless I drove through a time portal of some kind, I'm supposed to be in Mooseberry, Maine—population seventy-eight.

When my friend offered to lend me this place for the summer to decompress without hoardes of paparazzi shadowing my every movement, Arek was transparent about the nosey neighbors I'd encounter, the potholes in his driveway that appeared no matter how many times he'd patched them, and the gorgeous jetty off the back of the house. But what sold me on the place was its solitude. His seriousness when he informed me, "They've had an enormous population growth in the last few years. Big event getting the town sign updated and everything," was music to my ears.

"How many people used to live here?"

"Sixty-two and that's if Sula, the kids, and I weren't in residence," he names his wife of many years.

I lift a hand off the wheel and scrub it against my eyes to ensure I'm not hallucinating. No, the people are still there. Then, I have to hunt for parking which is why I'm both flabbergasted and irritated when I finally get in line to the place Are described as, "the only decent place to get food if you don't want to cook for yourself."

Is it some kind of special event where not only the entire town of Mooseberry must be eating out, but so must the surrounding towns.

I, who have never had to wait for a table in my life, am informed it might be close to two hours before I'm sat. "Less if you don't mind eating at the counter," the hostess snaps her gum at me.

"That's fine."

"Then here's your post card. On the back is a number we'll call out when we're ready to seat you."

"Thanks." Even as I move away, the next harried couple is already pushing their way forward to get their name on a still expanding list of potential patrons. It makes me intrigued.

Curious.

And considering what I do for a living, I'm halfway tempted to get a crew out here to shoot B-roll for a future episode featuring this little treasure in the woods.

But right now, after everything that happened, I value my sanity more.

After all, it's not every day the great-grandson of a US senator, the heir to billions, and one of the most famous faces on FoodNetwork—a man who has lived in the spotlight for his entire life—is contemplating walking away from it all.

ACKNOWLEDGMENTS

Nathan, I love you now, always, forever. You're always my hero.

To my son, if I had to guess, right now you're playing Fortnite and don't care that Mom's writing something sloppy into a book just for you. I love you.

Mom, you've always held my hand during my worst moments. I love you.

To Jen and my Meows, I can't wait to see you and love all of you always and forever.

Amy, Kristin, Dawn—you know from the bottom of my heart what it took for this one to be finished. Next time, remind me I do not need a stress reliever in the middle. LOL

To my editing team, thank you for the additional love, support, and late night sanity check. XOXO.

A&K, my personal saviors! I love you both!

To Holly Malgieri, thank you for NEVER letting me down! I love you, my twin!

To photographer Wander Aguiar, Andrey Bahia, Jenny Flores, and Donna Lathan, I love you all!

To my cover designer, Deborah Bradseth, for every gorgeous cover that makes me fall in love with the series all over again! XOXO

To the entire Foreword PR team, thank you for your love and heart.

To Gel, at Tempting Illustrations, thank you!

To my friends Holder and Skorniak for always making me smile. Thank you for letting me bring you into the Amaryllis universe.

Finally, my readers, I am overwhelmed by your love of Amaryllis. Thank you for your support, for choosing to read my words, and for taking the time to review each of my books.

ALSO BY TRACEY JERALD

AMARYLLIS HERITAGE SERIES

Free to Fall

Free to Judge

Free to Taste (Coming in 2026)

AMARYLLIS SERIES

Free to Dream

Free to Run

Free to Rejoice

Free to Breathe

Free to Believe

Free to Live

Free to Dance

Free to Wish

Free to Protect

Free to Reunite

SEVEN VIRTUES SERIES

Starting this fall!

MIDAS SERIES

Perfect Proposal

Perfect Assumption

Perfect Composition

Perfect Order

Perfect Satisfaction

Perfectly Free

Perfect Pitch

Perfect Pursuit

Perfect Secret (Coming in 2026)

GLACIER ADVENTURE SERIES

Return by Fire—Available in audio!

Return by Air—Available in audio!

Return by Land

Return by Sea

DEVOTION SERIES

Ripple Effect

Flood Tide

Troubled Water (Coming in 2026)

NEW YORK MINUTE (INDEPENDENT STANDALONES)

Close Match

The Ultimate Challenge

Go to https://www.traceyjerald.com/ for all buy links!

ABOUT THE AUTHOR

It began when Tracey made up stories in her head as she biked around her neighborhood in Connecticut. Writing, always a passion, interfered with her life when she started rewrote the ends of books instead of finishing college assignments. After all, what was more important, a happily ever after or Greek mythology?

Eventually, she realized the answer was both when she wrote the Amaryllis Series.

With over 300,000 copies of her work read worldwide, Tracey's collection of contemporary romance and women's fiction is available on Amazon.com and free on kindleunlimited. This includes her best-selling Amaryllis Series, Midas Series and Glacier Adventure Series. She has over twenty-five books in print and has participated in several anthologies for reader pleasure as well as charity.

Tracey is dedicated to her own happily ever after, having been married since 2007. She and her husband have one son who is as addicted to his Fortnite as his mama is to coffee.

When she's not busy with her family or writing, Tracey can be found in her home in north Florida plotting her next story, training for a runDisney event, and feeding her addiction to HGTV.

www.ingramcontent.com/pod-product-compliance
Lightning Source LLC
Chambersburg PA
CBHW050918030726
47503CB00007BB/2354